Novis

Rachel Tonks Hill

Cover design by Rebecacovers

www.racheltonkshill.com

For Yoon Ha Lee, who gave me the idea,
and for Jay, who encouraged me to complete it.

This book was based on and inspired by

the epic Old English poem, Beowulf.

CONTENTS

CHAPTER ONE

ROS

The vodka burned all the way down her throat, probably killing her taste buds as it went. It was the cheapest stuff she could get, and likely to dissolve her insides, but it was effective at getting a person drunk. Which was exactly what she needed right now.

Ros Lamarr and her crew had been on Erebus Station between jobs for six weeks now, and that was about five weeks too long for her liking. She needed to be out there, preferably shooting things, not sat on her ass feeling useless. Hence the cheap vodka.

She gestured to the barmaid for a refill.

The second shot went down easier than the first. Maybe because her tongue had gone numb. A pleasant buzz settled in Ros's stomach, her limbs feeling loose. She was on her way to being drunk.

She sat back on her shitty barstool and observed her surroundings.

Most of her crew were scattered through the station bar with the same idea she'd had. Gabby Hernandez was off to her left, wearing a dress that was a little too nice for an establishment like this, surrounded by a dozen hangers on of various genders, who were admiring Gabby's impressive musculature. Ros made a mental note to find her earplugs tonight; Gabby was her best friend but she could get awful loud when she got lucky.

Elsewhere in the bar she could hear Mila fending off

her own hangers on as she was trying to enjoy a much better quality vodka than the one her boss was drinking. Ros snickered when she heard Mila loudly exclaim "listen son, there's only two things that get me going; cleaning my weapons and killing a man. Can you guess which one I'm leaning towards right now?" Woman was sixty if she was a day but damn if she wasn't still a looker. Too bad for the two guys trying their luck she just wasn't interested. Mila was their ace sniper in more ways than one.

Ros had known her four years, and that joke was still funny.

"Another drink please," Ros said, shaking her empty glass at the lady behind the bar. Her current best friend.

"For a few extra credits you can have the rest of the bottle," she said. "You seem determined to pickle your liver anyhow."

It sounded like an excellent suggestion and Ros took her up on it. Two more shots took the edge off the crawling feeling under her skin. She wasn't made for being stuck on station and she hated not having a job. It wasn't so much the recycled air and artificial gravity that got to her—she was used to that on the *Mercenary Star*—it was more the feeling of uselessness that crept into her veins and made her itch. The feeling made her reckless, and a reckless merc quickly became a dead merc.

Dissolving her stomach lining was the lesser of two evils in Ros's professional opinion.

Gabby picked her way through the bar, two of her new friends at her side. Ros felt sorry for anyone still on the *Star*; things were about to get loud. The alcohol had fuzzed her mind a little and she couldn't remember which members of her crew were where. She could have sworn the twins had joined the party headed to the bar, but they were nowhere to be seen.

She decided to think about that later and chased the worry with another shot of vodka.

There was still a bit of battery acid left in her bottle when an extremely drunk bloke tripped over his own feet and practically fell on top of the bar next to her. Ros eyed the man, assessing for threats. He was big, well muscled. Most likely a merc like her. And judging from the smell of whiskey that seemed to be seeping out of every pore, he was a bunch more drunk than she was. He wouldn't pose much of a threat to Ros, but if he harassed the lady behind the bar...

"Oi tits!" he yelled, proving Ros's suspicions about him entirely correct, "gizza drink."

Ros closed her eyes. She was glad she'd worn shorts today; her knife would be within easy reach should she need it. She really hoped she wouldn't.

The barmaid sauntered over to the gentleman, a bored look on her face. "No. You've had enough by the looks of you." Her voice was calm, strong. Anyone with any sense would realise she meant business.

Sadly, her new friend didn't seem to be a person with very much sense.

"Aw come on toots," he said, slurring his words and spraying a fine alcoholic mist of spit everywhere. "Just one for the road?"

The lady behind the bar wiped off her face. "No. And if you ask again, I'll have security escort you out."

That was when the man made a fatal mistake; he reached out and clamped a hand on the barmaid's arm. "Gimme a fucking drink you fucking bitch," he snapped, face turning red.

Ros was on her feet in a flash.

"Apologise to the lady," she said, her voice little more than a feral growl.

He turned to face her. "Fuck you too you uppity bitch."

Ros smiled nastily. "I was hoping you'd say something like that."

Before the man could react Ros had snatched up her almost empty vodka bottle and smashed him round the back of the head with it. It made the most satisfying sound as it shattered into a million tiny cubes, the blow startling him but the safety glass ensuring his skin didn't end up broken.

Ros was okay with that; head wounds had a tendency to make an unnecessary amount of mess.

While the drunk was still reeling from the bottle to the head, she picked him up by the shirt front, slamming him down on the floor with enough force to wind a rhinoceros. Her foot slammed down on his chest, encouraging him to stay exactly where he was.

"Now you wait there for security," Ros said with a sickly sweet false smile.

The bastard didn't have the good sense to do as he was told.

He grabbed her by the ankle and yanked. Ros couldn't

keep her balance properly on her prosthetic leg and went crashing to the ground, narrowly avoiding smashing her head on the bar.

All the breath rushed out of Ros's lungs and before she could recover, there was a couple of hundred pounds of drunken asshole sat on her chest. He levelled a punch at Ros's face but she was still fast enough to block him, vodka filled bloodstream or not. Through the roaring in her ears she dimly heard Mila shouting something in Russian and fervently hoped the daft old bat wouldn't get involved.

She wanted this over and done with as quickly as possible without it turning into a bloodbath. People *died* when Mila waded into a bar fight.

Ros sent her fist crashing into the man's face. He let out a guttural grunt and a torrent of blood gushed from his nose. Combined with the alcohol and the head injury from before his reactions were slow enough for Ros to throw him off her and scrabble to her feet.

The fight should have been over then, but the damn fool just didn't know when to quit.

How he knew about the concealed knife in her fake leg Ros would never know but he lunged for the compartment and had it open before she could stop him. With a flick of his wrist the blade popped open and now he was an armed drunk, angry as all hell.

"You just fucking stay back you bitch!" he yelled, waving her own knife at her erratically.

Out of the corner of her eye Ros could see two security goons approaching but they hung back, keeping

5

the crowd away. It looked like they'd rather leave the knife-wielding shithead to her. Perhaps her reputation had preceded her.

"You really don't want to do this," Ros said, narrowing her eyes.

The pleasant buzz of drunkenness had dissipated by now, replaced by the hungry roar of adrenaline. If she couldn't be working, then this at least was something. She felt more alive than she had in weeks.

She cast her eyes around the near silent bar, looking for allies. Lizzie Park, her engineer and the best scout she'd ever hired, had materialised from somewhere to physically restrain Mila. It was probably the only reason the old lady hadn't flat out murdered the drunk for assaulting her Captain. None of the rest of her crew were around.

Ros wished Gabby hadn't slipped off earlier. It would have been good to have her long time friend by her side for a fight like this.

The drunk lunged with the knife and Ros could tell from the way he was holding it he didn't have much experience with small blades. She blocked the blow easily, but the blade went through her shirt like a hot knife through butter and she felt blood running down her arm.

Experienced or not the bastard could still kill her if he got lucky. That knife was five inches of the finest carbon-steel money could buy and Ros had spent many hours sharpening it to a lethal point. She knew *exactly* how much damage it could do to her insides if she let it.

She resolved not to let it.

The man attacked again, slashing wildly. Ros caught him by the wrist this time and twisted his arm up behind him, stopping him from using the knife.

"I'd drop it if I were you," she said in his ear. The knife was trapped between his back in her chest, the arm next to useless.

"Fuck you," he said, and drove his head backward. The back of his skull clipped her chin and split her lip, gushing blood. Copper exploded on her tongue as she staggered back.

Somehow she kept the bastard in a hold.

"I liked this fucking shirt," she growled through the blood pouring from her face.

Now pissed beyond belief, she twisted the man's arm just a little further than it could go, snapping his wrist. She heard the sound of the bone fracturing and it was just as satisfying as the cry of pain the man emitted. The knife dropped uselessly to the floor and Ros felt his knees go; the fight was over.

Security seemed to sense this as well and broke away from the crowd. "We'll take it from here ma'am," one bloke said. He didn't sound at all apologetic for being willing to her get stabbed rather than wade into the fight himself.

Ros grunted and pushed the drunk at them, bending down to pick her knife up. She wiped the blade on her shirt since it was covered in blood anyway and popped the blade back in.

The drunk howled as he was cuffed with no

consideration of his broken wrist. The second security goon eyed her knife from a safe distance of a few feet away. "You got a licence to be carrying weaponry like that?" he asked.

She sighed and dug into her pocket for her mercenary registration, flashing it at the security guys impatiently. "Happy now?"

Their eyebrows climbed up into their hairlines as they read her ID and they nodded. "Everything looks fine," said goon number one. "Sorry for the trouble Captain Lamarr. You want to press charges against this asshole?"

Ros waved away the concern, and they dragged him off, reading him his rights as they went. She sat back down at the bar, wiping at her cut lip.

The barmaid she'd gotten injured defending popped back up seemingly from nowhere and Ros grunted for another drink.

"Technically I should bar you," said the bartender, "but since you were saving my ass, I'll let you off this once. Here, on the house." She plopped a part bottle of a slightly better quality vodka in front of Ros and slipped off to serve someone else.

She unscrewed the cap and took a deep swig, wincing as the alcohol burned at her cut lip. At least she was sure the wound was clean now. She poured a little on her arm too.

"AJ's gonna be mad at me," she muttered to herself as she wiped blood streaked vodka from her chin.

Down the other end of the bar Lizzie was gesturing

wildly at Mila, probably trying to persuade her to head back to the ship before she murdered someone. The Russian was as stubborn as they came and it was a pain in the ass to make her do something she didn't want to. She sat back down at the bar and Ros sent the vodka bottle sliding down to her.

Mila took the cap off, raised the bottle in salute and said "na zdrovye," before taking a long swig. The bottle came back significantly emptier.

She reached for the bottle but it was snatched from the bar before she could grab it. Ros turned to give whoever thought it was a good idea to pinch her booze a piece of her mind but stopped short when she saw who the culprit was.

Matty Taylor. Her second-in-command.

"You should be more careful. I just decked a guy for less."

"I thought that was you in the middle of that brawl."

Ros grunted.

"Come on boss. Six foot black lady with a shaved head pile driving a guy into the ground? Had to be you."

She narrowed her eyes at him. Man had a point, but that didn't mean she had to admit it. "If you were in here that early how come you didn't help?"

Matty shrugged. "You looked like you were handling it." He took a swig from her bottle and passed it back. "Besides, I was keeping an eye on Lizzie and Mila. Brave girl trying to stop the old bat from wading into a fight."

Lizzie wasn't the youngest on the crew but she was the greenest. Which was probably why Matty thought he could get away with calling her 'girl'. Ros didn't bother correcting him; Lizzie would have to deal with him sooner or later and Ros saw putting up with her lieutenant's bullshit as a rite of passage for everyone in her crew. They'd end up dealing with worse out on a job.

Mind you, if she could deal with Ludmila Yevgeniena after a vodka bender then an officer's son with a stick up his arse should be no problem. Ros didn't say that out loud though.

"What do you want Taylor?" she said. "I'm trying to get drunk here."

"Got something better than booze, boss. I've got us a job."

Ros perked up at that. "What kind of job?"

"See for yourself." Matty handed her a tablet with the job description pulled up. She scanned the document quickly and then went over it again, just to be sure.

"You're kidding me."

"I swear I'm not boss."

"Novis colony? Fucking Novis colony?"

A frown formed between Matty's eyebrows. "Yeah. Something wrong with Novis colony boss?"

Ros groaned. How could he not know about Novis? Every good merc in the business knew the story. "You do know the colony is cursed right? Every single merc crew that's gone out there over the last five years has been slaughtered."

"The ad said something about the casualty rate. That's why the hazard pay is so high I assume?"

Ros nodded vigorously.

"I didn't think an element of danger usually bothered you, boss. I mean, you're Captain Ros fucking Lamarr. You're the best mercenary Captain in the entire Commonwealth, your record speaks for itself."

He had a point. "True, but we've never gone up against anything like Novis colony before." There was a kernel of excitement growing in her belly though. Novis would be a hell of a challenge, and Ros found she wanted to see if she was up to it. No matter the danger it would be better than drinking Erebus Station dry for another six goddamn weeks.

"It's your call boss. The pay's good but if you think the risk is too great–"

"We'll do it," Ros said suddenly, unaware she'd actually decided. "We've got a good crew and I'm tired of doing milk runs for shitty pay. Get back to the governor and tell them we'll take it. I'll let the boys know we've got work."

"Will do boss." Matty took his tablet back and headed out of the bar.

Ros drained the bottle of vodka—it would have been rude to leave a gift behind and she couldn't take open bottles out onto the main concourse—and left it on the bar with a thank you. She wobbled as she a made her way down the bar, probably a combination of shitty vodka and the after-effects of the fight.

"Did I hear Taylor say we have job?" Mila asked, not looking up from her glass.

"You heard right."

"Lots of things to kill?"

"Looks like it."

"Good."

Ros couldn't stop herself from grinning at that. "Make sure Lizzie gets back to the *Star* okay, would you?"

"Lizzie is grown woman," Mila said watching her Captain out of the corner of her eye. "She can take care of herself."

She certainly could if she could wrangle a half cut Russian sniper itching for a fight. And it looked like Lizzie had earned Mila's respect in the process.

"Don't stay out too late," Ros warned. "And don't do anything I wouldn't do."

"I wouldn't do half the things you *would* do, Captain," Mila replied, deadpan.

Ros allowed herself a laugh and staggered back to her ship.

The *Mercenary Star* looked a lot like the standard Commonwealth cargo ship; short, squat and utilitarian. What the *Star* had that a normal cargo hauler didn't was several tons of upgraded weaponry peppering her hull. The Erebus Station Irregulars' logo was painted along the side, underneath her name and registration information. She didn't look like much, but she was Ros's baby.

She was home.

The docking bay the *Star* sat in wasn't too far from the bar, for which Ros was eternally grateful to the stationmaster. Her legs were a lot more drunk than the rest of her. She stepped through the airlock and was greeted by the sound of Tchaikovsky's 1812 Overture blasting over the ship wide speakers.

Ears ringing in time with the brass and drums, Ros staggered to the med bay. "You boys better not be blowing stuff up." She knew what Ewan was like left to his own devices. And when listening to that song.

"Your ship's fine, Captain," said AJ, who was sat on a bed with a pile of knitting in his lap. "Ewan promised to behave himself, didn't you mein Lieber?"

"Aye," said the large ginger Scotsman in the chair next to him. "AJ wouldn't even let me take inventory in the armoury while you were on station." He picked at the sleeve of his sweater—which was bright pink with little hearts on and clashed horribly with his hair—smoothing down the material where it covered the stump of his arm. "Spoilsport," he finished, shooting a dirty look at his boyfriend.

"What's with the music then?" Ros asked, just as the final crescendo started.

"Hernandez," the two men said in unison.

"Ah." In all the excitement from the fight and the job she'd forgotten that Gabby had brought some friends back for the night.

AJ put his knitting down as the brass died away and looked at Ros. "What happened to you Kapitän? You look like you have been in a fight." His big bushy eyebrows knitted together, his cybernetic eye focussing on her lip, no doubt assessing the damage.

"That's cos I was." She braced herself for the inevitable lecture from her medic.

He just sighed. "What happened?"

"Some drunk was being an asshole, so I knocked him

down a peg or two."

AJ's gaze shifted to her arm and his eyes narrowed. "Shirt off Kapitän, this needs dealing with." He spoke in the sort of tone one might use with a truculent toddler and Ros knew there would be no putting him off; she might be the Captain but her medical officer outranked her when it came to the health of the crew.

She pulled her shirt off and sat down on the spare bed. Ewan was still in the room but she didn't much care; on a ship this small everyone saw everyone else naked sooner or later. It was no big deal.

Doctor Schneider hummed to himself as he cleaned and dressed Ros's arm and glued her lip up. The damn glue stung more than the vodka had.

"There, good as new," said AJ when he was done. He reached into a foot locker and tossed her a plain black t-shirt. "Try not to get into any more fights, hmmm?"

"Should be okay on that front doc, we're shipping out soon."

"We got a job?" asked Ewan, his face bright and the excitement in his voice unmistakable.

"We got a job," she confirmed. "Taylor's finishing up the formalities now. I want to get going as soon as we're resupplied and the stationmaster's given us clearance."

"Where are we going?" asked Ewan, looking very boyish with his sweater and the huge grin on his face.

"Novis colony."

The two men shared a look Ros couldn't read.

"I think I must have misheard you, Kapitän, I thought you said we'd taken a job at Novis colony."

"That's correct."

AJ swore in German, while Ewan just looked at her with a strange expression on his face, as though he couldn't work out if she'd gone up or down in his estimation. "You're having a crack at breaking the curse?" he said quietly.

"We are yeah. Besides, I'm going stir-crazy sitting on station all day. It's about time we had a challenge."

"I'll put in an order for extra medical supplies," AJ said mildly. Ros was mostly just glad she'd escaped a lecture. For now.

Ewan rubbed his hand through his beard. "Novis colony's a couple o' weeks out," he said. "And there's some rough territory between here and there."

"You'll need plenty of ammo for your toys, I know. Send me a wish list ASAP, both of you, and I'll see what we can get on station." She looked Ewan right in the eye and poked him in the chest for emphasis. "Nothing too expensive you hear? And I don't care what we're going up against you don't need an EMP mine the size of my bathroom."

Ros thought she heard him mutter "you spoil all my fun," but gave him the benefit of the doubt.

"Do you know where Tariq and Noora went?" she asked AJ. "I haven't seen them since I headed out and I need to talk to them about navigation as soon as I can."

"I thought the twins were with you?" said AJ, his eyebrows knitting together. "Ah, they'll turn up sooner or later. You know how those two are."

She did. They were the best pilot/navigator combo

she'd ever had but they could be incredibly insular when they wanted to be. They were protective of each other and where one went so did the other. AJ was right though; they'd turn up at some point. And then they'd work out a route to Novis that was ten times better than anything Ros could come up with.

Ros sighed to herself. She loved her crew. They were family. She hoped she was doing the right thing, taking them on a run like this. They were mercenaries, and they knew the risks; any job they took could get them killed. That's why the pay was so good. But this one felt different somehow. Normally Ros hated taking jobs on colonies where the word "curse" had been thrown around, but she needed to do something. If she stayed on Erebus station much longer she'd only get into more fights and eventually station security would have to arrest her. Spending time in a concrete cube six feet in every direction wasn't her idea of fun.

No, she'd get them all off station, get them whipped back into shape and get them shooting at something. It would be good for the whole crew.

"You reckon it'll be safe to head back to my quarters now?" Ros asked.

Ewan snorted. "Probably, though with Gabby you never know."

"Give the girl a break," said AJ, slapping Ewan on the back with his massive hand. "You unwind by blowing things up, Sergeant Hernandez unwinds by–"

"–Blowing other things," Ewan interrupted with a cackle.

"I'll tell her you said that, Burns," Ros warned and Ewan paled. Which was impressive given his skin was the colour of skimmed milk normally. AJ just laughed.

"Let Gabriela have her fun," he said. "Then you and I can have our fun too, ja?" He waggled his eyebrows at Ewan, causing a blush to creep out from the top of his beard.

Ros knew when she wasn't wanted and said her goodbyes.

The boys shut the music off before she got back to her cabin and the ship settled into a reassuring quiet. Lying back in her bunk with her cut lips burning and Gabby's snores drifting through the bulkhead, Ros wondered at how calm she was.

This was a big job, no doubt about it, but Matty hadn't been exaggerating when he'd called her the best merc Captain in the Commonwealth. And she'd put together a hell of a crew. They could do this, she knew in deep down in her bones. This would be the ultimate test, of her abilities, of her crew. It felt a little bit like destiny.

She was ready for Novis Colony. Was Novis Colony ready for her?

CHAPTER TWO

GABBY

The purple-black swirl of hyperspace hung malevolent against the transparent metal of the cockpit, like an oil slick on dark water. Gabby hated hyperspace.

It didn't matter how many times she travelled through it her discomfort never went away. There was just something... off about it. Something missing that she was used to in normal space but had never quite managed to put her finger on. It might be the only way to travel but being stuck inside their own miniature universe set Gabby's nerves on edge and made her teeth feel funny.

At least she dealt with it better than the Captain.

Ros was like a caged predator in hyperspace, all nervous energy and coiled muscles, ready to tear apart anyone who got too close. Gabby leaned against the bulkhead just inside the cockpit, watching as Ros micromanaged the twins' navigating and piloting.

"How long until we get to Novis colony?" Ros asked. She was wringing her hands together, twisting her fingers into all sorts of weird shapes.

"Bukra, inshallah," Tariq said, never taking his eyes from his console. Tomorrow. Ros's shoulders seemed to tense up even further at that news instead of relaxing.

"Ay capitán," Gabby called, "¿Qué tal?"

"Feeling un poco loco," Ros said with a sigh. She turned to face Gabby. She had bags under her eyes and there was a lot of tension in her jaw. "I hate this part.

Travelling to a job is almost worse than not having a job."

"You need to relax. Come on, I've just the thing."

Ros hesitated for a moment until Noora turned around, the bright orange of her hijab a strange contrast against the purple outside. "Please get her out of our hair Gabby," she said as her brother snickered. She shot Tariq a dirty look. "You know what I mean." She turned back to Gabby. "She's not doing anyone any good up here, least of all herself."

"Fine, I know when I'm not wanted," Ros said, but the grumpy look on her face was mostly for show. Gabby grinned; she liked it when she got her own way. Ros flicked the comms switch. "Hey Matty, you're in charge. Try not to break my ship."

"No promises boss," came the staticky reply.

"We'll be dropping out of hyperspace in an hour or so," said Tariq.

"I think I can keep her occupied that long," said Gabby, grabbing Ros by the hand and dragging her away.

Later, after she'd fucked her Captain into a sweaty, gibbering mess (and Ros had returned the favour), Gabby sat back to admire her handiwork. Ros's limb were much looser now, her shoulders less hunched over, and there was a genuine smile on her face as she fought to get her breath back.

"Thanks Gabby, I didn't realise how much I needed that."

She shrugged. "That's what friends are for."

And they were friends, despite the occasional round of mind blowing sex. They were great in bed together but had learned long ago that they weren't really compatible romantically. Mostly because deep down Ros was a great big mushball and Gabby didn't really do the whole romance thing. So they kept it at the friends with benefits stage (a phrase Gabby hated because there were many benefits to being friends with someone, whether you were having sex with them or not).

The ship wide comm clicked on. "Dropping out of hyperspace in sixty seconds," came Noora's voice. "Everyone grab onto something secure."

Neither Ros nor Gabby moved from where they were, nor went to put clothes on. They just reached up for the handholds built into the wall above the bunk and hung on until the shuddering stopped. Entering and exiting hyperspace was always a little rough, but Noora and Tariq were the best at what they did; hyperspace transitions these days were almost smooth.

As soon as it was safe to stand Ros ambled over to the comms. "I think that was your best one yet guys. ETA for arrival at Novis colony?"

"We came out of hyperspace a little further out than we planned," said Tariq, "but my estimate should still be correct. I anticipate landing sometime around noon tomorrow, provided we don't run into any trouble in the meantime."

"I hate it when he says things like that," Gabby grumbled. They *always* ran into trouble shortly afterwards.

She glanced out the small porthole Ros had in her cabin, one perk of being Captain. They'd dropped out of hyperspace in the middle of the system's Oort cloud, and instead of swirling purple the view outside was of ice and rocks of various sizes. Gabby felt better already.

Although the orgasm she'd recently had might have helped with that.

Ros turned around and grinned at her. "Looks like we still have time to kill. Wanna go for another round?"

"Always."

They were just getting nicely settled in when the *Mercenary Star* gave a sudden lurch, powerful enough to throw them both off the bunk. Ros lunged for the comms.

"Tariq, what the fuck was that?" she yelled.

"Pulse cannon," came the shouted reply. "We've got company."

"Why didn't we see them coming?"

"Ice is messing our sensors up, I'm trying to compensate."

"Shit!" She flicked the comms over. "Ewan, get your arse in gear. We need to return fire."

"Aye Captain!"

Gabby scrabbled for her clothes, her heart beating wildly in her chest. Neither of them would have time to put their armoured suits on, which could be a problem if their new friends got close enough to board.

"What do you think? Raiders?" Gabby said, pulling her bra back on.

"Maybe. Taylor said there was all sorts of shit in Novis's outer solar system. Why the fuck anyone thought this was a good place for a colony I don't know."

Gabby did, but she kept her mouth shut. Contradicting

her Captain when she was gearing up for a fight was a terrible plan.

Resources. Everything in space came down to resources; who had them and who wanted them.

Whoever was shooting at the *Mercenary Star* no doubt wanted whatever they thought might be on board.

The ship rocked with another impact.

Or perhaps they wanted to turn the *Star* into so much molten slag.

Gabby pulled her dress on and sprinted for the door. At least her cabin was next door; she didn't have to go far to grab her guns. Kicking the foot locker open she dragged her pulse rifle out, quickly checking it was in working order. She sent a quick prayer to God that she was so fastidious when it came to weapon maintenance. Gabby shouldered her rifle and strapped her pistol holster to her thigh. After a moment's thought she dragged the chest plate of her armoured suit on over her head; it wouldn't be as effective on its own but in a pinch it might mean the difference between life and death.

She considered putting her helmet on too but without powering the full suit up it would be more of a hindrance than a help.

The ship rocked again, the rumble of shearing and buckled metal rising from the depths of the ship. Tariq swore over the comm.

Definitely in a pinch right now.

"Gabby you ready?" Ros yelled from the corridor.

"Locked and loaded Captain."

"Good, come with me."

The Captain jogged down the corridor—fully dressed but with no armour—headed towards the cargo bay. If they boarded, if they were after whatever the *Star* was carrying, that would be the most likely point of entry. The deck plating thrummed as they returned fire at last.

"Take that ye wee fucken bawbags," Ewan screamed, loud enough to be heard ship wide without the comms. At least someone was having fun.

When they got to the cargo bay four of their mercs were already there, suited up and ready for action.

"Donkin, Ayres, Potts, you're over there," barked the Captain, gesturing to the far side of the bay. "Kendall you're with us. Take cover and keep your eyes peeled."

Kendall handed both Ros and Gabby in ear comms so they could communicate with the rest of their shipmates. Ros pressed a finger to her ear. "Mila, are you covering the exit from the cargo bay?"

"Da."

"If anything gets past us, make sure it dies."

"I will rain death and destruction down on them Captain."

Ros smiled, tight-lipped and grim. "Good, and Mila?"

"Da?"

"Try not to blow any holes in my ship."

The Russian didn't answer.

Another impact rocked the ship, sending the mercs in the cargo bay sprawling. Whoever was shooting at them was getting closer.

"Don't you fucken do that you fucken piece of shit," Ewan yelled. Kendall shifted nervously inside his suit.

Gabby took a deep breath and reached out to steady the young man. The last thing they needed was a nervous merc.

Nervous mercs got people killed.

"Tariq, Noora," Ros hollered into her mic. "Any chance of evasive manoeuvres?"

"Negative Captain," Noora replied. "None of the nearby gravity wells are big enough for us to do anything with. Our best chance is in outrunning them."

"Get Lizzie to give you all the speed she can and see if you can persuade them to come at us through cargo bay. Show them our belly."

"Aye Captain."

Ewan whooped as another volley of fire from the *Star* hit their pursuers.

The minutes stretched out, every second feeling like an entire year. Gabby focussed on keeping her breathing even, hyper-aware of every breath she took. The silence was oppressive, broken only by the occasional rumble of an explosion and Ewan's screamed obscenities.

A metallic clang echoed around the cargo bay; something had latched on to the hull.

"They're coming," Gabby whispered.

"Everyone ready," said Ros, voice as steady as a gunslinger's hand.

Sweat dripped down the back of Gabby's neck, making her shiver. She hoped whoever was making a mess of the paint work out there didn't blow the airlocks. The guys in the suits would be fine if they did, but she and Ros would be dead.

"Three hostiles destroyed Captain," said Tariq down the comms, "but we've got one attached. They should be coming your way."

"Anyone far enough away for Ewan to shoot at?" He'd been quiet for a while which was always worrying.

"Sorry Captain," Ewan replied. "Nothing in my sights. The bastards are all yours."

The clanking grew louder, followed by the grating sound of the outer airlock being forced open. Gabby crossed herself and said a quick prayer.

If she died today, it wouldn't be from exposure to vacuum.

"Here they come," Ros warned.

The inner airlock burst open and then everything was chaos. A loud chittering started up, making it hard to hear anything through the comms.

"XyrQ!" Gabby yelled as she opened fire.

Fucking eight feet praying mantises. Covered from top to bottom in a shiny black carapace as strong as steel, the only places they were vulnerable were at the joints and around the eyes. And the bastards wore helmets when they went raiding.

Gabby fired off a three round burst, hitting one of the insects in the joint between the thorax and foreleg, blasting the thing's arm off. The bug screeched and fell back, only to be replaced with another one.

She shook her shoulder out, wincing slightly at the pain. She was used to her suit absorbing the force of the kickback and hadn't compensated. There would be a hell of a bruise there later. She made sure not to make that mistake again.

One of the suited mercs yelled down the comms as they sprayed the enemy with a lengthy uncontrolled burst. As many rounds went into the bulkhead as hit the insects.

"Get yourself under control Donkin," Ros yelled over the roar of gunfire.

Donkin's weapon jammed, and she panicked, panting breaths coming over the comm and she hyperventilated. Gabby groaned. Damn rookie could be the end of all of them.

She grabbed a flash grenade from Kendall's weapon belt and dialled the charge back so it wouldn't blow a hole in the hull. Gabby flicked the switch and then tossed it into the crowd of XyrQ calling "fire in the hole!"

Every single one of the mercs took cover, shielding their eyes. Gabby was first up, punching holes in the now significantly thinned crowd of mantises. Her ears were ringing a little, but she could handle it. Her clip ran out, and she ducked behind a storage crate to reload. All around her the bark of gunfire continued.

The air stank of charred insect and metal.

Surging up from cover Gabby came face to face with a bug that had made it through the herd. One of the raptorial forelegs lashed out, smashing Gabby in the chest with all the force of a speeding bullet. She went flying.

She hit the bulkhead at the other side of the cargo bay with an unsettling crunch.

"Gabby!" Ros screamed as one of the other mercs yelled "Hernandez!" She wasn't sure which. Her hearing wasn't working properly.

The rest of her wasn't doing so well either.

Breathing hurt and her head felt like it was filled with glue. She'd hit it against the bulkhead. She thought. She couldn't quite remember.

The mantis that had punched her went down in a hail of gunfire from Ros and Kendall.

Unconsciousness hovered around the edge of her awareness, black and beckoning, but Gabby knew she couldn't give in to it. She was a soldier, and the fight wasn't over yet.

She anchored her rifle at her hip and kept firing, keeping to short bursts only when she was sure none of her allies were in the way.

Gabby's world contracted to just three things: breathe in, squeeze trigger, breathe out. Breathe in, squeeze trigger, breathe out.

She heard Ros screaming something but couldn't make out any actual words; all she could hear was a persistent buzzing noise. Several mantis heads exploded as high speed rounds tore through them. Mila had descended from her perch to lend a hand.

Then Ewan came barrelling into the cargo bay, mouth open wide in an incoherent roar. Three flash grenades went off in quick succession, demolishing the line of advancing XyrQ. Unprepared, Gabby didn't close her eyes in time and spots danced in front of her eyes.

When her vision cleared the torrent of bugs was pouring back through the airlock being chased by an angry Scotsman with explosives. He tossed another couple of grenades through the airlock and then three armoured figures went after them, picking off any remaining XyrQ.

Damn bugs never surrendered.

Her finger was still pressed against the trigger of her rifle but it just clicked uselessly, the magazine long since emptied.

Ros ran to her side, fingers fumbling with a medkit. "Gabby! Gabby can you hear me?"

Those were definitely words, she thought.

The Captain pulled a syringe out of the medical kit and jabbed it unceremoniously into Gabby's neck.

"Ay Dios mio!" she yelled, seeking away from her friend.

As the high-grade painkillers and stimulants worked their way into her system everything seemed to shift into focus. Breathing was still difficult but her everything didn't hurt so much. Gabby felt a loopy smile take over her face. The drugs were definitely working.

"Feeling better?" Ros asked, frowning.

"A little. I'm glad I remembered to put my chest plate on or I'd be nothing more than a red stain on the wall."

Ros's frown deepened. "Please don't joke about that." She grabbed Gabby by the elbow and helped her to her feet. Pain shot across her ribs, bright and insistent, but it soon disappeared into the narcotics induced haze of numbness.

She spent a moment wrestling with her thoughts once she was on her feet. Her brain still felt thick and sticky, like it was working at about half its usual speed. "Anyone else get hurt?" she asked, relatively sure she hadn't slurred any of the words.

"Ayres took a blow to the chest too, but the impact gel in his undersuit did its job. He'll be fine." Ros's voice cracked as she choked up. "You got lucky this time, Hernandez."

"I don't feel that lucky." She looked down at her chest plate, which now sported a dent so large it was a wonder she could breathe at all. "Suit's gonna need fixing."

"Let's get you patched up first." She slung Gabby's arm around her shoulders.

Gabby leaned heavily on her friend as they made their way to the med bay. AJ clucked and fussed like a mother hen when they got there, making sure she was settled on a bed as quickly as possible. It took a combined effort from him and Ros to get the dented chest plate off. That was when Gabby discovered just how much it hurt to raise her arms above her head.

Breathing was a lot easier with it off so it was worth it.

"I'll get engineering to make you a new one," said Ros looking at the sad remains of part of Gabby's beloved armour.

AJ approached with a pair of scissors and she sighed, ignored the spike of pain that caused. "I liked this dress," she said, hearing the pout in her own voice.

"I will knit you a new sweater to make up for it," AJ said, making short work of the dress, which had once borne a pattern of flowers in pastel shades but was now mostly covered in insect gore.

Livid bruises had already sprung up on Gabby's skin. She wondered if that damn mantis had broken every single one of her ribs.

"Not all of them," AJ said after waving about sixteen different diagnostic tools in her general direction. "Your sternum is intact too, which is good."

He lathered Gabby's chest in numbing gel and set to work with the bone knitter. She closed her eyes and leaned back in the bed, allowing the comforting warmth to wash over her. When he was finished Gabby still hurt, but she felt much better.

"You will need a few days to let your body heal on its own," he said, "but then you should be back to normal. Take it easy until you're fully healed. I do not want to hear of you doing anything reckless to set yourself back."

"Yes mother," Gabby grumbled, resisting the urge to roll her eyes.

"I mean it," said AJ wagging his finger at her. "No shooting, no gymnastics and no bedroom acrobatics. Let yourself heal."

"I'll keep an eye on her doc," said Ros, helping Gabby off the bed. "Make sure she gets some rest."

AJ nodded once and tossed Gabby a shirt, which Ros had to help her into.

The Captain escorted Gabby all the way back to her cabin, arm wrapped gently around her side the whole time. Ros settled Gabby into her bunk and pulled up a chair. Gabby had a sneaky suspicion she was planning on watching over her all night.

"You scared me you know, when you went down,"

said Ros quietly, a small frown on her face. "I thought you were dead."

That made two of us, Gabby thought. "Nah," she said out loud, "we've been through worse together." She eyed Ros's prosthetic leg, allowing a mischievous smile to take over her face. "I mean, neither of us even lost a limb this time."

Ros's laughter was a little hesitant, but it was genuine.

The comm buzzed and Ros jumped, apparently having forgotten she still had her earpiece in. Gabby's seemed to have disappeared somewhere along the way and she didn't much care.

"Go ahead," said Ros, pulling her earpiece out and flipping the main comm switch in the cabin.

"How's our patient Captain?" said Noora.

"I'll live," Gabby called.

"Broke most of her ribs but she'll be fine in a couple of days. How's Ayres?"

"Bruised but otherwise fine."

"Any idea where our insectoid friends came from?"

"Tariq's been checking the local news bulletins. There's a base somewhere in the outer solar system but no one's found it yet. Looking at previous reports I'd say we got most of the bastards."

"Keep an eye out for more anyway."

"Will do Captain."

"How's the *Star* looking?"

"Minimal damage according to Lizzie. Those pulse cannons of theirs were more noise than anything else. We'll put in for repairs when we get to Novis."

"Understood. Keep me posted. Lamarr out."

Ros turned the comm off and slumped forwards in her chair, covering her face with her hands.

"You okay jefa? You look like shit."

The Captain lowered her hands and raised an eyebrow as if to say *you can talk*. After a moment she sighed and leaned back. "I'm just wondering what I've got this crew into. I mean, we've not even reached Novis colony yet and you could have died and we could have lost the ship. Maybe this place really is cursed."

"Maybe it is, maybe it isn't. We're all still in one piece and that's what matters."

Ros just grunted at her.

"You'll have to pull yourself together before we get to the colony," Gabby warned.

"I know," said Ros, and she sounded miserable, the vowels stretched almost into a plaintive whine. She'd sounded like that the night she'd lost her leg; small, broken, unsure of herself.

Struggling with the ache in her ribs, Gabby sat up. "Look, if anyone can break the curse they say this colony has its you. You're the best in the business. Except for me," she said cheekily, letting a grin take over her face.

Ros smiled. "You're not Captain of your own crew though."

"Only cos I hate the paperwork," Gabby pointed out. "Besides, if I ran my own crew there'd be no one to kick your ass into gear."

"Remind me again why you're not my second-in-command?"

"I didn't want the job, there's almost as much paper pushing as when you're Captain. Besides, Taylor looks prettier on the recruitment posters."

"That's a lie and you know it."

"Oh alright. He's your second cos I thought we'd get more business with a man in one of the top positions. And I was right."

"Of course you were."

"Now, pull yourself together. The folks down on Nova colony are expecting Ros fucking Lamarr and her Irregulars. Who are you to disappoint them?"

The Captain's smile turned into a full blown grin.

"You're right as usual," said Ros with a dramatic sigh. "What would I do without you?"

"Let's hope you never have to find out. Now come here. My ribs still hurt and the amount of heat you kick out will help me keep comfortable."

Ros rolled her eyes but rose from the chair and climbed into the bunk with Gabby, who'd lain back down. She wrapped her arms around her Captain and snuggled up. Ros's muscles were as tight as they'd been earlier that day.

"Damn XyrQ undid all my good work and I can't even do anything about it," she grumbled.

"Just go to sleep," Ros shot back. "I need you back in fighting shape ASAP. Who knows what we'll be up against when we get to the planet."

Gabby flicked the lights off. "I'm sure we'll be able to handle it, whatever it is. Buenos noches Capitan."

"'Night," came the sleepy reply.

Ros fell asleep almost immediately but the ache in Gabby's chest kept her awake long into the night. Eventually she slipped into a troubled sleep, full of dreams about strange monsters. She woke up as Ros rolled out of the bunk to answer the comm.

"What is it Taylor?"

"Thought you'd want to know Captain. We're here."

CHAPTER THREE

ISOBEL

Novis Colony's spaceport smelled of engine grease, hot metal and the acrid tang of spent hyperdrive fuel. It had never been Isobel's favourite place to spend time, mostly because the risk of ruining her suit there was always high, but she was there to meet invited guests. She had a job to do, and she would put up with the noisome hustle and bustle of the spaceport to do it.

The *Mercenary Star* had landed an hour ago, slightly damaged according to the orbital controllers who had brought her in. A XyrQ raid after they dropped out of hyperspace. Isobel was concerned; the XyrQ were getting bolder and bolder. She sighed. Something to deal with *after* the problem she'd hired the mercenaries for.

Speaking of which, it was probably time for her to introduce herself to them.

Entering the berth assigned to the *Star* Isobel noticed a handful of people bustling around, checking the ship over and unloading equipment as they shouted to each other in half a dozen languages. Her gaze was drawn to a tall black woman with a buzzcut and cheekbones that looked sharp enough to cut glass. She stood in the middle of the room barking orders this way and that. With a black t-shirt tucked into khaki cargo pants tucked into boots, she was undoubtedly ex-military and looked like she meant business.

This must be the Captain.

Her reputation had preceded her; everyone in the Commonwealth knew of Captain Lamarr and her Erebus Station Irregulars. Career military with a distinguished record, she was honourably discharged after losing her leg. She set up the Irregulars after less than a year freelancing as a merc and they had a one hundred percent mission success rate, with minimal fatalities. That was why Isobel had taken them on.

Her registration papers and mission records hadn't prepared Isobel for just how good looking she was. She knew she was staring but she couldn't seem to help it.

A pretty Hispanic woman shouted something in Spanish, jerking her head in Isobel's direction, which got the Captain's attention. Lamarr looked right at Isobel and she felt a jolt in her chest, startled by the intensity of the woman's gaze.

It was a miracle she didn't trip over her own feet as she made her way over. Isobel held her hand out. "Captain Rosalind Lamarr I presume?"

The other woman winced, but shook Isobel's hand anyway. "Only my ma ever called me Rosalind, and then only when I fucked something up. Call me Ros."

Isobel winced internally. Screwing up a first official meeting with someone wasn't like her. Screwing up her personal life maybe, but never work. She tried to put it behind her.

"My apologies Ros. I'm Assistant Governor Isobel Devereux. I believe I spoke to your second-in-command."

Ros nodded and jerked her head at a couple of people milling around behind her. "Oi Matty, Gabby, get over here." The pretty Hispanic lady Isobel had noticed before came over, followed by a white man who was handsome enough, she supposed. "Assistant Governor Devereux, may I introduce Lieutenant Matthew Taylor, my second-in-command, and Sergeant Gabriela Hernandez, who makes sure Matty does as he's told."

Matthew stepped forward and took Isobel's hand, kissing it. "Charmed," he said with a smile that probably made a lot of women weak at the knees.

"Likewise," Isobel replied, not meaning it in the slightest.

Gabriela just gave her a respectful nod though it was accompanied by a speculative look. Isobel found that a lot less obnoxious than the Lieutenant's behaviour. She turned her attention back to the Captain. "I heard you ran into some trouble when you dropped out of hyperspace. I hope you didn't take too much damage."

"Gabby bust a few ribs and there were a few bruises here and there. Other than that the XyrQ mostly made a mess of the paintwork." Ros grinned. "My gunner's pretty good; only one of their ships even got close."

"I'm glad to hear it. When you're ready, you and your crew are invited to the governor's house for dinner. I'd like to go over some of the details of your assignment and my father would like to meet you. He's sorry he couldn't come meet you himself but the foreman of one of the refining plants had a small emergency that needed seeing to. You're welcome to come up to the house whenever you're ready."

Ros opened her mouth to reply but was interrupted

by Hernandez. "We've got everything covered here, jefa. You go with the nice lady to her house and we'll join you when Ewan's stopped complaining."

The two women shared a look Isobel couldn't interpret. If Gabriela Hernandez was who Isobel thought she was, then she'd known the Captain a very long time and was just as decorated. She wondered what she was up to.

"Alright," said Ros, still looking at Gabriela with barely concealed suspicion on her face. "If you can make sure there's someone to escort these reprobates–I mean, highly trained professionals–up later I would be pleased to accompany you, Assistant Governor."

"I'll see what I can do," said Isobela, biting back a grin. Something was going on, and judging by the way Taylor was looking backwards and forwards between his Captain and the sergeant, he was just as confused as she was. "Shall we?"

Ros followed Isobel as she escorted the Captain through the spaceport. Outside the planet's surface was dry and dusty, but the heat wasn't unbearable. Isobel could feel a slight crackle in the air that promised a storm later, and with it, rain.

"It's not far," she said to Ros. "I thought we might walk."

"Fine by me," she replied, shoving her hands into her pockets. The Captain's boots thumped against the packed dirt road, almost hypnotising in their regularity. "If you don't mind my asking," she said after a few hundred yards or so, "if things are bad enough here to warrant calling it a curse, why stay?"

Isobel sighed. She'd had this discussion with her father a hundred times over the last three years and it always ended up in a heated argument. "Novis has several rich mineral deposits, including metals used in starship manufacture and the production of hyperdrive fuel. The companies that sponsored this colony's founding still believe the potential benefits outweigh the costs."

"Even considering the mortality rate of the mercenaries they're paying for?" Ros asked with a frown.

"Even so."

The two women were quiet for a moment, which Isobel found surprisingly comfortable considering they'd just met. Ros was a solid, reassuring presence. Isobel felt like nothing could touch her as long as she was by her side.

"How bad is it out here?" Ros asked quietly. "I mean, I've heard rumours but by the time scuttlebutt gets out as far as Erebus station most of it's bullshit. What are we dealing with here?"

Isobel sighed. "It's bad. Initial planetary survey somehow missed an indigenous life form. Which wasn't a problem until we started mining. Apparently this creature didn't take too kindly to us digging up the planet."

There was a frown on Ros's face as she listened to what Isobel had to say. Her hands were clasped behind her back in the at ease position, which suggested she hadn't heard anything she and her mercs couldn't deal with. Yet.

"There's just the one life form?"

"That we know of. Only one ever attacks at any one time. If there are more out there I couldn't say."

"And what kind of damage is it capable of?"

"I'll show you."

The main settlement of Novis colony was half a mile or so down the road from the spaceport to minimise noise pollution for the residents. Most of the buildings were boxy prefabs that had been shipped to the planet packed flat and could go up in less than a day. It didn't look like much but for Isobel it was home.

"That wall looks new," Ros commented as they entered the gates of the settlement.

"They are. Originally we didn't put a protective wall around the town but after the first attacks… well. Not that it's done that much good. We have to replace sections of the wall after every attack."

"That's nanofibre reinforced steel and concrete," Ros said, looking utterly astonished.

"Yes. Yes it is," Isobel replied, her tone grim.

She led Ros into what had once been the living quarters for one of the scientific teams doing surveys for new mineral deposits. Now it was mostly just a mess.

"Well shit," said Ros as she saw the devastation.

Where once there'd been a cluster of metal boxes that had provided living and working areas for a dozen people was now a pile of twisted metal. The prefabs had been ripped to shreds, the furniture and equipment inside smashed. There were dark stains spattered across the metal that hinted at the fate of the occupants.

Isobel had nearly thrown up the first time she'd seen it. This was her fourth visit to the site; she was pretty much immune to the horror by now. She wished she wasn't.

Ros turned to her, wide eyed and possibly a little frightened. "Did you have mercs on duty during the attack?" Isobel nodded. "What happened to them?"

"Same thing they happened to the people in those buildings," Isobel said darkly. She remembered hearing the screams that night, every one of them cut short abruptly. She'd just lain in her bunk, tears running down her face unable to do anything to save them. Isobel wasn't a soldier, she was a politician, a bureaucrat. The only thing she could do was hire people more qualified than she to take care of the problem, and hope they succeeded.

Which was the reason Ros and her crew were here.

Isobel shook off the memories of their night, focusing on the present and the woman in front of her. Ros was kneeling in the dust, examining claw marks that had been torn into three inch thick steel as easily as if it were paper.

"I'll need all the information you have on this creature. Anything at all. And as much detail about each attack as you can give me. The smallest detail could make a difference."

"I'll liaise with Lieutenant Taylor. You'll have access to everything we have."

Ros smiled, but it was devoid of humour and happiness. Her eyes looked dull and if she'd been anyone else Isobel might have said there were tears in them. "Good. Thank you. Now if you don't mind, I need a fucking drink."

Later, at the governor's house, both Isobel and Ros were a little less rattled. The whole gang had arrived and were in boisterous spirits, enjoying the relative freedom after two weeks cooped up on a spaceship. Not to mention their delight at a meal that wasn't powdered or out of a can.

The repairs had gone well though everyone involved in them had had to wash up and change between the finishing work and arriving for dinner. Sergeant Hernandez was now wearing a beautiful floral dress that showed of a pair of very shapely calves. Taylor had donned a collared shirt and some foul smelling cologne. Isobel desperately hoped it wasn't her he was trying to impress. The one-armed man with a shock of ginger hair and beard—who Isobel now knew to be called Ewan— and the six-and-a-half-foot slab of muscle who never left his side, who had been introduced as the long-suffering medic AJ, were wearing matching jumpers in a violent shade of green that were clearly hand knitted.

Despite the relaxed garb and good spirits, none of the Irregulars had had much to drink, taking only a few sips of wine before putting it to one side. Ros, in contrast to her earlier statement, had foregone the alcohol entirely, opting for a strong coffee instead. Mila had followed her Captain's example, as had the twins, Tariq and Noora.

They were an eclectic bunch; loud, foul-mouthed and completely without shame, but Isobel could see they were professionals. They were on the job and every one of them was ready to leap into action at a moment's notice.

Right now though, they were busy telling stories of their Captain's more memorable exploits.

"So there we were on Tartarus IV," said Ewan, clearly in his element. "And I mean, who names a planet after hell anyway?"

"Ewan," Ros scolded, leaning back in her chair with a smile on her face.

"Right. Sorry boss. Anyway, we'd cleared the colony sight of the native critters—nasty wee bastards they were, looked like spiders the size of a small dog and their bites stung like buggery."

"Liebchen, if that stings so much then I am doing something wrong, ja?" said AJ with a quirk of his lips. The whole table erupted in laughter.

Ewan scowled. "It's just a phrase."

"Ewan!" This time it was Lizzie chastising him to get back to the point. Isobel bit back a smile; man couldn't keep a story straight to save his life but he was utterly charming with it.

"So we'd blasted all the little creatures to smithereens and were about to pack up, job done, when out of nowhere appears this massive fucker, obviously the brood mother or something. I mean, we're talking the size of a house and she's a wee bit pissed we've just turned her kids to paste."

"It wasn't out of nowhere Ewan," said Gabby. "Damn thing rose out of the ground like something out of a story."

Ewan ignored her, focusing his gaze on Isobel, who

was utterly enraptured by the piecemeal way this story was being told. "Then this thing opens its jaws, well mandibles I suppose, and looks like it's going to swallow Matty whole. And there's no way the Captain's gonna let it eat the best paper-pusher she's ever had."

"Hey!" Taylor interrupted indignantly. "I'm good for more than just paperwork," he protested.

"Yeah?" Gabby said sweetly. "What else are you good for then?" She accompanied her question, which was practically a purr anyway, with a blatant assessment of his entire body. Colour sprang to his cheeks but he didn't speak again.

"What did the Captain do?" Isobel asked, eager to drag the mercenaries' attention back to the story. Her eyes flicked to the woman in question, who was watching everything with an indulgent smile.

"The creatures has Taylor in its fucking jaws and he's screaming down the comm–"

"–I was *not* screaming."

Ewan ignored him. "So the Captain fucking *climbs* up the bastard's leg, right up its body and onto the top of its head. She's wobbling all over, trying to keep her balance on this creature that's fucking *chomping* on her first mate."

"Thankfully the armour my crew wear is the best money can buy," Ros added. "Well worth every credit."

"I'll say," Matty agreed.

"Anyway," said Ewan, dragging everyone's attention back to himself. "The Captain pulls her rifle off her back–"

44

"–Margaret," Gabby interjected. "The rifle is called Margaret."

"Right," he said with a glare. "She takes *Margaret*—" and here he injected so much sarcasm into the name that Isobel nearly spat out her drink "—off her back, plants her feet and says 'put my secretary down.' Then she blows the thing's brains out and it drops Matty on his arse as it goes crashing to the ground."

"The bruises took weeks to heal," Taylor grumbled.

"The Captain though, she keeps her balance until the last possible moment, executes a perfect forward roll and jumps to her feet, walking away like she's leaving a fucking bar." Ewan finished with a flourish and Isobel had to suppress the urge to applaud.

"She's always had a flair for the dramatic," said Gabby, rolling her eyes. The gesture couldn't be mistaken for anything other than fond.

The Captain had her hands behind her head and a grin on her face like the Cheshire Cat, which made Isobel's stomach feel all floppy. Damn the woman was impressive.

"And how much of that story is true?" said a voice with a heavy French accent from behind Isobel. She jumped at the sound, knocking her wine glass over. She used her napkin to mop up the mess with as much dignity as she could muster.

"Every single word of it sir," said Ewan, sounding affronted that someone would dare doubt his story.

"Well," said AJ with a teasing glint in his eye, "the creature was perhaps not *quite* as large as a house."

"Everything else though, completely true," said Matty.

"Even the bits where I looked like a prat."

"Especially the bits where you look like a prat," said Lizzie, poking him in the side.

"Yeah. I wasn't kidding about Ros's flair for the dramatic," Gabby added. "No need for exaggeration there."

There was a mumble of agreement from the Irregulars and Isobel took advantage of it to make proper introductions. "May introduce my father? Governor Benoit Devereux."

Ros unfolded herself from her chair like a cat climbing out of a box, all languid limbs and predatory smile. Isobel tried to ignore the way it made her heart beat faster. She strode over to the Governor and stuck out her hand. "Captain Ros Lamarr," she said. She waved a hand at the rest of the table. "And these are the Erebus Station Irregulars."

"Charmed," said Governor Devereux with a smile. He sat down at the table next to Isobel, squeezing his daughter's hand lightly. "Don't stop on my account."

One of the serving staff put a plate in front of the Governor and he tucked in, gesturing at the mercenaries to get back to telling their tall tales.

"Do we have any stories suitable for telling in front of the Governor?" Ewan wondered out loud.

"I've got one," said Gabby, sitting forward and putting her elbows on the table. "From back in our military days."

"Gabby, no, not that one," Ros groaned. The sergeant shot her a wicked grin.

"So we're both raw recruits still, fresh out of basic

training and convinced we're God's gift to the galaxy." Gabby's gaze was sharp as she looked at her Captain, who had buried her face in her hands. "Our first tour of duty was out of Eternatis, suppressing rebels after the war."

"Was this after they tried to secede from the Commonwealth?" Isobel asked. She'd always enjoyed history, even if it could be bloody, and if two veterans of that momentous campaign were in the room with her... well, she would have a bit of a fangirl moment.

"The same," said Ros. "We didn't fight in the actual war, mind you."

"But you were there afterwards?" Ros nodded. "Most of my favourite battles happened after peace was officially declared anyway," said Isobel with a grin.

"Anyway," Gabby continued. "We're both idiot teenagers with their first set of mechanical armour and a big gun. We get intel from a local that there's a group of dissidents hiding up in the hills and that they're ambushing supply trains. Now, the locals didn't take too kindly to this."

"I imagine not," said Governor Devereux. "People get quite grumpy when their access to food and medicine is interrupted." Isobel knew he was speaking from experience there.

"And of course when you got this intel you went straight to your superior officers, right?" Ewan asked with a grin. Isobel didn't know if he'd heard this story before or if he knew where it was going because of how familiar he was with his comrades.

"Course we didn't" Ros scoffed.

"We decided that, since we were all of eighteen and basically invincible, we would deal with it ourselves." Gabby took a sip of her wine, either for fortification or just to make the pause more dramatic. Isobel was certainly on the edge of her seat. "So we troop up into the hills looking to shoot these pendejos and make names for ourselves."

"Except we were the pendejos in this case," Ros said. Her eyes glittered with some emotion Isobel didn't know her well enough to identify.

"We really were," Gabby agreed. "The locals had given us the impression that there were a handful of these guys at most but their estimates were really, really wrong."

"How many were there?" Isobel asked.

"Half a fucking army," Gabby said. "A few hundred rebels all camped in this ravine against two soldiers fresh out of training."

"Those are not good odds boss," said Ewan.

"No, no they're not," his Captain agreed.

"And being the brash young things you were, *that* was when you informed your superior officers and called for back up," said AJ. There was a smile lingering in the corner of his mouth that said he knew better.

"That would have been the sensible thing to do," Gabby admitted. "Instead Ros cooks up this plan where we use a few of our grenades to start a rock slide and bury the whole damn camp."

"How we managed to set those charges without being seen I'll ever know," said Ros. "Took us hours."

"So we get everything set and line up the shot to set off the chain reaction," Gabby continued. If it was possible her grin was even wider now, a clear indication she was reaching the climax of the story and the source of her Captain's embarrassment.

"What happened?" Isobel asked.

"Ros sneezes at the last fucking second and misses her shot, which alerted the whole damn camp."

"It's true, I did," Ros said, looking sheepish. Honestly it was kind of adorable.

"Well you survived, so something must have gone right," said Lizzie. The look on her face was all rapt attention, almost as keen as Isobel was. Clearly it was the first time she'd heard this particular tale.

"Yeah, but it wasn't for the want of trying," said Gabby. "I'm picking off the first few guys charging at us while Ros is desperately trying to get the shot off. She finally manages it, and because neither of us are demolitions experts, the rock slide doesn't happen at all like we planned."

"What happened?" Isobel's father asked in between bites.

"The entire canyon comes down," said Gabby, pulling a face. "So the rebels are running to escape the tonnes of rock falling down on their heads–"

"–she's not kidding that the entire canyon collapsed," said Ros looking sheepish. "Damn thing was a mile long and we turned it to dust. They heard the bang all the way back at camp."

"So we're trying to outrun both the rock slide and the rebels," Gabby added. "And *they* start shooting at us, determined that if they're going down, so are we. We're dodging falling rocks and gunfire, running as fast as we bloody can in heavy armour suits."

"Well you obviously outran them," Lizzie said.

Gabby nodded. "Thing is our entire regiment heard the initial explosion and were on their way to investigate. We come running out of what's left of the canyon, covered in dust and breathing heavily, with a handful of rebels on our tails."

"Which must have been a hell of a sight," Ros interjected.

"The few rebels that survived the rock slide see how many guns are pointing at them and promptly surrender. Our commander interrogates them herself and between them and our reports gets the whole story."

"What did your CO do?" Isobel asked.

"Gave us fucking promotions," said Gabby. "What we didn't realise at the time was that canyon was the main base of operations for the whole damn dissident movement and we'd knocked them out in one go. Within a month the Commonwealth had completely subdued the rebellion."

"They kept it quiet that two idiot recruits were responsible of course," Ros said. "And privately we got a bollocking, but other than that I think it turned out quite well."

Another round of applause broke out, and Isobel heard her father chuckle quietly. The woman they'd hired to deal with their problems seemed to have extremely good luck. She'd need it if the Irregulars were to have any chance of destroying the monster and surviving.

Isobel glanced over to where Ros was sat, looking both pleased and embarrassed by the attention. The Captain's gaze snapped to meet hers and Isobel felt a rush of excitement run down her spine. Her eyes were so dark they were almost black and Isobel thought she could very easily fall into them if she wasn't careful.

She shook herself to clear her thoughts.

The laughter had subsided and the faces around the table turned sombre.

"We should probably discuss your plan for dealing with the current issue," Isobel said. She watched as a shudder ran through Ros's body, no doubt as she remembered what she'd seen earlier that day.

"I received the information you sent," said Matty, leaning into Isobel's personal space with that god awful scent. "I have a few suggestions but I'm sure the Captain and I will review it fully tomorrow, come up with a proper plan."

"And if the creature attacks in the meantime?" Isobel asked.

Ros looked her dead in the eye. "Then we gear up and end it," she said.

"I believe you," Isobel said, and she did. She really, really did.

CHAPTER FOUR

ROS

The monster didn't appear that night, for which everyone was grateful. Reviewing the information taken from previous attacks suggested it was using natural tunnels surrounding the settlement to move around. Even Lizzie couldn't follow the trail back to its nest.

Since flushing it out of its den didn't seem to be an option, they set up patrol patterns in and around the colony. The drudgery of walking back and forth through the dusty town made them restless. After the battle with the XyrQ, and given Novis's reputation, every single one of them had expected more action than they'd seen so far.

Ros wasn't exempt from the tedium either. She maintained that a good Captain lead from the front and that was what she intended to do. She took her turn at the walking, even taking some of the shitty shifts to relieve her crew.

She'd decided that no one was to patrol alone, and she'd taken the midnight shift along with Gabby. Mila was up in one the guard tower that the Irregulars had thrown up after they arrived, staring at everything through the scope of her rifle. Lizzie had volunteered to make sure she wasn't alone; those two were getting on surprisingly well given the age difference. A second team comprising Donkin and Kendall were covering the other side of the settlement.

With luck, nothing could happen in Novis colony

without *one* of the teams noticing.

"Fuck," said Gabby, interrupting Ros's thoughts. "This sand gets everywhere. I'm sore and chafing in... places."

Ros snickered to herself, long since used to Gabby. "Maybe if you didn't wear dresses on your off hours," she said.

"Hey, my dresses make me feel pretty," Gabby said. Ros could hear the pout in her voice, even over the comms. "I'd just rather be chafing for more interesting reasons."

Ros laughed when she heard a disgusted noise from Mila echo over the comms. "Behave Hernandez, or our ace sniper might decide to use you as target practice."

"Fine. But I'm still wearing the dresses off duty. You've certainly never complained about the way I look in them."

"If that's what's important to you then fine, but don't complain to me when there's grit in your unmentionables." Ros wanted to laugh at her friend but she knew that would lead to more unprofessional behaviour. And she didn't want to annoy Mila any more than necessary. Instead she checked in with her eyes in the sky. "Status report Mila."

"Nyet. Nothing. I am tempted to play cards with Lizzie."

"That bored huh?" Ros said, allowing herself a chuckle.

"This is quietest job we've had since we did security detail for the Ambassador's spoiled brat."

Ros groaned, and she heard matching noises from

both Gabby and Lizzie. "Why did you say that Mila?" she asked, genuinely distressed. "Now everything's gonna go tits up."

"Hush. It will be fine," the Russian protested.

Ros didn't believe that for a second.

The second team chose that precise moment to radio in. "Uh, Captain," said Kendall. "I think there's something here you need to have a look at."

Ros and Gabby exchanged a look they both understood even through the visors of their suits; that sounded fucking ominous. One thing was sure, Ros was going to fucking kill Mila.

It only took five minutes to walk from one end of the colony to the other in powered armour. As they approached the second team's location, Ros could see the other two mercs crouching over something. It was too dark to see exactly what from this distance.

"I don't like this one bit jefa," Gabby said over their private channel.

"Neither do I," Ros replied.

Their team mates were crouched over a corpse. Because of course they were. It was rather difficult to tell that it had once been human given the state of it, only the distinctive shape of the skull giving it away.

"One of the civilians, we think," said Kendall, straightening up. "I wanted to check in with you before I radioed the barracks to see if our people are all accounted for."

"No one should have been out but us," said Gabby. "Curfew was two hours ago."

"Which means this poor sod might have been ripped out of their bed," said Ros. "Mila, you listening in on this?"

"Da."

"I am going to kill you."

"Fair." Ros could almost hear the shrug in her voice.

"Mila, Lizzie, I need a sweep of the compound from up high. Let me know if you see anything. You two," she said pointing at Kendall and Donkin, "go scout the living quarters and tell me if there's any damage. I'll radio our people."

The two mercs saluted their Captain and scuttled off to carry out their orders. Gabby held her ground. Ros heard a ping on their private channel.

"Why didn't we hear anything?" she asked, her voice low and quiet even though none of the others could hear them.

"I don't know," Ros said honestly. "But I mean to find out. But first..." She pinged Taylor's comm. He took a few seconds to answer and his voice was thick and groggy when he did.

"Taylor here," he said. "What's up boss?"

"We've got a man down situation. I need our people accounting for."

Ros heard the rustle of him jumping out of his bunk and when he spoke again his voice was much clearer. "Tariq is in here with me, so he's fine. Give me a minute on the others." Ros waited patiently to know her crew were all fine. It was her worst nightmare that one day she'd lose one of them to a mission and there would be nothing she could do to stop it. "I can hear Ewan snoring in the next room," Matty continued. "He and AJ are fine. Noora is fine, Donkin's with you, right?"

"Right," said Ros. "Mila, Gabby, Lizzie and Kendall are on duty too."

"Okay, I've got Potts, Ayres and Hampson. Jury, Smith, Siddiqui and Steel. That's everyone, right?"

Ros ran through her mental crew roster and breathed a sigh of relief. Ordinarily she'd be annoyed that he hadn't memorised the crew himself but in these sorts of situations it was best not to assume anything. "That's everyone," she said, relieved beyond measure. "Wake Ewan and AJ up and keep watch at the barracks just in case. Tell Ewan not to arm the cannon."

"He'll be annoyed about that." Ros could hear Taylor was grinning.

"He can deal with it. I don't want the whole colony waking up and I don't want him blowing up the barracks. I'll go break the bad news to the Governor."

"You mean his lovely assistant don't you?" Taylor asked. If he was waggling eyebrows Ros would cut him into one inch cubes.

"Focus Taylor. Someone is dead and we've got work to do. Lamarr out." Ros shut off the comm before she said something that would put her second into a bad mood for days.

"We really going up to the Governor's house for a wake up call? asked Gabby.

Ros nodded. "I don't have the private comm channel for either of them."

"You should work on that," said Gabby, and there was

a smug lilt to her voice that reminded her of Matty's just moments before.

"Not you too," she snapped.

"Sorry jefa," Gabby said, and her spine straightened infinitesimally as she stood to attention; her mind was back on the job.

"Let's go," she said and stomped off towards the Governor's house, Gabby trailing behind her.

They were only halfway there when Donkin screamed down the comms.

"Kendall? Captain? Hernandez? Oh god someone, anyone, help!"

Ros snapped into action. "Mila, Lizzie, give me a visual!" she yelled, racing across the compound to where Kendall's and Donkin's location markers were flashing.

"Nyet, I cannot see anything," Mila shouted back.

The sound of gunfire and a flash up ahead told Ros that at least one of her team was still alive and that they were in trouble. She flipped a switch and put her armour into power mode, letting her run faster. The cracking retort of Mila's sniper rifle rang out, followed by an unholy screech.

Ros wavered, temporarily stunned by the sound that had greyed out her suit's sensors. Everything was static, and she didn't know what the hell was going on.

"What the fuck was that?" Gabby shouted down the comm which was thankfully still operational.

"I don't fucking know!" Ros yelled back. Her heart was pounding, fear gripping her throat as she ran. She was moving as fast as she could, even for a human augmented with powered armour. If she went any faster the suit would start blaring warnings at her.

Mila's rifle sounded again, followed by another scream.

"How much fucking damage can this thing take?" she heard Lizzie shout.

Ros remembered the walls and the twisted remains of the research prefabs and too late realised that two people were nowhere near enough to hurt this thing.

She and Gabby pounded round a corner just in time to see another flash of rifle fire, this time from someone on the ground.

"Kendall!" Ros shouted but there was no answer.

Another suited body was on the floor and not moving; Donkin.

Ros's stomach plummeted to somewhere between her knees as she realised her worst nightmare had come true and then she pushed it aside. There was no time for emotions during battle. She had to react, to take action. While some of her people were still alive.

She pulled Margaret from her shoulder holster even as she caught sight of Gabby doing the same with her own rifle. For a second Ros was thrown back to every single battle she and Gabby had fought for the Commonwealth before reality reasserted itself. Her finger found the trigger and squeezed before she even realised she was aiming at a target.

Whatever it was it was hard to see in the dark, and Ros had no idea what it had looked like. Every other person who had ever seen it was dead. The information

Isobel had given her amounted to little more than a few scant impressions and was next to useless in a life or death situation.

"Gabby, flare!" she yelled as the shadow ran left, ducking between two of the disused prefabs.

The entire settlement lit up with an eerie red glow as Gabby's flare ignited in the sky and Ros got her first glimpse of the monster they were fighting. Her brain catalogued the details even as her instincts guided her arms into position to fire another round.

Four arms tipped with wicked looking claws; Ros already knew they could slice through steel. A snout like a crocodile filled with rows and rows of razor-sharp teeth. Powerful back legs and a thick, muscular tail completed the picture. The creature's skin was a purplish colour so dark it was almost black. No wonder it had been so difficult to see in the dark.

As the initial burst of brightness from the flare faded to a sustained glow Ros heard swearing in three different languages echo down the comms. She found she agreed.

The thing flinched at the burst of brightness in the sky and then steadied itself. It seemed to realise that there was nowhere to hide—and oh god that suggested a keen intelligence to the thing; no wonder it had been so difficult to deal with—and advanced towards the mercenaries again. It used its massive back legs to take a flying leap, easily twenty feet, which put it right in front of Kendall, who lit it up with sustained fire from his weapon.

One massive claw came up in the air and Ros saw

what would happen before it did.

"No!" she screamed, but there was nothing she could do.

The claws came slashing down and went through Kendall's suit like it was made of paper. A wet guttural scream sounded in the night air and then was cut off. Mila's rifle barked again and Ros saw this creature take the shot right in the back. It barely even flinched.

"Stupid fucking thing just die!" Gabby yelled as she advanced, gun spitting out fire and death.

It brushed off the hail of fire from Gabby's rifle as though it were nothing. Could nothing hurt the damn thing? Ros remembered the way it had flinched when the flare had gone up. Perhaps it was sensitive to bright lights.

At this point she was willing to try anything.

"Gabby, visor!" Ros yelled even as she flipped her own down. She was tempted to light up the super-heated filament of the blade in her arm but getting that close to the thing was a bad plan. Instead she pulled a flash grenade from her belt and pulled the ring, tossing the thing at the creature before following up with another burst of fire from Margaret.

The grenade went off with a full payload, blasting sand and rock everywhere. The creature didn't seem to notice the roar of fire, but it cowered away from the light. Another unholy shriek pierced the air and Ros's suit churned to static. When the light faded and her vision cleared she saw the creature running off down the street. Gabby set off in pursuit.

"Wait!" Ros barked. "See to our people. Lizzie, can you track it?"

"I've got a general direction and some telemetry. I'm doing what I can."

It would have to be enough. No matter the job her people came first. Gabby knelt next to Kendall's prone form, running her gloved hands over him to check for signs of life. She looked up at Ros and shook her head.

Ros took the news like a punch in the gut. She felt the overwhelming urge to vomit but somehow swallowed it. Her legs felt like they were made of treacle as she staggered over to where Donkin was, groping around in the darkness. Her fingers met something solid, and she turned her visor light on, hoping and praying she'd find signs of life.

She could have punched the air in celebration when she found a pulse. It was weak and thready, and there was a hell of a lot of dark stickiness all over Donkin's suit, but it was there. She was alive.

"AJ, I need you," Ros yelled, switching her comm to the medic's channel.

"Who is hurt?" came the answer, his voice gentle and wrapped reassuringly in his German accent.

"Donkin's down. Bad. I won't know more until you look at her."

"Can you move her?"

"I don't know," Ros replied honestly.

"I'm on my way. Ewan is coming too."

"Hurry."

Ros dumped Margaret on the ground next to her and

focused on stemming the flow of blood. The creature had slashed its way through her chest plate, but it looked like the blow hadn't gone as deep as the one that had killed Kendall. Donkin's breathing was shallow and rapid, and a sheen of sweat was visible on her face through the blood spattered visor.

Gabby came and stood next to her friend, a reassuring presence as Ros fought to keep one of her people alive. She crossed herself and Ros knew she would be feverishly muttering prayers in Spanish.

It was times like this that Ros wished she shared the faith her oldest friend held so dear.

The minutes stretched out into eternity as Ros counted the unsteady beat of Donkin's heart. At last she heard the distinctive sound of AJ and Ewan swearing in their own strange mix of German, English and Gaelic.

Ros had run out of swearwords that felt appropriate.

"Let's have a look at her," said AJ, pulling Ros's hands from the red slashes on Donkin's chest.

Gabby pulled her to her feet, and she followed the instructions, staring at her bloody hands, numb.

"Kendall?" Ewan asked quietly.

Ros shook her head sadly.

"Fuck."

Gabby held Ros's hand. She wasn't sure she could have remained standing otherwise.

AJ pulled Donkin's chest plate off and muttered something in German. Judging by the tone of his voice the situation wasn't good. Ewan moved next to his Captain and took her other hand.

Ros felt her eyes burn with oncoming tears and fought to keep them at bay. She wouldn't—she couldn't—cry in front of her crew. It just wasn't done.

The tears slipped loose anyway.

Suddenly it felt very stuffy inside her helmet and Ros's lungs demanded more air. She pulled her hand free from Ewan's grip tore the helmet from her head, dropping it in the dust. Only the iron grip of Gabby's fingers on her other hand kept her from following her helmet and falling to her knees.

"Nein!" AJ said and Ros's heart sped up. He pulled a dozen items out of his medkit and tossed them aside, useless. Finally he found what he was looking for, a syringe, and pressed it to Donkin's neck. She convulsed, limbs flailing every which way with no regard to who might be in the way. AJ received a fist to the abdomen with a soft "oof".

Ros wanted to go to her crewmember, instinct demanding she try to stop the fit, pin her legs down or something. But she knew it would do more harm than good. She squeezed Gabby's hand tighter and stayed back, letting AJ have space to do his job, to do what he could for Donkin.

When the convulsing stopped AJ pulled out his medical scanner, which beeped and flashed as he waved it over Donkin. Ros had never wanted to learn how to read medical diagnostic tools as much as she did now; the lights and noises their own language that would tell her whether Donkin would live or die.

AJ closed the scanner and sat back on his heels. He

looked up at Ros and there was such pity in his eyes she instantly knew.

She was gone.

"No!" Ros shouted, and it was more of a guttural roar than an actual word. Her knees gave out beneath her and she hit the ground, her descent slowed by the vice-like grip of Gabby's hand.

The tears came in earnest then and Ros found she didn't care. They streaked down her face as she sobbed out her grief for the people she'd lost; people who were dead because of her. The pain felt like a lump in her chest that grew bigger with every heaving breath. Eventually the pressure inside her grew too much to withstand, and she gave in.

She howled into the night.

Her vision blacked out as she fought to breathe properly. Dots swam in front of her eyes and for a moment she thought she might pass out. A hand on her shoulder—Ewan—steadied her, and she fought her way back to coherence.

When her vision cleared again Mila and Lizzie had joined them, the latter of whom also had tears streaking her cheeks. Ros saw Ewan wipe at his face too.

Neither Kendall nor Donkin had been with the Irregulars long, but they'd become family in that time. And neither of them deserved to die like that.

"Captain?" said Gabby, squeezing Ros's hand. Somehow her voice was steady and that brought Ros back to herself. Duty now, grief later.

She dragged herself back to her feet. "AJ, get them to

the medical centre. Novis must have somewhere to store the bodies until we can get them both home. And go pick up the poor bastard we found earlier. Get Mila and Lizzie to help when they're done tracking. Ewan, could you let the rest of the crew know?"

"Aye," he said, and his voice still sounded choked up with tears.

"Gabby, I need you with me. We need to go inform the Devereuxs." Ros scooped up her helmet and marched off towards the Governor's house, dragging Gabby along with her. She still hadn't let go of the Captain's hand.

Grief curdled to anger in Ros's gut which crystallised to stubborn determination. She'd come to Novis colony for the challenge, to see if she could beat the curse that had annihilated so many other mercenary bands. Now though, it was personal. In a single night this monster had doubled the Irregular's fatalities and that she would not stand for.

She swore she would end this creature if it was the last thing she did.

"You alright jefa?" Gabby asked quietly.

"No," Ros replied. "I have to–I have to tell their families. I think Kendall has —had—children. How do you break this kind of news to them?"

"He knew the risks when he signed up for this life," Gabby pointed out. Her tone was sharp as the knife Ros kept in her false leg. "We *all* know the risks before we sign on as mercs. You didn't decide that for him."

"But I brought him here," Ros argued. "And that was the decision that killed him."

Gabby shook her head. "He should have fallen back. I don't want to speak ill of the dead but he panicked. He knew there was back up and he stayed out there on his own. You didn't make that decision for him."

Ros felt a prickle in the corners of her eyes. She would cry again but not now. She'd do it later in the privacy of her bunk. And the she'd go kill something to make herself feel better. "At least Kendall went quick. Donkin…"

"AJ did all he could. Sometimes it isn't enough."

"I won't fail again. I won't," Ros said, sticking her chin out defiantly. The door of the Governor's house loomed before them, malicious and sinister. Once she was through that door the failure would be official. It would be real.

She'd engaged the creature she'd been hired to kill and failed. To make things worse, two of her people had died.

Ros wished she could have a stiff drink before having this conversation.

A servant opened the door, looking annoyed to be disturbed at this time of night. The annoyance fell away when he noticed the blood stains on Ros's armour. Gabby and Ros were ushered into the sitting room while he went to go wake the Governor and his daughter.

Ros fought the urge to fidget, settling instead for pacing up and down the room.

Isobel entered, alone, wearing a lilac robe that Ros would have appreciated in any other circumstance. There was a serious look on the woman's face that whatever two mercs wanted to say to her in the middle of the night, it wasn't good. Isobel's gaze lingered on Ros's bloody gauntlets.

Gauntlets that were covered in Donkin's blood. Ros tried not to think about that part.

"What's happened?" Isobel asked, her voice somehow calm and steady. Ros felt a rush of gratitude for that. She wasn't sure she could have dealt with a hysterical diplomat but Isobel's collected demeanour steadied her. "Is everyone alright?"

"No," Ros said, and she was surprised at how dead and devoid of emotion her voice was. "We discovered the body of one of your colonists. We were on our way to inform you when we made contact with the creature. Two of our people were lost."

"I'm sorry," Isobel said and, to her credit, Ros believed her. "Do you know which of our people was killed?"

Ros shook her head. "The remains will need identifying."

Isobel's jaw tensed. "And the creature?"

"Gone. My tracker is doing what she can to follow it."

Isobel nodded. "I'll wake our medic up and we'll begin the process of identifying the remains." She rubbed her face, looking exhausted and far older than she could actually be. No doubt it would be a long night for her. She walked to the door and paused just before leaving the room. "I am sorry for your loss Captain Lamarr," she said.

There was such genuine sympathy in her voice that Ros almost cried again. Instead she just nodded. "Thank you. Could you find time to meet with me tomorrow so we can discuss what happens next?"

A sigh. "I'll do what I can. Tomorrow is… likely to be long."

"I understand."

"Get some sleep Captain. If you can."

Ros wasn't sure how she got back to the barracks. She had the vague impression of Gabby dragging her along, of the sorrowful faces of the rest of the crew. She pulled her armour off piece by piece, tossing it into the corner to clean in the morning.

She hit the bunk and immediately started sobbing.

CHAPTER FIVE

ISOBEL

Captain Lamarr took the deaths of her crewmembers hard. In the days following she worked like a demon, attending the autopsies, writing messages to the families, collating every scrap of information she could find on the monster. Isobel had lent the Captain the use of an office in the Governor's house and she often found the other woman there in the middle of the night, writing furiously or else passed out on top of a pile of printouts and tablets.

Isobel was getting worried about her.

Which was ridiculous; the woman was practically a stranger. Still... Isobel couldn't deny her attraction to the striking mercenary. And the stories she'd heard and the depth of feeling she had for her crew only deepened the attraction. She'd seen the naked grief on Ros's face the night of the attack and had been moved by it.

There was no use pretending otherwise; Isobel was enamoured.

Which might go some way towards explaining why she was stood in the doorway watching her sleep like an absolute creep.

Ros was face down on the desk, her fingers loosely wrapped around a stylus and her cheek no doubt stuck to the screen of the tablet she was resting on. She was wearing a tank top that put the fine muscles of her arms on full display and Isobel couldn't stop herself from eyeing them appreciatively. Add in the slight puddle of drool on the desk and it was so unbearably adorable Isobel found it difficult to make herself wake the mercenary; if she was falling asleep in a chair (one that Isobel knew wasn't comfortable) then she obviously needed the rest.

On the other hand, she wouldn't be very rested when she woke up, and Isobel knew from experience that using a desk as a pillow resulted in all sorts of interesting neck and shoulder pain. It would be kinder to wake Ros and pack her off to her bunk, but Isobel's legs were strangely uncooperative.

Ros murmured and shifted in her sleep, a frown forming between her brows. Isobel was just about to leave her be and stop watching her sleep like some sort of stalker when she cried out, the noise unmistakable as one of distress. Ros's arm shot out, batting at some invisible enemy and she softly cried "no!"

She was having a nightmare.

Resolve crystallised in Isobel's chest and her feet took her across the room in one fluid motion. With no regard at all for her own health she tapped the Captain on the shoulder.

"Captain Lamarr?" she said tentatively. "Ros? Wake up, you're having a nightmare."

Another cry issued from Ros's mouth, this time sounding pained, and Isobel's heart raced. She gripped Ros's shoulder firmly and shook.

"Ros, wake up!"

The next thing she knew she was flat on her back on the study floor with a mercenary sat on her chest, an arm braced across her throat. Ros was wild-eyed and breathing heavily, but it was nothing compared to the panicked flutter of Isobel's heart in her chest. Damn her reflexes were quick. And she was so close Isobel could feel the other woman's breath against her cheek. Given their current position Isobel probably shouldn't be feeling a flicker of arousal at their proximity but apparently no one had informed her body.

Ros's eyes cleared as she took in her surroundings, fear slipping into confusion as she came fully awake.

"Assistant Governor Devereux?" Ros asked, her voice thick with both sleep and bewilderment.

"I think, given our current position, it would be fine for you to call me Isobel." She had always used humour to diffuse awkward situations and, despite the forearm lodged firmly against her windpipe, this situation was no different.

Ros started at that, finally seeming to realise how compromising their position was.

"Fuck," she swore, leaping backwards and to her feet faster than Isobel could follow. "I am so sorry." She offered her hand to help Isobel up, which she accepted gratefully.

"Don't worry about it," Isobel said, waving off the concern. Her back was a little bruised from hitting the floor at such speed but she was otherwise unharmed. "It was the risk I took when I decided to wake a soldier and a mercenary." She dusted her clothes off, trying to appear unaffected by the violent reaction to reassure her companion. Ros's shoulders were still tense and her gaze wary; obviously she wasn't as successful as she'd hoped.

"Did you need me for something?"

Isobel shook her head. "You sounded like you were having a nightmare. And I know from experience those desks aren't the most comfortable pillows."

Ros grimaced. "Yeah," she agreed. "I slept there last night, and I woke up with the worst crick in my neck I've ever had. Thanks for waking me despite, you know..." She trailed off, obviously unsure about how to refer to what had just happened. Technically it was assault, but Isobel was more than willing to let that slide given the circumstances.

"Does that happen often? The nightmares I mean?"

Ros glanced at the floor and played with her closely cropped hair; a nervous tick if Isobel had ever seen one. "Yeah, pretty often. I've seen a lot of things in my life that were nightmare worthy. And with what happened a few days ago..."

"I understand." She didn't really, but Isobel wanted to. She'd had to deal with a lot of the same things as Ros over the last few days; identifying the remains of the dead colonist, informing the family, etc. But in her case the dead man had never really been more than a name on a list, a face in the crowd. Kendall and Donkin had been part of Ros's crew and even though she'd only known the Irregulars a week or so she could tell they were like family. And they'd been under Ros's command, her protection and it was clear in the lines on her face that their deaths weighed heavily on her conscience.

Isobel should probably feel a little guilty she wasn't

more cut up about her dead colonist, but the truth was after nearly three years out here she was immune to it. Colonists ended up dead or missing on a weekly basis on Novis; in the beginning she'd cried for every one but at some point the heart grows hard, if only to protect itself. As much as she could see the Captain was in pain she wouldn't wish that kind of numbness on anyone.

Still, she wanted to help. If she could.

"Can I get you anything?" she asked. "A drink, something to eat?"

"No thank you," said Ros, though there was gratitude in her eyes.

"Well, you know where I am if you want to talk," she said, disappointed that their time together had been so brief. "Goodnight."

"Wait!" Ros said and then looked at her boots as though embarrassed by her outburst. "Some company would be nice for a little while."

Isobel felt a smile of genuine joy spread over face. "I would be happy to." She settled into the couch along the wall, gesturing at Ros to join her. "Do you want to talk about work?" Ros nodded. "Have you made much progress in locating the beast?"

Ros settled into the couch, her shoulders relaxing as she held forth on her quest to avenge her fallen crewmates. Lizzie, her tracker, had followed its trail to a cave entrance before she'd called off the search; being underground with an enemy that knew the terrain (and had just ripped apart two mercenaries in full armour) wasn't the best plan so she'd pulled back. Orbital scans by

Noora and Tariq using the *Mercenary Star*'s sensors had revealed the cave system to be massive, extending for miles around and below Novis Colony's main settlement. The sensors hadn't picked up any sign of the beast itself, but Ros had them maintain orbit with regular sensor sweeps hoping to find out more information.

"Gabby's given the thing a name too," said Ros, more relaxed and animated than she'd been at the start of the conversation. "She's started calling it 'el bestia del diablo'—the beast of the devil. The rest of the crew just call it the Hellbeast."

"It certainly seems appropriate," Isobel mused. They'd held off on giving the thing a name, beyond referring to it as the curse, mostly because they knew almost nothing about it. And because colonists were a superstitious bunch by nature (which is how rumours of the Novis Colony Curse had got started in the first place) and naming things gave them power. But Isobel had seen stills from the camera feeds on the mercs' suits that night and Hellbeast seemed to fit.

"Thank you," said Ros softly, reaching out to rest her hand on top of Isobel's. She tried not to give any outward sign of the sudden increase in her heart rate though it was possible Ros could feel the jump of her pulse at her wrist.

"For what?"

"For listening. For waking me up. For not getting mad that I pinned you to the floor and tried to strangle you." Ros shrugged, but her cheeks seemed a little darker than usual. Was she embarrassed? Isobel couldn't imagine the fabled Ros Lamarr being embarrassed about anything.

"It's fine. Really. A little easier on the throat and it would have been entirely my pleasure."

Ros's cheeks were definitely darker now, and she ducked her head, tucking her chin into her shoulder. The only word Isobel could think of to describe it was bashful, and she was utterly enchanted.

"Anyway," she said, not wanting to dwell on Ros's clear embarrassment. Just because Isobel was enamoured didn't mean Ros was too. "I should let you get some sleep. You shouldn't be out alone with no armour but I promise you this couch is fairly comfortable for sleeping on." Isobel stood up and made for the door, throwing a glance over her shoulder before she left the room. Ros was looking at her curiously, with her head tilted to one side and it made Isobel pause. She stood and crossed the room to Isobel.

"Thank you," she said softly, repeating her words, her tone even more gentle than it had been earlier. She reached out her hand and drew Isobel closer to her until she could feel the heat radiating off the mercenary's body. Ros pressed a brief, soft kiss to her cheek and Isobel felt her whole body react, head to toe. "I'll see you in the morning. Goodnight Isobel."

Her name sounded like a caress on Ros's tongue and it made Isobel want to fall into her arms, to kiss her with every ounce of passion she possessed. She resisted, pulling back until she was in her own space again.

"Goodnight," she returned, and she wasn't entirely sure her voice wasn't husky and roughened with desire. Judging by the darker than usual colour of Ros's eyes she'd noticed.

Isobel didn't exactly flee, but she did hurry away and back up the stairs before she did something impulsive ad ill-advised. Tripping up over the small piles of clothes strewn across her floor (she really needed to tidy those up soon) she flopped into bed, a languid smile on her face.

The last soft tendrils of arousal still curled through her body, making it hum rather pleasantly. Her dreams would be good tonight, she could tell. And in the morning, who knew?

She fell asleep still smiling

The next morning Isobel was still in a wonderful mood, and she was under no illusions that it had everything to do with the striking mercenary who had bestowed a kiss on her cheek. She'd had less chaste kisses from diplomats at functions but none of them had had such as lasting effect as Ros's kiss had.

Her good mood was obvious, and so much so that even her father noticed.

"Sleep well?" he asked, one eyebrow raised and a small smile in the corner of his mouth that told Isobel he knew exactly what was going on. And even if he didn't he had suspicions, which were right more often than not.

"Oui Papa. I slept very well, merci."

"And were you by yourself for this wonderful night's sleep?" There was a twinkle of mischief in his eyes and Isobel cursed her complexion as she felt her cheeks heat; the blush would no doubt be visible to her father.

"I assure you I was alone in my bed last night Papa," she insisted.

"Hmmm," he said. "No late night assignations at all then?"

"Well I wouldn't call it an 'assignation'," Isobel said and her father laughed. Isobel glared at him but there was no strength behind it.

"Isobel, chérie, you have always been obvious in your affections, and I have noticed the looks you have been giving Captain Lamarr when you think no one's looking."

"Of course you have," said Isobel, rolling her eyes. She couldn't be angry with him, not when he was correct. Her father leaned over in his chair and pressed a kiss to the top of her head.

"Just promise me you will be careful, chérie. Captain Lamarr is a mercenary by trade and a soldier by nature; she may not be the type to settle in one place."

"I know that," Isobel grumbled and then she sighed. "Anyway, talk of 'settling down' is a little presumptuous. I don't even know if she's interested in me."

"She has eyes, does she not?" her father said and then turned back to his breakfast, the conversation over.

Isobel picked at her cheese and meats after that, her appetite having disappeared. She'd been so caught up in the giddiness Ros made her feel she'd almost forgotten the thing she held most dearly of all; her duty. Ros—Captain Lamarr—was here to dispatch the Hellbeast plaguing Novis Colony so they could get back to the important work of mining much needed minerals for the Commonwealth. Countless colonists and two of Ros's own people had already died. Now was not the time for an ill-considered romance.

(There was a little voice in the back of her head that insisted this was *exactly* the time for a little romance. After all, with a monster on the loose no one really knew if they'd live to see the next day, so it made sense to live life to the fullest while they could. If that included a little romance then all the better. Isobel shook the idea away.)

After breakfast she went down to the Irregular's barracks looking for the Captain. There were a few threads from their conversation last night she wanted to revisit hoping to find the Hellbeast all the quicker. When she got there, however, Ros wasn't there. Hernandez sat at the small comms station the Irregulars had set up in the common room and Isobel could hear the faint crackle of conversation going backwards and forwards.

"She's not here chica," Gabby said. "She came in first thing this morning talking about some idea she'd had for trying to track el bestia del diablo. She's in orbit with Tariq and Noora on the *Star*."

Isobel tried to hide her disappointment at that but she had a sneaky suspicion she'd failed. "I had one or two ideas on that myself," she said, hoping her voice sounded neutral and businesslike. "It can wait. If you'll excuse me, there are things I should be doing."

"Nah chica, pull up a chair," said Gabby, kicking one towards Isobel. She was wearing fatigues and a t-shirt today and already that seemed strange to Isobel, she'd gotten so used to seeing her in a dress.

She took a seat on the gracelessly offered chair and said "you know if you like dresses I've got a couple of slinky black numbers you might like. I think they'll fit you around all your muscles."

Gabby let out a bark of laughter. "I'm more used to women trying to get me out of my clothes than put me in them, but thank you."

"I can see why." Isobel's attention might have been caught by someone else, but she couldn't deny Hernandez was a very attractive woman.

"Gracias. Now, is there something I can do for you while we wait for la jefa to check in?"

Isobel hesitated. As much as she wanted to pump Gabby for information about Ros (and get some clues on how she might go about winning her heart) she knew full well that the two women had been friends a long time. Anything she said to Gabby would get back to Ros.

"Don't worry chica, I never kiss and tell," Gabby said with an exaggerated wink. "What la jefa doesn't know can't hurt her, sí?"

Isobel didn't know what to say to that so she shrugged. "I was hoping to continue our conversation from last night is all."

"Oh so you're the reason Ros wasn't in her bunk last night?" Gabby asked with a grin. She waggled her eyebrows in a way that would be lascivious on a man but was somehow okay on her. There was genuine happiness in her voice which made Isobel feel okay about it. "Good for you."

"Well, I wouldn't say I was the reason. She fell asleep at her desk."

The grin abruptly vanished from Gabby's face. "Again? She's been doing that a lot since Kendall and

Donkin were killed. She's taking it hard."

"I got that impression. She was having a nightmare when I stuck my head in the office, so I woke her up."

Gabby whistled. "You're tougher than you look chica. I've seen Ros through more nightmares than I can count and I still have to think twice before I wake that girl up. What happened?" Isobel told her. "Ow. Well, you're still breathing so it can't have been that bad. I bet the view was nice from there, huh?" And suddenly the grin and eyebrows were back, like she'd never even been worried about her friend.

There was no point in lying; the view *had* been very nice. "It was yes."

"See, I knew you and the Capitan would hit it off."

Isobel hesitated then. There was a question she wanted to ask, but she wasn't sure she knew well enough to ask it without coming across as rude. She wasn't sure she wanted to know the answer either.

"You said you've woken Ros up out of nightmares before. Do you bunk up together often?" There, that sounded reasonable. Couched in diplomatic language, but reasonable.

Gabby narrowed her eyes at Isobel; she wasn't falling for it. "Cut the bullshit chica. What do you really want to ask me?"

Isobel took a deep breath. "Are you and Captain Lamarr involved?" She braced herself for the answer. If Ros and Gabby *were* an item there was no way in hell she stood a chance. Not with the length of time they'd known each other. And how good looking Gabby was. Isobel was insanely jealous of the definition in her leg muscles.

"If you mean romantically then no. We're best friends and have sex sometimes but that's it. I love her, but I don't really do the whole getting tied down thing. I wouldn't have thrown her at you if she and I were involved like that."

Isobel wasn't sure whether to be relieved or not. "Threw her at me?"

Gabby laughed. "That first day remember? In the spaceport? I convinced her to walk up to the house with you."

Isobel remembered. The company had been wonderful even if the scenery and conversational subject matter had left a little to be desired. She was just about to object to *anyone* being thrown at her when the comm crackled.

"*Mercenary Star* to Novis. Hernandez, you there?" Ros's voice was unmistakable.

"Aye Capitan. There's a beautiful lady here wanting to speak with you too." Gabby threw Isobel a wink as she said that and she grinned; the woman's humour was infectious.

A great put upon sigh rattled down the line. "Gabby you better not be talking about yourself again."

Another round of laughter. "Two beautiful ladies then," she said. "The Assistant Governor is here."

"Isobel's there?"

Isobel could have sworn there was a note of hope in Ros's voice as she said her name and that her tone softened just a little. She thought that might be a little too optimistic of her though.

"Sí," Gabby said. "Shall I leave the two of you alone?"

"Gabby, I'm in the cockpit with Tariq and Noora. Even if you fuck off, which I know you too well to believe you will, I wouldn't be alone."

"Spoilsport."

"Isobel, did you wan–need me for anything in particular?"

The twinkle in Gabby's eye told Isobel she'd caught that little slip. "I had more ideas on how we might track the Hellbeast." She glanced at Hernandez as she said the name and was rewarded with an amused smile. "I assume you're up there taking advantage of the *Star*'s sensors to locate our... problem?"

"Yeah," said Ros and then sighed. "We're not having much luck though. Whatever shit it is you're digging up down there is blinding our sensors. We can barely even get signals of human life from here."

"I thought that might be the case. Would it help if you had the initial scans done before the colony was founded? They're not completely accurate now but they might help you compensate for some of the noise."

"That... that sounds really useful, actually. Thanks." Ros's voice sounded a lot brighter than it had before. She said something Isobel couldn't hear—presumably talking to the other two occupants of the ship—and then the comm crackled again. "The twins say those scans would be our best chance of finding anything from orbit. Get them to Lizzie see if she can do anything with them."

"Will do," Isobel, feeling pleased that she could be

useful. Her objective achieved, she didn't quite want to end the call just yet. There was a warm feeling in her stomach from hearing Ros's voice and she wanted to prolong it.

Unfortunately Gabby chose that moment to speak up. "Hey jefa, I think the lady governor deserves a reward for being so helpful. How about a kiss?"

"Hernandez," Ros said, and her tone of voice was so severe that Isobel felt the urge to snap to attention. Gabby's face dropped the grin, and she held her hands up in surrender even though the Captain couldn't see them; she clearly knew she'd gone too far.

"Lo siento Capitan. Won't happen again." Isobel believed her. Hopefully Ros would too.

"Glad to hear it. Isobel, sorry about my Sergeant. Sometimes she forgets she's not the same rank as me any more."

"You two were the same rank?" Isobel asked, genuinely curious now.

"Sí. We both ended up Sergeants before we were discharged. Then she decided to cheat and get a ship so she could be Captain."

Ros's laughter rattled down the comm. "It wasn't cheating Gabby. I filled in all the paperwork for both the *Star* and the Irregulars. I earned my rank fair and square."

Gabby rolled her eyes at Isobel. "It's the only reason Matty's second-in-command instead of me. I hate doing the paperwork. But he's a good boy and does what I tell him so everything works out."

"I should go get those scans..." Isobel said, and there

was a pang of sadness at that. She could happily sit here and banter with these two women all day. But alas, there were things for her to do. An assistant governor's time was never her own.

"I should let you get back to work," said Ros, and it was possible she sounded as sorrowful as Isobel felt. "*Mercenary Star* out." The comm clicked off and Isobel was on her own with Gabby again. Gabby who was looking at her as though she was a logic puzzle she couldn't work out.

"What? she asked, well aware she was being rude, but she didn't like being stared at.

"I think you'll be good for our Capitan," Gabby said with a curt nod. "You watch, we'll make an Irregular of you yet."

Isobel was sure that was a compliment of the highest calibre but she didn't know how to deal with it. She nodded awkwardly and all but fled Hernandez's keen gaze.

The conversation hadn't been a complete bust though, she mused as she walked back to the governor's house. She'd let Ros know about the scans and found out that, whatever the exact nature of the relationship between the Captain and Hernandez, it wasn't romantic. Now she just needed to decide what to do with that knowledge.

She shook her head. These mercenaries would be trouble, she could tell. Somehow she couldn't bring herself to mind.

CHAPTER SIX

GABBY

The scans that Isobel provided allowed the Irregulars to rule out a bunch of places the Hellbeast definitely *wasn't*. Which was somewhat useful, Gabby had to concede.

On the other hand, finding out where the thing actually was meant diving into practically unnavigable cave systems with little more than the light of a torch to see by. Gabby wasn't too happy about that. It wasn't that she was claustrophobic; it was more that she didn't enjoy being in the dark underground looking for a creature that could rip though her armour, especially when said creature was almost black.

She had an aversion to situations she considered to be suicide runs. Gabby had made this point to Ros. Repeatedly. But the Captain was still in mourning for her two lost crew members and wasn't at her most rational.

"Should have sealed the deal with the Assistant Governor, she might be less angry then," Gabby mumbled under her breath.

"Sorry, what was that?" asked Ewan, glancing at her through his visor.

"I said the Captain should have slept with the Assistant Governor. She makes fewer reckless decisions when she's getting laid on the regular."

Ewan snorted. "I thought you were in charge of the solution to that particular problem of the Captain's."

"Yeah well, usually I am. But I make it a policy not to seduce anyone who's making gooey eyes at someone else."

"The Captain *has* seemed a little smitten," Ewan agreed.

"Shut up you two," Lizzy interjected, "I think it's romantic."

Ewan and Gabby shared a look that said 'youngsters' and rolled their eyes.

"I saw that," Lizzie said.

"How? Dios mio I can barely see what I'm treading in let alone what facial expression Ewan's making. Although knowing him he's looking lovingly at his cannon and stroking it erotically."

"I am not!" he protested but Gabby heard the scrape of metal on metal as his arms went back to his sides.

Gabby just grinned to herself.

"If you three have finished being unprofessional," Ros said down the comm.

"Never Captain," Ewan said, and Gabby could hear the smirk in his voice. Gabby flicked her comm to the private channel she'd set up for her team so they could talk without getting shouted at. There was only cave wall and darkness to look at, anyway. And Gabby needed a distraction before she started screaming and never stopped.

"Hey Ewan," she said. "How come you never got a regular prosthetic for your arm?"

"Are you kidding Hernandez? You've seen what this baby can do, right?" he said, patting the cannon attached to his stump affectionately. Gabby had heard him use that tone of voice before, but normally he was talking about AJ and not an inanimate object.

"I have, in fact, seen what she can do. Frequently." Ewan had been with the Irregulars since the group's inception and, since he'd lost his arm long before he joined, Gabby had seen the cannon used hundreds of times over the years. She appreciated the sheer bloody mess it could make. Damn thing had saved her life more times than she could count.

"Well then, you know why. I don't understand why anyone would choose to have just an arm when they could have this baby instead." he hoisted the cannon up onto his shoulder and gaze at it proudly.

"Even though you had to have a metal plate attached to your stump to stop the kickback shattering your shoulder? Lizzie said.

"Even so."

"Come on Ewan." said Gabby. "You know as well as I do that you could get a regular prosthetic arm to attach to your plate and then you could have the best of both worlds. The Captain would probably help you with the cost."

"Ah but then I'd lose precious seconds strapping this baby on," he said. Ewan shrugged. "I wanted the cannon, so I learned to do everything one handed. I don't understand why it's such a big deal."

"Whatever makes you happy you ginger nut," Gabby said.

"Very funny Hernandez." He sounded pissed at the

insult, but that was part of the game with Ewan. They'd traded insults so often over the years they'd passed through offensive and were just straight up affectionate now.

"Quiet you two," Lizzie hissed down the comm. She crouched a few feet ahead of them looking intently into the darkness.

Gabby stilled, the grin sliding off her face. Lizzie was the best tracker they'd ever had; if she thought she'd spotted something, then they'd better fucking pay attention.

"What is it?" she said. "What can you see?"

"I can't *see* anything but there's... something. A feeling," Lizzie said, whispering even though no sound could escape their suits except through the comms.

Gabby and Ewan shared a look. She knew that being a mercenary and staying alive was as much instinct and trusting your gut as anything else, and Ewan knew it too. If Lizzie's gut was telling her something wasn't right, then they'd better trust that before they ended up a pile of gore.

"I'm gonna check in with the boss." Gabby flicked her comm over to the universal channel. "Hernandez to Lamarr. Come in Captain."

"Lamarr here. You have something Gabby?"

"Sort of. Lizzie's concerned about something."

"What you got Lizzie?"

"The rocks in this part of the cavern aren't sitting right," she said. "It doesn't look natural. They've been disturbed."

"Our creature?" Gabby asked.

"I think so." Lizzie reached out and touched a rock in front of her, and her suit glove came back with something on it. Something black and sticky and almost certainly organic.

"Is that... blood?" Ewan asked.

"Looks like it. But if our Hellbeast came through here after the fight why hasn't it dried yet?" Lizzie asked. She looked up at Gabby with a crease between her eyebrows she would have found adorable under other circumstances. Such as on a beach, half naked with an alcoholic drink in one hand. Gabby shook the thought away; it wasn't helping right now.

"It's possible that this thing's clotting mechanism is wildly different from anything we've ever seen before, but I can't think of any advantage for that," Ros said. Her voice kind of trailed off, and Gabby felt there was something she wasn't saying.

"Or?" she prompted.

"Or it could be more recent."

"Great," said Ewan. "Just great."

"What's up with you?" Gabby asked.

"Well, you don't think a big fucking thing like that would just blunder around injuring itself on rocks do you? I saw the footage and what it did to those poor kids. If that *is* blood, and it *is* recent then there's something out there capable of fucking up our Hellbeast," he said.

"Which means..." Gabby trailed off. Hardly daring to voice the thought.

"Which means there might be more than one of

them," Ros said, and her tone was grim.

"Now let's not go jumping to conclusions," Lizzie said. "We've seen no evidence of multiple creatures, and neither have the colonists. That thing took like four shots from Mila's sniper rifle, plus countless shots from you guys on the ground. We definitely injured it. It's not beyond the realm of possibility that one of the creature's wounds got reopened somehow."

"It's possible," Ros agree. "But I'm not taking any chances. We fall back to the rendezvous point. Taylor, Mubarak, Potts, you listening to this?"

"Aye Captain," Taylor said. "Falling back to rendezvous point."

"Great. Mila, Noora and I will meet you there. Hernandez."

"Sí Capitan?"

"You get your team back safely too. I want everyone home in one piece, you hear me?"

"Sí."

Lizzie rose from her crouch and took point as they made their way back through the darkness to the rendezvous. Gabby could feel the hair on the back of her neck standing on end; every instinct was on high alert, convinced that something might leap out at them at any moment.

The three of them crept forward a few feet at a time. Gabby was looking every which way, peering into the gloom to see whether they were being followed. Trouble was her imagination was conjuring up plenty of things she was sure weren't there.

Still, she kept one hand on her gun, Just in case.

Her own breathing was loud within the confines of her suit and somehow the air tasted stale. Gabby shook herself. It wasn't like her to be almost hyperventilating on a mission. Good mercenaries, mercenaries who wanted to live a long time, did all their panicking *after* the mission. And yet here she was, one strange shadow away from an outright panic attack.

And with the way the three sets of torches were interacting, every shadow seemed strange.

They grew against the wall and lurched sideways as the light fell on outcroppings of rocks and piles of minerals and stalagthingies. Gabby's heart was racing and she could feel a sheen of perspiration all over her face.

I'm not panicking, I'm not panicking, she thought to herself.

She'd just about persuaded her heart rate to go back to normal when Ewan fired his cannon at something to the side. It was a low powered shot since there'd been little charge up time but the sound still reverberated around the close tunnels until Gabby's ears rang.

Adrenaline shot through her and she damn near pissed herself. Panicked fingers scrabbled for her gun but when the dust cleared, there was nothing there.

Anger replaced the fear and Gabby lashed out. "What the fuck Ewan?" she practically screamed down the comm.

"I thought I saw something," he yelled back. Judging by his tone of voice he was just as rattled as Gabby was.

"I don't care what you thought you saw," Gabby shouted, seething mad. "You can't just go off half-cocked like that. There are fucking procedures for a reason and that reason is so I don't take your fucking head off."

Lizzie tried to butt in. "Uh guys." Both of them ignored her.

"What was I doing? I was making sure none of us got our fucking hearts ripped out by that fucking monster. But then that's not a concern for you is it, *Gabriela*? You don't have one."

"Guys!" Lizzie shouted.

Gabby growled. "You fucking take that back you ginger cunt." She shoved him hard in the chest plate, but he didn't move; his armour kept him steady.

"Shut the fuck up!" Lizzie shouted, and Gabby and Ewan finally heard her over the haze of anger and the blood rushing in their ears. "We're not alone," she said, and she sounded every inch the teenager she actually was.

A cold feeling of horror crept down the back of Gabby's neck. What the fuck was wrong with her? She never got this distracted while on a mission. She was better than that. Judging by the look on Ewan's face, he was having the same revelation.

"What do you see Lizzie?" Gabby whispered, even though the volume of her voice on the comm didn't matter.

"Something's moving," she replied, and she sounded terrified. "Something dark. I can't see much."

"Where?" Ewan asked, his voice much calmer than the

last time Gabby had heard it. Lizzie gestured off to the group's nine o'clock.

"Okay," said Gabby. "Slowly move your torches in that direction. Start on three: one, two, three." The torches crept round at a tortuous pace. Gabby thought her heart might explode it was beating so fast.

The shadows shifted, growing and lengthening as the torches swung around. At about ten on the clock the cave wall gave way, opening out into blackness and empty space that seemed to swallow the light. Crouched in the middle of the dark was the Hellbeast breathing heavily, its crocodile jaws dripping. There were marks on its purple-black carapace that looked like wounds from Mila's rifle. This was their quarry alright.

The mercenaries stared at the Hellbeast. The Hellbeast stared back.

No one seemed to dare move.

"Back up slowly," Gabby said, continuing to whisper. "Don't startle it."

Ewan said something in Gaelic that was definitely swearing.

"Gabby," Lizzie said plaintively. She sounded as terrified as Gabby felt.

One step back. Two.

The Hellbeast didn't move.

Three, four, five.

It stayed still.

The other wall of the tunnel was coming up fast behind them. They'd have to take their eyes off it sooner or later if they wanted to get out of there.

Sweat dripped down Gabby's neck, the inside of her suit hot and humid.

"On my mark, we break for the rendezvous point," she said.

The Hellbeast screamed.

"Mark!"

The mercenaries took off at a run, and Gabby thought she heard the Hellbeast follow. She didn't look back to find out for sure. She was too busy running for her life.

Lizzie was out in front of the group, smaller and lighter in her armour than the other two. But she was also less used to running and tired more quickly. Gabby did her best to keep Lizzie from falling behind. She was not losing anyone.

They ran and ran. Turning corners blindly.

"Which way Lizzie?" Gabby yelled.

"This way," she shouted back, taking a right.

"Captain," Ewan shouted down the comm. "We're headed your way at speed. And we've got company."

"Roger that," said Ros. She sounded calm enough over the comm, but that was no guarantee of anything.

The three of them plunged forwards into the dark, hoping against hope their allies could do something about the monster they were currently acting as bait for.

They turned another corner, dove down another tunnel and then Gabby could see it; the faint glow of light in the small cavern they'd chosen as a staging ground, far ahead. She pushed her legs harder, her suit whirring and grinding as it fought to keep up.

And then Lizzie tripped.

She went down on her knees with a clatter and Gabby almost fell over her. Ewan shot past them and then paused. "Keep running," Gabby yelled. He hesitated but did as he was told, heading for the bright light and the promise of back up.

Gabby steadied herself and then dragged Lizzie to her feet.

"Leave me!" Lizzie said.

"I'm not losing anyone today," Gabby said through gritted teeth. She set Lizzie on her feet and started moving forward again. The first step Lizzie took she cried out and nearly went down again. Only the fact Gabby hadn't let go of her yet stopped her from falling over again.

"My ankle," she said, and Gabby could hear the tears choking her voice.

"It's probably just sprained," Gabby said in what she hoped was a reassuring voice. "AJ will fix you up no problemo."

Behind them, the Hellbest screamed.

"Leave me!" Lizzie shouted. "I'll only slow you down."

"I don't leave people behind," Gabby said.

Resolve crystallised in her chest. She'd seen what the Hellbeast could do, even to someone in top of the range armour like she was wearing, but she wasn't afraid. Not any more. She felt a cool, calm feeling wash over her, starting from where the panic had been roiling her stomach. She was a soldier, a comrade was down, and she would do whatever it took to get her back to base safely.

And if she couldn't do that then at least they wouldn't

die alone.

"Don't you dare die for me," Lizzie said and then hissed as she tried to take another step.

Gabby slung Lizzie's arm around her shoulders and held on tight. Then she swung them round, so they were facing direction of the Hellbeast's advance, the rendezvous point and their allies at their back.

"What are you doing? I can't walk backwards," Lizzie protested.

"Just move," Gabby said, and pulled her gun from her hip. Her voice was harsh, she knew, but coddling Lizzie now would get them both killed. Contrary to her protests, she could in fact walk backwards. For a certain definition of walking. Gabby flicked the comm with her thumb. "Ros, can you hear me?"

"I can hear you," she said. She sounded worried. "Where are you? We can see Ewan but not you and Lizzie."

"Lizzie fell. I'm helping her get back to camp but we can hear the Hellbeast following us. We could do with some back up, someone to buy us time."

"Should have kept Ewan with you," Ros chided. "Ewan, can you stay where you are? I'm coming to meet you. Arm the cannon."

"Aye Captain."

"Taylor, with me. Gabby, keep moving as long as you can."

"We will."

"You should have just left me," said Lizzie through tears and gritted teeth. Gabby reviewed her assessment it was just sprained; if it hurt that much to put weight on it in armour then there was a good chance it was broken.

"I need your sharp eyes Lizzie," Gabby said, ignoring her fear and self-deprecation and giving her something to focus on instead. "You're the only one who can see this thing in the dark. I need you looking out for me, can you do that?"

They took several steps backwards into the unknown dark before Lizzie nodded. "I can do that." Her voice sounded steadier already, her breathing more even.

Gabby's heart was beating quickly but now it was anticipation rather than fear. Despite the pitch black and the monster out for their blood, she felt more in control of the situation.

"There," Lizzie said, pointing straight ahead. "It's hanging back, well outside the light of our torches. I think it can tell I'm injured. It certainly seems to be stalking us."

As though it had heard Lizzie's words and wanted to prove her wrong, it screamed again and lurched forwards. Gabby reacted before she could even think, firing three bursts from her hip. She hit with every single shot.

It didn't seem to injure the creature, but it recoiled away from the muzzle flash.

"Gabby," Lizzie said. Her breathing had sped up and Gabby could tell she was heading back towards panic.

On the other hand, she was perfectly calm and still. Her gun hand didn't waver as she put three more rounds into the Hellbeast.

"I wish we knew where its vulnerable spots were,"

she complained.

"I'm not convinced it has any," Lizzie said bitterly.

Gabby kept them walking backwards at a steady pace, Lizzie held firmly by her side. Every few steps she fired another three round burst into the darkness, just to keep the creature at bay. The tactic wouldn't work forever though; either she'd run out of ammo or the Hellbeast would realise she wasn't doing any damage. She wasn't sure which would happen first.

"Come on Ros, where are you?"

"Right here," said a voice down the comm just as she heard footsteps behind her.

"Looks like the cavalry's here," she said happily.

The Hellbeast let loose another ungodly scream.

"Ewan!" Gabby wasn't sure who yelled his name, but he snapped into action. His arm cannon thrummed with energy as it powered up for a really impressive shot.

"Down in front," he yelled and Gabby hit the deck, pulling Lizzie down with her. The cannon went off with a boom that echoed off the walls and shook the ground Gabby was lying on.

When the dust settled, she looked up. The Hellbeast was still standing, only now it looked pissed.

"Well fuck," Ewan said at the same time as Gabby yelled "will nothing kill this fucking thing?"

"Everyone fall back," Ros said. "Retreat. Ewan; cover fire."

"Aye."

The next shot that went over Gabby's head was significantly lower powered than the ground shaking one.

Still, it was enough to make the Hellbeast fall back a few steps, hissing as it went.

Gabby pulled Lizzie to her feet again. "Come on kid," she said, "we're nearly there."

Lizzie gave her a smile that was more a grimace, and she looked pale and greenish even through her helmet visor. Taylor jogged up to them. "Let me take her," he said.

Gabby glanced at Lizzie, who nodded. Matty pulled her onto his back for a crude piggyback, hindered by his bulky powered armour. Once Lizzie was secure (comfort was a secondary concern for everyone by this point) he set off back to the rendezvous at a jog.

The Hellbeast was advancing again.

Gabby holstered her pistol and pulled her rifle from her back. Ros did the same.

The two of them fell into a familiar rhythm of laying down cover fire for a retreat. Gabby would hit the Hellbeast with a three round burst and then pause while Ros hit it with her own burst. They moved backwards bit by bit, keeping the creature pinned down under continuous fire the whole time. Every time it tried to get round them Ewan let loose with another underpowered shot from his cannon to persuade it otherwise. Gabby lost herself in the dance, the steps long ago ingrained in her muscles and her brain. She almost didn't notice they'd reached the cavern with the rendezvous point and back up.

She was vaguely aware of Taylor putting Lizzie on a stretcher and Tariq and Noora getting her out of there. That made tactical sense; they were essentially a team down but they'd lost the least combat experienced three of the group. She shook away the thought both Kendall and Donkin had had plenty of combat experience. The remaining six of them should be able to take the monster down. She hoped.

"Plan?" Gabby said, risking a sideways look at Ros.

The Captain quickly glanced at the roof of the cave and then her attention snapped back to the enemy. "Let's bring the house down."

Gabby grinned to herself even as she heard Ewan whoop with excitement.

"The colonist's resources?" Mila asked, the only dissenting voice in the crowd.

"They can worry about digging them out once this thing is dead," Ros said.

Taylor and Potts had joined in laying down suppression fire and the four of them were doing a good job of keeping the Hellbeast at bay even if they weren't doing much damage.

Ros quickly outlined the plan and, while it wasn't the best she'd ever come up with, it wasn't the worst. And she certainly had experience in creative demolition.

In between bursts of fire Gabby pulled grenades from her belt and armed them, but didn't set the timer. Ros, Matty and Ollie were doing the same, dropping the grenades to the cave floor as they retreated towards the cave entrance, back towards the light where they would have the advantage. Mila and Ewan were doing the same with the cave ceiling, coating their grenades in ultra strong adhesive before throwing them upwards.

The Hellbeast stubbornly kept coming after them, not a fucking clue in the world what they were doing.

"Come on you bastard," Gabby muttered as the put another few rounds into its impenetrable hide.

They were almost to the cave entrance now and Gabby's grenade belt was nearly empty.

"Power her up Ewan! Mila, ready your shot," the Captain called.

"Right between the eyes," the Russian said, her voice cold and steady. Gabby hoped she never ended up on the woman's bad side.

Ewan's cannon loosed a high-pitched whirr as it charged to its maximum setting.

"On the count of three," said the Captain. "One, two, three."

The mercenaries burst into action. Mila's rifle barked twice in quick succession and the Hellbeast stumbled as it was hit in the face with powerful concussive rounds. Gabby saw the first one hit but not the second; she was too busy running towards the light with Ros, Taylor and Ollie.

Bright sunlight nearly blinded her as she emerged from the darkness. She flipped the sun filter down on her visor and kept running; she needed to be as far away from the cave entrance as possible.

Ros dived behind a pile of rocks and Gabby followed suit just as she heard the boom of Ewan's cannon going off. There was a pause that felt like an age and the she heard a second explosion, and a third. The planned chain reaction roared to life, grenades popping like popcorn in a microwave, the explosions almost drowned out by the sound of shattering and falling rock.

Ewan and Mila made it to cover just as a last decisive boom turned the entrance to the cave system to rubble and dust.

Gabby held her breath, senses alert for any sign of the monster. Nothing. She shared a look with Ros who signalled they she couldn't detect anything either.

The dust settled and nothing moved. No screams pierced the air. No rocks moved ominously. They'd done it.

Gabby let out a whoop of celebration. They had done it.

CHAPTER SEVEN

ROS

Ros fought to get her breath back as the dust settled all around them. That had been one hell of any explosion. She was glad of the air filters in her suit, otherwise she'd be choking on particles of rock as she breathed deeply, desperately trying to get air into her lungs.

Her eyes were trained on the pile of shattered rock that had been a cave entrance a few minutes ago, searching the rubble for any sign that their enemy might have survived.

Nothing moved. The only thing she could hear was the harsh rasp of her breathing.

Gabby glanced at Ros, her eyes asking if she could see anything. Ros signalled in the negative. All she could see hear and smell was explosive and charred rock. No sign of the bastard Hellbeast. It looked like they'd done it.

She heard Gabby whoop in triumph down the comm. Ewan quickly joined in, leaping to his feet and shouting in the direction of their dead prey in a mixture of languages; Ros only recognised a handful of the words but all of them were rude. Matty was laughing and telling Ewan not to let his cannon off (possibly a euphemism, it was often better not to ask with those two) while Mila sat regally on the floor, already checking her gun for damage.

Ros couldn't believe it had worked. Gabby had been kind enough not to say anything, but she had a history of things not going as planned when explosives were involved. It was a fucking miracle the cave had collapsed in almost the exact way she'd pictured, let alone the fact that the Hellbeast had been trapped under a few tonnes of rock.

She stepped forwards, slowly, each foot planted with caution; Ros didn't trust her luck and wasn't about to call victory, despite the noise her Irregulars were making. She'd seen the mess the Hellbeast had made of Donkin and Kendall's bodies, she'd seen it take any number of shots from Mila's rifle without so much as missing a step; she wouldn't call the mission a success until she saw the body with her own eyes.

Her professional reputation was at stake, not to mention the restless souls of two mercenaries who's deaths weight heavy on her conscience.

"Taylor," she barked down the comm, stopping him from celebrating mid jump. "Get on the radio to the rest of the team. I want to know how Lizzie is and we'll need extra helping hands for clean-up."

"Yes Captain," he said, legs automatically snapping together as he stood to attention.

"Something the matter Capitan?" Gabby asked on their private channel, coming to stand by her side. Ros didn't take her eyes off the pile of rubble.

"I don't trust the situation. I won't believe it's dead until we've dug the body out and I've seen it with my own eyes."

Gabby just nodded, her face grim. For all that she'd been the first to celebrate, Gabby knew she had a pragmatic head on her shoulders; if her Captain wasn't convinced their target was dead, then neither was she.

"Ewan, stop your fucking bawling and pull the shovels out," she said, switching back to the general comm. "I want to make damn sure we got that thing."

"Aye Captain," he said.

"In the meantime I suppose I should go give the Assistant Governor and update." Gabby shot her a soft, secret smile through her helmet, but said nothing.

"Lizzie's fine," Matty said stepping back into the conversation. "AJ says the ankle is broken but it should respond to the bone knitter just fine. She'll be back on her feet in a couple of days. Tariq and Noora are on their way back with Siddiqui and some heavy lifting equipment."

"Good, good," Ros muttered under her breath, already planning the logistics of the next few days. Dealing with the paperwork, making sure they got paid, R&R for the crew, having Donkin and Kendall's bodies sent home... There was a lot to do.

As Ros turned to walk away, she heard the last thing she wanted to hear; the sound of rocks falling rolling down the side of the pile. Something under the mound of rubble was moving.

"What the..." she heard Ewan mutter

Her suit flashed a warning at her and she whipped back around, heart in her throat. No... it couldn't be...

An all too familiar scream split the air as something burst upwards out of the rubble, rocks of all sizes flying everywhere. Ros's sensors went to static at the sound.

"How the fuck did it survive *that*?" Matty yelled.

Ros had no idea, but her stomach felt like it had gone

on vacation somewhere between her feet.

At least the Hellbeast seemed to have been injured this time. One of its forelegs was practically hanging off, and its snout was bent at a precarious angle. Black gore was dripping from its torso—it looked like some of the protective scutes on its back had come apart—and it was limping. It was hurt bad and pissed off about it.

"Mila!" Ros shouted as she went for her rifle; Margaret was off her shoulder and powered up in seconds.

A rifle shot split the air, and the Hellbeast screamed as its bad arm came off entirely. A stream of angry Russian came down the comm but Ros knew the job was far from done. They were out in the open and had daylight on their side but this creature was still standing after having a couple of tonnes of rock dropped on its head; this wasn't going to be easy.

"Flanking patterns," Ros called. "Gabby, Ollie, go left. Taylor, you're with me. Ewan, Mila, keep down the centre."

Ros got confirmation from her people as the teams split off, circling round the beast which had a wary look in its eye. She didn't like the intelligence the damn thing kept displaying.

"Padre nuestro que estás en los cielos, santificado sea tu Nombre," Gabby muttered under her breath. Ros wasn't sure whether she was on their private channel or the general one but she hoped God was on their side for this fight; they needed all the help they could get.

Ewan's cannon sang as it powered up. The Hellbeast

cocked its head to one side, dark eyes fixed firmly on Ewan as it backed up a few steps, feet slipping on the rubble. It seemed wary of the centre team, was it possible it was aware who was to blame for its current injuries? That level of intelligence was unnerving but they could use it. Potentially.

"Ewan, Mila, use your fire to drive it towards Gabby and Ollie," Ros barked. Another shot rang out with a crack, whizzing past the Hellbeast's face. Ros saw the creature move left in response. "Yes! Keep going," she cried. "Taylor and I will try to get behind it."

The Irregulars all did their jobs well, Ewan and Mila working to move the Hellbeast where they wanted it while Gabby and Ollie lay in wait. Ros and Taylor circled round the pile of rubble eyes peeled for any weak spot they could find.

Unfortunately for them, the Hellbeast had a mind of its own and didn't want to play by the rules.

Ros and Taylor hadn't yet moved into position behind it when the Hellbeast let out another scream that shorted the cameras and sensors on her suit. When the static subsided enough to see again the Hellbeast was bounding towards where Gabby and Potts were lying in wait. They were well trained though, and were on their feet in a flash, firing their weapons to keep the monster at bay.

The damn thing just shrugged it off.

Ros took off at a run, trying to get to her best friend to help her but her suit had no way of compensating for the uneven terrain and it was slow going. The Hellbeast was faster; Ros wouldn't get there in time to help her friend.

"Gabby!" she yelled as the Hellbeast turned and knocked the other mercenaries off their feet with a vicious swipe of its tail. Nether Gabby nor Potts got back up.

Ros's vision went red. Margaret was in her hand and she was firing before she even thought about it. If Gabby was dead...

No, she couldn't think about that. She wasn't dead. She couldn't be. Ros didn't know what she'd do without her.

She advanced on the Hellbeast, finger on Margaret's trigger, constant fire peppering the creature's hide. It didn't seem to care.

"Why won't you just die?" Ros spat.

Whether the thing could hear her or not she couldn't tell, but it whipped round and fixed its glare on Ros.

"Yeah come on you scaly fucking bastard," she screamed, loud enough to make the comms buzz. "Come and get me."

The thing advanced on her. Ros didn't relent, either with her weapons fire or her swearing.

"Uh boss," Taylor said, sounding like a scared little kid. "Are you sure it's a good idea to goad this thing?"

"Either help me shoot this fucker or shut the fuck up Matty," Ros snapped. Gabby still hadn't got up and her heart was pounding like she'd run a marathon. There was a horrible sick feeling in her stomach that got worse with every second Hernandez was down. "Ewan, Mila, cover fire. I'm going after our guys."

"On it boss!" Ewan said and let loose with a stream of

Gaelic insults. A steady tide of Russian joined it and between the two of them it was a wonder the air didn't turn blue.

Ros slipped Margaret back onto her shoulder as Matty finally started firing at the Hellbeast. The damn thing charged at her but she dived out of the way, rolling down the side of the rubble-pile. Her head hit the back of her helmet as she landed and she bit her tongue. Copper warmth filled her mouth, but she swallowed it; it was never a good idea to spit with your visor down and she didn't have time to open it, not when Gabby needed her.

"You alright boss?" Matty called.

She pushed herself onto her knees. "I'm fine," Ros said. She could still taste blood and her head hurt but none of that mattered. "Keep that thing's attention on you." She found her feet again and took off at a run, her gait unhindered by unsteady terrain as she went around the pile of boulders.

Between the three of them they kept the Hellbeast's attention long enough for Ros to get to Gabby. She flicked her heads up display to show vital signs for her team members but at that moment the creature let out another scream, turning everything to static.

"For fuck's sake," Ros bellowed. She was utterly fucking terrified at this point; Gabby was still down, as was Potts, and that wasn't a good sign. Could their bastard prey give her a minute to check whether her people were still alive?

Apparently not.

The sensors on Ros's helmet went back to normal,

and she scrabbled closer, but before she could take any readings Matty gave a shout.

"Boss look out!"

Ros ducked, acting on pure instinct and that was what saved her. Razor-sharp claws whistled through the air where her head had been just moments before. She hit the ground with a jolt and immediately scrabbled for her weapon; her fingers fumbled with the straps on Margaret's holster.

Her blood ran hot in her veins, her chest pounding from the adrenaline. She couldn't make her fingers work. Why couldn't she make her fingers work? Gabby was still down; the display on Ros's suit told her she was still alive but not why she hadn't got up yet. For all Ros knew Gabby could be bleeding out inside her suit, or into her brain.

She shook herself. She couldn't think about that. Not when three of her mercs were still very much alive. Finally, and with great effort, she found her feet again. Margaret came loose from her holster and she was ready to join the fight again.

While she was down the Hellbeast had been drawn away by Ewan and Matty. Mila was stood at a distance taking what shots she could without endangering her squad mates. The two men were drawing the creature back and forth between the two of them; from what Ros could tell they were trying to tire it out. As her hearing came back properly, she could hear the constant stream of taunts and swearwords being tossed between the two men, the crack of Mila's rifle and the boom of Ewan's cannon. How hard had she hit her head, anyway?

"Need some help there fellas?" she asked.

"Wouldn't say no," Matty shot back. He sounded out of breath. They'd really been making the Hellbeast work, and yet it barely seemed to notice. It waved its remaining three arms in front of it, trying to bat away the shots Ewan and Matty were sending its way. Only Mila's shots seemed to do any damage, and then it was too little. They could do this for days and barely scratch the bastard thing.

"Hasn't anyone found a weak spot?" Ros asked, jogging lightly to take her place in the back and forth tactics they'd set up.

"Nyet," said Mila as she lined up another shot. The crack of the rifle nearly deafened Ros but the Hellbeast barely seemed to feel it. "I keep trying Captain."

Ewan let off another round from his arm cannon (was he still keeping them underpowered on purpose? He couldn't have much charge left) and that seemed to piss the monster off. It let out another scream—thankfully Ros's sensors didn't short out this time—and darted forwards, headed straight for Ewan. Ros tried to call out, to warn him, but there wasn't time. The creature's jaws clamped down on his cannon with an audible crunch and lifted him clear into the air.

"Ewan!" Ros cried.

The Hellbeast continued chewing on his prosthetic and picked Ewan up, swinging him from side to side in the air. If it kept this up, he would lose the rest of his arm. Ros wanted to get a shot off, to help her friend, but there was no way of making sure Ewan didn't get hurt in the crossfire.

"Oh no you don't you fucken bawbag," the Scotsman shouted. His bushy ginger eyebrows were creased in concentration and his face was red from exertion. He looked pissed off as all hell.

The cannon hummed as Ewan powered it up (and how he could do that while being flung through the air on a shoulder that *had* to be dislocated Ros would never know). The Hellbeast didn't seem to notice.

Ewan fired his cannon, and it went off with a loud crackathoom. The big ginger bastard was blown backwards out of the Hellbeast's mouth and went flying towards a nearby rock.

There was a scream in Ros's throat, desperate to be let loose but there wasn't time for that. The Hellbeast was spitting back ichor and chunks of flesh but the damn thing was still standing. Three of her people were now down and Ros had had enough.

Margaret sang, high-pitched and familiar as she laid into the Hellbeast. Matty joined in with a roar and even Mila let loose another volley of invective as she joined in the fight. Everyone in the Irregulars fucking loved Ewan, and if he was hurt...

Somehow, in between the rage and the sheet terror that threatened to make her vomit, Ros found the breath to call out. "Ewan, you alive you bastard?"

"Aye Captain," came the reply, and Ros couldn't remember the last time she'd felt so damned relieved. "I'm afraid I'm out of this fight though."

"You sit tight," Ros said. "AJ will kill me if anything happens to you." Margaret barked once, twice, three times and still the Hellbeast didn't give in. "If you can move see if there's anything you can do for Hernandez and Potts."

"Aye," Ewan said. Ros had never heard him sound so weary.

Her eyes flicked toward her downed soldiers and that was all the advantage the Hellbeast needed. It gave up trying to dance around the hail of fire coming its way and pounced for Ros.

"Boss!" Matty yelled as he dived in front of her taking the blow for her.

"No!" Ros yelled, but it was too late.

The Hellbeast struck Matty with a swipe of its claws, knocking him off his feet even as she heard the tearing of the metal of his suit. He tumbled a few feet, his weapon clattering uselessly to the side, and then was still.

Ros screamed.

Rage blinded her. It was just her and Mila now and that wasn't fucking good enough. She wouldn't stand by while her entire crew was slaughtered.

With a bellow Ros charged for the Hellbeast, ducking and weaving around blows from his claws and tail alike. She couldn't hear anything down the comm; the only sound in her head was the scream that had been fighting its way out of her throat.

Ros took a rolling dive over the creature's muscular tail and, for the first time, found herself behind it. Its back was armoured, almost like armadillos, and in a flash Ros knew what she had to do. There was probably a weak spot at the join between the armoured plates and the rest of its body, one she'd be able to take advantage of.

She looked at the creature's back and knew she'd be able to climb it.

She'd climbed worse.

Ros didn't think, the only thing keeping her going was rage and adrenaline, everything coming through as pure instinct. Ros holstered Margaret—she was running hot and needed a break anyway—and took a flying leap onto the Hellbeast's back. The protective bands moved as it tried frantically to get her off. Ros could feel the impact of Mila's concussive rounds hitting the beast, and she knew at least one of her allies was still standing.

It swiped with its tail, trying to knock Ros to the ground, but it couldn't reach. It tried with one of its remaining claws and had more success. Ros's suit beeped frantically at her as the razor-sharp claws tore through her leg. She laughed; it was the leg she'd lost already and all the Hellbeast had accomplished was ripping new scars into her prosthetic. Her stump might sting later but right now she couldn't feel anything over the rush of adrenaline in her system.

She hoped there would be a later.

After what felt like hours Ros finally pulled herself onto the Hellbeast's shoulders, looking down over the battlefield from their enemy's perspective. Damn thing was tall. Matty was off to the side, his suit crimson with blood. Ros put it out of her mind.

Only one thing mattered now; killing the beast.

She pressed a control to flick out the super-heated blade hidden in the arm of her suit and fired it up. The filament glowed red and then went to white as it came up to temperature. The blade burned so bright Ros had to put down the sun visor on her helmet to see at all.

Holding on to the Hellbeast's head with one hand, she drew the blade back, readying for the final blow.

"This one's for Matty," she yelled, and stabbed downwards with all her remaining strength.

The super-heated edge of the blade ate through the Hellbeast's flesh like it was butter.

The creature screamed loud enough to not only short out the circuits on Ros's suit but to make her ears ring and her head go fuzzy. She thought she could hear Mila groaning down the comm—no doubt suffering as much of a headache as Ros was—but with the incessant noise knocking her brain around she couldn't tell.

She pushed harder.

Black goo bubbled up from the gaping wound in the Hellbeast's neck, charred and smelling like a barbecue gone wrong. Still Ros leaned her weigh onto her blade. The gauntleted fist of her suit sank into the Hellbeast's flesh and it let out another gurgling scream.

Finally, finally she was doing some damage.

Ros pressed even harder. She didn't know how deep her blade had gone but the creature was thrashing and bucking, desperate to throw her off. Her arm was anchored deep within its chest cavity however, and she was going nowhere.

The beast fell to its knees and Ros was almost flung from her perch.

Pulling on her remaining strength she bent her arm at

the elbow, drawing the super-heated edge of the blade up and out. She didn't stop until she saw the glowing tip protruding from the Hellbeast's flesh, spattered with blackened gore.

With a flourish she pulled her arm out, nearly severing the beasts head as she did so. Her blade's heating filament had burnt out, and the edges turned black and brittle. Ros jumped off the beast's back even as it slumped to the side, definitely dead.

She'd turned its insides to soup; there was no way it was getting back up after that.

Just in case, she ordered Mila to put a full clip of concussive rounds through its brain, which the Russian did with an air of sadistic glee.

The Hellbeast was dead.

Ros almost fell to her knees in relief, but there was still work to do.

Ewan had crawled over to where Hernandez and Potts were still lying n the ground, leaving Ros free to rush to Matty's side.

The poor bastard was still alive.

"Matty," she called, as she ran to him, popping her blade back into its holster and tearing her helmet off. The stench of burning metal and cooked flesh hit her nostrils making her choke on her own bile, but she only cared about her idiot second-in-command.

"Captain," he choked, the sound wet and gurgling low in his chest. The Hellbeast had caught him right through the torso, the thick carbon-steel of his massive suits armour plating no match for those deadly claws. The wound weren't as deep as those she'd seen on Kendall's body but they were deep enough. He was bleeding out, his lungs fulfilling with blood and suffocating.

Where the hell was AJ?

"Get the medic!" Ros cried, her voice hoarse from all the screaming she'd done in her final battle with the beast. She pulled Matty to her chest, cradling in her arms. She desperately wanted to stem the bleeding but there was no time to pull her gauntlets off.

"No good cap'n," Matty said, slurring his words a little. "I'm a goner."

"Don't you talk like that," Ros said, choking on the words. "You're not dead until AJ says you are." Something hot and wet was running down her face and she realised she was crying.

Matty coughed and when it stopped his lips were red with blood. He licked them and grimaced at the taste.

"Why?" Ros asked, desperate. "Why would you do that for me? You didn't have to take that blow."

He smiled, but it was lopsided, like he was forgetting how his face muscles worked. "Yeah, I did. You're the boss," he said, like that explained everything.

He coughed again, a longer fit this time and Ros was afraid he would stop breathing before the end of it. When he took a gasping rattle of a breath after the coughing subsided her heart nearly stopped. "Just tell me I did good boss," he said. His voice was getting thready and weak and she knew it wouldn't be long now; AJ wouldn't get here in time and even if he did, there was nothing he could do for Matty.

"You did good Taylor," Ros said, somehow managing a smile. "You're a fucking idiot, but you did good."

He grinned at that, his teeth red. "Was the best secretary you ever had, huh?"

"You were never just a secretary Matty, never," Ros said fiercely. Suddenly it was important to her he understood that before he died. "You were always more than that and you know it."

Ros's eyes stung, but the tears kept coming. Matty just nodded and looked away, staring into the distance. He was still staring when his final breath rattled out of him and his body grew still.

Ros screamed. Her throat felt like it was bleeding but she didn't care.

The bastard had died for her, and she would never forgive him.

"Capitan?" said a tentative voice at her side, and Ros would have cried if she wasn't already. She looked up from the body cradled against her chest into familiar eyes. Gabby was okay.

Somehow the relief of that knowledge didn't outweigh her grief.

It brought her to her senses long enough to realise she was still a Captain, and she still had a job to do. She laid Matty's body back down and pulled her gauntlets off so she could close his eyes. At her side, Gabby was muttering the last rites under her breath.

Ros got to her feet and wiped her face. Her eyes felt all puffy and sore, but she'd live. Matty wouldn't. It took a moment for her to pull herself together.

"What happened to you?" Ros asked, noticing for the first time that Gabby wasn't wearing her armour.

"Something in my suit fried when I went down and everything locked up. I couldn't move, couldn't even activate the comm. I was fucking terrified until Ewan flipped the emergency release and let me out."

"Potts?" Ros asked. She wasn't sure she could deal with losing another merc today.

"Head injury. He's still out but AJ's on his way. We'll know more when he arrives."

Ros nodded. "We uh. We need to sort out the body," she said. Her mouth didn't want to work properly.

"We'll sort it," Gabby said gently. "We'll do right by Matty," she promised.

Ros barely heard her. Her eyes had flickered back to the Hellbeast's charred remains. Rage bubbled up inside her again as hot and intense as it had during the battle. Before she knew what she was doing she'd hobbled over to the monstrous body and was laying into it, kicking it with energy she shouldn't still have. Her bad leg threatened to buckle under her but she kept going, pounding into the creature's hide with every ounce of hate she possessed. Gabby just watched her.

It was a long time before she could bring herself to stop.

CHAPTER EIGHT

ISOBEL

The whole colony had an air of celebration in the aftermath of Captain Lamarr's victory. The Hellbeast, as it had become known, had plagued Novis almost since its founding and to be rid of it, finally, was a huge relief for all the settlers.

Not to mention the Governor and his daughter.

The relief Isobel felt was almost tangible in its intensity. No more writing to colonist's relatives to break the bad news; no more begging the Commonwealth government for more funding to entice people to settle here; no more meetings with their corporate sponsors to discuss the lives and deaths of people she'd known, lived and worked with in terms of profit margins and asset loss.

It was done. Over. She could finally relax.

She'd always been a people person and kept an eye on the mood of the colony from the moment she was appointed her father's assistant. Isobel knew the colonists would need some sort of official celebration, some time where they could let their hair down and cut loose, knowing they were safe. So she persuaded her father to obtain funding for a proper party, here at the Governor's mansion.

Food and wine (actual proper alcohol, Isobel didn't know the last time she'd had some) flowed easily and there were smiles all round. The Erebus Station Irregulars, now the heroes of Novis Colony, had also been invited and were the centre of attention as the surviving colonists sought to congratulate their saviours. Everyone was having a wonderful time.

Everyone except for Captain Lamarr that was.

Ros had been quiet and withdrawn since the Hellbeast had finally been defeated. She'd gone to the Governor's mansion on foot and presented Benoit and Isobel with one of the creature's severed arms; a gruesome trophy and proof it had indeed been killed. The mercenary Captain's face had been puffy, her eyes red rimmed and Isobel knew then that the cost of victory had been high. She'd asked Ros about her crew and, tight-lipped, she'd explained that she'd lost her second-in-command in the battle. Isobel had wanted to say something, anything, to comfort her, but the merc had stormed out before she could find the words. Isobel hadn't spoken to Ros since; all communication had been through Gabby Hernandez, who was now second-in-command.

At some point during their acquaintance she had developed an almost supernatural ability to know where the mercenary Captain was at all times, so of course she noticed when Ros vacated the corner she'd been scowling in all night and slipped out into the garden. Her fingers itched; she wanted to go after her, but she was mid conversation with the twins, Tariq and Noora Mubarak, and it would have been rude to leave them. Not that she wasn't enjoying their interaction immensely.

According to the Irregulars the Mubarak twins were quiet and insular but Isobel hadn't found this to be the case at all. Tariq said little but when he did, he had a biting wit. And despite seeming serious and focused on the mission he'd spent the evening teaching Isobel how to swear in Arabic (not that she was sure *when* she'd have the opportunity to say rude things about people's mums in another language). Noora was a little more outgoing than her brother and had been shyly flirting with Isobel all evening. Isobel had spent enough time around Gabby Hernandez to recognise the flirting techniques as hers and wondered if there was history there or whether she'd just picked up a tip or two along the way.

The Irregulars had also said it could be difficult to get any personal information from either of them but they had already informed Isobel that they were identical twins, not fraternal. She'd wondered how that worked for a moment and then the penny dropped.

"One of us is trans," Noora had said with a grin. "No, we're not telling you which."

Isobel asked no more questions about their genders, figuring it was their business whether they told her the full story or not. She felt honoured that they'd confided that in her after only knowing them a few days and wondered what assholes they'd encountered in the past that made them so protective of each other. Isobel wanted to hit them on the twins' behalf, and she wasn't a violent person.

When her attention finally flickered back to the conversation, Noora was looking at her with an expression that was half sadness, half amusement. Isobel immediately felt guilty for not having been paying attention.

"I'm sorry what were you saying?" she asked.

"It's okay," Noora said, her accent curling around the vowels in a way Isobel would have found deeply attractive if her attention wasn't elsewhere. "You should go after her."

"But–"

"Go after her, habibti," Noora said with a smile. "I can make a tactical retreat."

Isobel felt bad for her. There was no guarantee Ros would welcome her attention and there was a very attractive, interesting woman in front of her who was obviously keen on getting to know her better. But the heart wants what the heart wants, as the saying goes, and Isobel's had belonged to Ros Lamarr from the moment she'd laid eyes on her. "Sure?"

"Sure. Captain's been withdrawn since Matty died. Go see if you can cheer her up."

"I'll talk to you later," Isobel said, and she meant it. This was a young woman she wanted to keep as a friend.

Noora smiled and turned to her brother, the two of them slipping back into their native Arabic. Isobel grabbed her drink and followed in Ros's footsteps.

She leaned against the door frame, wine glass in her hand, looking out over the garden. It was mostly a practical space, used for growing food and other useful plants for the colony's use, but she'd tied hard to make the space beautiful. Peaceful. She'd succeeded judging by the way Ros sat on a small rock with her feet dangling in one of the irrigation canals. Isobel had always found the sound of running water soothing and it looked like Ros did too. She wanted to go talk to the Captain, an ache in her chest when she thought of the hurt she must be feeling, but she hardly knew the woman. It wasn't her place to help.

She wanted to though. So very badly.

Despite the encouragement Noora had given her, she hesitated.

Isobel felt the warm brush of fabric against her arm and tore her eyes away from the mercenary Captain in the garden; it was Gabriela Hernandez, and her eyes too were fixed on Ros.

"She's been like this for days," she said quietly, so her voice wouldn't carry. "Ever since the incident. She won't sleep, won't eat, won't talk to me. She just sits there and broods. It's not healthy."

"You're worried."

"Damn right I'm worried," Gabby said, somehow expressing her anger without raising her voice. "She's my Captain, but she's also my friend. I just want her to be okay."

Gabby seemed to deflate a little then and Isobel found herself at a loss. She knew how to deal with people in many situations but somehow she didn't know what to do now; when people were hurting, and she wanted to reach out, to comfort, but daren't because they were practically strangers.

"Can't you pull her out of it?" Isobel asked, knowing it was foolish even before the words left her mouth.

"Believe me, I've tried," she said, and Isobel could

practically feel the frustration pouring of Gabby in that moment. "I guess this is just one of those things she's gotta work out for herself. As much as it hurts to see her like this."

Isobel knew how she felt.

Gabby looked at Isobel slyly out of the corner of her eye, a small smirk tugging at her lips. "I don't think she'd turn down *your* company though."

Something in Isobel's chest flip-flopped at the implications of that, but she pushed it away. "Why me? What do you think I can do to help when she won't let you in?"

"I've known Rosalind Lamarr a long time," she said, "and sometimes I think I know her better than she knows herself. I can read that woman like a book, and I know what she looks like when she's smitten with someone. That–" she said, pointing at the figure on the rock "–isn't all grief, trust me."

Isobel didn't know quite how to respond to that so she settled for swallowing awkwardly.

After a moment Gabby continued. "Did you know that before this mission she'd only ever lost two crew members?"

"I did." That information was freely available in the Irregulars' public records, and it had been one reason Isobel had hired the crew in the first place.

"She's taking it hard that she's doubled that on this mission, not to mention losing Matty," Gabby continued. "She always had a soft spot for the little shit," she said with a smile on her face. Judging by the tone of her voice

Ros wasn't the only one with a soft spot for the late Lieutenant Taylor.

"When you say 'soft spot'..." Isobel said. She knew she sounded jealous, but she couldn't quite seem to hold it in.'

Gabby stifled a laugh in her palm. "No no, it was never like that. He was more like a brother, for both of us. He was the first hire we made back when we set the Irregulars up. It's gonna be hard to adjust to him not being there." Isobel murmured her agreement. "Anyway, Ros is all about the women. One woman in particular if you catch my meaning. I think she might find Matty's loss a little easier to deal with if you were there," Gabby said softly and for all the innuendo in her voice before, Isobel could tell she meant it. Ros Lamarr was as infatuated with Isobel as Isobel was with her. At least, according to her oldest friend. That was enough encouragement for Isobel. "Go to her," Gabby said, eyes soft in the moonlight.

So Isobel did.

She approached carefully, trying to make her approach seem casual rather than deliberate. She didn't want to startle Ros from her thoughts. Partly because she didn't want to and partly because she knew what happened when you startled people with military training. It didn't really matter; with the way Ros was staring at the water like she could set it on fire with her mind she probably wouldn't have noticed half a battalion marching past.

Isobel paused as she reached the rock Ros was using as a bench, suddenly unsure. She looked around to get reassurance from Gabby but she was nowhere to be seen.

She took a sip from her glass, telling herself she didn't need Dutch courage (though she knew full well she did) and opened her mouth to speak.

"Is this seat taken?" Isobel asked quietly.

Ros started and stumbled to get her words out. "Yes! I mean... no it's not taken. You may sit. If you would like."

Isobel just smiled and took a seat not too close to Ros as to seem improper but not so far away that there could be physical contact if that was desired. "You're missing your own party," she said gently, not wanting it to sound like an accusation. She didn't blame Ros for wanting time to herself and needed to get that across.

"Yeah. Needed some fresh air. Too many people." She tried to smile at Isobel but even she could tell it was forced. There were shadows under Ros's eyes that hadn't been there a week ago, and her eyes looked bloodshot. Gabby had been right; she wasn't sleeping.

Her heart constricted and Isobel felt an overwhelming need to fix things. She wasn't quite sure how to go about that. So the pair just sat in silence for a while, listening to the running water.

It didn't feel as awkward as it maybe should have.

"I'm sorry about Lieutenant Taylor," Isobel said quietly, wanting to get that conversational elephant out of the way as early in the conversation as possible. "Your other people too."

Ros nodded and her jaw tightened. "Thanks," she said stiffly. "They were good people. All of them." she went back to staring at the water.

Isobel took a sip of her wine and then nudged Ros,

offering her the glass. She was almost surprised when Ros accepted it, took a sip and handed it back. They passed the wine back and forth for a while in silence. It was oddly intimate considering the two women hadn't known each other long.

Eventually the wine dwindled to a few dregs, and while Isobel thought that was probably her cue to leave Ros be and go find another drink, she really didn't want to.

"How are you holding up?" she asked instead.

Ros sighed, the sound rattling up from deep within her. "Not great," she said, and Isobel heard honesty in her voice. She sounded tired, worn.

"Anything I can do?"

"Just... being here helps for some reason."

Isobel smiled. "Gabby thought it might."

The look Ros gave her at that was more resigned than surprised but there was still a certain amount of shock there. Possibly because Isobel was willing to admit it. "Gabby is meddling again." There was a harshness to her voice then, and the thought struck Isobel that Ros might think she was only there because Gabby had made her.

"She just wants to help," she said. "I was dithering about whether to come to you and she gave me the nudge I needed."

"You wanted to keep me company?" She sounded surprised.

She nodded. "I don't like seeing you so withdrawn," she said honestly. "I wanted to see if I could help."

"You are helping," Ros said, nudging Isobel's arm with

her own. She didn't move back into her own space afterwards, instead leaving her arm resting against Isobel's. She could feel the warmth radiating off the other woman's body, which was pleasant in the cool night air of Novis.

Isobel's heart raced at the contact, pounding even faster when she realised Ros could probably feel it too.

"Your heart's racing," Ros murmured after a while.

"I'm nervous."

"Not used to being so close to a bad ass gun-toting mercenary?" Ros said, but the joke fell a little flat. There was doubt in her eyes and her posture shifted subtly to be more defensive. Isobel wouldn't have noticed if she hadn't had years of training in the art of reading people through their body language.

"More like I'm not used to being so close to a woman I'm attracted to," she said.

Ros shot her a look that was all surprise. A smile slowly spread across her face, lighting up her eyes in a way that chased away the shadows under them. Isobel knew then that even if the feelings swirling around in her chest weren't reciprocated, Ros was pleased by the revelation.

"So you're attracted to me, huh?" said Ros with a cheeky wink.

"Of course I am," Isobel replied. "Have you *seen* you?"

Ros looked incredibly pleased by that remark. "Why thank you, Assistant Governor Devereux. That's one of the nicest compliments I've ever received."

"Call me Isobel," she said as she leaned closer, unable

to stand the distance between them. "Or Izzy, if you really want."

"Izzy?" Ros breathed. Their faces were close together now; Isobel could almost taste the wine on her breath.

"My mother used to call me that. I don't let many people use it," Isobel said, wanting Ros to know how special she was, how she'd lit her heart up from the moment she'd first laid eyes on the mercenary. Ros's hand drifted up to caress Isobel's cheek gently and a shiver of pleasure ran down her spine.

"I feel privileged, Izzy." the tender look in her eyes was all honesty.

Isobel leaned impossibly closer. "You know we shouldn't really do this," she said, watching Ros shiver as her breath ghosted across her lips. "Bad form to fraternise with an employee."

"Jobs over, money's in the bank," Ros said, her lips curling up into the beginning of a wicked grin. "I'm not your employee any more.

"Well then, by all means," she breathed. Ros closed the space between them.

Kissing Ros Lamarr was like nothing Isobel had ever experienced before. The woman kissed with her whole body, pressing the length of her against Isobel until she thought she might combust. Her hands were in Isobel's hair, caressing her face, never staying in one spot for long. Her lips were rough and chapped but Isobel didn't care, the kiss was so so gentle, and those lips were the sweetest thing she'd ever tasted.

Isobel let out a sound that was half gasp, half moan,

unable to help herself. Ros took advantage of Isobel's open mouth to slide her tongue along her lower lip, seeking permission. Isobel felt like lightning was running down her spine. She pulled Ros closer, kissing her with every ounce of passion she possessed, which turned out to be quite a lot.

By the time they parted, breathing heavily and wearing ridiculous grins, Isobel had ended up sat in Ros's lap. She would have felt embarrassed about that, but given she'd just had one of the best kisses of her life she didn't really care.

"I've wanted to do that for a while," Isobel admitted.

"Me too," Ros said, and for a moment the happiness in her eyes chased away the shadows.

As they returned Isobel found herself wanting to chase them off again. Unable to think of a better way, she leaned in and kissed Ros again.

Isobel had meant to kiss Ros gently, to assure her that things would be okay and there were feelings here besides just wanting to kiss her senseless, but she quickly lost all control. Desire licked at her, urging her to kiss Ros harder, faster, to press closer. She nipped at Ros's lower lip with her teeth, dragging an undignified noise of pleasure from the Captain. She was lost, utterly lost in kissing this woman.

She ran her hands over Ros's short hair, longer now and shaggier than when she'd first arrived, ghosting her fingers gently over her ears and she pressed hot kisses to Ros's jawline, to her neck. Ros shivered and moaned.

Isobel was just wondering about the wisdom of

dragging Ros to her private chambers and skipping the rest of the party when Ros slowed the kiss and pulled away. She looked at Isobel with dark eyes, pupils wide with what could only be desire, and possibly something else Isobel couldn't quite read.

"Not that this isn't a wonderful way to pass the time," Ros said, her voice rough and low. It was the sexiest thing Isobel had ever heard. "But I think people might notice if we're missing from the party much longer."

As much as she hated to admit it, she knew Ros was right. Isobel was being a poor host as it was by being out here. Still, she wasn't quite ready for the moment to end.

She pressed a gentle kiss to Ros's mouth, very different from the ones they'd shared so far. This kiss spoke of feelings beneath the ragged desire in her chest, a promise that this wouldn't be the last time. When she was satisfied Ros had gotten the message (and she had, judging by the wide eyes look she was giving Isobel) she clambered out of Ros's lap and helped her to her feet. Isobel tutted when the mercenary shoved her boots back on without even bothering to try drying her feet off, which just earned her a wicked grin.

Isobel wanted nothing more than to head back to the party hand in hand, but she knew that couldn't happen. "We should probably go back separately," she said, the sadness in her voice barging its way to the forefront without her permission.

"Probably," Ros agreed. "I want to do this again sometime."

"I'll pencil you in," Isobel said dryly as she made her

way back into the mansion, via a bathroom to check her face bore no irreparable evidence of what she'd been up to.

When she slipped back into the party, it looked like no one had noticed her absence. Her father was holding court with several settlers who looked distinctly several sheets to the wind while the rest of them fawned over the Irregulars. Isobel got wicked grins from both Gabby and Noora, and then again when Ros sauntered back in, hands in her pocket like she hadn't a care in the world, but either no one else had noticed she was even gone or they didn't care. Isobel snagged another glass of wine and made another circuit of the room, stopping to speak to everyone there.

Ros had finally joined the party and was surrounded by a small gaggle of admirers, asking for stories of the Irregulars' exploits. Isobel made her way over to them while trying not to make it obvious that was where she desperately wanted to be (which probably meant she was being obvious about it) just in time for someone to asked how the crew got their name.

"So, Captain Lamarr, how did your company get the name 'Erebus Station Irregulars'?" one colonist asked, John, Isobel thought he was called.

Ros shrugged, a lopsided grin on her face. "I needed to name the something to register, and I was on Erebus Station at the time."

John nodded as though this was an eminently sensible decision. "And are you called the Irregulars because of your unconventional tactics?"

"Nah, I named us after the fact that my period never comes when I expect it to…" John blinked at that clearly surprised, and Ros's grin grew a fraction wider before she ruined it by bursting out laughing. "Of course it's because of our tactics. You should've seen your face though." John laughed along, but he looked distinctly uncomfortable.

"But Captain," Mila said, a look of confusion on her face. "There is nothing irregular about our tactics. We go in, shoot everything that moves and get paid."

This prompted another round of laughter from the group during which Ros met Isobel's gaze. It was hot and full of promise and it took all of Isobel's willpower to drag herself away. The slightest jerk of Ros's head indicated she wanted them to get out of there so Isobel finished her drink and went to say goodnight to her father. The party would do just fine without her.

It was very hard not to look like she was rushing. She wanted nothing more than to find out what Ros had planned, and her skin tingled as she considered the possibilities. She was on her way out, having said goodnight to everyone she was required to, when Gabby Hernandez collared her.

"Captain's looking a lot happier," she said simply.

"Yes," Isobel said, hoping the sudden rush of heat in her cheeks wasn't visible as a blush.

"Told you she'd let you help," Gabby said, a satisfied smile spreading over her face. She looked like a cat that had got into the cream. "Go get her tiger." She stepped aside so Isobel could pass.

"Thank you," Isobel said, and Gabby just nodded at

her. She slipped back into the party and was immediately surrounded by people clamouring for her attention. She wondered which of them would end up in her bed and then she decided a better use of her time was wondering who might end up in her own.

Just the thought of it was enough to make her hurry. Ros was waiting for her when she reached her chambers.

"I hope this isn't too presumptuous," the Captain said softly. The light of Novis's moon streamed in through the window, making Ros look almost ethereal. Isobel forgot how to breathe for a moment.

"You are beautiful, Captain Lamarr."

"So are you, Izzy." Ros looked ridiculously pleased to be allowed to use the pet name.

Isobel took a step towards her and then Ros was in her arms, kissing her with the same intensity she had earlier. Isobel had had lovers before, but she was sure none of them had ever kissed her like this, like she was the only person in the universe. She certainly hadn't had anyone focus so intently on just kissing her when they'd got to her bedroom. Ros kissed her like she could do it forever and that would be enough for her. It was intoxicating.

She scraped enough brainpower that wasn't focusing on the sensation of Ros's lips against hers to manoeuvre the other woman towards the bed. Ros's legs hit the bed and her knees gave way, the two women falling in a heap with a laugh. They rolled so Ros could settle against Isobel's side and continue kissing her. Eventually they both needed air and Isobel pulled away, looking at Ros, trying to memorise every inch of her face. The atmosphere was electric.

When Ros let out an unexpectedly loud yawn, Isobel couldn't help it; she burst out laughing.

"Sorry," Ros said sheepishly. She couldn't quite meet Isobel's eyes. "Mood ruined, I know."

"Oh chérie, you haven't ruined anything," Isobel said, using two fingers under Ros's chin to force her to meet her gaze. "You haven't been sleeping, I know."

"I wanted everything to be perfect," she grumbled. Isobel pressed another kiss to her lips to stop her.

"This *is* perfect," she assured. "There is time. Come, sleep."

Ros did just that. They settled into Isobel's bed in just their underwear, arms wrapped around each other. Ros was asleep in moments. Isobel had never felt so safe, so content to just sleep as she did in Ros's arms that night. She drifted off into pleasant dreams of what the future might hold for them.

It therefore came as a shock when she was woken early the next morning by a frantic banging on the door.

"Ms Devereux! Ms Devereux," said a voice on the other side of the door.

Isobel quickly threw on a robe and crossed the room. Ros propped herself up on one elbow, a curious look on her face.

"Yes?" Isobel said, opening the door just far enough to talk to the servant without revealing the guest in her bed.

"Ms Devereux you should come with me," he said. There was a terrified look in his eyes and tear tracks down his face. Isobel felt her stomach plummet.

"Why? What's happened?"

The man wouldn't look her in the eye. "Ms Devereux I'm so sorry, it's your father. He's been killed."

CHAPTER NINE

ROS

There was so much blood Ros could hardly believe her eyes. It didn't even look like there was a person in there.

Isobel was a mess. She'd wanted to see the body for herself, what was left of it anyway, and Ros had gone with her, damn the consequences of people finding out she'd spent the night in the Assistant Governor's bed.

When they'd got there it had been all too obvious what had happened. Ros had seen these kinds of injury before, and the wide slash marks in the furniture and walls were all too familiar.

Gabby had been right. There was another Hellbeast out there somewhere.

Ros was too occupied comforting Isobel in the immediate aftermath. The woman was a diplomat, a bureaucrat; she wasn't used to seeing the sheer level of gore on display and had thrown up. Ros knew from bitter experience that all the exposure to gruesome sights in the world didn't help when it was someone you loved. Isobel clung to her, sobbing as she cried for her father.

No one seems to know what to do, the servants who'd found the... remains looking to Isobel for leadership she wasn't in any state to give. For lack of better options, Ros took charge of the situation.

"Get in touch with my people," she said to the man who'd dragged Isobel (and by extension, her too) out of bed and into this waking nightmare. "My second Ma–" she choked on the name, having momentarily forgotten he was dead. "*Gabby* will organise a search party, and security for the room. We need to be *very* careful how we let this news get out. Also tell my medic I want him to deal with this, and discreetly. Understand?" The man nodded. "Yes sir," he said, even though Ros held no rank over him.

"They'll all be horribly hungover so it might take a couple of tries to rouse them. Let no one into this room apart from myself or the Assistant Governor until Gabby gets here, are we clear?" "Crystal."

"Good. In the meantime I'll get Isobel out of here. She doesn't need to look at this any more." Isobel was on the floor by this point, sobbing so hard Ros feared she might make herself sick again. It was clear she wasn't going anywhere under her own steam in a hurry. Ros scooped her up and carried her, bridal style, back to her room, where she gently placed her in the shower. By this point the sobs had diminished to the odd hiccup, and Isobel could get a few words out.

"Papa," she wailed pitifully.

"Shhh," Ros soothed, her heart twisting at the sight of the other woman in such emotional pain. "It's gonna be okay," she said, trying to make Isobel believe even though she wasn't sure herself. "I'm gonna take care of you." Isobel just clung to her desperately, her chest heaving as she fought to get air back into her lungs.

"Come on Izzy," Ros said, "let's get you out of these clothes." They were covered in blood and vomit and Ros knew from experience that everything would feel just a little better when Isobel was clean.

Isobel laughed at that, a half hysterical sound that set Ros's teeth on edge. "This wasn't exactly how I pictured you saying those words." "It wasn't how I imagined it either," Ros admitted, pulling Isobel's robe off and tossing it towards the sink.

"I'm sorry," Isobel mumbled into Ros's shoulder. "Not exactly the morning after either of us wanted." "*You're* sorry?" Ros's mouth hung open in disbelief. "You have *nothing* to be sorry for sweetheart." The endearment slipped out of her mouth without permission from her brain, but she didn't want to take it back. "Come on. Let's get you cleaned up." Ros pulled Isobel's underwear off and pulled her to her feet. She switched the spray on and was about to give Isobel her privacy when a hand grasped at her elbow.

"Don't leave me," Isobel begged, her eyes pleading. She sounded small and scared. "please." "I won't, I promise," Ros said easily. She slipped out of her own clothes (which she'd hastily thrown back on after they'd received the bad news) and slipped into the shower with Isobel. Despite the fact they were both naked, it was one of the least sexy things Ros had ever experienced. Isobel clung to her the whole time, intermittently sobbing and letting out grief-stricken screams. All Ros could do was hold her tight, and hope she'd be okay.

(In a hypothetical alternate universe somewhere, Ros hoped another version of her and Isobel were are also sharing a shower, the kind that might be expected after sharing a bed with someone for the first time. Ros wished with all her heart they were in that universe instead, not because that other, potential Ros might be having amazing sex with a beautiful woman, but because in that world Isobel would still have her father. That was all she wanted for Isobel right now.) After the shower Ros dried Isobel off as well as she could considering the other woman's flailing, uncooperative limbs. She found clean nightclothes in a drawer and then she put Isobel to bed so she could sleep off her grief for a few hours. By the time Isobel had dropped off to sleep Ros was back in her own clothes and at the mercy of her thoughts.

This was her fault. She hadn't done her job properly.

She'd known about the possibility of another monster out there but had done nothing to investigate the matter, too wrapped up in her own grief. If she'd just stopped to think for a moment, then Isobel's father might still be alive.

She was pulled from her thoughts by a knock on the door. Since it wasn't her place to tell people whether they could or couldn't enter Isobel's bedroom she answered it and slipped outside. It was Gabby, her face pale and her eyes drawn, but her eyes were bright.

"How's she doing?" Gabby asked quietly.

"Not good," Ros replied honestly. "I should have talked her out of going to the scene but I'd just woken up. I wasn't thinking." "Shitty morning after huh?" Gabby joked, but there was no humour to it.

"Nothing ha– we didn't..." Ros trailed off, running her hand through her short hair. "anyway, I'm glad we didn't do anything. I'd hate for Isobel to have the guilt of knowing she was getting laid while her father was dying on top of everything else." Gabby pulled a face that wasn't quite agreement but wasn't disagreement either. "You have anything yet?" "AJ's collecting the body—what's left of it anyway—right now. Ewan and Mila are making sure no one gets in or out of the governor's room without your say so. Lizzie's talking to the servants, see if anyone heard or saw anything last night but so far nothing." Ros nodded, rolling this new information around in her brain as she considered her options. "Get Tariq and Noora up if they aren't already. We need them on the *Star* looking for our elusive monster." "Already done jefa," Gabby said. "Neither of them think we'll find any more than we did last time, but it's worth a shot." Ros nodded again, her brow furrowed in thought. "What are you thinking Capitan?" "Job's not done Gabby. We were supposed to make this colony safe, and we failed." "You're going after it." It wasn't a question; Gabby knew Ros too well for there to be any doubt.

"I am gonna find the piece of shit creature that took Isobel's father away from her and I'm gonna tear it into pieces." She was angry now, so angry she could hardly breathe. She hadn't felt like this since the day Matty died. She needed to hit something, or someone.

"Ros, Ros breathe," Gabby said, taking hold of her Captain's biceps. "You can't go after this thing without a clear head. All that's gonna achieve is getting you killed too and I'm not exaggerating when I say I couldn't cope if I lost you. You need to take a moment to think, be there for your girl while she buries her papi, and then you can murder the bastard. Sí?" Ros was shaking her head even before Gabby had finished speaking. "I'm not sure we have that long Gabs. You've been to the scene right?" Hernandez nodded. "It's fucking mess in there, but it was so methodical. That was precision butchery in there. And no one heard or saw anything. If this thing was angry because we killed its mate or its kid or whatever the hell the other thing was, there was a room full of people it could have slaughtered. But it didn't. It chose a victim with great care to create the biggest impact. And it made damn sure no one saw it." "But... that level of intelligence..."

"Puts this thing on the same level as humans, I know. It's sentient and, given what it's done to this colony, makes it pretty much evil in my book." "But–"

"No!" Ros interrupted, shouting at the top of her lungs. "If it was just a beast pissed off because we're in its territory I could cope with that, but this thing has shown enough intelligence it could probably communicate with us if it wanted to. But instead it has hunted down and murdered colonists in their beds, and from what we can tell the damn thing hasn't even been feeding on the bodies. It's just sport. Tell me Gabby, if it were a human being doing this what would you call it?" "I'd call it a fucking serial killer."

"Exactly. This thing is evil, and we need to take it down." Gabby sighed, and Ros knew she'd surrendered. "Fine," she said. "We'll get this thing. You wanted to break the curse, and it looks like that's not done yet. But please, wait until after the funeral to go hunting. Isobel is gonna need you, and you're no good to her if you get yourself killed." Ros paused. The last thing she wanted was to cause Isobel any more pain. "Okay. I'll wait until after the funeral. But in the meantime I want this colony defending. Set up patrol routes and shifts. We know how to kill these things now, that's something." "The colonists will want to know what's going on when they see a bunch of mercs patrolling in full armour. What do we tell them?" "You'll think of something." Ros sighed, suddenly feeling all the fatigue of the last few days pile on her at once. She swayed slightly and Gabby had to catch her arm.

"You alright jefa?"

"Yeah," Ros insisted. "I'm good"

"Go get a couple hours sleep with your girl in there," Gabby said softly. "We'll deal with things out here." Ros just nodded at her friend, grateful beyond measure she understood. She slipped back into Isobel's room. She was still asleep, tangled up in the covers. Ros pulled her boots and shirt off and crawled in next to her. She was asleep before her head had even hit the pillow.

***

Ros hated funerals, even when it was for people she didn't know very well.

The last week had been hard. Isobel had withdrawn into herself and had only really come out to feverishly organise her father's funeral and then she became quiet again. Ros wasn't sure what she was supposed to do. She'd done her best to be there for Isobel, make sure she ate and slept and washed regularly, and made sure she knew Ros was there for her if she needed it. She was never sure if she was overstepping her bounds, acutely aware that all there was between them was a handful of kisses and the fact they'd shared a bed the night Isobel's father had died. In terms of declaration of feelings or statement of commitment, there wasn't really a term that covered what the two of them were, and Ros knew Isobel was in no state emotionally to be making those kinds of decision.

Still, Isobel seemed to want Ros to stay close to her, so that's what she'd done.

The Irregulars had handled almost everything else, from breaking the news to hungover colonists who thought all their troubles were behind them to running security for the entire colony and preparing the remains for burial, they'd done it all. Ros was proud of her crew, even given the circumstances that had forced them to step up to the plate.

They had all wanted to attend the funeral, in solidarity with their Captain and her sort-of-girlfriend. Gabby had even made sure everyone dressed for the occasion and Ros wasn't sure she'd ever seen her crew look so smart. Only the heavy weapons attached to the Irregulars' belts hinted that being out in the open for a funeral wasn't necessarily safe.

Isobel stood pressed against Ros's right side, holding her hand so tightly it hurt. Ros didn't say anything. Isobel had got through the brief service without her voice cracking but now there were silent tears running down her face as the attendees filed past the tiny urn and said their goodbyes. Gabby saluted the urn before crossing herself and murmuring a prayer; Ros's crew had elected her their representative, and she was speaking on behalf of all the Irregulars.

When everyone was done, and the urn had been buried (Isobel had insisted her father be buried close to the colony that had practically been his life's work) Ros tugged on their joined hands. "Come on," she said. "Let's get out of here." Isobel just nodded and allowed herself to be led away.

There was a wake being held (in the same hall that had held a celebration barely a week before) but Isobel didn't look like she was up for it. To be honest, she looked about ready to pass out.

The woman had lost an alarming amount of weight in the last week, the hollowness of her cheeks made worse by the dark shadows under her eyes. She wasn't sleeping, which Ros knew because she was spending every night in Isobel's bed, wracked by nightmares that pulled her from unconsciousness sweating and screaming.

Ros had done what she could, but she increasingly felt like whatever she did, it wasn't enough. And there was a persistent itch in the back of her mind, prodding her to get out of there and *do* something. She didn't have any experience in dealing with a grieving partner, especially when she wasn't certain that's what they were to each other. She mostly just wanted to shoot something. *That* she could do.

The funeral was over now. She'd promised Gabby

she'd wait that long. She could hunt the bastard down.

Later, because right now Isobel still needed her, and all Ros could do was try her best.

She pulled her suit tie off and loosened her shirt. Isobel sat in her bed, staring blankly at the wall, still wearing her black dress.

"Come on, sweetheart." Ros murmured. "How about a nap? You should get out of that dress and sleep." Isobel shook her head. "There's too much to do. I can't." "You don't have to do it all right now babe. Come and rest with me." Ros laid down on the bed and opened her arms. Isobel remained where she was.

"I've been... lax this past week, but that stops now," she said. Ros didn't know whether she was talking to her or to herself. "In the absence of a properly appointed Governor those duties fall to the Assistant Governor. Me." "Izzy..." Ros said. She could see where this was going. She'd done it herself after losing people; she'd thrown herself into work hoping it would ease the pain but all it had achieved was wearing her down.

"No," Isobel said. "Ros, I need to do this. For my father. For myself." "Okay," Ros said, letting out a frustrated breath. "But you can take a nap right now. Shoulder the burdens of an entire colony later. You need to rest." Isobel hesitated but ultimately she pulled off her dress and crawled into Ros's arms. They laid there for a while, listening to each other's breathing while Ros stroked up and down Isobel's back. Ros thought Isobel was asleep, but then she shifted so she was looking at Ros, her eyes burning into her.

"Izzy?" she asked, unsure what that look meant.

"Kiss me," Isobel demanded.

"Izzy…" Ros said slowly. "I don't think that's a good–"

"Kiss me," Isobel said again, more insistent this time. Her hand was fisted in Ros's shirt, pulling hard enough to be uncomfortable. Ros paused. "Please," Isobel said, and it came out so softly, almost a whimper, and Ros was helpless.

She loved this woman, she knew that now, and she would do anything to make her happy. She kissed her.

It wasn't their first kiss by any means, but it was the most passionate they'd shared since the night before Isobel's father had been killed. Isobel tugged at Ros's shirt, shifting to lie on top of her. Her tongue was in her mouth and Ros's brain buzzed with pleasure. This was bliss.

Ros broke the kiss reluctantly. "Izzy, we should back off," she said, hear breaths coming rough and heavy. Isobel had kissed her way down Ros's jaw and now she looked up at the mercenary with hurt in her eyes.

"Don't you want me?"

"You look me in the eye and tell me I don't want you right now," Ros said. "I want you so much it hurts, but now is not the time. You just buried your father, Izzy."

Isobel looked down, her grip of Ros's now creased shirt loosening. "I know. I wanted to forget for a little while. Is that wrong of me?"

Ros shook her head. "No, no it's not. But it's not a healthy coping mechanism and I don't want our first time together to be for the wrong reasons. I'd feel a little bit used if we had sex right now, I won't lie."

Isobel burst into tears, so Ros pulled her close. She was soaking Ros's dress shirt with her tears, but she didn't care; she just held on tightly and let her cry. It lasted a while, the sobs making Isobel's body shake. Ros made soothing noises and rubbed her back, her heart breaking for the woman in her arms. Eventually Isobel slipped into a fitful sleep, leaving Ros wide awake and brooding.

She still blamed herself for the death of Benoit Devereux. If she'd been less wrapped up in her own grief over Matty, she might have thought to check out the hypothesis that there was another creature. Lizzie had said there was no evidence of that, and she was right, but they should still have ruled out the possibility. There was no excuse for leaving the colony at risk because they'd taken casualties.

With another pang of guilt Ros remembered that Potts was still in the *Mercenary Star*'s infirmary. AJ was keeping him in a medical coma while the swelling in his brain went down. There was no guarantee he would pull through, though AJ Schneider was one of the best doctors in the business. She hoped he would. And she swore she wouldn't lose any more people on this job. Even if it cost her her own life.

Isobel stirred in her sleep, murmuring and fidgeting as her brow furrowed; no doubt the beginning of another nightmare. Ros pressed a kiss to her temple and stroked her back. That seemed to settle her, and she drifted off again, face peaceful once more.

Love. Ros hadn't been expecting that when she'd taken this job.

Even a week ago she wouldn't have been certain that was what this was but in her mind, in her heart, there was no doubt. Isobel was going through hell right now and Ros had been at her side every step of the way, supporting her, trying to make the grieving process as easy as possible. And she still felt like that wasn't enough; she wanted to do more, wanted to make it so this beautiful wonderful woman never had to hurt again.

It was a little intimidating, the strength of these feelings Ros had for Isobel. She was a mercenary, and she'd been a soldier before that; she'd spent her life travelling the galaxy, shooting people and creatures. Most of her love affairs had been brief, often a single night, before she inevitably moved on. Getting attached was a bad plan when they could end up dead, or you could.

But with Isobel...

They hadn't even had sex and Ros was more invested in this "relationship" (if that was what this even was, everything was still so nebulous, undefined) than pretty much any other in her life. The only exception to that was Gabby, her oldest friend, whom she loved absolutely but who didn't want romance and never had. Starting a merc band with Gabby was about the biggest declaration of commitment Ros would ever get from her, and it was one of the best decisions she'd ever made.

Isobel represented possibility, and that was a little overwhelming. For the first time in her life Ros wanted to stay in one place because that was where Isobel was. She wanted everything with this woman in her arms, wanted to *be* everything to her. She would give Isobel the stars if she asked for them and not think twice about the effort involved.

And she had no idea if she felt the same way.

Ros couldn't bring Isobel's father back, as much as she wanted to, but she could bring down the creature that had killed him. She'd sworn that the morning after the party, when waking up is Isobel's arms for the first time had been overshadowed by tragedy.

She would find this creature and kill it, so it couldn't hurt anyone ever again.

Her thoughts turned to Gabby. And Ewan and Mila and AJ and Lizzie, Tariq and Noora. Her crew, her family. They would have her back in this if she asked them. Every single one of her Irregulars would go to the mat for their Captain and Ros knew it. But the memory of Matty's last words, the way he'd said that he *had* to give his life for hers as though there had been no other choice, still haunted her. She couldn't ask it of them, wouldn't ask it of them. No more people would die for her or because of her. This was her burden, and she would bear it alone.

She looked down at Isobel, still sleeping on her chest. Beautiful, fragile Isobel, who could read body language and facial features as easily as Ros could read written words. Isobel who was always so meticulous and put-together when on official duty but who's personal quarters—which Ros had practically been living in for the last week—were an absolute, fucking disaster. Isobel who had decided less than an hour after her father's funeral that it was time to suck it up and shoulder the burdens her father had carried his whole life. Isobel who Ros had known less than a month and who she already loved.

Isobel was still as she slept, the earlier nightmare having been chased away. And she looked so at home curled into Ros's side, like she belonged there. Ros wanted to keep her right where she was for a very, very long time. But her colony, the colony she'd run with her father, the colony she'd hired Ros to protect, was still cursed. There was still a monster out there, and it was Ros's responsibility to take it down. She would do this for Isobel, because she loved her, and she would do it alone, because she loved her mercenaries.

Ros pressed a kiss to Isobel's temple and slipped out from under her. She grumbled a little at the disturbance but didn't wake, and soon she settled back down.

"I'll be back if I can, Izzy," Ros whispered. Suddenly there was too much emotion in her chest, and it made it hard to breathe. It felt like a hundred words were trapped in her throat, dying to get out, but she couldn't bring herself to let them; once they were out they couldn't be unsaid. She had to tell Izzy how she felt, but speaking the words to her sleeping form wasn't enough, and she couldn't find her voice.

There was a tablet somewhere on Isobel's infuriatingly messy desk, and it took Ros a moment to find it. The words came a little easier when she was writing them down. She didn't allow herself time to think about what she was saying, just let her heart pour out and onto the electronic device. Satisfied she had adequately explained herself, she set the tablet on the pillow next to Isobel. Unable to suppress the urge, she leaned over and pressed a soft, chaste kiss to Isobel's lips. She sighed in her sleep, a smile playing around her mouth.

"I love you," Ros whispered.

And then, before she could change her mind, she slipped out of the room. She needed to grab her gear, and then she had a monster to kill.

CHAPTER TEN

GABBY

The first sign Gabby got that anything was amiss was the startled scream from the Assistant Governor's room.

She'd slipped upstairs to check in on Ros—and by extension, Isobel—when she heard it. Fearing the worst she set off at a run, pistol in her hand. Gabby all but kicked the bedroom door down and stood there panting, adrenaline rushing through her veins, as her eyes frantically searched the room for danger.

Isobel was unharmed but alone, sat on the bed in just her underwear. It took Gabby a few moments to realise what was wrong with that picture.

"Where's Ros?" she asked, confused. Her gun was still in her hand, hovering just above the holster, ready in case any new threat appeared.

"She's gone," Isobel said, and she sounded utterly wretched. Gabby had seen her deal with her grief over losing her father by leaning on Ros, but she had no idea just how much the woman had depended on the Captain until now; it sounded like she was taking Ros leaving harder than her father's death. Gabby thought she knew what that meant, but it wasn't her place to say.

That didn't stop her wanting to ask a million questions.

"What do you mean 'gone'?" was what Gabby actually said.

"I mean gone," Isobel repeated. She seemed a little

calmer with every passing moment, pulling herself together with an ease that spoke of years practising a public face. "See for yourself."

Isobel tossed a tablet at Gabby—she hadn't even noticed she'd been holding anything until then—and she barely caught it.

What she read on the screen horrified her and sent her into a string of swearwords in every language she could think of. Isobel seemed shocked at the outburst.

"Sorry," Gabby said, wincing a little but still utterly livid. "This is just... fucking typical of Ros. She thinks she's got to carry the whole world on her shoulders, she never thinks to ask for help. Not even when people will willingly give it." Gabby deflated a little as she realised she could have prevented this. "I'm sorry Isobel. I knew she wanted to go after the other monster and I convinced her to wait until after the funeral. I didn't think she'd be so fucking literal."

"It's not your fault," Isobel said. She was sitting up in the bed with her legs tucked against her chest. She looked small, fragile, but there was a spark of stubbornness in her eyes that had been missing for the past week. "We'll find her."

Gabby ignored that last part; of course they'd fucking find her. Not finding Ros wasn't even an option. "I thought Ros would be too preoccupied looking after you to go off half-cocked like this."

Isobel's eyes went wide, as though something had just occurred to her. "She was but... earlier I was talking about wanting to take on my father's duties now the funeral was over. If she thought I didn't need her any more..."

Gabby slapped her own forehead at the thought of what was going through her best friend's head right now. "Stubborn fucking puta," she yelled, frustration boiling up inside her. "She could have come to *me* instead of running off on her own. What does she think I'm here for?"

Isobel was looking at Gabby with wide eyes full of tears. "Does she think I don't need her any more? I do. I still do." Gabby perched on the edge of the bed and tentatively reached out a hand to offer comfort. Isobel grabbed hold of it and squeezed hard.

"I don't know if you read the same letter I did, but I did not get the impression Ros thinks you don't need her. If anything she thinks you need her to do this. *She* needs to do this."

"But... why?"

"Because that woman is in love with you, or did you not read that part?"

"No I did," Isobel said, her cheeks turning a little pink. "I think I–"

"No, no. That's for you to say to Ros, not me," Gabby interjected. "Ros loves you, and if there's one thing she's good at it's taking care of the people she loves. Throw in a little guilt and the fact her professional pride is at stake here and you've got a recipe for disaster."

"Why would she go alone though? She's seen what these creatures can do."

Because she's a fucking fool, Gabby thought. "She has. And she's also lost too many people to them. She thinks she's protecting us." She stood up suddenly and let out a frustrated growl. "Do you know what time it was when you last saw her? Knowing how much of a head start she has would be good."

Isobel shook her head. "No, sorry. I was a bit of a mess."

"That's alright. Look, I need to go talk to my crew, but I don't want to leave you alone." Just in case you decide to do something foolish too, Gabby thought to herself. "Is there anyone I can send up to stay with you? A servant or even one of the Irregulars? You were getting on pretty well with Noora, weren't you?"

Isobel flushed again. "Yeah, I was. She kept flirting with me though."

Despite the seriousness of the situation, Gabby couldn't help but grin. "Good on her. You let her down gently I hope?" Isobel nodded. "Good. I can ask her to come sit with you if you like?"

"Let me throw some clothes on first," Isobel insisted, "then you can send her up."

"Will you be okay on your own for a minute?"

"I'll be fine." She didn't have the look of a woman who would run out the door the minute she was alone so Gabby took her at her word.

She nodded and slipped out the door, giving the woman her privacy. It took all her self-discipline not to punch several holes in the wall as she made her way back downstairs. How could Ros do this? They were supposed to be a team. But no, Ros had to play the hero, had to be all noble and try to sacrifice herself.

She fought to get her face back to neutral before she

entered the hall in the Governor's mansion. The last thing Gabby wanted to do was let anyone know something was wrong. Ros had been the glue keeping the entire colony together for the last week and the news she'd disappeared, gone off to get herself killed, could be disastrous for morale.

Noora was in a corner with her brother, who looked like he was trying (unsuccessfully) to flirt with Lizzie. Gabby made her way over and leaned close to murmur in Noora's ear.

"I need you to do me a favour," she said. "Ros has decided to go AWOL and I don't want Ms Devereux left alone while we mount a search. Can you head upstairs and go keep her company for a bit?"

"Sure thing boss," Noora whispered back. Gabby could see there were questions in her eyes—where had Ros gone and why?—but she kept them to herself. She apologised to the group and slipped away. Tariq and Lizzie gave their Lieutenant a strange look, but she waved them off. Lizzie and Tariq were both good people but if she was going to talk Ros out of doing something foolish and potentially suicidal she needed to bring out the big guns. She needed Ewan and AJ and Mila.

The three of them were across the other side of the room with a small group of the more prominent colonists. Mila looked like she was fending off a couple of admirers (when would people learn?) much to Ewan's amusement. She made her way over there, remembering to stop and murmur a few words of condolence to the people she met along the way so as not to make it look like anything was wrong.

"Sorry to interrupt, but can I borrow you three a moment?" Gabby asked, looking at her crew members each in turn.

"Something the matter Gabriela?" AJ asked, his eyebrows creasing. She realised he'd probably seen Noora slip off; that eye of his missed very little.

"Nothing major. Just need to check in," she replied, trying to keep her voice friendly and upbeat. "The garden?"

The four mercenaries made their way outside, Mila grumbling the whole way about young men who didn't understand the meaning of the word no. She might be full of complaints, but Gabby could tell the Russian was grateful for the distraction. Once outside and well away from prying ears AJ stopped Gabby in her tracks and looked at her seriously.

"Okay boss, what's wrong? You wouldn't pull the three of us out of there without a good reason."

"Yeah," Ewan agreed. "Something wrong with the Captain?"

"Ros has gone AWOL," Gabby admitted. "Slipped out while Isobel was asleep. From what I can tell she's gone after the second monster."

The response was instantaneous and predictable; loud curses in three separate languages. Gabby knew exactly how they felt.

"What is plan, Lieutenant?" Mila asked. She was the first to quit swearing. Ewan, predictably, was the last.

"I need one of you to go to the barracks and check the

gear, make sure she hasn't gone off unarmed and unarmoured. We need to search the *Star* too. We don't know how much of a head start Ros has but I'm hoping we can catch her before she does anything too foolish."

"I will go to barracks," Mila volunteered. "If she is there I will kill her myself." The look on her face suggested the sniper was completely serious.

"No!" Gabby protested.

"Fine. Just a little punching then," Mila said. It was probably the best deal Gabby was likely to get. She nodded her agreement.

"AJ, will you come with me to the *Star*? I want to check the equipment lockers and see if she's accessed the sensors recently."

"What do you want me to do Gabs?" Ewan asked.

"Go with Mila, if she'll have you." Gabby looked at the Russian, quirking her eyebrow in question. She received a terse nod in return. "We'll cover less ground in pairs but we'll have a better chance of subduing Ros if there's two of us. If there's no sign of her at the barracks, get suited up and come meet AJ and me at the *Star*. We'll search on foot if we have to." The other three nodded. "Alright, you have your orders. Fall out."

Ewan and Mila went off in the direction of the barracks the Irregulars had been using, bickering the entire way, while AJ and Gabby set off for the spaceport and the *Mercenary Star*. AJ eyed Gabby thoughtfully for a while before speaking up in his low rumble.

"Something must have set the Kapitan off," he said. "You know more than you let on back there." Gabby just nodded. "Gabriela..." AJ said, "tell me what's going on."

"Take one part guilt over Matty's death, one part falling in love with Isobel Devereux, mix in a dash of over-protectiveness and sprinkle with hurt professional pride and what do you get?"

AJ sucked in a breath between his teeth. "I know that recipe. It ends up with a dead Kapitan and the break up of our little family."

"Exactly"

"Gabriela?"

"AJ?"

"Do you think we'll find her in time?"

"I hope to God we do. I'm not sure I can live without that woman any more."

AJ lay a hand on Gabby's arm, his fingers gentle despite their size. "She will be okay, I think. You have her back and always will, and she has the rest of us as well, even if she has forgotten about that for the moment. We will find our brave leader, we will find this other creature, and we will make this colony safe. I believe that with my whole heart."

Tears sprang into Gabby's eyes. AJ had a way of making her feel better even when she was hurting emotionally. That was why he was such a good doctor, she supposed.

"Thanks AJ."

"Any time, liebchen."

The spaceport was sparsely staffed, most of the people on Novis having been given the day off so they could mourn their Governor. Those who were left on duty were blank-faced and red-eyed, their minds clearly elsewhere. AJ and Gabby got into the *Star*'s berth with only the minimum of security checks. Gabby thought about asking whether anyone had seen Ros, but she was hoping to keep the Captain's disappearance quiet as long as she could, even if it meant doing things the hard way.

Climbing the landing ramp into the bowels of the ship, Gabby cocked her head to the side, listening for any signs of movement within.

Nothing.

She sighed. "If she was here, then she's gone now."

"Or she's playing a great game of hide and seek," AJ said dryly. Gabby snorted at that, but said nothing.

They checked the armoury first and found it empty. AJ checked the inventory and cross-checked with the contents of the weapons lockers. "It looks like everything is here. Whatever weapons the Kapitan has with her, she didn't get them from here."

Gabby checked the weapons lockers in the changing rooms next; there was nothing missing from there either, and there was no sign the Captain had even been on the ship recently. "Let's get to the cockpit, check the sensor logs," Gabby said and she could hear the dejection in her own voice. She'd been hoping to head Ros off at the pass, not go chasing after her all across the planet, but that was looking unlikely.

They made their way through the ship, checking in any rooms they passed as they went. Gabby thought she didn't work with AJ often enough, which wasn't surprising given she was on the front like punching people and he was in charge of patching her up when she was done. It was a shame; they made a good team, working quietly and efficiently

"So..." he said after a good five minutes without speaking. "The Kapitan and the Assistant Governor, huh?"

"That's right."

"How do you feel about that?"

Gabby stopped dead in her tracks and gave AJ an incredulous look. "Why would it affect me?"

AJ shrugged. "I know the two of you aren't exclusive, and I can't say I understand that but each to their own. Whatever makes you happy. But in all the time I've known the two of you I haven't seen this. Playmates for both of you, sure, but falling in love? That I have not seen. It has the potential to change things, nein?"

She nodded slowly. "I guess it does."

"So I say it again: how do you feel about that?"

She paused, considering. Gabby hadn't thought about how this might affect her, too busy trying to make sure the Captain was happy. "I'm pleased for Ros," she said. "I mean, I've been pushing her at Isobel Devereux more or less since we landed, hoping they'd get together."

"Well it seems that they have, and the Kapitan at least is serious about it."

Gabby nodded. She paused, thinking, emotions churning inside her. She'd never been good at dealing with them, tried to push them down where she wouldn't have to, but now that AJ had asked she couldn't deny that the thought of Ros running off and getting herself killed because she'd fallen in love made her feel... something.

"I love her," Gabby said, suddenly feeling like it was important she got that out there. "I mean, I've never really known how all that works but it seems the best way to sum up how I feel; I love her. I always have and I always will, but I can't give her what she needs. Romance and monogamy and commitment, they're not me. I can't do it. We've been fucking on and off since we were seventeen and she's my best friend, but..."

"That is a long time to maintain any kind of relationship. You say commitment is not for you but I think maybe you are committed already, just perhaps not in the way many people would expect you to be." AJ tapped his chin with his finger, apparently deep in thought.

"I guess you're right. I've stood by her side for nearly two decades. I started the Irregulars with her—started a family basically." The more she thought about it the more she realised AJ was right; she was already committed, in a sense, and that had never made her feel even a shred of the anxiety that the idea of marriage or anything like it did. This sort of commitment she could cope with.

"And do you think the Kapitan's relationship for Ms Devereux will change any of that? Do you think it will change what you are to each other?" He was looking at her with both eyes, and Gabby felt like the bastard could see right into her soul.

She shook her head, no, but suddenly she wasn't so sure. "I mean... there's another person involved now. I don't know what Isobel does or doesn't want, or how Ros might react to that." For the first time she understood what the pain in her chest was; it was fear, and it had been steadily growing since she'd found out Ros loved Isobel enough to go charging head first into danger without thinking. For so long Gabby had been the only one she'd do that for and the idea that now there were two people Ros would give her life for felt... odd. Was she jealous? She wasn't sure. Was she terrified for her friend? Definitely.

She felt lost, unsteady, like the ground under her feet might give way any second. Gabby didn't like it one bit. She shook the strange feeling off, telling herself she needed to concentrate on the task at hand. She could work out her feelings later. "It's not gonna matter if we don't find Ros before she does something foolish," she said resolutely, marching off in the direction of the cockpit.

AJ followed her at a more sedate pace and leaned against the cockpit door while Gabby was viciously stabbing at the sensor control panel. "Do you know what I think? I think Ros understands that romance isn't something you can do; she knows very well what you can and cannot give her, and she loves you anyway. I think that just because she is being a dummkopf for Isobel Devereux doesn't mean she wouldn't do the same for you. And I think we need to find the Kapitan so you can all have a sit down and discuss where this is going to go."

Gabby poked the console so hard her finger hurt. He was right, of course he was, she just didn't want to admit it. The sensor logs flooded the screen and Gabby scanned them quickly, trying to make sense of the data so she could tell when they were last used.

"You know, Ewan and I have been together for nearly ten years now," AJ said, a slow, fond smile spreading over his face. "Nothing about us is conventional. He is a one-armed soldier who likes blowing things up far too much and I am a doctor who looks nothing like people expect a doctor to look. I knit my boyfriend ridiculous sweaters and he wears them with glee, even when I make them clash with his hair. I love that man with all my heart, and sometimes I hate him, but we are happy. Does it matter that our arrangement looks strange from the outside? Not to me. All that matters is we are happy.

"When we find the Kapitan you sit down with her and this Ms Devereux and you work out an arrangement that makes you all happy. And if it does not look conventional from the outside? Who cares? I will have Ewan punch anyone who says anything."

Gabby laughed at that, she couldn't help herself. "Thanks AJ, I needed that."

"Any time," he said with a grin. "I know that you are more than capable of hitting people yourself, but sometimes it is nice to have someone do it for you, ja?"

"Ja. Here we go." The sensor logs had finished rolling across the viewscreen and Gabby finally had the information she needed. "Ros *was* here. She accessed the sensors about an hour ago. Looks like she used the information we got from the Hellbeast's autopsy to refine the search parameters. Narrowed it down to a search grid a couple of kilometres square."

"Where is it?" AJ asked, focused now.

"Five clicks or so from here. In her suit Ros could be

at the search zone by now."

"Then I think it is time to check in with our friends and then suit up."

"You don't have to come with me," Gabby protested.

AJ gave her a look that promised he would accept no nonsense. "We cannot guarantee we will find the Kapitan before she finds the creature. Who better to take with you than a medic?"

Gabby felt a little foolish that she hadn't thought of that. "Okay, you have a point. Call your boyfriend."

AJ did, and without argument too. There was a brief exchange of cute nicknames (and Gabby could have lived without the knowledge that Ewan referred to AJ as his "big squishy teddy bear" as could Mila judging by the gagging and retching noises coming over the comm) before Gabby decided she would take over. She grabbed AJ's comm before she found out more information about his and Ewan's love life than she ever needed to know.

"If you two are *quite* done flirting," she said, shooting AJ an irritated glare. He shrugged at her, clearly unrepentant. "Tell me what you found."

"The Captain's suit is gone," Ewan replied, his voice suddenly serious. "So are her weapons. Siddiqui said she saw her shipping out but the Captain ordered her to stay put and keep quiet."

"Girl didn't even want to tell us she'd seen the Captain," Mila grumbled. "She only spilled when I threatened to pull her fingernails out one by one."

"Remind me never to tell her any sensitive information," Gabby murmured. AJ smirked at her.

"You find anything at the ship boss?" Ewan asked, his voice eager.

"Got a search area for both the monster and Ros. She has an hour's head start on us so she could be there by now."

"We're going after her, right?" Ewan asked. Gabby could almost see the furrow in his ginger eyebrows.

"Of course we are, mein Lieber," AJ interjected. "The lieutenant wanted to go alone like our Kapitan but I have persuaded her otherwise."

"Good," Mila said. "We would have come with you, anyway."

Tears pricked at the corners of Gabby's eyes; she'd seen this level of loyalty directed towards Ros before, but she'd never been on the receiving end. It made her feel something big inside her chest, something she didn't have time to work out right now. Not when Ros was in danger.

"Fine," she said, trying to hide the hitch in her voice. "Mila, Ewan, suit up. AJ and I will bring some extra munitions from the ship. Bring our gear too and we'll meet you on the road between the colony and the spaceport. I'm sending you the coordinates for the rendezvous. You copy?"

"Aye."

"Da."

"We'll see you on the road then. Hernandez out." She flipped the comm off and handed it back to its rightful owner.

"You okay Gabriela?" AJ was looking at her with concern in his eyes.

"I will be once we find Ros," she said truthfully. "Go get whatever you think we'll need from sickbay, I'm going to pick up some toys for Ewan from the armoury. I'll meet you at the ramp in ten minutes, sí?"

"Ja," he replied, snapping off a salute that probably should have been sarcastic but was oddly genuine. He headed off to the medbay as directed.

On her own for the moment, Gabby gave herself permission to breathe. There was still a lot of fear tangled up in her gut with a bunch of other emotions, but having a plan of action and a direction to go in helped.

"Hang on Ros," she said to herself. "We're coming for you."

She could only pray they weren't too late.

CHAPTER ELEVEN

ROS

Ros was starting to think this might have been a bad idea.

Somewhere between picking up her suit and her search area (another cave system, lovely) she had lost the fire in her belly and the conviction in her heart. She knew that this creature needed to die, but she was regretting not at least calling Gabby in to help.

She felt so very alone, and that allowed the doubt to creep in.

The night vision filter on her helmet (installed by Lizzie after the last fight) allowed Ros to see in the dark but it cast everything in a creepy green glow. It wasn't helping with her nerves. She swallowed her fear and tightened her grip on Margaret, pressing on; she'd already made her choice, it was too late to back out now.

Ros knew there were several square kilometres of caves and tunnels to search, and realistically it could be hours before she found her prey. Part of her mind hoped her friends, her family, would come for her before then, but another part, the part that was currently in charge of her decision making processes, wanted them to stay the fuck away. No one else could get hurt because of her, she thought. No one.

Except her.

It was quiet in the tunnels, the only sound Ros could hear the steady thump of her boots on rock and the slightly ragged sound of her own breathing, loud inside her helmet.

"Come on you bastard, where are you?" she whispered.

Her sensors were all on full, her suit projecting a loose map of the tunnels onto her visor. There was no sign of any other living creature within a half kilometre radius of her current position. Not even any native insects or anything, which was unusual. Concerning.

Ros pressed onward.

After another thirty minutes' fruitless searching Ros was getting jumpy. Every odd little shadow, every strange echo sent her pulse racing. It was only her many years of discipline that stopped her from firing off a couple of rounds into the darkness every time she was startled.

If her old commanding officer could see her now, Ros knew she'd be disappointed.

On her own in enemy territory with no backup, jumping at shadows. How far she had fallen. She was supposed to be Captain Ros Lamarr, best mercenary Captain in the Commonwealth. She wasn't making a good case for that right now.

"I should turn back," she told herself. "Isobel will have noticed I'm gone by now. She'll have alerted the others. They'll be coming for me."

But there was a horrible little voice in her mind that told her they wouldn't. No one would miss her. No one would come for her. In fact, it was probably for the best if she died all alone out here. She wouldn't be able to hurt anyone ever again that way.

Objectively she knew that wasn't the truth, but her thoughts had been a mess since Matty had died. There was a very real darkness to them she couldn't shake. Looking after Isobel had made things easier for a while, but she didn't need her any more. The guilt that had been festering had bloomed suddenly and had driven everything else out, like the emotional equivalent of a corpse flower. She couldn't think, and when Ros couldn't think she *acted*, often with disastrous consequences.

"I should get back," Ros said, sterner this time, but she didn't listen to herself. She was astute enough to recognise that she'd made a terrible fucking decision, but somehow she couldn't bring herself to act on that. Turning back was for cowards, she thought. The only way out of this was forward.

Ros shook her head, trying to clear her fuzzy thoughts. She felt drunk even though she'd not had any alcohol since the night of the celebration; since the night she'd kissed Isobel for the first time. It felt like there were too many thoughts in her head, and she couldn't keep track of them all. The only thing she had any real handle on was her anger, and it was this that had driven her to this point, to a potentially suicidal mission against an enemy she knew was much stronger than her.

Her thoughts drifted to Gabby.

Gabby would be mad at her, no doubt about it. And, despite the blackness in her mind and the doubt in her heart, she knew Gabby would mount a rescue. That woman loved her, Ros knew that, even if it wasn't quite the way lifelong best friends who occasionally slept together usually loved each other.

(The two of them were practically married, Ros knew, and in another lifetime they probably would have been, but that sort of thing wasn't for Gabby. Ros had always known that and was okay with it. If Gabby were any other way she wouldn't be herself, and Ros wouldn't love her so damned much).

Gabby was probably on her way already, Ros reasoned. She would probably have roped the others in too; Ewan and Mila at the very least, and AJ in case she got herself injured. In trying to keep them safe Ros would end up putting them in danger anyway, and another layer of guilt settled over her mind.

The tunnels remained empty. Her sensors told her nothing. There wasn't anything here.

Even with her thoughts in turmoil, Ros knew when to make a tactical retreat. It was time to head home, apologise for worrying the people she loved and make a new plan of action. A better one that didn't involve anyone putting themselves in unnecessary danger. It was alright to turn back, Ros told herself. It was okay to admit she'd been wrong.

Her footsteps faltered. She came to a halt. It took a huge amount of effort, but she turned herself around. The part of her brain that insisted she deserved this fate, deserved to die alone was screaming at her, but she ignored it. Ros stepped forwards, heading back the way she'd come. Heading home.

Forcing herself to do the right thing took so much of her concentration she wasn't paying attention to her heads up display.

Her proximity sensors beeped out a warning just seconds before something collided with her, knocking her to the ground.

Ros's head smashed against the inside of her helmet, dazing her. She shook herself to try to clear her vision.

There it was.

Four arms, like the other one. Crocodile snout, tail. Skin covered in armoured plates that made it practically invulnerable. This one was much bigger than the one they'd killed before, and that had taken six of them working together.

Ros was fucked.

It was looking at her with undeniable intelligence in its eyes, head cocked to one side as though it was curious. Maybe it was considering Ros for lunch.

She scrambled to her feet as fast as she could, fingers fumbling for the safety catch on Margaret. Ros knew the rifle would do little damage to the creature, but it might keep it distracted long enough for her to escape.

Adrenaline flooded Ros's system and her fight-or-flight response was telling her to get the fuck out of there. She wasn't sure she'd have much of a choice.

The creature let out a scream that curdled Ros's blood and fritzed her suit's systems. She was driven to her knees by the intense headache the scream caused, her helmet going black. Panic welled up in Ros's throat like vomit. She couldn't see, and if she couldn't see she could neither fight nor run. She was as good as dead.

Margaret was in her hands though, and the creature's

screams had never affected their weapons before. Ros squeezed the trigger, letting off a volley of fire she felt but could neither see nor hear.

Abruptly the screaming stopped, and Ros's suit came back online. Now she could see again she shouldered Margaret for a proper burst of fire.

The creature was nowhere to be seen. That... was not a good sign.

How could something so big disappear?

Ros did the only sensible thing she could think of; she turned and ran.

She didn't get very far before something slammed into her again, throwing her against the wall, sending Margaret clattering to the ground. Her suit's sensors didn't even have time to warn her it moved so fast. This time when her head struck the inside of her helmet she saw stars.

A concussion would make this a very interesting fight.

"You want to play do you?" she growled, "then let's play."

She pulled a pair of flash grenades from her belt, pulled the pins and threw them, shutting her eyes against the flash she knew was coming. They went off with a bang that echoed in the small tunnels, and the creature screamed again.

This time she was ready for it.

She didn't need to see to release the catch on her blade; she knew her suit as well as she knew her own body. The blade slid from its sheathe and into her waiting hand. Ros charged forwards as soon as the static across her visor cleared enough to see.

Apparently the creature hadn't been expecting the attack; Ros took a flying leap at it and ignited her blade, its super-heated edge slicing through the creature's arm with very little trouble.

"That one's for Ollie!" she screamed.

The creature reacted by flinging out one of its remaining arms, catching Ros in the shoulder with its razor-sharp claws. The metal of her armour tore open with screech but the reinforced nanofibres of the suit she wore underneath just about held.

Blood dripped from a small wound near the crease of her armpit, burning hot with pain, but it could have been much worse; it could have caught the arm holding the still burning blade.

"Is that all you've got?" she shouted at the creature. In hindsight she should have known better.

The creature growled low in its throat, the sound sending static ghosting across Ros's visor but not properly shorting it out. The next thing she knew she was flat on her back with the creature on her chest, jaws snapping at her face. Her blade slipped from her grasp cutting into her right thigh before spinning across the stone floor out of reach.

Ros screamed.

Fire raced down her leg as the blade made short work of her suit. The upgrades Lizzie had designed to tackle the Hellbeast's thick armour apparently worked just as well on carbon-steel.

She didn't have time to stop and assess the damage,

not with a large amount of razor-sharp teeth snapping at her face. Ros had no doubt that if they got close enough, those teeth would make even shorter work of her armour than her sword had.

Instinct took over, and she grabbed the creature's jaws with her gauntleted hands, struggling as hard as she could to keep those deadly teeth away from her vital organs.

She only had so much strength in her arms though, her left shoulder already wounded, and her suit could only assist her so far. Eventually she would tire or the servos on her suit would give out or the creature would scream and short everything again and then she'd be dead.

Ros suddenly found that she didn't want to die after all. And if it was her time, if this was the way she had to go, she was determined to take this bastard with her.

A groan escaped her lips as she pulled her left hand away, leaving only her right fighting off the jaws that wanted to tear her apart. She wouldn't be able to keep it at bay for long, she knew.

Ros used her free hand to pull another flash grenade from her belt and popped the pin with her thumb. Then she shoved her hand into the creature's jaws, ignoring the crunch of teeth around her armour. Quickly letting go of the grenade she pulled her arm out and clamped the creature's jaw shut, containing the explosion.

"This one's for Isobel's dad!"

The grenade went off with a bang that almost tore a hole in Ros's helmet. Ignoring the fresh head injury, she rolled out from under the creature as soon as its weight shifted, reaching for her short sword.

Thankfully the blade was still burning.

She struggled to her feet, her injured leg almost giving out under her, and took stock of her enemy.

The creature was in a bad way; besides the limb Ros had removed earlier the grenade in its mouth had done a lot of damage. The lower part of its jaw was hanging loose and dripping foul black blood. There was a lump of flesh on the ground at its feet that might have been its tongue once upon a time, but it was difficult to tell.

Any other creature would have been killed by a grenade going off inside its mouth, but not this thing. It was still standing and was looking at Ros with what could only be described as hate in its eyes. Ros had known these creatures were intelligent—scarily so—but to see a human emotion in its alien eyes was unsettling.

There was no doubt in Ros's mind any more; this creature knew exactly what it was doing when it had killed Benoit Devereux. It had chosen its target carefully for maximum impact and then carried out a precision attack any special ops group would be proud of. It had known exactly what it was doing, and that made it evil.

It had to die. No matter the cost.

"Let's finish this," Ros said.

She couldn't charge the monster, not with her leg burning the way it did—how deep had her blade gone anyway?—but she didn't need to. The creature made a horrible gurgling sound that might have been a laugh and then rushed her.

Ros was ready for it.

She swung her blade high, going for the creature's neck. Her aim was true but the thick armour plates took the brunt of the damage. She hadn't damaged the flesh underneath she could tell.

The creature veered away from the bright light and source of pain, giving Ros the chance to ready another swing.

Her sword bit into its chest as the creature charged again, and Ros threw her whole weight behind the blow, trying to push the blade as deep as possible, to do the maximum amount of damage. Judging by the wet scream the creature let off, it was working.

Its remaining arms flailed around it, trying to bat Ros away. She stood her ground and let her armour take the damage. Just a little longer...

Her blade sputtered out and caught fast. She couldn't get it to go any deeper, no matter how hard she pushed.

The creature seemed to realise this at the same moment she did and swung again, managing a much more coordinated blow this time. Instinct took over as Ros let go of her sword and dropped into a roll, narrowly avoiding the claws coming her way. She executed the roll but with her injured leg she couldn't channel the momentum and find her feet again.

Her limbs felt like porridge, thick and useless, and she ended up face down on the tunnel floor.

She didn't have time to berate herself for the failure. Sharp claws dug into the back of her suit, smashing the servos and cutting her skin. Ros screamed.

The creature dragged her across the floor, the metal of her suit scraping noisily against the rock. Ros couldn't think, couldn't move. Everything hurt. She could feel blood seeping across her back, wet and hot, whether from the claws or the jagged metal that had once been her armoured suit she couldn't tell.

Her back hurt. Her shoulder hurt. Her leg hurt. Her head hurt. She was out of weapons, out of options. Out of time.

This was it.

The creature pulled upward, lifting Ros off the ground. It twisted its arm, adjusting its grip so Ros was face to face with it. One clawed hand was wrapped around her front, claws digging into her back. She could see its face now, see the victorious glint in its eyes. It was almost as though the creature was gloating.

"Fuck you!" Ros spat, covering the inside of her helmet with a fine spray of blood and spit. When had her mouth started bleeding, anyway?

Another horrendous sound gurgled up from the monster's mouth. It was laughing at her. The damn thing has a sword jammed in its chest and was missing half its jaw, not to mention one of its arms and it was *laughing* at her.

"Oh hell no," she managed to say. The claws in her back tightened and breathing became that much harder. Black dots appeared in front of her eyes as she gasped for air. Unconsciousness beckoned, followed shortly by death.

She could tell these were her final moments, so she

dragged her thoughts to Gabby, and Isobel. She wondered if they would lean on each other in their grief over her death. She hoped so. Gabby had the rest of the Irregulars to turn to, but Isobel had no one.

Ros still didn't even know if Isobel loved her. That might be her greatest regret.

Something in her chest snapped as the creature's grip tightened, her ribs most likely. She was almost beyond caring.

She thought she heard voices, the sound of heavy footsteps rushing towards her, but she was probably imagining it. Wishful thinking in her last few moments, hoping her friends had come for her.

An explosion sounded in the small space, almost deafening Ros, and she could have sworn that sounded exactly like Ewan's cannon. The creature screamed, blinding Ros's sensors and senses alike, and by the time her brain caught up with what was happening, she was on the floor and Ewan was wrestling with the creature.

Gabby knelt down beside her with her visor flipped up and Ros didn't think she'd ever seen anything so beautiful in her life. "You came for me," Ros choked, her lungs screaming with every syllable.

"Of course I came for you," Gabby said, and if her voice was softer than usual it was buried under the ringing in Ros's ears. "Just hang on Ros, we'll get you out of this."

Then she was up and away, and Ros called after her, not wanting to be separated again. AJs face swam into view. His eyes were full of a mixture of worry and relief.

"You just take it easy, liebchen," he said. "Let the

others deal with the monster while I look after you."

Ros shook her head, making herself dizzy. "Have to help." She was slurring, but that wasn't important. What was important was making sure none of her friends got hurt saving her sorry ass. "Need to finish this."

She heard Ewan whoop with delight and the crack of Mila's rifle, followed by a string of swears in Russian. If any of them got hurt now because of her...

"Help me up," Ros demanded. AJ looked like he wanted to argue, but he did as he was told. And if AJs strong arms were the only thing keeping Ros upright, he was kind enough not to say anything.

Margaret lay on the floor a few feet away, somehow miraculously unharmed in the fight between Ros and the creature. She reached out with her right arm, grunting in pain and frustration when she couldn't reach it. AJ scooped the rifle up and set it in her hand, bracing the butt of the rifle against his own body so the kickback wouldn't hurt Ros any more than she already was.

Gabby had her own blade out and ignited and she was running around the creature slashing at anything she could reach. She must have caught something vital because the creature's leg gave out under it and it collapsed to one knee with a scream. Ewan took the opportunity to literally shove his cannon arm in the creature's shattered maw, letting loose a series of shots that should have turned its skull to paste. Somehow the bastard was still standing.

"That's it baby," Ewan crooned to his favourite weapon, "revenge at last."

Mila let loose another shot that hit the creature in the eye socket and it swayed drunkenly, clearly hurt. Gabby drew her arm back, readying for the final blow.

"Everyone step back," AJ called, his deep voice sounding far too large for the small space they were in. "The boss needs to finish this one." Gabby and Ewan stepped out of the way, eyeing their target warily. The creature didn't try to escape; it just sat there, staring at Ros with its one remaining eye.

It was almost as if it knew this was the end.

Ros was mere seconds from passing out but she managed to charge Margaret and aim for the mess of gristle and blood that had once been the creature's jaw. AJ had to help her keep a grip on the weapon and keep it steady.

"This one's for Matty," Ros gasped, and squeezed the trigger.

Thanks to AJs support her shot sailed true, slamming into the creature's face. Ros thought she heard something break—possibly the thing's neck—and then it was over. The malevolence disappeared from its eyes and it swayed once before collapsing forward onto the ground.

Ros felt her own legs give way with sheer relief, and would have faceplanted herself if not for AJ lifting her up, armour and all, and holding her tightly to his chest.

"Rest now Kapitan," he said softly. "It is over."

As if to punctuate his words, the sound of Ewan's cannon and Mila's rifle rang out three times each, making damned sure the thing was dead.

Suddenly consciousness felt like too much of a burden

to maintain and Ros let herself drift in and out of awareness as AJ peeled off her armour and got her on a stretcher. Gabby and Ewan carried her out of the tunnel system as AJ worked to stop the bleeding and stabilise her wounds.

She must have passed out properly at some point because the next thing she knew it was daylight and she was strapped to the back of one of the colony's rovers, a drip attached to her arm. Gabby was sat over her, her lips moving as she said something Ros couldn't quite hear but knew to be a prayer; she'd watched Gabby praying often enough over the years to know the gist of the movements her lips made. Mila was sat on Ros's other side, scowling.

Mila noticed Ros was awake first and nudged Gabby.

"Hey, how you feeling?" Gabby asked, her voice a lot more gentle than Ros probably deserved.

"Okay," Ros rasped out. Breathing and talking was still problematic, but other than that she actually felt pretty good. AJ had the best painkillers.

"Good," Gabby said and promptly punched Ros in the upper arm. "Don't you *ever* do that to me again."

Ros flinched from the blow, which made her ribs move. She gasped in pain, which attracted AJs attention from the front of the vehicle.

"Do not injure my patient any further Gabriela," he said, sounding cross. "I have not yet determined the full extent of the damage."

Gabby apologised to him but she didn't look the least bit sorry. Ros, on the other hand, very much was.

"I'm sorry," she ground out. "I shouldn't have gone

without you."

"Damn right you shouldn't have," Gabby replied hotly. "You're lucky to still be alive."

"I know," Ros said, and closed her eyes against the wave of pain in her chest. When she opened them again Gabby was looking at her like she was trying to memorise her features. Ros couldn't remember having been on the receiving end of such a look from Gabby before and she wasn't sure what it meant. She knew there was something she needed to say before she passed out again. "Hey Gabs?"

"Yeah?"

"I love you," Ros said. "I thought you should know that."

"I do know that," Gabby said, and then hesitated. Her eyes flickered to the front of the vehicle, and she must have found whatever she was looking for because her gaze was firm when it returned to Ros. "I love you too. Even though you ran off without me."

"S'rry," Ros said, slurring as the painkiller tried to pull her back into unconsciousness.

"Sleep now," Gabby said gently. "We'll get you back to the colony and patch you up so you can work on apologising to Isobel as well."

Ros nodded and shut her eyes. She was hovering right on the edge of unconsciousness when she felt someone lean close to whisper in her ear.

"If you ever do this again, I will kill you myself," said Mila, sounding one hundred percent serious about it.

Ros thought that sounded reasonable.

CHAPTER TWELVE

ISOBEL

Ros looked so small, lying in bed like that.

Isobel had almost convinced herself that the woman was invincible, but here was irrefutable evidence she wasn't, and it made her heart ache. Ros had come back from her ill-advised field trip with a concussion, six broken ribs, a lacerated back and a deep cauterised wound to her thigh. Not to mention half a dozen other small injuries; cuts and bruises and grazes. Her suit of armour was practically a write-off. She was lucky to be alive.

The monster that had plagued Novis Colony for years was dead, the curse potentially broken, and yet all Isobel, now Governor Devereux, cared about was the fact Ros had come back to her. Battered and bruised but in one piece.

Doctor Schneider (who had insisted Isobel call him AJ) had put Ros in a medically induced coma almost as soon as they were back at the colony. To allow her head injury to heal, he'd said, but also to stop the stubborn woman from trying to get out of bed and go kill something else before she was ready. Isobel had barely left her side since she'd been brought in, choosing to do what work she could from Captain Lamarr's bedside.

She didn't have an assistant to take some of the work from her shoulders, but there were plenty of people willing to help her as she transitioned into her new role.

The Irregulars had been indispensable in helping rebuild the colony so far. Gabby had them doing grunt work to keep them occupied, hauling building materials and putting up new prefabs to prepare for new colonists (because apparently bored mercenaries were a dangerous thing). Tariq and Noora (the latter of whom had been instrumental in helping Isobel keep her head while Ros had been missing) were doing regular sensor sweeps of the entire planet, looking for any signs of more creatures. So far their search hadn't turned anything up, but after last time they wanted to be sure.

"I have to," Noora had said when Isobel had asked her friend why she was spending so much time in orbit. "If there are any more of those creatures out there we need to know. Captain hates leaving a job half done. Besides," she'd said over the comm, a grin in her voice that Isobel knew only too well by now, "we don't want the Captain running off and getting hurt again before you can do the dirty with her."

Isobel had felt her face heat at that, glad of the fact Noora couldn't see her blush. How it had got out that she and Ros hadn't actually had sex yet, she had no idea (though she suspected Gabby's involvement) but the Irregulars weren't being shy about teasing her for it. She thought it might be a coping mechanism while their Captain was out of commission, but it also made her feel accepted by the crew. The Irregulars were starting to feel like family.

She sighed and put her paperwork down, glancing over at where Ros lay in her bed, hooked up to half a dozen monitors. AJ had reduced the medication that was keeping her unconscious the previous day, so Ros might wake up at any time. Isobel felt nervous about it. She hadn't spoken to the mercenary since before she'd snuck out to kill a monster on her own and she wasn't sure what she would say. Ros had basically declared her love for Isobel, both in the note she'd left and in her actions. Isobel wasn't as sure, still sorting out what she was feeling. And Gabriela Hernandez wasn't exactly making it easy for her to figure out.

As if summoned by Isobel's thoughts, Gabby walked into the room and plopped down in a chair next to Isobel. She'd obviously just had a shower, her hair was still damp, and she smelled of soap, and she was wearing a beautiful summer dress. The look on her face, however, was serious. Isobel knew from the long conversations she'd had at Ros's bedside that the Lieutenant felt betrayed that Ros had gone after the monster without her. Isobel also knew that wasn't the full extent of the issue; she knew Gabby well enough to read her facial features by now and she could tell something else was bothering her, and she had a good idea what it was.

If her hunch was correct, it could put one hell of a spanner in the works regarding her and Ros. So far she'd kept quiet, but Isobel wasn't sure how long she'd be able to keep that up.

"How's she doing?" Gabby asked quietly, her eyes never leaving the figure lying in the bed.

"The same. AJ said her brain activity looked promising when he checked in earlier; she was showing signs of coming out of the coma. But when she might wake up is out of his hands. All we can do is give her time."

Gabby nodded but her face looked strained. She wanted to talk to Ros, desperately, that much Isobel knew. She felt exactly the same.

"Gabby..." she started and then trailed off. What was she planning on saying exactly?

"Isobel?" Gabby replied, her eyes finally leaving Ros's face and locking onto Isobel's. "Something the matter?"

"Yes. No. Well, sort of?" She sighed. "To be perfectly honest, I don't know."

"Wanna talk about it?" Isobel's immediate instinct was to say yes, but she wasn't sure she could talk about it to Gabby yet. Gabby noticed her hesitation and carried on. "I know I'm not always the best shoulder to cry on, I sometimes don't understand emotions the same way others do. It's okay if you don't know if you can talk to me. I suggest you try AJ. He's great at this stuff."

"I do want to talk to you, Gabby," Isobel said, and she meant it. However this turned out Gabby would play an important part in her life, Isobel knew. She didn't want to isolate the woman. "I just... I think I need to sort my own head out first. Does that make sense?"

Gabby nodded. "Try going for a walk. Helps me when I need to think. Then go find AJ. He's helped me sort out my head in the last week or so," she said. "I'll look after Ros while you're away."

Isobel hesitated again. She'd basically only left Ros's side to use the bathroom. What if she woke up while she was away? She desperately wanted to be by Ros's side when she woke up. *If* she woke up, said a nasty little voice in her mind. She wanted hers to be the first face Ros saw, but she knew she was no good to the woman if she couldn't sort her own head out.

She sighed. "Call me if anything happens," she said, standing up and leaving the room. Gabby grunted an affirmative response, her gaze locked on Ros once more.

It turned out Gabby was right about one thing; a walk in the garden helped clear Isobel's head. The fresh air blew away some of the cobwebs her thoughts kept getting stuck on. As she walked past the irrigation system, memories of her first kiss with Ros fresh in her mind, her thoughts turned to the all important question; was she in love with Ros Lamarr?

What should have been a simple question was tangled up in the mess of grief her father's death had left her with. Isobel thought back to how things had been before Benoit Devereux had been killed. She'd liked Ros, felt drawn to her. She'd enjoyed kissing her, a lot, and had been more than willing to let the mercenary bed her. She was attracted, certainly, and she liked her, but was it love?

She thought it might be.

It would be a lot easier for Isobel to decide how she'd felt if she'd been in love before. She'd had relationships before, with both men and women, but her work had always come first. Those previous relationships had inevitably fizzled out when the promise of infrequent sex had become insufficient reward for the effort of maintaining the relationship. Isobel had never been particularly emotionally invested in those relationships.

And yet... what she felt for Ros had already surpassed anything she'd known before. She was more invested in a woman she'd known a month, with whom she'd shared a handful of kisses and not much else, than she'd been in her last girlfriend, who she'd been with over a year. Was it love? It was entirely possible. The idea both thrilled and scared her.

Isobel shook herself. She should take Gabby up on her suggestion of talking to AJ. The man was in a long-term romantic relationship himself, at the very least he might be able to tell her if she was in love.

AJ had been bunking in the servant's quarters at the Governor's mansion since Ros had been brought in, so he was never more than a minute or so away from his patient (Potts had come out of his coma four days ago, much to the relief of the Irregulars, so he was free to tend to Ros more closely). He was easy enough to find; just follow the loud swearing in a strong Scottish accent and where Ewan was, AJ was sure to be close by.

Ewan was lounging on the bunk Isobel was sure had been claimed by AJ while his boyfriend sat in a chair, knitting something in the ugliest orange wool she'd ever seen. She desperately hoped whatever it was it wasn't for Ewan; it would look *horrible* next to his hair.

"Ah, Ms Devereux," AJ said as she hovered in the doorway. He was one of the few people who had yet to address her by her new title, something she was immensely grateful for. "What might I be able to do for you?"

"I was hoping we could talk." Her gaze flicked to

Ewan. "In private?"

Ewan just grinned in response. "I know when I'm not wanted," he said, but Isobel could tell he wasn't hurt. He was far too easy-going for that.

"I will see you later, mein Lieber," AJ said softly.

Ewan blew him a kiss and slipped out shutting the door behind him. AJ put his knitting down and fixed his gaze on Isobel, giving her his whole attention. For a moment Isobel wondered exactly what his bionic eye could see when it looked at her, but then she decided she didn't want to know.

"How is my patient?" he asked, brow furrowed in concern. "Everything is okay I trust?"

"Ros seems fine," Isobel rushed to reassure him. "Still the same when I left. I was hoping to talk to you about... well about me. Gabby said you were good at this sort of stuff," she said, not bothering to elaborate on what 'stuff' he was supposed to be good at. If he was as perceptive as Gabby had suggested he'd know what she was talking about anyway.

AJ smiled kindly. "I do what I can, and I have pointed out the obvious to our dear Gabriela when she is being oblivious. Although in her case it is mostly hitting her around the head until she sees sense. I trust I will not need to do this for you, hmmm?"

"Depends how stubborn my brain ends up being," she muttered, making AJ chuckle.

"We shall see. What 'stuff' is it that Gabriela thinks I can help you with? You are trying to sort out your feelings for our dear Kapitan, are you not?"

Isobel looked at him with her mouth open. "How did you...?"

"I have eyes, liebchen. I notice things. And you and the Kapitan are not, as they say, very subtle."

Isobel felt herself flush at that, cheeks burning with shame. Not that she and the Kapitan had a thing going on, but that she hadn't been very subtle about it. She was a diplomat; she should know better.

"What is it that has you concerned?" AJ asked.

"I'm trying to... ascertain... the exact nature of my feelings for Ros."

"You and Gabriela, you are as bad as each other. Honestly, the Kapitan sure knows how to pick them." He rolled his eyes at Isobel, but she never got the impression he was laughing at her. It was quite nice actually. "What exactly are you having difficulties with?

"I'm trying to work out if, if I love her," she said quietly. "What does it feel like? Being in love?"

"You have never been in love before?" AJ looked surprised, but there was no pity in his gaze, no judgement. Isobel wondered if the man had a mean bone in his body. She shook her head. "That is a shame," he said. "But perhaps it is simply that you have not met anyone worthy of your love. Until now," he added with a sly grin. "You think you might be in love with our Kapitan?"

"It's possible," Isobel admitted. "But I want to be certain before I say anything to her. And... it might be nice to know more about Gabby and Ros too, before I commit myself to anything. I don't want to get hurt."

"Sit, liebchen," AJ said, gesturing at the bed. Isobel did

as she was told. "You have come because you want my advice, ja?" She nodded. "Then my advice is this: whatever it is you feel for the Kapitan I do not think she will hurt you. She is a good person, and she loves deeply and without restraint. I have known her for ten years now, and I can honestly say she is one of the best people I have ever known. Your heart, should you choose to give it to her, will be in safe hands."

Isobel hummed non-committally, wringing her hands. AJ's words were all well and good but it didn't help her decide whether she wanted to give her heart to Ros, or tell her if she already had. She said as much to him.

"Okay, let's diagnose you then," AJ said, leaning back in his chair. "What are your symptoms?"

"Rapid heartbeat, fluttering stomach, breathing faster when I'm around her." Isobel paused, thinking. "Sheer terror when I realised she'd gone after the monster on her own. More relieved than I've ever felt in my life when she came back alive." She paused again. Her heart was beating quickly just talking about it, and there were words just behind her teeth, fighting to get out.

Isobel cleared her throat. "I've been putting aside my duties to stay by her side and I've never done that before. I want to know her, to be as close as possible." She bit her lip. "I want her in my life, permanently, but... if she'd rather be with Gabby, if that would make her happy... That's all I want. For Ros to be happy whether that's with me or not."

AJ stroked his chin and hummed as though considering Isobel's words. "Do you want my professional opinion? As both a doctor and a person who has extensive experience of romantic relationships?" She nodded vigorously. "It sounds to me that you are very much in love with our Kapitan."

"But I've only known her a month! Surely that's not long enough to... to..." Isobel couldn't quite bring herself to get the words out.

"The heart is a very fickle organ, believe me. Emotionally speaking at any rate. The heart wants what the heart wants, as the saying goes, and it appears as though your heart wants our Kapitan."

Isobel took a deep breath. She was in love with Ros Lamarr. Her head buzzed with the knowledge, her heart racing in her chest and yet... she thought that admitting to herself she had fallen in love would be more of a revelation. Somehow it wasn't. The realisation of her feelings simply felt like the next step on a journey she'd been making for a long time now. It felt inevitable, like coming home.

She was in love with Ros, and she felt great about it. Elated even. Then she remembered the other issue at hand and her heart fell.

"What about Gabby?" she asked.

"What about her?"

"I mean, where does she fit into this whole situation?"

"That is not something I can tell you, I am afraid. The answers to that question can only come from Gabriela, and from Ros. The three of you need to sit down and have an honest conversation sometime soon, ja?"

"Yeah, I guess we do," Isobel said.

"I will give you the same advice I gave Gabriela when she was having trouble. Do not worry about other people. What matters is that you and the Kapitan and Gabriela find an arrangement that makes you all happy. If it does not look conventional from the outside, so what? Anyone who wants to give you Scheisse for that will have to deal with Ewan, and they will have to deal with me."

Isobel took a deep breath, tossing AJ's advice around in her head. She could do this. She could deal with conversation, with people. She could negotiate with the best of them. However the other two women felt about each other, surely they could come to some agreement that would make them all happy. Compromises might have to be made but... she was in love for the first time in her life. Whatever compromises she needed to make to make for a relationship with Ros to work would surely be worth it.

"Okay," she said, and her voice was steadier than it had been in a while. "I guess the only thing I can do for now is wait for Ros to wake up. There's not a lot I can do until she's in a position to talk."

"Nein, you are wrong there, liebchen. There is much you can be doing. Be kind to Gabriela, she is hurting as well. And talk to her. If my hunch is correct, and they almost always are, you and our dear Gabriela will need to learn how to communicate closely to keep the Kapitan in line."

He smiled widely at Isobel, his eyes twinkling. She decided that she really, really liked AJ. She liked all the Irregulars really, but there was an inner circle of people around Ros, who loved her best and would go to the ends of the galaxy for her, who had accepted Isobel into the fold so easily. It felt like having a family, which was startling in the wake of her father's death. Startling, but not unwelcome.

Isobel had the sudden overwhelming urge to hug AJ, so she did. He patted her on the back with one of his massive, deceptively gentle hands.

"Thank you," she said, her eyes filling with tears. "You've been a great help."

"It is what I am here for," he said, still smiling. "Now, shall we go check on my patient? If I leave her too long I am half convinced she will wake up and try to go off hunting something else. That woman does not like being cooped up in bed."

Isobel thought AJ must be psychic or something; when they got back upstairs Ros was not only awake but trying to climb out of bed. Gabby was doing what she could to convince her Captain she should stay put, but apparently Ros was feeling extra stubborn and resisted.

"That is quite enough of that," AJ said, raising his voice slightly so it rang out above the sound of machinery and Gabby and Ros arguing. "Kapitan you are not to move from that bed until I say you can. Do not make me get the restraints out, you know Ewan doesn't like it when I have to use our toys on someone else."

Isobel felt herself flush. That was *far* too much information about someone else's sex life for her to be comfortable but it seemed to do the trick. Ros shut up and laid back down, glaring at the ceiling like she could set it on fire with her mind. Gabby just stood there smirking.

AJ muttered under his breath about reckless Captains who didn't know how to take care of themselves as he pottered around performing checks on Ros. Isobel tuned him out and slid into the chair next to the bed, taking Ros's hand in her own.

"Hey," she said, softer than she'd intended. "How are you feeling?"

Ros met her gaze and smiled even though AJ was changing her bandages. "I feel like I've been run over by a herd of something. You're a sight for sore eyes though." Isobel felt her cheeks heat yet again and shot a look in Gabby's direction. Herndandez just smiled.

"It's good to see you awake. You had us all worried for a while." Isobel felt tears prickling at the corners of her eyes. "You had me worried."

"Hey, it's okay," Ros said, reaching up to stroke Isobel's cheek. "I'm alright. I'm pretty tough and besides; I'm too pretty to die."

Isobel laughed at that, and out of the corner of her eye she saw Gabby's smile get bigger. AJ finished his checks and announced that Ros had sustained no lasting damage on her foolish quest but that she should stay on bed rest for a few more days.

"I am counting on you two to make sure she behaves," he said, pointing a finger at both Gabby and Isobel. "You make sure she stays in that bed. Now, if you'll excuse me, I should go find my boyfriend." He left the room and Isobel was suddenly acutely aware that she was on her own with the two people who held her future happiness in their hands for the first time. Well, while all three were awake at any rate. She shifted in her chair, suddenly nervous.

Gabby didn't seem to have any such problem. She pulled another chair up to the bed and sat down next to Isobel, resting her hand gently by Ros's thigh. Ros gave Gabby a smile and then turned her attention to Isobel.

"I owe you an apology," she said. "I shouldn't have snuck out on you like that, it wasn't fair. I get like that sometimes; I just need to *do* something and I don't always think about the consequences properly. I've already apologised to Gabby for running off without her to back me up, but I'm sorry for making you worry as well. I'll try not to do it again."

"You better not," Isobel said, feeling tears well up again. She remembered waking up and Ros being gone, the other side of the bed cold for the first time in a week. She remembered a brief moment of panic, looking around the room for her before spotting the tablet Ros had left behind. She remembered reading the message, being bowled over by what the letter said. She remembered screaming for lack of any other ideas how to deal with it.

She should have realised she was in love with Ros long before AJ helped her work it out.

"I love you," she said softly, looking Ros dead in the eye. "But if you ever do anything like that again I will not be responsible for my actions, you understand?"

"Message received and understood Captain," Ros said through the grin that was slowly spreading over her face. "I love you too." Her gaze shifted to where Gabby was sat with a matching smile. "You okay with me loving her too?" she asked, jerking her head towards Gabby.

"Yeah, I am," Isobel said, surprised to find she meant it. She didn't remember making that decision but apparently she had. "I mean, we'll need to have a proper conversation about how this will work, but I don't want you and Gabby to end what you have because of me." She looked at Gabby, wonderful beautiful Gabby, who had gone after Ros, who was the reason Ros was here and still alive. "We'll work something out. We can all be happy. If that's what both of you want."

"I want," Ros said, looking at Isobel and Gabby in turn. "I want you both very much."

"I want it too," Gabby said. "Like you said, we'll sort out the specifics later, when Ros is well again. I want to keep what I have with Ros and I want the two of you to love each other. I don't see why we can't have that."

"That settles it then," Isobel said, extending her other hand out for Gabby to take, and she did. "We're doing this." Ros moved her other hand to rest on top of Gabby's by her leg, despite the discomfort that passed over her face as she did so. It felt almost like they were shaking on it, sealing the deal.

They sat there together, a little circle of love and hope, until Ros fell asleep again. Watching Ros sleep, holding Gabby's hand, it felt right to Isobel.

It felt like home. It felt like family.

CHAPTER THIRTEEN

ROS

It was another week before Ros was allowed to get out of bed. Apparently the wound to her thigh was worse than she'd thought and AJ didn't want her putting weight on it before it was ready and blah blah blah. Honestly Ros stopped listening to him after the third lecture about how she'd almost died and she should take it easy.

She hated being on bed rest. She needed to be up and about, *doing* things. Even with Gabby and Isobel keeping her pretty much constant company she was *bored*. And she wanted to see just how bad the damage to her suit was. But mostly she was bored. Her trigger finger itched something rotten, but she was stuck in bed until AJ gave her the okay to be up and about.

He'd threatened to get the restraints out and as much as she loved the man, she really didn't see him that way. So she stayed put, and Gabby and Isobel were in charge of keeping her entertained.

Ros let a dreamy smile drift across her face as she thought of the two women she loved best. On that front at least, everything was going great.

For the first time in all the time they'd known each other she and Gabby had a somewhat formal arrangement. Gabby had admitted she loved Ros, even if it wasn't in a romantic sense, and they had agreed to continue their long-standing arrangement when it came to sex; Gabby would fuck her Captain when she felt she needed it but would also have other playmates. As long as those playmates understood that Gabby wasn't after anything romantic or long-term then everything would be fine. The only person Gabby wanted a long-term relationship with was Ros and she wanted the relationship they'd had all along; professional partners, best friends and occasional fuck-buddies.

Ros didn't quite understand how that worked but she figured it didn't matter. She loved Gabby and if Gabby was happy that was all that mattered.

And things with Isobel were going great too. Isobel was soft and sweet and so tender with Ros and was very much accepting of all the mushy romantic stuff she'd never been able to do with Gabby. Ros's injuries prevented them from doing much of anything, but if the make out sessions they'd snuck in when AJ wasn't looking were anything to go by, their sex life promised fireworks.

Gabby and Isobel were getting along great too. Ros wasn't entirely sure what arrangement the two of them had come to but she knew it wasn't her business unless they made it her business. Given the speculative looks Isobel kept sneaking at Gabby she wouldn't be at all surprised if a third dimension ended up being added to their arrangement. Ros didn't care though; for the moment she was happy, almost blissfully so. Even if she still had to use crutches to get around.

Her busted ribs made even what little she could do painful. AJ might have worked wonders with the bone knitter, but they still hurt. It was a handy reminder not to do anything else foolish. (Sure wouldn't put it past the man to have healed her ribs *just* enough so they still hurt. AJ was lovely, but he wasn't above making sure he got his point across with some petty revenge every now and again. And if Ros was honest with herself, she fucking deserved it this time.)

Bored with staring at the same four walls Ros made a break for the garden. She needed the fresh air and craved the soothing sound of the irrigation system. But first she had to get past AJ and make it down the stairs.

Part one was easy enough since her doctor was currently enjoying some downtime with his boyfriend. The stairs were a bit trickier. Her thigh burned with every step she took, the after-effects of both the initial injury and the resulting surgery still very much making themselves felt. Still, Ros got herself downstairs and into the garden without running into anyone or screaming so she counted that as a win.

Once she was seated on the same rock Isobel had found her on the night they'd first kissed, she decided she was staying put. The sun was warm, the breeze was cool, and the air didn't smell like disinfectant, which was a vast improvement over where she had been. And if anyone noticed she was missing and worried, she wasn't that hard to find. They'd know she couldn't get far, anyway.

How long she sat there before Isobel found her she wasn't sure.

"I thought I might find you here," Isobel said, sounding amused. "AJ's not thrilled with you for disappearing on him."

"AJ can bite me," Ros said, not opening her eyes. "I

needed a change of scenery."

"Yes because you've not seen enough of the insides of your eyelids over the past couple of weeks."

Ros opened her eyes and grinned. "I was just resting. Getting out here took more energy than I expected."

"Well it would do," Isobel said. She didn't sound mad, or even that surprised. Just resigned. "You were in a medically induced coma a week ago. It's going to take a while to bounce back from that." Her voice gentler then, dropping into a more affectionate tone. "I wish you'd be kinder to yourself sometimes. You push yourself too hard."

"Yeah, I know. Gabby's been telling me for years. This is the first time her being right has hurt so much though." As though to drive the point home, Ros's leg twinged painfully. How long has it been since she'd last had pain relief? She wasn't sure. Too long probably. But she was outside in the sunshine with Isobel and that was worth a little pain.

Something must have shown on her face though because Isobel asked "Are you alright?"

"Yeah, I could use some more drugs but I don't wanna move."

"I could go get AJ," Isobel offered.

"You do that and he'll shout at me for being outside then drag me back to bed and I don't want that. I can deal for a bit."

Isobel frowned. "What can I do to help?"

"I've heard kisses are great for pain relief," Ros said with a wicked grin. "How about some of those?"

Isobel rolled her eyes, but scooted closer and leaned in anyway. The kissing went great until Isobel shifted to put her arm around Ros and set her ribs off. Ros hissed in pain but kept kissing, enjoying the smell and taste and feel of Isobel too much to let something as trivial as pain stop her. She could only keep going for so long though, and eventually they moved apart to lie back with their fingers entwined. Isobel had a goofy looking grin on her face and Ros knew hers matched.

"So," Isobel said when they'd been quiet for a while. "What happens next?"

Ros struggled upright, a frown taking over her face. "What do you mean?"

Isobel was no longer meeting her gaze. "I mean, AJ's got a few weeks of physical therapy planned while he weans you off the painkillers, but at some point he'll declare you fit for duty. What happens then?" The question of what happens to us was unspoken but hung in the air between them.

"Hey, look at me." Ros reached to pull Isobel's chin up with two fingers. "What's wrong?"

"I just–" She sighed. "Even with everything that's happened the last few weeks I don't remember the last time I was as happy as I am when I'm with you. And I guess I'm just scared that when you're cleared for active duty you'll head off back out to the stars on another adventure and forget all about me."

"Never," Ros said, putting as much conviction as she could into the words. "I could never forget about you," she insisted.

"I guess I need a little reassurance is all, and I'd like to know what happens next for us. Will you go home?" Isobel asked, her voice thick.

"You mean back to Erebus Station?" Isobel nodded. "Erebus Station isn't home Izzy."

Isobel looked confused. "But...?"

Ros shook her head. "It was a port of call, the best place to put in when we were between missions because they didn't mind a bunch of drunk mercenaries on their downtime and there were always plenty of jobs available, the type where people don't ask too many questions, but it wasn't home." Ros shifted to cup Isobel's cheek in her hand and gazed into her eyes. "Home is wherever I can put the *Mercenary Star* down and the last time I checked you had a perfectly functional spaceport here on Novis. So if you're asking where I'm gonna go when I'm between jobs the answer is here, if you'll have me." The way Isobel's face broke out in a smile was as much relief as it was happiness told Ros she'd been worrying about this for a while.

"Of course I'll have you," she said. "I want nothing more than to be with you as long as you'll have me."

"You'll be stuck with her a long time," came Gabby's amused voice from the side. "She has a habit of turning up and never leaving. I've been trying to get rid of her for years." Ros turned to look at Gabby and saw she had a smile on her face that was completely at odd with her words.

"Liar," she said. "If anything it's me that's been trying to get rid of you," she teased.

"Careful," Gabby said, looking at Isobel. "She'll drag you with her when she gets invalided out of the army and insist you start a mercenary crew with her and then you'll never get rid of her."

"I dunno, sounds alright to me," Isobel said, snuggling into Ros's side, gently, so as not to aggravate her ribs further. "Two mercenary bands sounds like a lot of work though, maybe we could think of some other way to symbolise commitment?"

Ros felt her heart pound in her chest. Combining that comment with the one about Isobel staying as long as Ros would have her, it sounded a lot like a suggestion of marriage, which she was in no way ready for. That someone would even be willing to joke about that though was... intoxicating, if a little terrifying. Tamping down on the feelings of uncertainty, Ros eyed Gabby with as much disdain as she could muster, which given Gabby was one of her favourite people, wasn't very much at all. "Did you want something, Hernandez?"

"AJ sent me looking for you," she said, everything about her voice and postures screaming that she wasn't bothered in the slightest by Ros's attempt at a commanding tone of voice. "He's upset that his patient gave him the slip and sent me after you."

"Five more minutes?" Ros whined. "The sun is warm, and the air doesn't smell like disinfectant and there's a pretty lady who keeps kissing me. Surely he knows all that is good for me."

"Sure it's good for you," Isobel said, "but only if you're taking care of yourself too. Come on, you needed more painkillers earlier. Let's get you back inside."

"Oh, I see how it is," Ros said with a mock pout. "You're all ganging up on me. Why did I ever agree to this arrangement?"

"Because you love us," Gabby said simply. "Now come on."

Ros hated to admit it but it took both of them to help her up and off the rock. Everything had seized up while she'd been sat there and she was well overdue for more drugs, meaning that everything that could hurt, did. She wasn't sure she'd have made it back inside at all if not for Iosbel and Gabby keeping her upright and steadying her. It was an excellent metaphor, she thought as she fought a wave of dizziness. Maybe she should write that down.

"Ah, there is my patient," AJ said as Ros stumbled back in to her hospital room. "You are overdue your medication. I imagine you are feeling those injuries of yours again, ja?"

"I have no idea what you're talking about. I've never felt better," Ros said, lying through her teeth. Getting back up the stairs had been harder than getting down, even with help, and she knew full well AJ could see both the sweat on her forehead and the way her hands were shaking; that damn eye of his missed nothing.

Mercifully, no one said anything and soon Ros was back in bed, her veins full of powerful narcotics and unconsciousness beckoning. "Stay with me?" she mumbled, looking at both Isobel and Gabby.

"We're not going anywhere," Gabby said. "You just rest now."

"Kay," Ros said, her voice sounding very far away. Her lips felt oddly loose and they weren't responding properly. "Love you both."

"Love you too," Isobel said as darkness claimed Ros. Gabby just smiled.

***

"Come now Kapitan, you must put your weight on it," AJ said, his voice somehow still full of boundless patience despite the way his patient was behaving.

"But it hurts" Ros protested, angrily. She hated feeling weak, hated feeling unable to do simple things like walk.

"Of course it hurts," AJ shot back. "You had a super-heated sword blade eat most of its way through your thigh. Now concentrate and put some weight on your leg."

AJ was horrible at physical therapy. Actually that wasn't true; as with all aspects of his job he was very good at it, but when it came to getting his patients back on their feet he was a stern taskmaster who brooked no argument. Ros was glad she hadn't had him for PT after she'd lost her leg; she would probably have beaten him to death with her new prosthetic.

"Ugh, I hate you so much right now," Ros said as she grit her teeth and slowly transferred her weight to both legs. Her thigh burned with the effort but she kept going until her foot was flat to the floor.

"Do you want to get back to work or not?" AJ asked. "Because I do. You are driving everyone up the wall while you are stuck in bed and I tell you it will be easier to fix your mobility issues than try to patch you up after Gabriela has lost her temper with you."

Ros hated to admit it, but AJ had a point. Gabby had snapped at her pretty hard the night before, which wasn't like her at all. Her second was evidently still a little mad that Ros had run off without her and got herself in this state in the first place.

"Gabby will come round," Isobel said gently from where she was sat watching the proceedings. Moral support, she'd said when she demanded to be allowed into the session. "She just hates to see you hurting and isn't sure how to deal with that."

And that was another thing; she wasn't sure what was happening between Isobel and Gabby but it was slightly unnerving. It was great to see the two people she loved most in the world getting along so well, getting to know each other enough that Isobel could read Gabby's moods almost as well as Ros could, but it was also a little strange. Not to mention irritating when they ganged up on her. She'd never done anything like the arrangement they'd made with the three of them and wasn't sure what to expect. Whatever happened, it would be an adventure, and Ros looked forward to it.

Not to mention she had an ongoing wager with herself on whether Gabby and Isobel would end up hooking up as well.

After half an hour of torture (at least from Ros's perspective) AJ told her she could call it a day.

"You are doing well Kapitan, but you could be progressing faster. If you do not stick to your exercises it will take you much longer to get back to work."

Exhausted and grumpy, Ros snapped back sarcastically. "I have powered armour AJ, I don't need to be able to walk."

He gave her a look that could peel paint. "Your current set of armour is barely any use for scrap metal, and there is no way I will let you get fitted for a new set until you can walk unaided without pain relief. Suck it up Kapitan and do your exercises. You–" he pointed at Isobel "–make sure she does as she's told. I am going for a drink and to find my boyfriend."

"Tough crowd," Ros said, grinning at Isobel to cover up how much pain she was in.

"He's right you know," Isobel said. "You want to get back out there but you need to be in the best shape you can be before you go charging into your next fight."

"I know he's right," Ros said with a sigh. "I'm just... not used this. This is probably the worst I've ever been hurt, even considering the time I lost my leg. And I'm not used to being so... useless for so long."

Isobel sidled up and slipped an arm about Ros's waist. Thankfully her ribs were feeling much better by now. "You're not useless. Not at all," she said, her voice soft and sincere. "Come on. Let's get you back into bed for a bit."

Ros just nodded as she allowed Isobel to take some of her weight and guide her back to bed. "Stay with me?" she said, hating that her voice sounded so small and unsure.

"Always," Isobel replied, sliding in under the covers.

They laid there for a long time, wrapped up together, listening to their own breathing. After a while Ros shifted, restless. "You know I love you right?" she said quietly.

"Yeah, I do. You okay?"

Ros's armed tightened around Isobel. "I will be."

"What do you need?"

"Just you." Ros scooted closer and pressed a kiss to Isobel's neck, just under the corner of her jaw and felt the pulse there speed up. "Izzy," Ros breathed.

"Sorry," she whispered. "I'll just... I'll get it under control in a minute. It's fine." Her pulse remained rapid, erratic.

"Don't pull away. Tell me what you want. Tell me what you need."

"I want you Ros," Isobel whispered, her voice raw and thick, like something was about to burst out of her and she was desperately trying to control it. "But I don't want to risk hurting you. I'll be fine."

Ros believed her. There was nothing wrong with a little bit of frustrated desire and she would have let it go were it not for the answering heat low in her own belly. Injuries be damned, she wanted Isobel too. "I'm sure we can work around my wounds," she said, letting her voice drop into a husk so Isobel would know she was in the same position. Her fingers found the gap between Isobel's shirt and her pants and eagerly explored the tiny sliver of exposed skin. Isobel shivered in response.

"If you're sure," she said.

"I'm sure. We'll go slow. We'll be careful. Tell me if you want me to stop."

"I will," Isobel said as she allowed her fingers to slip under Ros's shirt. Ros felt her breath hitch. "Let me know if you're uncomfortable at all, with anything."

"Promise, now will you kiss me, please?"

Isobel kissed her, hard, though her body remained gentle. There was a tension between them that Ros hadn't felt since the night of Benoit Devereux's funeral. The air sang with desire, the two of them in complete harmony. Isobel dragged her mouth away from Ros's, her breaths coming fast.

"I'm so glad you didn't let us do this the day of the funeral," she said, as though she'd been reading Ros's thoughts. "It wasn't the right time then, I know that now. This, *this* is right."

The truth of Isobel's words felt inescapable to Ros, the weight of them comfortable. This, between the two of them, was magic. There were no other words to describe it. Ros kissed Isobel again, trying to tell her with her kisses what her words could not.

They shed their doubts along with their clothes. Naked, Isobel was beautiful to behold, and Ros was suddenly self-conscious about her own body. She knew what Isobel could see, and she felt like it wasn't enough. There were fresh scars across her back from the Hellbeast's claws, still livid and red. But there were also older marks, places where the skin was puckered and torn, evidence of a life lived violently.

"Hey, you okay?" Isobel asked, voice little more than a whisper.

"Yeah," Ros said, her voice catching in her throat. "Just self-conscious I guess."

"About your scars?" Ros nodded. Isobel's fingers

moved over the marks on her back, her touch so impossibly light that the hyper-sensitive skin nearly screamed at her. "They're beautiful Ros. *You're* beautiful."

Ros could count on one hand the number of partners she'd had that had told her that and meant it, as she could tell Isobel meant it. She threw herself into their next kiss, trying to convey what she felt even though she didn't have words that were adequate. They fell into a rhythm together, communicating with words and gestures what they wanted, what they needed.

...

"Do you want to take your leg off?"

"Not this time. Leave it on... Might wanna take the knife out the secret compartment though."

"Yeah, that's really not my thing."

...

"Is this okay?"

"More than okay."

"I'm not hurting you?"

"No, just keep going. Don't you ever stop."

...

"Fuck! Right there. Wait. Shit. Stop!"

"What's the matter? Are you okay?"

"Cramp in my bad thigh. Give me a minute."

"Take as long as you need."
"It's okay, I think I'm ready to start again."

...

"Fuck that was... That was..."
"Pretty good?"
"Try amazing. My turn now though."

...

"Is this okay?"
"Yes. I like that. A little faster."
"Like that?"
"Yes. Now a little to the left."
"You're or mine?"
"Mine. Fuck! Right there."
"If you like that then I know a few other things you might like."

...

"Fuck! Ros!"
"You like that huh?"
"Yes!"
"Shall I keep going?"
"Yes!"

...

"Sacré bleu you're good at that."

"Plenty of practice. Plus Gabby taught me a few tricks."

"Remind me to thank her."

"I will. Again?"

"Non. I think quatre petit mort is enough for now."

"I suppose it's not bad for our first go together."

"Not bad?"

"Izzy, my love, I have so much to show you."

...

Ros was almost asleep when she heard the door open and gently close again. There were only three people who would come into her room unannounced and one of them was currently wrapped around her arm and breathing against her neck.

"AJ if that's you you can fuck off," Ros mumbled.

"Good job I'm not AJ then," Gabby said with a chuckle. "He'd blow his lid if he found the two of you all naked under there. You been fucking?"

"Yeah."

"Oh." Gabby's voice sounded disappointed and it was enough to bring Ros fully awake.

"Gabs? You okay?"

"Yeah, I was just gonna, come have a nap with you or something but... It's fine. You're busy. I'll just..."

She hesitated and Ros could tell she was on the verge of leaving. Gabby wasn't ordinarily a cuddly, affectionate person, even immediately after sex, but since Ros had been injured she'd often woken up with Gabby's arm slung over her. It was like she wanted to know where Ros was and make sure she was safe at all times. It was incredibly endearing.

She was just about to tell Gabby not to leave, but Isobel beat her to it.

"Tell her to stop being silly and get in here," she muttered grumpily into Ros's shoulder. "Bed's more than big enough for three."

"If you're sure," Gabby said, sounding hesitant. They'd have to work on that. After a nap though.

"You better do as the lady says," Ros said, throwing a bit of her command voice into her words. It worked because Gabby quickly stripped down to her underwear and climbed in, pressing her back to Ros's stomach. Isobel reached out and laced her fingers with Gabby's. They were definitely going to end up a thing.

It was surprisingly comfortable and not awkward considering it was the first time they'd done this. Three sets of breathing fell into sync and Ros felt herself drifting off again, warm and safe between two of her favourite people.

"A white woman, a black woman and a Latina women climb into bed together," Gabby said suddenly, breaking the silence. "Stop me if you've heard this one…"

"Gabby?" Ros grumbled.

"Sí?"

"Shut the fuck up."

"Sí Capitan."

Ros smiled and snuggled deeper into her partners' embrace. She could get used to this, she really could.

CHAPTER FOURTEEN

GABBY

Six months later

Hyperspace swirled pretty and sinister against the cockpit viewscreen but Gabby wasn't watching it for once. Her eyes were fixed firmly on Ros, who was practically vibrating with excitement.

It wasn't the normal level of Ros being jittery in hyperspace either. This was well beyond that, the product of eight long, hard weeks away from Novis Colony and Isobel. Even their usual tumble had done nothing to stop the fidgeting; she'd gotten back out of bed and gone straight back to pacing up and down the cockpit.

"Will you sit down?" she said, patience finally snapping. "You're giving me a headache." Gabby had missed Isobel too, but she was damned if she would admit that.

"Sorry," Ros said sheepishly, sitting down as she'd been ordered. "I'm just... anxious to get back home."

Over in the other corner of the cockpit, Noora was smirking. "I've never seen you this excited to get home, Captain," she said.

"It's different when you have someone waiting for you," Tariq, his tone so certain and final it made Gabby wonder if he was talking from personal experience. She didn't pry though.

"Yeah," Ros agreed, running a hand through hair that

was definitely overdue a trim. "Erebus station was never really home anyway, not the way Novis has become home already. And yeah, it really makes a difference knowing I get to see Isobel again soon. It's been so long!"

"Not much longer," Tariq said, talking buttons on his console. "Exiting hyperspace in three, two, one…"

The oily swirl of hyperspace gave way to the star dotted black of normal space and Gabby breathed a sigh of relief. Something in the cockpit started beeping.

"What's that?" Ros asked, clearly still strung tighter than was healthy.

"Message beacon," Noora said calmly. "Warning us about XyrQ activity in the area."

Gabby frowned. "They're getting awfully close to the colony now," she said. "How far out from Novis are we?"

"Do you want the actual distance," Tariq asked dryly, "or something that'll actually make sense to you?"

"The second one," Gabby grumbled.

"We're about five hours out from the colony at our current speed," he said. He'd gotten a lot better at calculating their hyperspace exits over the last six months. Gabby fully expected he'd jump directly into orbit one day.

Ros was frowning at the middle distance.

"Ay Capitan, what's the face for?"

"That's too close, far, far too close. The XyrQ normally stick to raiding the outer limits of a system where inexperienced pilots and first timers make the exit from hyperspace. This close to the colony there's too much traffic for them, and it's harder to escape the armed patrols. Something's up. Something bad."

Gabby knew the look Ros had on her face; she'd seen it a thousand times before they went into battle together. She grabbed the nearest comm panel. "Ewan will you go man your guns for me? We might have something for you to shoot at soon."

"Aye," came the simple reply. Less than a minute later Gabby heard the sound of the main pulse cannon powering up.

"Bastard was probably just waiting for me to give that order," she muttered to herself. "Fucking Scotsmen with itchy trigger fingers." She looked over to where Ros stood. Ordinarily the Captain would have had a smile on her face or a response to the joke, but she was still frowning.

"Anything on the sensor's Tariq?" she asked, completely ignoring what Gabby had just said.

"Nothing yet Captain," he said. "Wait! Two signals, coming in fast."

Gabby grabbed the comms again. "Ewan, get ready, we've got incoming."

"Aye, I see them."

"They're XyrQ by the look of them," Noora said, concentrating hard on her own panel. "And in bad shape. Someone's taken pot shots at them already."

"Makes that easier for us," Gabby said.

Ros shook her head. "Means they're more desperate, and that makes them dangerous."

"Want me to suit up Capitan?" Gabby asked, resting a hand on Ros's arm to soothe whatever was going in the woman's brain. "I mean, this is one of my favourite dresses but if you think we're at risk of boarding, I'll suit up and ruin it." It was one of Ros's favourite dresses too, mostly because of the low neckline, but it was just a thing. It could be replaced.

"Wait," Ros said. "Noora, those ships showing any signs of slowing down?"

"None at all. Looks like they're running away from something. Five minutes until contact."

Those five minutes felt like forever, the tension in the cockpit climbing as time crawled on. Ros stood stock still in the middle of it all, a frown on her face as she stared at the two dots on the screen that were getting closer and closer.

"They're powering up weapons," Noora, said, her her voice strung tight. "Slowing to attack speed."

"Ewan!" Gabby yelled into the comms.

"I've got the bastards!" the Scotsmen yelled back. Gabby heard the Mercenary Star's pulse cannons firing and felt the impact of return fire. The ship shook three times and then nothing.

"Did he get them?" Ros asked.

"Negative," Noora replied. "They basically did a strafing run on us and continued on to the outer solar system. Wherever they're going, they're in a hell of a hurry to get there."

Ros's frown deepened. "I don't like this at all." She grabbed the comm. "Ewan, you keep your pasty white ass in that chair in case we get more company," she said.

"Aye Captain."

"Tariq, Noora, let's continue on to the colony. Keep an

eye out for any other ships and let me know if anything turns up. I don't care if it looks friendly or not, if it's on our sensors I want to know about it, yeah?"

"Aiwa," the twins said in unison.

"Gabby, with me." Ros marched out of the cockpit and down the corridors to her quarters. Gabby followed a few metres behind, worried. It wasn't like Ros to initiate sex like this, and certainly not after a near battle, which meant that more likely something was on her mind she didn't want the rest of the crew to overhear.

Almost as soon as the door sealed behind them Ros turned to Gabby, an unhappy look on her face and said "I don't like this at all."

"Me neither Capitan," Gabby said honestly. There was a crawling feeling down the back of her neck; something was going on in their home system and they didn't have all the facts. "We've fought XyrQ before. That wasn't their usual tactics."

"That's what bothers me," Ros said, sitting on the edge of her bed and rubbing at her face. "They're too deep in the system, too close to the colony and ignoring a prize like us is just not like them. One of those ships should have attempted to board us."

"Or at least made more of an effort to disable us. That felt more like a courtesy than anything else."

"Exactly. Which means they had some other objective, some other purpose, and I want to know what it was."

Gabby did too. Partly because when the XyrQ got organised and planned things out it ended badly for whoever they were targeting. The bastards never gave up once they had their eye on an objective, and they never surrendered. If they had designs on Novis Colony, then the entire system was about to turn into a bloodbath.

"We can't do much without more information," Gabby pointed out, not unreasonably. Apparently it wasn't what Ros wanted to hear.

"This is my home," she shouted, punching her bed in frustration. "The people I love are counting on me to keep them safe."

"Us," Gabby said firmly. "The people we love are counting on us to keep them safe. Don't you even think about going off on your own again. Whatever the XyrQ have planned we'll stop, together."

"Together," Ros said, managing a weak smile. "Together."

Ros still looked troubled, but the slightly manic gleam had left her eyes. The chances of her running off to do something foolishly heroic were slim. For today at least.

"Come on," Gabby said, clapping her Captain on the arm. "We can't do anything without more information. Let's get back to the cockpit and see if we can't find out more information."

Ros nodded, her face still troubled, but she willingly followed Gabby out of her quarters.

They got their answers a few hours later when they came across a trio of ships. One was a crippled cargo ship more or less drifting in space and it was accompanied by two of the short range patrol ships from Novis. Ros grabbed the comm the moment they were within visual range.

"This is the Mercenary Star to damaged cargo ship. Anyone alive over there needing assistance?"

The message that came back crackled badly, the voice behind it was weary and held an accent Gabby didn't recognise, but it belonged to someone who was very much alive. "This is Captain De Costa of the Freightliner Master of Souls. Our engines are more or less shot, any help you could offer would be very much appreciated."

"Let me know what you need and if it's in our power you can have it. Do you need me to send my medic over?"

"Affirmative," replied Captain De Costa. "Our own doctor survived the attack but we have many wounded. She could definitely do with a hand."

"Noted. I can also send my engineer over with him if you like."

The sigh that rattled down the shaky comm signal was one of sheer, unadulterated relief. "Much appreciated Capitan." She paused a moment before continuing. Gabby took the opportunity to message AJ and Lizzy (and Mila, because these days wherever Lizzy went, so did Mila). "Mercenary Star, huh? Am I addressing Captain Ros Lamarr then? The Captain Ros Lamarr?"

Gabby had to resist the urge to laugh at the exaggerated eye roll Ros made in response to that. Their reputation often came in handy but sometimes it also really irritated her. It was honestly kind of adorable that Ros really had no idea how badass she was, or that she had genuinely earned her reputation. The note of awe in Captain De Costa's voice was there for a reason.

"The one and only," Ros replied. "Mind telling me

what happened?"

"XyrQ" De Costa spat, and Gabby could immediately tell that the Captain had encountered them before. Survivors of XyrQ attacks almost always had a special note of hatred in their voices forever after.

"We made contact with two XryQ ships on our way into the system. Were they your attackers?" Ros kept the seething anger out of her voice, but Gabby could see it in the tense lines of her face.

"Affirmative. Two XryQ ships came out of nowhere and crippled our engines before we could react. I've never known such a precision attack before."

"Were there boarding parties?" Ros asked earnestly. "Did they take any of your cargo?"

"One boarding party from each ship," De Costa confirmed. "They caught us in a pincer movement, putting holes in the hull either side of the cargo bay. We lost a lot of good people down there," she said bitterly. "We've been preoccupied with getting ourselves back on our feet and treating our wounded. We know the bugs took something but we haven't had the time to do a full inventory."

The worried look was back on Ros's face, and all Gabby wanted to do was reach out and offer comfort, but she couldn't. Ros was in full Captain mode, and lives were on the line here. It wouldn't be appropriate. She'd comfort the Captain later, when she could hold Ros close as she let whatever emotion she was putting aside now spill out of her.

"That kind of precision attack isn't like the XyrQ," Ros

said. "The hit and run I've seen before but they normally take everything they can get their hands on, and leave precious few survivors behind. This sounds like they were after something in particular."

"Agreed," said Captain De Costa.

Just then Gabby received word from AJ that their party was ready to depart and informed Ros.

"Alright Captain," she said. "My people are on their way. Let me know when we have an ETA for repairs and we'll coordinate with your escorts to get you out of here. We'll get you to Novis, don't worry."

"Thank you Mercenary Star. De Costa out."

Ros blew out a shaky breath after the comm had disconnected. "Fucking XyrQ," she said, closing her eyes for a moment before getting back to the job at hand.

"Tariq, Noora, you keep an eye on the sensors. If anything so much moves in this system I want to know about it. Make sure Ewan stays where he is; I want to be ready in case of another attack." They both confirmed their orders and Ros switched her gaze to Gabby. "Our priority here is getting the Master of Souls repaired and her survivors tended to, but as soon as possible I want to know what's missing from their cargo bay. I want to what those bastards were after."

"Sí, Capitan," Gabby said.

"You have the bridge," Ros said, and stalked out of the cockpit. Even if she hadn't just been left in charge, Gabby wouldn't have dared follow.

***

When Lizzy had finally finished crawling through the bowels of the Master of Souls' engine room, her conclusion was exactly the same as the ship's engineer; it was completely and utterly fucked. The XyrQ had executed the kind of precision attack that would be impressive for a Commonwealth military ship and had more or less turned the engines "to paste" as Lizzy put it. There was no way in hell the Master of Souls was going anywhere under its own steam in a hurry. Gabby was the one who had to contact Novis Spaceport and tell them the bad news. She was also the one who had to break it to Ros.

Ros, who was already frustrated beyond belief. Ros whom she found pacing up and down in her quarters like an animal in a zoo.

Her attention snapped to Gabby the minute she walked in the door.

"Well?" she demanded, and Gabby couldn't remember the last time Ros had used that kind of impatient tone with her, if ever.

"Not good. We're going to have to tow them back, Capitan."

Ros growled with frustration, looking like she was a hair's breadth away from punching the bulkhead. Gabby quickly explained the situation, hoping to head off any more bursts of bad temper by providing more facts. The anger slipped from Ros's face when she heard it was looking like a couple of days before any of them would arrive at the colony, the rage replaced by a look of sheer longing.

"Just a few more days, Capitan," Gabby said, trying to

pitch her voice to soothing rather than patronising. "I miss Isobel too."

And it was true, she did. Gabby had never been one to get emotionally attached to her lovers. The only person who'd made her want to stick around after sex was Ros, with whom she'd been best friends for the better part of two decades; with whom she'd built a thriving business, a family. But what they were building with Isobel on Novis was unlike anything Gabby had ever known, and she shared much of Ros's impatience to get back there. To get back to Isobel.

To get home. Gabby hadn't had a home anywhere else but where Ros bunked down for almost as long as she could remember. Now she had a place she could call home, she was just as eager as Ros to get back there. But having a certain... detachment from the heated emotions that normally went along with relationships like theirs allowed her to keep her head that much cooler than Ros. There was still much to do here, with the Master of Souls, and though this wasn't a job as such, they couldn't abandon her. She explained as much to Ros.

"I know, it's just..." Ros ran her hand over the top of her head, through hair that desperately needed cutting again; none of them had had much time for personal grooming on this last job. "It's a few days too long. I need to see her Gabby, with my own eyes. Hear her voice. It feels wrong, going for so long without that."

"I understand," Gabby said, even though she wasn't certain she did. "I don't feel right either. But I've never allowed anything to stand in the way of my duty, and I don't intend to start now. I'm not gonna let you start either. We'll see Isobel soon enough; in the meantime, there's work to do."

Ros nodded, some of the vulnerability slipping from her, giving way to her Captain persona. "We still need to know what those bastards were after, and I've a feeling I'm not gonna like the answer."

"I get that impression too," Gabby said with a wry smile.

"Inform the crew that medical support and repairs are our current priority. As soon as she's sturdy enough, we'll get her out of here. The moment we can spare the personnel, I want a complete inventory of the Master of Souls' cargo bays, and I want them cross-checked with their manifest." She sighed, her face looking old and weary all of a sudden. "As soon as possible I want you to contact Novis Traffic Control, see if they can get me some face time with Izzy, I have some apologies to make."

"Sí Capitan," Gabby said, giving her a soft smile. "I'll do that. You gonna be okay?"

"I'll be fine, for now," Ros said. "Though I would appreciate company later. For now, there's work to do, and you see if you can get me that call. I'll be on the Souls helping with repairs if you need me."

With that she turned on her heels and left the room. Gabby stood for a moment in her Captain's quarters, wondering how much more of this Ros could take before breaking. She had a feeling she'd get her answer sooner rather than later.

***

Gabby looked at the data on the table in disbelief. It had been checked and double checked; it couldn't be wrong. And yet she very much wanted it to be. Nothing good could come of this, not with what the XyrQ had stolen from the Master of Souls.

The items missing from the manifest were mostly metals that were often used in spacecraft hulls and bulkheads, and a few tons of various ores that could be converted into fuel for hyperdrive engines.

"This makes no sense!" she said, gesturing at the tablets strewn across the table. "Why would the XyrQ be building ships? And where? Surely if they had a shipyard in this system we'd have noticed it."

Captain De Costa's face was set into a grim line. "Shipbuilding says invasion to me," she said. "Which doesn't look good for Novis Colony."

"You're damn right it doesn't." Gabby looked at Ros, who hadn't said a word since De Costa had brought them the data they'd been waiting on for days. "If the XyrQ are building an armada, we don't have enough ships in the system to protect the colony. And it could take weeks for back up to arrive, assuming we could get the Commonwealth to believe us at all." Her mind was already working double-time, trying to plan for every possible scenario, every possible disaster. "I mean, we could always evacuate…" she said, already knowing that wasn't an option. Isobel wouldn't leave the colony she and her father had worked so hard to build, and most of the colonists were loyal to their Governor; they wouldn't leave either.

And Gabby knew that if Isobel stayed, so would Ros. So would she.

"It makes no sense," Ros said finally, shaking her head. "This isn't typical behaviour for the XyrQ"

De Costa frowned. "Explain."

"The XyrQ don't build ships, they steal them," Ros elaborated. "Occasionally they cobble ships together from floating wrecks and half destroyed parts, but I've never known them to actually build one from scratch. If these XyrQ are building, if they're operating so far beyond their usual tactics then there's no telling what might happen." Her voice was stiff, contained, and Gabby knew she wanted nothing more than to lash out, to let her anger loose on something anyone. But she couldn't, not when she was in Captain mode. So she kept herself under control, and the tension practically radiated from her. Gabby wanted to reach out, to soothe and help and protect, but with Captain De Costa in the room she had to keep strict protocol. Later, she kept telling herself.

Ros's gaze shifted from the tablets on the table to the wall of the Master of Souls' briefing room, where a map of the Novis system had been projected. There was something else Ros wanted to say, some other possibility she was considering but didn't want to say out loud. The words looked like they were caught behind her teeth, in the tension of her jaw.

"Capitan?" Gabby asked. "Was there something else?"

"The XyrQ could be building ships, or…"

"Or? De Costa prodded.

"The materials they took... They could also be used to build a bomb."

De Costa sucked in a startled breath but Gabby kept her head. "What kind of bomb?"

Ros met her gaze, and the look in her eyes wasn't pleasant. "The kind of bomb that could wipe out most of the system."

"Well fuck," Gabby said, the words escaping before she had a chance to rein them in. No wonder Ros had been so worried. She took a deep breath, trying to steady the pit of dread that had opened up in her stomach. "So, what do we do now?"

"We assume the worst, and prepare for it," she said, her voice threaded with steel; it was the tone she used right before going into battle. "Whatever the XyrQ are doing with those materials, it isn't good, and we're sitting ducks for another potential attack here. So we get the Master of Souls to Novis as fast as we can; we can finish the repairs there. After that I need to speak with the Governor."

Gabby suppressed a wince. If Ros was referring to Isobel by her title, even though everyone present knew about their relationship, then she was further in business mode than Gabby thought. And that wasn't necessarily a good thing.

"And then, Capitan?" she prompted.

There was nothing but burning hatred in Ros's eyes as she answered: "then we find them and end them."

De Costa gulped audibly. Gabby knew better than to

react outwardly. Inside though, her heart was hammering. She'd heard Ros use that kind of tone only once before, during their military days, and the memories weren't pleasant.

"Dismissed," Ros said, even though they were on the Souls and she had no authority to dismiss anyone. Despite that, De Costa dutifully filed out of the room. Gabby on the other hand did not, discomforted by her Captain's—her friend's, her lover's—attitude and demeanour.

"Ros..." she started.

"Leave it Gabriela," Ros said coldly. "Dismissed."

Gabby looked on in shock as Ros turned on her heel and marched out of the room. Against her better judgement, Gabby went after her.

"Captain?" she called down the corridor. She was ignored. "Ros? Rosalind!" she cried, her accent thick around the unfamiliarity of the word.

Ros whipped around to face her. "I said leave it," she snarled.

Gabby was a soldier through and through; she knew how to follow orders, and follow them well, but she also knew when to disobey those orders. Now was one of those times.

"What's gotten into you Ros?" she asked. "You've been on edge almost since we entered the system. No, since we got buzzed by those two ships. There's more to this than you're letting on.

Ros's fists were clenched at her sides, knuckles pale. "I don't see why I should put up with fucking aliens threatening my home my entire life," Ros said, lip curling with a snarl.

"That's what this is about?" Gabby said in disbelief. "Goddamn it Ros you are not your mother. This isn't Wagama. It's not your mother's fault these XyrQ hijos de putas are threatening Novis, and it's not your fault either."

That was entirely the wrong thing to say, judging by the way Ros exploded immediately afterwards.

"You know nothing about my childhood Gabriela," Ros spat. "Nothing!"

Gabby recoiled, partly because of the sheer amount of venom in her lover's voice and partly because that was plainly not true. Ros was beyond reason now, operating on instinct and adrenaline, fuelled by a pain that had been buried long before Gabby even knew her. She would have to be the level-headed one in this situation. So she reined in her own temper, vowing to herself that she'd take it out on some innocent rock formations when they landed. Later, when Ros was in less pain.

"Your mother knew the risks when Wagama was settled, every colonist does. It's not her fault things went so wrong."

"No, but she didn't have to drag me into it," Ros said coldly, her anger turning from fire to ice, but just as likely to burn. "She should have left when she found out she was pregnant. She should have–" She closed her eyes, swallowing thickly. Gabby thought she might be fighting down tears. "There was no one there to help Wagama when we needed it. I won't let Novis fall to the same fate." And with that she obviously considered the conversation over and walked away as fast as her prosthetic leg would allow her.

This time Gabby didn't follow.

"Gabriela?" said a soft voice from a nearby doorway. AJ. "Gabriela, you are crying. Is there anything I can do to help?"

Gabby furiously wiped away her tears. "No. Nothing."

"I could speak with our Kapitan, if you wished."

"Don't bother, it's not worth it," Gabby said and stormed off towards her quarters.

Once safely in her own space she let the tears fall. "It doesn't matter," she tried to tell herself. "It doesn't matter."

She'd never told a more bare-faced lie in her life.

CHAPTER FIFTEEN

ISOBEL

"She is being insufferable," she cried, throwing a handful of tablets down on the desk in Gabby's room. Honestly, she didn't give a damn about the potential damage. She flopped down onto the sofa with a huff.

Gabby didn't even look up from the weapon she was cleaning. "You don't need to tell me."

Isobel immediately felt bad; Gabby had been dealing with Ros's temper and her reticence longer than she had. "Sorry," she said, "I shouldn't be taking it out on you. It's not fair." It wasn't, and yet that was exactly what Ros was doing; taking it out on whoever was nearest whether they were strangers or the people she was supposed to love best.

"It's okay," Gabby said, the misery in her tone making it clear it very much wasn't. "What did she do now?"

"She wants to take half my ships with her on another sweep of the system. I told her no. She took them anyway."

Gabby winced at that. "How many is that now?"

Isobel sighed, the sound rattling up from deep inside. She was tired of this bullshit. "I think this is her twelfth recon run in three weeks. She refuses to believe there's nothing out there."

"Yeah well, that's Ros for you. Once she's got an idea in her head she's like a dog with a bone. Won't let it go." Gabby let out a nasty little laugh. "Usually that's a good thing, but this time..."

"She's not taking care of herself," Isobel said, voicing her fears for the first time. "She's not eating properly, she's not sleeping. And when she does, she's crashing in the barracks, not coming back to me." The knot of fear she'd been carrying the last few weeks tightened in her throat. "I'm worried."

Gabby finally put the gun down and met Isobel's gaze. The dark circles under her eyes matched the ones Isobel saw in the mirror every morning. "Me too chica, me too." She opened her arms, inviting Isobel for a hug. Gabby wasn't often physically affectionate outside of sex, but Isobel desperately needed human contact. She accepted the offer, snuggling gratefully into Gabby's shoulder, bare at the moment since she was wearing a strappy summer dress.

After a moment just enjoying the contact, Isobel continued. "I just... I can't shake off the feeling that all the work we've put into our relationship is unravelling." She hadn't spoken of her fear out loud before now, but with Gabby she felt safe enough to admit it.

"I know how you feel," Gabby said. "I've known Ros a long time, been to hell and back with her, *for* her, and right now it feels like she'd be more than willing to throw all of that away to find these bugs."

That thought wasn't reassuring to Isobel in the least. She loved Ros, knew Ros loved her, but their relationship was still relatively new in the grand scheme of things; it could still go so, so wrong so easily. But if Ros was pushing Gabby away, her friend, her partner, her lover of almost two decades; if she was putting all that at risk to find the XyrQ nest then what chance did she have of their relationship surviving?

Isobel let out an uncharacteristic growl of frustration.

"I just wish I knew *why* she was so determined."

Gabby pulled back from the hug slightly and gave her a look she couldn't quite interpret. "Did Ros ever tell you why she joined the Commonwealth military?"

Isobel shook her head. "She never really wanted to talk about her past, not that far back. The earliest she'd open up to me about was meeting you. Why? Do you know more?"

Gabby took a deep breath. "Sí," she said. "She doesn't like to talk about it, but I got her real drunk one night and the whole story came spilling out. She grew up on a colony a lot like this one, actually."

"She did?" Isobel asked, her interest piqued.

"Yeah," Gabby said. "Middle of nowhere, tons of resources for the Commonwealth and a Governor who cared a lot about the fate of the colony."

Isobel felt her cheeks heat at the sidelong compliment though her heart gave a sad pang when she realised the comment was as much about her late father as it was her. "What went wrong?" she asked, because of course something had gone wrong, or Ros wouldn't be in the state she was now.

"Commonwealth was trialling a new type of colony, something to do with power generators and self-sufficiency. I don't know all the details; Ros was just a kid at the time and she'd had half a bottle of vodka before she started talking. Let's just say that whatever they had was of great interest to the aliens living in the next system."

"XyrQ?" Isobel asked. If the bugs were responsible for whatever had happened to Ros's childhood home that would explain her recent foul mood and short temper.

Gabby shook her head. "Wasn't the XyrQ. I don't know who it was, but it wasn't the mantises that were responsible."

"What happened to the colony?" Isobel asked, even though she didn't really want the answer. She already knew it wasn't good, but she needed details, needed to better understand the woman she loved.

"Razed to the ground," Gabby said. She was avoiding Isobel's gaze, even though she kept stroking her shoulder gently, maintaining physical contact. "They asked the Commonwealth to help, but by the time they sent someone out it was already too late." Gabby gave a great rattling sigh and continued, her voice wobbling ever so slightly. "Ros was one of the few surviving colonists."

"And her parents?"

"Father was never in the picture. Her madre was killed in the attack. I've seen the sanitised version of the official report on Wagama; it says the Governor refused to leave her post and died defending the colony. Ros doesn't really remember much about the attack. PTSD basically. She grew up in the foster system in Commonwealth city after that, passed between families who didn't give a shit about her until she was old enough to enlist in the military. When I met her she said she'd joined up to 'see interesting places, meet new people and kill aliens.'"

Isobel blew out a long, measured breath. "And she's upset about the XyrQ attacking Novis because it reminds her too much of Wagama."

"Exactly," Gabby said. "Like I said, she doesn't talk about it much, and she finds it difficult to be reasonable when it comes to alien races preying on human settlements. She told me she feels like she has a home here and, honestly, I'm not sure she's had that since her madre died. This thing with the XyrQ is pretty much pushing all her buttons at once and its making her a little loco."

"Yeah, I think I understand why now." The wheels in Isobel's head were turning. She was a diplomat, a politician; she knew better than anyone that the first step in any negotiation was to understand the people you were negotiating with. Thanks to Gabby's disclosure, she felt she understood Ros a little better. Now all she needed to do was decide on a plan, identify what it was she wanted out of any negotiation with Ros and what chips she had to bargain with.

She wanted Ros to feel better that was certain. She wanted her partner back to her old self, to laugh and joke and make love with her again, instead of running herself ragged on a wild goose chase around the system when there was no guarantee the XyrQ were even up to something. She had plenty of chips to bargain with; her own love and concern for Ros's well-being, Gabby's concern and that of rest of the Irregulars, the lack of evidence the XyrQ even had a stronghold in the system and the finite resources the colony had available to devote to searching for it.

In a diplomatic situation this would be an almost ideal starting point for negotiations. But sorting out issues in romantic relationships weren't like hammering out a trade deal or securing extra funding from the Commonwealth bureaucratic machine. This would require a more delicate touch, and there was far more at stake here than in any negotiation she had even mediated in her life.

Isobel sighed. The train of thought running around in her head was doing her no good. Thinking about something else for a while would be beneficial. She seized on the first subject that came to mind.

"Why did you join the military?" she asked Gabby, honestly curious. That decision had led to her meeting Ros and eventually to all this.

"Not many choices for a Latina kid growing up in the slums on Central," Gabby said, once again avoiding Isobel's gaze. "It was either the military or the gangs, and while the gangs paid better I didn't wanna end up in prison so... here I am."

Isobel swallowed, suddenly uncomfortable with the implications of what Gabby had shared. It was all too easy for her to forget that things weren't always ideal in the Commonwealth. That, despite all their medical and technological advances, there were still those who had, and those who didn't.

Growing up in a political family had always allowed Isobel a measure of luxury. Even here on Novis, where she'd spent the last decade or so, she lived in comfort. Even when the dust storms roared up off the plains, or there was a mining incident, or when raiders made getting supplies difficult, she never had to go without. She would always have what she needed, and usually a little more, just because of who she was. She had all that, and often took it for granted. It sounded like Gabby hadn't had that growing up. The thought made her sad.

She mentioned none of that out loud; her struggle with her own privilege was hers to deal with, and Gabby didn't need to be burdened with it. Instead she said simply, "was it really that bad?"

Gabby shrugged. "I exaggerate a little but yeah. The gangs had a pretty firm hold on our neighbourhood, and law enforcement knew to stay away. They didn't do a damned thing when my brother was killed."

Isobel started at that. Gabby had been almost as reticent as Ros was when it came to talking about her past. Until that moment she hadn't even known Gabby had a brother, let alone that he was dead.

"Do you mind if I ask what happened? I mean, you don't have to tell me if you don't want."

"No, it's okay," she said, though the tension in her voice suggested it very much *wasn't* okay. "It happened a long time ago. Stupid pendejo borrowed money from one of their loan sharks and when he couldn't pay him back those hijos de putas made him transport chems for them to work off his debt. A canister broke in transit and you know how they make you transport them. He was dead before anyone could do anything to help. Massive overdose."

"Oh Gabby, I'm sorry."

"Nothing ever happened to them, no one was ever held responsible for his death, and to make matters worse the gangs tried to hold the family responsible for the outstanding debt. I came of age not long after and hopped the first transit out. I swore they weren't gonna get me like they got Santi." There were tears in Gabby's eyes and Isobel wanted nothing more than to brush them away and hold Gabby tight. She wasn't sure that would be appreciated, so she settled for taking Gabby's hand and lacing their fingers together, offering what comfort she could.

"Oh Gabby, I'm sorry."

"Sometimes it feels like my life didn't really start until I met Ros. Within our first year of service we were inseparable, we'd been awarded medals for our brave stupidity, and I'd paid off Santi's debt." Gabby smiled then, and the sight eased the anxiety in Isobel's heart just a little. "I haven't been home in a while, but I still send a cut of every paycheck to mi madre y abuela."

Isobel wasn't sure what to say in response to that kind of disclosure, so she kept quiet. They stayed that way for several minutes, the silence comfortable, filled only with the sound of their breathing. Out of nowhere Isobel remembered why she'd originally come to bother Gabby and heaved a great sigh. Gabby raised an eyebrow in question.

"What are we going to do about Ros?"

Gabby shrugged. "I don't know, chica," she said. "Wait

until everything goes sideways and pick up the pieces afterwards?"

"That plan doesn't reassure me very much."

"It's about the only way to deal with Ros. Trust me, I know."

Another sigh rattled its way up from the pit of anxiety in Isobel's chest. "If that's all we can really do, I suppose it'll have to be good enough." Isobel pressed a kiss to Gabby's cheek, causing her to look at the Governor with shock on her face.

"What was that for?"

"You're good people Gabby Hernandez," Isobel said putting her heart into every syllable, "and I love you. Every part of you, just the way you are."

Gabby's cheeks flushed, and she suddenly found the floor very interesting. "You're not so bad yourself," she replied. After a moment or two of less comfortable silence, Gabby cleared her throat loudly. "Right, I'm sure you have things you're supposed to be doing, and I better go flirt with Tariq to make myself feel better."

Isobel laughed at that. It didn't surprise her that Gabby used her flirtatious manner to mask some of her deeper emotions, but she had a question. "Tariq? Why Tariq?"

"It's always hilarious to watch him try to flirt back. The poor boy is so bad at it." Gabby got a sly look on her face then. "Besides, I think he's sweet on someone here on Novis and I wanna be the first to find out who."

Isobel laughed. "You are incorrigible."

Gabby shrugged. "So people keep saying." She

disentangled herself from Isobel, stood up and stretched. She was at the door when she paused and turned back. "I got them out you know," she said quietly. "My family. Bought them a small house away from the slums when I got out of the army. I couldn't do anything to save my brother, but I did everything I could to help them. Because they're family." She gave Isobel a hard stare that felt almost uncomfortable. "Ros is family too. I'll do anything to help her. Promise." And then she slipped out of the room, presumably to torment poor Tariq. Reluctantly, Isobel returned to her own duties.

Their newfound comfort and closeness lasted over the next few days. Gabby gravitated towards Isobel during her downtime and even slipped into bed with her every night, cuddling up close and staying there until morning. Isobel was learning that Gabby only sought physical contact like that when she was injured or worried. The situation with Ros definitely had her worried and Isobel found that the closeness helped her too.

Her relationship with Gabby had always been defined by their mutual relationships with Ros, and it was a comfort to Isobel that they were moving towards something of their own. It would never look like any of the relationships Isobel had had in the past, Gabby just didn't work that way, but Isobel increasingly found she was glad of that; what they had was theirs and theirs alone, and all the more precious for that.

Isobel should have known better than to think it could last. The peace was shattered four days later by Ros's return.

The first inkling she had that her girlfriend was home was when the sound of shouting in at least three different languages drifted into her office. Leaving her paperwork behind with a sigh, Isobel went to investigate. Sure enough, Ros was in the centre of the altercation, which turned out to be a screaming argument between the Captain and Noora. Gabby was there too, doing her best to interfere while Lizzy attempted to hold her back. The entire situation was a shitshow, a bomb just waiting to go off unless she defused it exactly right.

So of course the first thing out of mouth was "what the fuck is going on here?"

"She is being completely insufferable!" Noora cried. She was angry at her Captain, truly angry, and Isobel didn't think she'd ever seen that.

"Now where have I heard that before?" Gabby said bitterly.

Isobel shot her a look that clearly said stop as Lizzy yelled "Gabby!"

"We've barely been back an hour, and she already wants to get back out there!" Noora said, frustration bleeding from every single syllable. "I keep telling her, there's nothing out there."

"There is," Ros insisted. "The XyrQ have a nest in the system, I can feel it in my gut."

"Well I can't find it, and neither can the best trackers and navigators in the system," Noora replied. "So how about you calm your tits for five minutes so the rest of us can take a breath?"

Isobel had never seen a person with their hackles raised before but it accurately described Ros in that moment; her shoulders were up by her ears and her face was contorted in an angry snarl. If her hair had been longer it would probably be standing on end, making the mercenary Captain look even larger.

Noora didn't seem at all impressed by the display, standing casually with her weight all on one leg, her face displaying nothing short of utter contempt.

Isobel stepped between them before they could escalate to trading blows. "Noora, your attitude isn't helping at all. Cool it." Smugness radiated from Ros for a moment before Isobel rounded on her too. "And Ros, Noora's right; you need to take a break before you work yourself sick. If there is anything out there you're not gonna find it like this. We need more evidence. And there's no reason you can't get some goddamn sleep while you're waiting for that."

For a moment it almost worked, both of them relaxing visibly. Ros even took a step back from Noora, clearly backing down with her body language.

And then Gabby stepped back into the fray.

Lizzy, to her credit, tried to stop her, but Gabby in a full-on rage was like a runaway freight train; out of control, dangerous and likely to cause explosions when it finally hit something.

"Oh good, if you're finally listening to reason does that mean you're gonna stop pushing me the fuck away?" Hurt radiated from Gabby with every word, and Isobel's heart broke for her a little.

"What do you mean?" Ros asked, sounding genuinely confused. "I haven't been pushing you away."

"You left me behind," Gabby roared. "You said we'd deal with whatever was threatening our home *together* and you just left me behind."

"You didn't think there was any point in doing another sweep of the system," Ros protested.

Gabby wasn't having any of it. "That doesn't mean I don't want to be right there at your side, anyway. Fucking hell Ros, I thought we were supposed to be *partners*." And oh, if there weren't layers upon layers of meaning behind that one word. Isobel was beginning to understand that Ros Lamarr had the ability to hurt Gabby like no other person in the universe. She wished she could help, but this was between the two of them.

Ros seemed to visibly deflate at the accusation. "Gabs, I'm sorry. I didn't realise..."

Gabby said nothing, she just stared at Ros with anger in her eyes, breathing heavily. Isobel knew neither of them would get anything hashed out in their current state. They both needed rest. And she would make sure that happened even if she had to chain them both to a bed. She knew AJ had the equipment for that.

"Right then," she started, her Governor voice in place. "Both the Irregulars and the *Mercenary Star* are grounded until further notice. Don't look at me like that Ros, I'm the Governor, I can do that. You and Gabby are both going to get some rest and then we're all going to sit down and talk this through like adults. Understand?"

Ros nodded while Gabby just grunted, still staring at

her Captain. Isobel gave a look to Lizzy, who got the message.

"Come on Gabby," Lizzy said gently. "Let's get you settled down." She grabbed Gabby around the bicep and pulled her away. Gabby didn't even protest.

"You're coming with me," Isobel said to Ros, trying to soften the order a little. Ros just nodded, her eyes following Gabby down the corridor. "Come on," Isobel tried again, slipping hand into her girlfriend's. "You need to get some rest."

Ros stayed quiet all the way up to their bedroom where she sat down on the bed staring at her feet. Isobel bent down to undo Ros's boots for her. Now that her face wasn't warped with rage Isobel could see the exhaustion written all over it. Her cheekbones were far too prominent, and the dark circles under her eyes were more like a full set of luggage than just bags.

"I'm sorry," Ros croaked, her voice hoarse.

"I know," Isobel said. "And I forgive you, but it's really Gabby you should apologise to."

"I will, just–"

"*After* some sleep. Come on, you look exhausted."

Ros didn't protest, she simply curled up on top of the covers and was out as soon as her head hit the pillows. Isobel curled up around her, wondering how she could fix this.

Isobel was jolted from her impromptu nap a few hours later by the bedroom door opening. Gabby slinked in with a guilty look on her face. Isobel immediately knew she'd given Lizzie the slip and wasn't supposed to be here.

"If you think you're starting round two you've got another think coming," Isobel warned in a harsh whisper, not wanting to wake Ros up.

"I'm not, I promise," Gabby said, holding her hands up in surrender. "I just want to talk to her."

"She's still asleep."

"No I'm not," Ros said, her voice raspy. "will you let her in if I promise to behave?"

Isobel had a feeling she might end up regretting the decision, but she nodded her assent.

Gabby shuffled over to the bed, looking every bit as exhausted as Ros. Isobel wondered how she'd missed that over the last few days. She stood up, intending to give the other two women some space, but Ros reached out and grabbed her hand.

"Don't go," she said, her voice pleading. Isobel wasn't sure why Ros was so insistent about this; perhaps she was afraid of another temper flare up without her stabilising presence but in the end it didn't really matter. Ros had asked her to stay, so she would.

Isobel nodded and made for the sofa she kept in her room. "I'll be over here if you need me."

"Gracias," Gabby said as she passed by. Isobel pressed a kiss to her cheek, letting her know through action that she was more than welcome, that she could always rely on her.

"I'm sorry," she heard Ros say in a choked voice as Gabby settled onto the bed. "I've been an ass."

"Don't you dare leave me behind again," Gabby said fiercely, clutching Ros to her. "We're a team. You said we'd always be a team."

"We are," Ros sobbed. "I won't do it again, I promise."

Something tense inside Isobel loosened then; they'd be okay now, they all would. Ros and Gabby continued to talk it out, conversing quietly in Spanish. Lulled by the cadence of words she didn't understand, Isobel drifted off to sleep on the sofa.

She woke up the next morning sandwiched between Gabby and Ros in bed—one of her favourite places to be. "I take it we've made up then?" she mumbled sleepily.

"Sí," Gabby said into the crook of Isobel's neck.

"We've come to something of an agreement," Ros added, turning over so she was facing Isobel.

"Oh?" Isobel felt she probably needed caffeine for whatever conversation they were about to have, but she knew she wasn't gonna get it.

"Gabby and I have agreed—together—that we'll do one more sweep of the system, using only the Irregulars' resources. If I still haven't found anything by then I'm not going to. So I'll come back to Novis and wait for whatever happens next."

"Whatever happens next?" Isobel questioned sleepily. Definitely not enough caffeine.

"I still think the XryQ are up to something and I'm not going to leave my home undefended while they get up to it. So, the sweeps stop, the running myself ragged stops, the alienating the people I love stops, but I won't take any jobs out of system until I'm confident Novis is safe. Does that sound okay to you?"

"It would sound better after a few more hours sleep,"

Isobel grumbled. "But yes. As your girlfriend and the Governor of the colony you're going to be pacing up and down for who knows how long, that sounds like a good plan. If Gabby agrees."

"I do. And I'm going with her next time she goes into space. That part was non-negotiable." Gabby's voice was sharp, and Isobel knew then that while Ros had been forgiven, the hurt she'd caused Gabby wouldn't soon be forgotten.

"When are you setting out?" Isbel said with a yawn.

"Not for a couple of days yet," Ros said softly, stroking Isobel's hair.

"Oh good, does that mean I can get some more sleep?"

"It does," Ros said, a smile tugging at the corner of her mouth. "Sweet dreams my love, we'll be here when you wake up."

Isobel was out like a light, safe and warm and loved.

Things were considerably calmer over the next few days. Neither Lizzy or Noora seemed to hold a grudge for the screaming match they'd been involved in and the rest of the Irregulars were more settled. AJ had commended Isobel on her handling of the situation, which had been resolved without bloodshed or the use of firearms. Apparently that wasn't always the case with the Irregulars. Isobel was mostly just proud of herself for dealing with it without AJ's help. Somehow she got the impression he'd appointed himself the doting father of the ragtag band of misfits Ros had assembled and he was the one normally tasked with sorting them out.

She imagined it was a nice change for AJ not to have

to be the sensible one for once.

The *Mercenary Star* left on its last sweep of the system as planned and things settled even further. Isobel was fully expecting Ros to come back after forty eight hours or so, empty handed. So when she received an urgent message from the *Star* after a tedious meeting with the head of Novis' mining operations, Isobel's senses were immediately on alert. She immediately locked herself in her office to view it.

Ros's face appeared on screen, worried and drawn, as though all the progress of the last week had been undone. Her message was simple and devastating.

"Isobel, we've found them."

CHAPTER SIXTEEN

GABBY

Of course it wasn't that simple. It never was.

Ros wanted to go after them immediately, go storming into their stronghold and, knowing her thought process recently, go out in a blaze of glory. Gabby would have been the first to veto that idea but someone beat her to it.

"Absolutely not!" said Noora hotly.

Ros looked at her as though seeing her pilot for the first time. "I beg your pardon," she said, her voice low and dangerous, the way it got just before she turned someone to a bloody pulp. Noora didn't seem fazed by the obvious threat written across Ros's face.

"We know nothing about their base apart from its location. Nothing on their numbers or the layout, not to mention what they're building there. If they are building weapons, then walking in there with no intel is suicide. And even if they're not building weapons, it's still basically a death wish, heading into a XyrQ nest like that."

"But–" Ros tried to protest.

Gabby cut her off. "No buts, Capitan," she said. "Noora is right. The only thing we know is where they are and that they almost certainly outnumber us. This isn't a fight we can win on brute strength. We need to be clever about this. Any chance of back up?" she said, turning to address Isobel.

She sighed. "I've contacted the Commonwealth but

given all the other skirmishes going on at the moment I'm afraid we're low on their list of priorities. They'll send someone, but it could be weeks before they set off, let alone get here."

"Unacceptable," Ros growled. "We can't just sit here and wait for the Commonwealth to get off their asses and *do something*."

"No one is proposing that we do," Noora shot back. Her face was as hard and determined as Gabby had ever seen, and in a match of wills Ros was no longer the guaranteed victor. Gabby smiled to herself despite the seriousness of the situation; the girl had developed some backbone.

"What *is* the proposal then?" Isobel asked. She sounded almost as frustrated as Ros. Gabby knew she was worried about her colonists, and the merchants who kept them supplied; they'd spent more than a few evenings up late talking about that. Gabby placed a hand on Isobel's shoulder, letting her know she was there, that Isobel had her full support, even if her girlfriend was too busy trying to be a hero to do what was supposed to be her job in that respect.

Still, Gabby wasn't sure she could entirely blame Ros for her reaction. Tragic back story and all that. But it meant that she had to step up to the plate and be the leader Ros usually was, the leader she was too compromised to be right now.

"We can't beat them in a straight fight," she said, stepping back into the conversation to defuse what was rapidly devolving into another argument between Ros and Noora. "They have the numbers and they're on their home turf. That means we have to fight smarter. Noora, what do we know about that rock they're camped in?"

"It's more ice than rock really," Noora said, tapping the tablet in her hand to bring up the telemetry readouts from her flypast. "Right on the edge this system's Oort cloud. The high water content made it difficult to scan more than a few kilometres deep in the time we had, and the scans didn't tell us much. Whatever they're doing it can't be generating much heat since there was no sign of any steam plumes emanating from the surface."

"Seems strange that the insects would build a base in a giant ball of ice," Ros commented, stroking her chin thoughtfully. "Surely they're more susceptible to the cold than we are, and I know I'd be freezing my tits off living out there."

Noora shrugged. "We really don't know all that much about the XyrQ–"

"Except that they like to kill any diplomats we send to talk to them," said Ewan, contributing something other than a vicious scowl for the first time since the meeting began.

Noora shot him a look that could melt lead. "–how their society functions or even their biology. We don't even know where their home planet is," she continued, pointedly looking at Ewan the whole time. "For all we know they could be perfectly at home in the ice."

"So we still have next to nothing," Ros said, her temper about three seconds from boiling over. "How are we supposed to beat them?"

"We play dirty," Mila said, looking up from where she'd been turning a knife over in her hands. "Small groups, hit and run, mapping out their stronghold as we go."

"I mean the layout is likely to comprise a series of tunnels, judging from the density readings we got," Noora added. "It could work."

"I'm not sure I like the idea," Isobel said, her face twisting with anxiety.

"That's why you're the diplomat and we're the mercenaries love," Ros said with an unpleasant smile.

Isobel ignored her. "I mean what you're proposing is guerrilla warfare. Hunting them down in their *home*. The Commonwealth–"

"Isn't gonna get here fast enough," Ros interrupted, the hard look back on her face. "If we wait on this who knows how many more people will die? How many more tons of materiel are gonna get stolen? We need to take them out *now*."

Isobel shook her head. "The legalities of what you're proposing..."

"Aren't a problem," Gabby said, trying to sound a lot more reassuring than Ros had. "They've been preying on Commonwealth vessels for months. As far as the law is concerned they have committed acts of war and we are authorised to use any means at our disposal to defend the colony. The Commonwealth will back us to the hilt on this."

She didn't add that the Commonwealth had done far more shady things than what Mila had proposed. She'd taken part in a number of those things herself. Isobel was a diplomat though, and she had a trust in the government and the idea of due process that Gabby had lost long ago. She didn't have the heart to shatter Isobel's idealism. Thankfully neither did anyone else.

By the time Gabby had pulled herself out her dark thoughts and paid attention to the conversation again, they were onto discussing the details of their plan: find somewhere on the surface of the XyrQ's ball of ice to set up a base camp and send multiple small groups into their stronghold at a time to worry at their defences, divide and conquer and all that. Noora was relatively confident she and Tariq could land them on the planetesimal's surface without being detected, using the high levels of water and other ices that had prevented detailed scans to their advantage.

The meeting broke up and everyone went their separate ways. Isobel had duties to attend to, which left Ros at something of a loose end. She still had a brooding look on her face, her eyebrows creased into a little frown and Gabby knew that couldn't lead to anything good. Time for a little diversion.

"Come on," she said, taking hold of Ros's hand and dragging her towards the staircase.

"What are you doing?" Ros asked. There was a hint of anger in her voice but mostly she sounded weary. Gabby knew how she felt; she wanted this over with as soon as possible.

"Stopping you from doing something foolish," she replied. Ros opened her mouth to argue but Gabby cut her off. "I know you, Ros," she said. "You're still itching to get out there as soon as you can, with or without backup. You're all tense, like a snake ready to strike and I intend to do something about that. As it happens, I know a few sure-fire ways of getting you to be less tense."

Ros grumbled a little, but she agreed anyway. An hour and a half later she was looking a lot less tense. Gabby laid back on the bed feeling pleased with herself. The slight breeze coming in from the window cooled the sheen of sweat on her skin making her shiver, but she didn't cover up. She felt too damn good to move right now.

"Thanks," Ros said, fiddling with the straps to put her prosthetic leg back on. "I think I needed that."

"You did," Gabby said. "Now, you wanna tell me what's got you tense in the first place?"

Ros hesitated, then sighed. "I just, I hate the waiting. Feels the same as being in hyperspace. My home, people I love are in danger and I can't *do* anything. I feel powerless."

"You are doing something though," Gabby insisted. "Making plans is doing something. You know as well as I do that planning is critical for any mission. You've been doing this for years, Ros, what's got you so wound up you can't remember your basic training?" Gabby kept her voice soft, knowing that if she was even the tiniest bit harsh right now Ros would freeze up and they'd get nowhere.

"You know why I'm so determined so stop whatever the XyrQ have planned for this system," Ros said tersely.

"Wagama," Gabby acknowledged, ignoring the way

Ros's spine stiffened at the name of her childhood home. "I understand why you feel you need to fight the mantises, but I don't understand why you're trying to kill yourself doing it. I've known you twenty years Ros and I've never seen you like this. What's eating you?"

Ros was silent for a moment, staring intently at a patch on the floor as though it held the answers to the mysteries of life. Finally she sighed, and the remaining tension Gabby hadn't fucked away drained from her body.

"Everything's been going so well," Ros said sadly. "I don't remember being this happy before in my life."

"And you're trying to sabotage that?"

"No!" Ros practically shouted. "At least... not intentionally." She looked a little lost sitting there with her head buried in her hands. Gabby had never seen her look like that in all the time they'd known each other and honestly it was a little frightening.

Ros appeared to be at a loss for a few more moments before her shoulders slumped in defeat. "The last six months," she started, her voice cracking, "have been wonderful. I've had you and the Irregulars, someone who *really* loves me and a home to call my own for the first time in decades. And I don't feel like I'm equipped to deal with that. I don't know if I know *how* to be happy." She looked miserable sat there, and Gabby wanted nothing more than to fix things, but she wasn't sure how. Or even if she could.

"That's the problem, you're too happy?" she said, with more sarcasm than she intended.

Ros's head snapped up. "No! Yes. I don't know." She pulled an utterly miserable face. "I– I'm happy, so happy Gabs, I don't even know how to put it in words. My life just doesn't work like this. Since I lost my ma I've been passed from pillar to post; by the system, in the army. When we started the Irregulars, I felt like I was finally in control of my life, in a way I never had before. I felt like something empty inside me had been filled. Maybe not completely, but enough. And it never occurred to me to ask for more."

"And now?" Gabby asked, pushing aside the thought that the Irregulars weren't enough for Ros, that *she* wasn't enough. That wasn't what Ros was saying, and besides, she'd long known she couldn't give Ros what she needed, not in a romantic way. Isobel could though, and she was beyond grateful that she and Ros hadn't had to give up what *they* had as part of the bargain.

"Now I feel so full, of love, of joy, it's like I never had that hole inside me at all. That scares me." Ros sighed, the sound coming up from deep within her chest. "And I feel so guilty about it."

"What the ever-loving fuck do you have to feel guilty about?" Gabby said, the words falling out of her mouth before she could consult her brain.

"Matty," Ros said simply.

Gabby felt like she'd been punched in the gut; she'd all but forgotten about her fallen comrade. Forgotten that she'd never wanted to be second-in-command and that she'd inherited the job the old-fashioned way. "Shit," she said. Suddenly things made a little more sense. Ros was nowhere near over his death.

"Yeah," Ros said miserably. "And it's not just Matty. Donkin, Kendall... Izzy's dad..." Ros trailed off and the fist in Gabby's gut squeezed.

"Dios mio," she muttered as everything finally clicked into place. Ros continued as though she hadn't heard her.

"I'm the happiest I've ever been in my life Gabs but at what cost? People *died*–" Ros choked on her words as tears ran freely down her cheeks. "Isobel shouldn't even be able to look at me," she continued through her sobs. "Her father is dead, and it's my fault. I didn't do my job properly, and it cost Benoit his life. By all rights Isobel should hate me and, and–"

"She doesn't," Gabby said softly. "She loves you."

"She shouldn't!" Ros roared, pounding her fists into the bed. "She shouldn't want to be anywhere near me and instead she gives me a home, makes me the happiest I've ever been and I don't deserve it. I don't deserve it." Ros broke down then, choking sobs ripping through her chest and making her breathing irregular.

Gabby moved to the edge of the bed and laid a hand on Ros's arm. Ros, to her credit, only flinched slightly. At a loss as to what to do, Gabby just sat there, lightly touching Ros while she cried her eyes out. She had no words that might make this better. Gabby had dealt with survivor's guilt a dozen or so times in her career, both her own and others, and it never got any easier. There was nothing she could say that would make this any better. The only thing that really helped was time, so time was what Gabby gave her.

Eventually Ros was all cried out and curled up into a ball, falling into a fitful sleep. Gabby gently rearranged her on the bed so she'd be more comfortable and then just sat there brooding. How could she have missed this? Her Captain had been in pain for six months and she hadn't noticed. Gabby felt her own flash of guilt at that. Then again, Ros was good at hiding things when she wanted to. Perhaps there hadn't been anything to notice.

There was a soft knock on the door and then Isobel stuck her head round. "Thought I'd find you in here," she said, entering the room properly, not remotely bothered by the fact Gabby and Ros were both naked as the day they were born. "Ros seemed like she could do with a distraction earlier." She stopped abruptly then, apparently noticing Ros's less than peaceful expression for the first time. "Is she alright?"

Gabby shook her head. "I don't think she's been alright for a long time."

Isobel demanded an explanation for that statement, and by the time Gabby had relayed her entire discussion with Ros she was feeling drained.

"How could we have missed this?" Isobel asked, a distraught look on her face.

"Ros is good at hiding things when she wants to. It's part of what makes her a good merc."

"She honestly thinks I should blame her for my father's death?"

"She does."

Isobel let out a string of words in a language Gabby didn't quite recognise, though they were certainly swearwords. She wasn't sure which of the Irregulars Isobel had been spending far too much time with, present company excepted, but the crew were apparently a bad influence on her.

"That is the most ridiculous thing I have ever heard," Isobel continued. "None of us had any idea there was more than one of those monsters out there, so why should she have magically known? I miss my Pa, of course I do, but that in no way diminishes how I feel about Ros. And I in no way blame her for his death. It was tragic, but no one was responsible. Not even Ros can shoulder the blame for everything."

"She tries her hardest to," Gabby said with a long-suffering sigh. She'd been putting up with Ros's shit for over twenty years now, and while she wouldn't change it for the world, it did sometimes wear a person down.

"How are you doing?" Isobel asked softly, settling onto the bed next to Gabby.

"Bien," she replied. "Eager to get out there and put these insects in the ground. Hopefully things will get back to something resembling normal then. And maybe we'll get a chance to sort this one out," she said, nudging Ros gently. Apparently it was enough to wake her.

"Isobel?" Ros said sleepily.

"Shhh, ma chérie, I'm here." Ros grunted and reached out a hand to grab Isobel's wrist, falling back to sleep almost immediately afterwards. Isobel sighed. "Well I guess I'm not going anywhere."

Gabby couldn't help but grin a little. "Stay then, it's getting late. We'll deal with everything in the morning."

Isobel didn't need any further persuading. She stripped down quickly, somehow getting everything off without disturbing Ros's iron grip on her arm. Between the two of them they manoeuvred Ros so she was on the bed properly and lay down either side of her.

"We'll take care of you," Isobel whispered, pressing a kiss to Ros's temple. "Won't we Gabby?"

"Sí," she replied. "We've got your back Capitan. You just sleep."

Shortly afterwards Gabby followed her own advice.

Ros was in somewhat better spirits the next day, no doubt helped by the fact Isobel had had time to play before she had to get to work. The Captain was practically whistling as she strolled downstairs to meet with the rest of the Irregulars. Gabby didn't bother to hide her grin.

"Aye, *someone* had a good night," Ewan teased the moment Ros walked through the door.

"Shut it Burns," Ros shot back, her good mood not diminishing one jot.

Gabby felt her grin get even wider. Isobel *had* done a good job of reassuring Ros that she loved her and held no grudge regarding her father's death. The Captain would probably be on cloud nine for days. So would Gabby for that matter.

"When's the wedding," Ewan said, completely ignoring his Captain's orders. Ros's ears went a few shades darker than usual, the only sign she was embarrassed by Ewan's words.

"Leave her be liebchen," said AJ, chastising his boyfriend. "The Kapitan is entitled to her happiness, nein?"

Ewan grumbled a little, but it was good natured. Gabby decided they'd all had enough fun at Ros's expense and got down to business. "Alright you lot, show me what you've got."

It turned out that while Gabby was distracting the Captain so she didn't run off to do anything foolish, the rest of the crew had put together a comprehensive battle plan for tackling the XyrQ. Based on Mila's suggestion in their meeting yesterday, the plan included a preliminary time line for the action (to be amended as they received more data on the ball of rock they were working on) a current inventory of the Irregular's munitions and supplies and a requisition order for anything else they might need from the Governor. Gabby was impressed; perhaps she should drag the Captain off and leave the crew to their own devices more often.

"What do you think?" Gabby asked Ros as she read through the plans.

"It's good. This is doable," she replied, her Captain face perfectly in place. "We've even got suggestions for team breakdowns and how many teams to send out at once to cause maximum confusion." She frowned. "You haven't put Lizzie and Mila together. Something going on that I need to know about?"

"Nyet," Mila replied as Lizzie shook her head. "I thought Burns and I would make more effective team for this mission."

"Maximum amount of bang for your buck," Ewan said with a grin.

"I'm paired with Noora," Lizzie said, gesturing at the tablet Ros had in her hands. "The two of us should be less easily detected than that big Scottish bastard over there. We're going to get in as close as possible and do as much recon as we can. Engage the enemy only if necessary."

Gabby and Ros exchanged an impressed glance. Everything had been taken care of, every contingency planned for. All they had to do was sign off on it.

"I don't know why they even need us," Gabby said, trying not to let her smile take over her face. "They've covered everything on their own."

"Do not be so hard on yourself Gabriela," AJ said. "You and the Kapitan, you are the heart of our little family."

"Not to mention the most effective team we've got," Ewan added. "There's a reason we've assigned you the most incursions; you're bloody good the pair of ya."

"Yeah," Lizzie agreed. "We wouldn't be the Irregulars without you two." Mila made a grunting noise that could have been agreement.

Ros smiled at that. "Well then, I better go get this signed off by the Governor. You lot make preparations."

"Yes Captain," came the answering chorus in several accents. Gabby hung back after Ros had left.

"Thanks for that guys. I think she needed the vote of confidence. And having a plan ready to go is a weight off her shoulders, not to mention it stops her champing at the bit to get going."

"It is the least we can do," said AJ. "We meant every word of what we said, and do not forget that this is our home too. We want to take down these insects just as badly as the Kapitan does."

"Aye, and if we can be a little more objective than the Cap' is right now, then it is our duty to take care of things," Ewan said.

Gabby felt a stinging sensation in her eyes, but she refused to let them fall in front of her crew, her friends, her family. She had chosen these people, and they'd chosen her right back. "Alright you lot," she said, blinking back the irritating moisture threatening to fall down her face. "You heard the Capitan, get going. It's your plan, you know what needs doing, get to it."

They did as they were told though the salute Ewan gave her was more sarcastic than respectful. She followed the group, intending to help as much as possible; the quicker they got out there the quicker they could come home. There was no way Isobel wouldn't sign off on the plan; they'd be hard pressed to come up with anything better. Gabby straightened her spine in preparation; the hunt was on.

CHAPTER SEVENTEEN

ROS

It was fucking freezing. They'd been on the XyrQ's ball of ice for three days now, and already Ros was sick of the damned cold. Freezing her tits off indeed. She stamped her feet to get the feeling back into her toes.

"I know a few things that would warm us up," Gabby said teasingly, her breath condensing in front of her with every word.

Ros groaned. "I cannot overstate how much I don't want to be naked right now." She was wearing about four extra layers as it was, there was no way she was taking any of them off.

"Who says we need to get naked?" Gabby waggled her eyebrows along with the words. Ros let out a bark of laughter.

"The answer's still no."

"Suit yourself," Gabby said with a shrug. "I can always go see if Tariq wants to play."

"No chance," Ros shot back. "Not when his sister's out there. Besides, doesn't he have a boyfriend or something?"

Gabby's eyes light up in delight but the comms crackled before she could say anything. "Mubarak to base, come in base camp."

"This is base camp," Ros said, ignoring Gabby's slight pout that she wouldn't get to ask her questions. "Go ahead Noora."

"All clear out here. Five more miles of tunnels mapped out. We've found some outposts and machinery but we've not encountered any actual XyrQ yet. Lizzie thinks there's a central cavern somewhere in this ball of ice but we've found no sign of it. We're go for phase two."

"Phase two is go. I'll alert the rest of the crew. You two get back here for some rest."

"Will do Captain. Mubarak out."

"Time for some fun?" Gabby said hopefully.

"Time for some fun," Ros agreed. She raised her voice, calling out across the base camp. "Ewan, Mila, suit up. Ayres, Potts, Siddiqui, Manning, you're up. Four teams, hit and run. Do as much damage as possible then get out of there. Operational radio silence. You know what to do."

She and Gabby ended up suiting up next to Ewan and Mila. Her suit had been fixed months back, but it still felt good sliding into it, like coming home to an old friend. Her fond reunion with the power armour that made her a near invincible killing machine was only slightly ruined by Ewan's constant grumbling.

"You're a sniper Mila, what are you doing suiting up for close quarters combat?" he said, poking fun at his teammate.

"I can kill a man from three hundred metres," Mila said matter-of-factly, "what makes you think I cannot kill him from three?"

Ewan paused and cocked his head to one side. "Is there a particular reason you're always talking about killing a man?" he asked.

"Da," Mila said, sliding a razor-sharp dagger into a

sheath on her leg. Then she straightened up and walked away without another word.

"That woman scares me," Ewan said, the look on his face making it clear he wasn't joking.

Ros fought the urge to laugh. "Me too, Ewan. Me too."

Fifteen minutes later she was suited up and out in the tunnels with Gabby at her side. Every sense was on high alert, straining to detect any sign of the XyrQ. A slight shudder ran down her spine as she remembered what had happened last time she'd been a tunnel. At least she wasn't cold any more.

Gabby, who was on point, moved to the next junction and peered round the corner. She signalled that the coast was clear. Ros hated being on radio silence. She much preferred laughing and joking along with Gabby as they worked, but it was the right decision tactically. They knew almost nothing about the XyrQ's stronghold, including what frequencies they might be using for comms. The ice would limit the distance their signal would travel, but they couldn't risk the bugs tapping into their frequency. They'd lose the element of surprise, the uncertainty over numbers, everything.

The tunnel opened out into a small cavern with an abandoned installation in it. Looked like a guard outpost and a few vehicles. They were all in good repair, so there was a chance they weren't abandoned, just not in use right now.

She and Gabby crept up to the outpost and set the charges. Enough explosives to render everything unusable while making a nice bang. They'd heard the rumble of another team's explosives going off; the hope was that multiple teams setting off multiple charges would not only cause confusion for the XyrQ but also divide their forces.

The charges laid, Ros crept back to cover, Gabby close behind her. She held five fingers up to start the countdown. When she got to zero, the entire cavern exploded. Peering round the corner Ros was pleased to see they'd judged the charges right; enough to destroy whatever equipment was there but not enough to bring tons of ice down on their heads.

Now came the hardest part of the plan, the waiting.

The plan was to wait fifteen minutes after each detonation to see if there was a response by the XyrQ. If there was then they'd pick off as many of them as possible. If there was no response in that time frame they'd retreat from their position and return to base camp to pick up more explosives. The idea was to do the maximum amount of damage in a short space of time, all while hiding the truth about their numbers from the enemy. It was a good plan, and Ros was impressed with Mila and the rest of the Irregulars for putting it together. It didn't make the waiting any easier.

Ros's HUD told her eight and a half minutes had passed when Gabby signalled that she had something. They hunkered down even more. Sure enough, less than thirty seconds later a gaggle of insects burst from the other end of the cavern.

Ros signalled to Gabby to hold; she wanted them to be as close as possible before they opened fire.

Twenty metres away. The XyrQ were methodically investigating the cavern, clearly rattled.

Fifteen metres away. Ros pulled out a flash grenade, signalling to Gabby to do the same.

Ten metres away. The lead XyrQ was headed right for them, obviously having realised that location would be ideal for cover, for a trap.

Five metres away. Ros gave the signal to open fire.

She and Gabby threw their grenades at exactly the same time before quickly pulling down the visors on their helmets.

The grenades went off with another huge bang, practically disintegrating the nosy lead XyrQ. As soon as the flash had faded Ros was up above her cover, emptying Margaret into any target she could see. Gabby was right behind her. Four bugs went down before they had chance to react.

Thrown into chaos, the enemy ranks broke. Some insects turned tail and ran back the way they'd come; Ros casually mowed them down. Others, in their confusion, headed towards where she and Gabby were hiding; Gabby took care of those.

It was astounding really, after so many years fighting together Ros and Gabby could read each other so easily, even through their body armour. They divided up tasks quickly and efficiently, all without a single word between them. In a matter of minutes they were picking off the stragglers, the rest of the XyrQ either dead or dying.

The poor bugs had never stood a chance.

When it was over Ros nodded once to Gabby and they

both left their cover, weapons at the ready. They did a quick sweep of the cavern, checking the headcount and putting any survivors out of their misery, and then they were on their way back to base camp.

Forty two XyrQ dead and several tons of materiel destroyed in under thirty minutes, all without a single word.

By the time they got back to camp Ros was almost giddy, buoyed up by a successful first mission. They both tore their helmets off as soon as they could, and judging by the grin on Gabby's face, she felt exactly the same.

"We've still got it," Gabby said, eyes bright.

"Yeah we do," Ros replied, putting her hand up for a heavily armoured hi-five. "Any other teams back yet?" she said, addressing AJ, who was the de facto commander at base camp when she and Gabby were out on patrol.

"Siddiqui and Manning got back a little over ten minutes ago," he said, not bothering to look up from his knitting. Ros couldn't really begrudge him something to keep his hands busy; he wasn't really needed unless (until) someone got hurt and with Ewan out there in the tunnels he'd need something to keep the worrying to a minimum. "The other teams are still out." A muffled explosion echoed through the tunnels. Even from this distance Ros could tell it was somewhat larger than the one she and Gabby had set off. "That'll be Ewan and Mila," AJ said with a sigh.

Gabby snickered while Ros tried to bite back a grin.

Sure enough, half an hour later Ewan and Mila came thundering down the tunnels, Ewan in his enormous suit designed to hold the weight of his cannon prosthetic and Mila in a much sleeker, more lightweight set of armour. Like Ros and Gabby before them, they pulled their helmets off as soon as they were inside the perimeter of base camp. The two of them immediately began bickering like an old married couple.

"She is fucking crazy," Ewan practically bellowed. His face was red from exertion and his beard and hair were plastered to his skin with sweat. Mila by contrast looked like she'd done nothing more strenuous than take a meandering walk.

"*I'm* crazy?" the Russian barked back. "I am not the one who decided to use twice the agreed amount of explosives."

"I thought their boom sounded a little larger than it should," Gabby commented mildly.

"Well I'm not the one who decided to stay and fight even though there were three times the number of XyrQ expected," Ewan roared, standing chest to chest with Mila. Even though Ewan was about a foot and a half taller and twice her weight, Mila didn't look intimidated in the slightest. If it came down to a fight between them Ros's money was on the tiny angry Russian lady, hands down, arm cannon or no arm cannon.

"I have seen worse odds," Mila said calmly.

"Worse odds? That damned bug almost took my fucking head off!"

It was obvious this argument was more than just the run-of-the-mill post-mission bickering that was so common among the Irregulars. This wasn't about blowing off steam; this was serious. Fortunately Ros wasn't the only one who realised that, both AJ and Lizzie moving in to placate their respective partners.

"Alright that's enough!" Ros snapped. "You two, take a step back from each other and stop calling each other crazy. That's not okay and you know that." They followed their Captain's order but still didn't back down entirely, both of them glaring at the other with as much ferocity as they could muster. Ros was surprised their suits didn't melt. "What happened out there? Ewan?"

"More XyrQ responded to our action than we thought they would," he said. "We ended up with about a hundred bugs converging on our position but Mila refused to retreat."

"They all died, did they not?" she asked, as coolly as one might enquire about the weather.

"Mila," Ros growled in warning. "Is it true you used more ordnance than authorised? Ewan?"

At least he had the grace to look sheepish. "I did. There was more materiel in our assigned location than we thought there would be, so I added in a little extra spice."

"Your objective was to disable, not to disintegrate," Ros said with a sigh. "Both of you are at fault here." Both of them protested but Ros cut them off; she wasn't going to put up with any more of their bullshit. "Shut it the pair of you. Ewan, if you hadn't made such a big boom you might not have brought so many bugs down on your heads. And Mila, you should have retreated when Ewan wanted to. I don't care if you think you can deal with the situation, we're not taking any unnecessary risks on this mission. Now, both of you, take half an hour to cool down and then we'll have a proper debrief. Dismissed."

Reluctantly, and with a lot of grumbling, Ewan and Mila did as they were told, slinking off with their partners in tow. This left Ros alone with Gabby, who had seemed a lot more amused with the situation than Ros thought was warranted.

"Thanks for the back up there," she said pointedly. Gabby ignored the sarcasm.

"Oh come on, where's your sense of humour? This is perfectly normal behaviour for these two. If Ewan wasn't as gay as the day is long they'd have gotten married years ago so they could argue more effectively and conveniently and you know it."

Ros sighed. "I don't like fifty-to-one odds Gabs. Not when we're dealing with the mantises."

Gabby shrugged at her. "It came out alright in the end, usually does with those two. Stop dwelling on could have beens. You know that's not going to do you any good. They both came back; that's the important thing."

Ros hated to admit it but Gabby was right. They could plan for as many contingencies as they wanted to but at the end of the day what they did was utterly unpredictable. There were always things that they could have done differently, done better, and if she focused on that she'd go mad. Not to mention render herself completely ineffective as a leader.

"I just want to make sure we take everyone home after this one," she said sadly. "And not in a body bag either."

"I know Ros, I know," Gabby said seriously, meeting Ros's gaze with a soft look.

The moment was only slightly ruined by the sound of the remaining team's ordnance going off.

By the time Ayres and Potts got back to camp Ros had extracted a sensible report from Ewan and Mila and they were mostly speaking civilly again. They were four for four on the days' missions, which meant it was time for Gabby and Ros to put their heads together and evaluate what could be done better.

"You think we should increase the team sizes?" Ros asked as she pored over Mila's original plans. "One of our teams *was* almost overrun."

Gabby shook her head. "I think two people works well. Ewan and Mila ran into trouble because he was a little overzealous with the explosives, and between his cannon and Mila's crack shooting they were fine. He won't do it again because he knows Mila will actually kill him if he does. And AJ will never forgive him if he lets that happen. Besides, two is a good number if anyone does have to make a retreat; it's easier to lose a tail in this maze of ice with smaller numbers."

Ros nodded, acknowledging all of Gabby's points. She still kind of wanted to increase the team sizes, just to keep everyone safe, but she could acknowledge that had more to do with her own issues regarding this mission than it did anything tactical. She would cede to Gabby's decision on this one.

"So more of the same. We hit them hard, hit them fast,

as many teams as we can and make the targets as random as possible. I want to keep the XyrQ guessing about our numbers."

Between the two of them they hammered out a course of action, taking into account the new variables they'd discovered. They decided they could risk leaving fewer mercenaries to defend the camp so they could send more teams out at a time; the more they could divide the enemy forces the better each teams' odds of victory.

Everything went according to that plan for the next few days, surprisingly so. The Irregulars worked around the clock, heading into the tunnels in shifts, hoping to keep the XyrQ on the defensive, harried and exhausted. There was still no sign of a central chamber, nor had they gained many clues about what the XyrQ were up to. Much of the equipment they'd destroyed appeared to be for excavation, but why the XyrQ were digging up this particular space rock remained elusive.

"Are they mining?" Gabby asked as she and Ros suited up for their mission that day.

Ros shrugged, though the effect was dampened by the mechanised armour she was most of the way through putting on. "I can't think of anything this ice ball might have that Novis wouldn't have in greater abundance. At least we've not seen any evidence they're building an armada out here." Ros was beyond relieved about that though she wasn't entirely comfortable with not knowing what they *were* up to.

"Thank the Lord for small mercies," Gabby said before putting her helmet on. She crossed herself as she did before every mission. "Locked and loaded?"

"Let's do this," Ros said, donning her own helmet.

Back out in the tunnels they were under radio silence again. Which meant that Ros couldn't let Gabby know about the creeping sensation crawling down the back of her neck. Something felt different, off, and it wasn't just that their target for the day was much further into the tunnels than before. It wasn't a feeling of getting close to their goal but something else. Something bad.

Ros signalled to Gabby to be careful and carried on.

Everything looked like it had on their previous runs. The tunnels were still icy and fucking cold, there was still the occasional cavern or more open tunnel filled with smashed metal and dead XyrQ. Everything looked normal. And yet Ros couldn't shake the feeling that something was wrong. Her heartbeat was much higher than normal though not quite high enough that her suit was sounding a warning.

They arrived at their target for the day and Ros signalled for Gabby to come to a halt.

Today's cavern was much bigger than those they'd hit previously, and while the others had contained small outposts and various pieces of equipment, this one looked like it had been used as living quarters. Heat lamps were scattered about, surrounded by object that could have been seats if this were a human camp. The excavation equipment was much larger too, and though Ros couldn't tell why, she got the distinct impression this cavern had been in use much more recently than any of the others. Yet it was completely empty now. Add in the fact that there were multiple exits from this cavern and there was only one conclusion Ros could draw; this was the perfect set up for an ambush.

The creeping sensation of something being wrong increased. Ros risked using the comms, flicking it to her and Gabby's private channel.

"I don't like this," she said, ignoring the way Gabby startled at the sudden break in silence. "Smells like a trap."

"Yeah," Gabby agreed. "You must be concerned if you're willing to break your own order for radio silence."

Ros nodded. "How do we approach this?"

"We've still got a mission to complete, and a gut feeling isn't a compelling reason to retreat. We continue as planned, but stay on alert. This could go tits up at any second."

"Agreed. Let's blow up as much as we can and then get out of here. Return to radio silence unless absolutely necessary. Lamarr out."

Ros gave the signal to continue and the two of them crept forward, gazes sweeping the cavern for any sign of trouble, their suits' sensors on high alert. Gabby laid explosives in the most tactically advantageous positions, but Ros held back, still not sure about this. As she approached one of the heat lamps she finally got a concrete sign that all was not as it seemed. The temperature readout on her HUD indicated the lamp was still warm, recently used.

She signalled Gabby over, who noticed the same thing. Ros could see her frown even through the visor of her suit. Gabby signalled back that they should continue and despite every instinct screaming at her to retreat, Ros proceeded with the plan. There was no way this wasn't a trap, but the first step to turning the situation to their advantage was knowing that it was a trap.

Explosives laid, Ros and Gabby scrambled for cover, bracing themselves for the detonation. Ros held five fingers up to start the countdown and at zero pressed the button. The ensuing explosion felt like it rocked the entire planetessimal.

This time the reaction from the XyrQ was instantaneous.

They came pouring into the cavern with an unholy screech. It seemed like there were hundreds of the bastards coming at them from every direction.

"Trap!" Ros yelled, breaking comms silence once again. Then she was fighting for her life, popping up from her cover for the briefest second to let off a few rounds before ducking behind the ice once again. For every XyrQ she put down it seemed like there were three or four took its place.

It wasn't looking good.

"Lamarr to all teams," she shouted on the general channel. "Request immediate back up at my location. All teams converge on my coordinates." The comms just crackled ominously, no reply from any of the other teams.

Gabby popped up from behind the ice to mow down another six bugs. "It's no use," she cried, "they won't get here in time. We have to get out of here."

Ros didn't answer, too busy trying to keep the XyrQ

from overwhelming them. She knew Gabby was right though. She'd killed at least twenty of the bastards and they kept coming. The sensors on her suit were struggling to get an accurate body count, but the numbers it kept displaying weren't good. Sooner or later the XyrQ would wear them down and then they'd be nothing but paste on the icy floor.

There was only one thing they could do.

"All teams, full retreat," she roared, popping up to take down a few more bugs. They were getting far too close now, almost in range of their powerful forearms. "Repeat: all teams retreat. Return to base."

There was a muffled sound down the comms that *might* have been Ewan swearing his agreement, but Ros was too busy trying not to get killed to really listen. Gabby laid down cover fire while she moved backwards into the tunnels and then Ros returned the favour. The air was thick with gunfire and the screeches of dying mantises.

"Fire in the hole!" Gabby said, lobbing a flash grenade into the tangle of bugs pouring into the tunnel after them. Both she and Ros used the slight lull after it went off to retreat further down the tunnel.

"Lamarr to basecamp," Ros said when she had breath enough to speak. "All available personnel suit up and ready defences. All teams in full retreat with enemy in pursuit. Repeat: everyone suit up. We're headed your way and we're bringing the party with us."

Ros lost track of time after that, everything narrowing to the same actions over and over again: cover Gabby as she moved backwards through the tunnels, then run as fast as she could while Gabby covered her. Occasionally one of them tossed a flash grenade at their pursuers so they could both retreat at the same time. The bodies piled up but the pack of XyrQ never seemed to get any thinner.

"How many of the fuckers are there?" Ros shouted in frustration. Gabby didn't reply, she was too busy muttering the Lord's Prayer under her breath, alternating it with that Psalm about the valley of the shadow of death. Ros could have done without that to be honest, but she didn't have the breath to spare to chastise Gabby for it.

She'd been on hundreds of missions with Gabby and could count on her fingers the number of times she'd found it necessary to pray in the middle of a mission. Things were really not looking good.

Just as Ros started to lose her grip on hope, she heard the boom of Ewan's cannon echoing through the tunnels. Instinctively she headed towards the sound of back up. Several long minutes later, she and Gabby burst into a parallel tunnel where Ewan and Mila were in a similar situation.

"Nice to see ya Captain," Ewan yelled. "Looks like these bastards are smarter than we gave them credit for." He fired his arm-mounted cannon again, blasting through the wall of insect chasing them. In the ensuing chaos, Mila mowed down more of the enemy with an efficiency that was almost frightening. They were an effective team despite their almost constant bickering.

Ros and Gabby both tossed flash grenades at the same time, partially collapsing the side tunnel they'd just come through and buying them more time.

"Any sign of the other teams?" Ros asked when she had chance.

"Nyet."

"Nothing but insect all the way," Ewan added. "You're the first humans we've seen since we left camp."

Ros nodded slowly as she put another few rounds in an enemy carapace. "We need to regroup," she shouted as the surge of XyrQ increased once more.

"Back to camp then," Ewan said. "After you Captain." He punctuated his statement with another cannon blast.

Bolstered by the extra backup, Ros dived down the tunnels like a woman possessed. She just hoped there would still be a basecamp left when they got there.

CHAPTER EIGHTEEN

GABBY

Everything was a mess when they got back to camp.

AJ, bless him, was trying to mount some semblance of a defence with the remaining mercs, but he was a doctor, not a strategist. One of the other teams had made it back, Ayres and Potts, and had brought their own gaggle of XyrQ with them.

Gabby took one look at the situation and realised that everything was going to go tits up very quickly without proper instruction. Fortunately, that was what they had Ros for.

"Captain on deck!" Gabby yelled down the comms by way of announcing their presence. Everyone who was able to stood to attention.

"Alright Irregulars, lets sort this mess out," Ros said brusquely. "AJ, thank you for your help but I'm gonna need you in sickbay now. Ewan, go man your turret, see if you can't plug that hole that's leaking bugs. Mila, I want you up high with your rifle. The rest of you on me, single line around camp shoulder to shoulder. Let's form a shield wall and buy the others time. Go go go!"

The Irregulars scrambled to follow their orders and in a matter of minutes Ros turned a rout waiting to happen into a decent defence. Gabby had time to sneak in a quick smile before all her attention was focussed on shooting XyrQ and staying alive; Ros really was the best in the business.

Ewan's cannon echoed around the valley Noora had landed the *Star* in, followed quickly by the crack of Mila's rifle.

The XyrQ seemed to realise that order had been restored and their current tactics weren't going to be any more use. They hung back in the tunnels, waiting and chittering among themselves. The Irregulars had no such restraint: Gabby shouldered her weapon and fired at every piece of black carapace that moved; Ewan's turret went off in short bursts, quickly blasting through the ice and rock the XyrQ were hiding in; Mila's rifle went off at much more irregular intervals, but every time it did it was followed by the dying screech of at least one bug.

Just moments ago the Irregulars had been on the back foot, disorganised and practically defeated, now they were on the verge of a decisive victory.

"Flash grenade time Capitan?" Gabby asked with a grin.

"Aye," Ros said, completely focused. "Irregulars, flash grenades, on three. One, two, three!"

The entire shield wall tossed their grenades at the same time and they went off with a flash almost as bright as a sun. By the time Gabby could see again the tunnel the XyrQ had been coming through was a pile of ice and dust. They were safe for now.

A cheer went up from the Irregulars.

"Alright, don't get cocky," Ros barked. "I want guards posted at every remaining entrance to the tunnels; the insects are bound to try another way. Anyone who's injured go see AJ. Ayres, Potts, with me. Ewan, Mila, meet us in the cargo bay. I want to know what the fuck went wrong."

Everyone moved to follow the Captain's orders as fast as they could, the adrenaline from the battle still flowing strong. Gabby was pleased to see only a couple of people limping off to sickbay; fewer injuries was always good.

In the cargo bay Gabby took her helmet off, the suit hissing slightly as it readjusted to the outisde pressure. Ros on the other hand practically tore hers off and threw it into a corner. She was pissed.

"Okay, someone talk to me. What the hell happened out there?" Ros growled.

"It was an ambush Captain," Ewan said. "They jumped on us the moment we set the charges off and practically chased us down the tunnels. There were far too many of them for it to have been anything other than planned."

"The same thing happened to us," Gabby said. "Potts?"

"Same here, sir," Ollie said. "We barely made it out of there alive."

"Has anyone heard from the other team?" Ros asked darkly. "Any word from either Manning or Siddiqui?" Everyone shook their heads.

"Not a sausage," said Ewan. "We heard your orders loud and clear Captain, but there wasn't a peep out of anyone else."

Ros stiffened, her body language signalling that she wanted nothing more than to go after her crew. Hate and frustration rolled off her in waves.

"We're two people down then," Gabby said, stating the obvious to give Ros time to get herself under control.

"And assuming some of the XyrQ survived the tunnel collapse, they now have our location."

"We could move somewhere else?" Ayres suggested somewhat timidly.

"Not an option," Ros snapped. "Our two missing people may have been captured by the XyrQ—" *or worse* Gabby mentally added "—but there's every chance they're still out there. Lying low until the danger has passed, or still trying to give the XyrQ the slip. If there's even the slightest chance they're still out there we need to stay put so they can find us. This is where they'll come back to if they're able and I won't risk them finding an empty valley and thinking we left them behind. The Erebus Station Irregulars don't *do* that."

"Where do we go from here then?" Mila asked. "Our plan was good one but obviously no longer viable."

"We have to operate on a number of assumptions," Gabby said. "One, that our people are still out there and trying to get back to us. Two, that the XyrQ now have our location, and a good idea of our strength and capabilities. They'll be back, and in greater numbers. We need to be ready for them."

Just then the comm crackled. "Sorry to interrupt Kapitan," AJ said. "But I thought you should know that everyone has been patched up. A few cuts and bruises, nothing more serious than a sprained ankle."

"Good, thank you AJ," Ros said, some of the tension bleeding out of her. She might be missing two crew members, but everyone else was fine. "You want to join us in the cargo bay?"

"I will be right there. AJ out."

Ros sighed, though she didn't seem to get any relief from it. Gabby wished she could drag her off for a little "relaxation" but there simply wasn't time. No, Ros would remain tense as all hell until he mission was over and then relieve it all in one go. Judging by how tightly Ros was holding her shoulders, both Isobel and Gabby would be walking funny by the time Ros let herself relax properly. She was looking forward to it.

Gabby dragged her attention back to the present just as AJ walked into the cargo bay. He looked harried and weary; command was really not his strong suit and the situation the camp had been in when they'd got there was well beyond his experience level, which explained why he looked like shit. Ewan slid his arm around his boyfriend's waist.

"What went wrong?" Ros asked AJ, looking him dead in the eye. Apparently it was a "no mercy for anyone" sort of day.

"You left a medic in charge, that's what went wrong," AJ shot back acidly, apparently in no mood to tolerate Ros's bullshit. That was good; they might actually be able to get something done.

"You were the ranking officer–" Ros started.

"Who has no experience organising troops for battle," AJ pointed out. "You left me with some of the greenest mercs in the group, and people whose expertise lies outside of combat. Noora and Lizzie were the most experienced people I had, and they were fresh off a recon mission and resting. I did the best I could with what I had."

"And you did pretty well," Gabby jumped in. She could see the way Ros was bristling and knew AJ was gonna get it in the neck if they weren't careful, and the poor guy didn't deserve that. "No fatalities and only minor injuries; that's good going for a commander with any amount of combat experience."

"Thank you Gabriela," AJ said, beaming. Ewan shot her a grateful look too.

At least Ros was sensible enough to know when she was outnumbered. "Fine," she said grudgingly. "We came out of that situation better than we could have, and a lot of that's down to AJ. How do we stop this sort of thing happening again?"

"I hate to say this Kapitan, but we need another senior officer with combat experience," AJ said cautiously. "We need a replacement for Matthew."

"No." Ros's reply was instantaneous, and Gabby could see the flash of grief and anger in her eyes. "Out of the question."

"Ros, come on," Gabby said, a pleading note in her voice. "You know he's right. I can handle the paperwork even though I hate doing it. That's not a problem. But you can't deny that our missions over the last six months would have gone a lot easier with another experienced merc on the crew. Someone with the kind of experience we have. Someone who can lead teams on their own. We need the extra help."

"Now is not the time," Ros ground out. Her teeth were gritted so hard it was a wonder she didn't shatter them and her eyes were wild. She knew it was ridiculous to hold out on this, it was written all over her face, and Gabby knew her well enough to read that level of desperation with ease. But she also knew her well enough to know Ros wasn't about to give this one up without a fight, not when she felt so strongly about it.

"Now might not be the time to recruit a new person," Gabby allowed, "but it's sure as shit the right time to talk about this. You saw how badly things were going when we got back to camp. AJ did his best but you can't put a medic in charge of inexperienced mercs and expect to come out on top. If we hadn't arrived when we had the entire crew could have been wiped out."

She saw a shudder run down Ros's spine at that, and Ewan pulled AJ even closer, obviously affected by the idea he could have lost his boyfriend. He might be a big fuck off Scotsman with an enormous ginger beard, but losing AJ would destroy him, no matter how tough he talked.

Gabby saw the moment Ros relented; her how body slumped ever so slightly as though in defeat.

"Alright," she said, "We'll look into it. *After* we're done with these fucking bugs. Now, if everyone is done questioning my command decisions, do you think we could come up with a plan for how we're actually going to defeat them?"

There was a general murmur of assent from everyone in the cargo bay.

"Good," Ros said. "Anyone have any ideas? Mila?"

"They have our location, an idea of our numbers and are wise to our plan."

"Not to mention two of our people," Ewan interrupted. Gabby was glad no one seemed to be assuming that Manning and Siddiqui were dead.

"Da. The bugs, they have all the cards here, and we have nothing."

Ros growled, her hand balling into fists at her side. "Will someone give me *something*?"

"If it weren't for our missing people I'd suggest blowing this rock to hell and getting out of here," Ewan said. "But if there's even the smallest chance they're still alive, we need to try to rescue them."

"How?" AJ asked. "We don't know where they are, or even where the XyrQ are based. We can't just go in blind, we'll lose too many people that way."

"We could–" Gabby started, but she was interrupted by the comm.

"I hate to interrupt Captain," came Lizzie's voice, far too rapid and high-pitched for it to be anything good, "but we've got trouble out here. They're back." The sound of gunfire echoed down the comm as though to reinforce that point.

"Shit!" Ros said at the same time as everyone else uttered their own profanities. Between them they swore in about five different languages, which Gabby might have found impressive if things hadn't been so dire.

"Helmets back on," Gabby said, finding her command voice quicker than Ros did. "They've got us on the defensive. We can argue about plans if we get through this with our skins intact."

Everyone scrambled to obey and was out the door in

a flash. Everyone except Ros, who looked a little lost. Gabby reached out to touch her hand even though the gesture wasn't nearly as effective through the layers of latex and carbon-steel that made up their armour.

"Hey," she said soothingly, "it's okay. We fought the bugs back last time and we'll do it again. Then we'll come up with a brilliant plan to rescue our people and defeat the XyrQ once and for all before going home to a hero's welcome.

Ros gave her a helpless look. "What if that's not what happens?" she asked, her voice smaller than Gabby could ever remember it being. She was rattled and unsure of herself, and that worried Gabby. Ros was the solid ground she had built the rest of her life around, and it suddenly not being so solid threatened to pull her under too.

"It will happen," Gabby insisted, making sure her voice was more confident than she currently felt. "We're the Erebus Station Irregulars and you're Captain Ros Lamarr; how can we not win?"

Ros sighed. "What if I'm not Captain Ros Lamarr, Greatest Mercenary Captain in the Galaxy? What if I'm just me? Plain old Ros."

"You're both," Gabby said softly. "That's why I love you." Ros looked up sharply, a startled look on her face. Gabby suddenly realised that was the first time she'd ever admitted that out loud in front of Ros. Now wasn't the time for heartfelt declarations though; now was the time for action. "Come on," she said, thinking that if she acted like it was no big deal then Ros would too. "Let's go be badass."

A shadow of a grin appeared on Ros's face just before she put her helmet on. They bumped their gloved fists together and pulled their weapons from their shoulders before heading back outside to assess the situation.

It was worse than they thought.

The XyrQ were pouring out of all the remaining tunnels into the ice in numbers that were frankly mind-boggling. There were a couple of dozen dead already and yet they kept coming. Two suited forms lay face down on the ice but there wasn't time to find out who they were or if they were still alive.

"Ideas Capitan?" Gabby asked.

Ros seemed to flounder for a second, the helplessness from the cargo bay still with her, before she found herself.

"I need eyes up high," she said, flicking the comm on. "Mila, can you get on top of the *Star*, give me an aerial view?"

"Da, Captain."

"Ewan, where's your cannon?"

"Here Captain," he said coming to her side.

"I need you to concentrate on trying to collapse those tunnels. Give them fewer exits."

"Aye cap'n."

"Lizzie, Noora, where are you?"

"Here Captain," they both said in unison.

"I want you two to keep close to the ship, pick off any bugs that make it past the front lines. Lizzie, Mila's been helping you with your marksmanship yes?"

"Da," Lizzie said with a cheeky grin curling around her lips.

"Good, put that to good use. Noora, where's your brother?"

"Still inside the ship," she replied. "He's put himself in charge of resupplying ammunition. He'll be safer that way inshallah."

"Good, good," Ros replied distractedly, her eyes roving across the battlefield.

"¿Que tal hoy Capitan?" she asked, worried.

"I'll be fine," Ros said, brushing off Gabby's concern, which only made her more worried. "Irregulars," she continued on the general comm channel, "form up. I want you in pairs where possible, behind cover. Your priority is to keep your partner safe. Don't take any unnecessary risks. Lamarr out."

"And what are we doing?" Gabby asked using their private channel. She'd not received any orders so far and while she was perfectly capable of deciding for herself what needed doing, she was curious as to what Ros might have in mind.

"Taking an unnecessary risk," Ros said with a smile that chilled Gabby to her core. The last time she'd seen that smile was just before Ros had lost her leg. "Follow me."

Gabby did as she was told, ignoring the unsettled feeling in her stomach. They made their way across the valley, taking out XyrQ as and when the opportunity arose. The Irregulars had rallied somewhat with their Captain's support and were now holding their ground. The two mercs who'd been on the ice when they'd first exited the ship were now back behind the line of the

Irregulars' fire, and at least one of them was sitting up. Ewan's screamed profanities could be heard even without the comms activated, and the booming retort of his arm-mounted cannon rang out at steady intervals.

The tide was slowly turning in their favour.

Ros led Gabby out of the valley and started to climb, heading out to the side before turning towards the enemy line.

"What are we doing?" Gabby asked again, having received a less than satisfactory answer the first time she'd asked.

"Pincer movement," Ros said, her gaze focused on something ahead of them. "When we were in the tunnels before I noticed some shafts above us that were open to the sky. We're going to use those to surprise the hell out of the bugs."

"That's—" *a terrible fucking plan* "—not a bad idea actually," Gabby said, hoping she sounded like she meant it. It sounded like a sure-fire way to get killed to her, but if she had to die, she'd much rather it was fighting by Ros's side so she said nothing.

The ice grew steep before long, too steep to climb without help. Gabby pulled a tool from her belt and fired a cable deep into the ice overhead. Fortunately the climb wasn't so steep she needed her auto-ascender; they could pull themselves up by hand. The ice flattened out before long, and they kept going.

They found a hole in the ice that looked big enough for them to fit through. Gabby's suit sensors told her there was movement in tunnels below but not much else that was useful, like how many eight foot mantises they were about to jump in the middle of.

"You ready?" Ros asked.

"Not even a little bit," Gabby said. She reloaded her gun anyway.

"On my mark then. Three, two, one, jump!"

Ros went first and Gabby followed hot on her tail. The ice scraped unpleasantly against her armour as she slid down the short, steep slide they were on. The noise rattled inside Gabby's head. Then the slide gave way, and she dropped ten or so feet to the tunnel floor, landing heavily. The servos in her suit were the only thing that stopped her pitching forwards and landing on her face. She recovered quickly and joined her Captain, who had already taken down half a dozen or so of the mantises.

Everything was a blur after that. There were bugs in front of them, bugs behind, bugs fucking everywhere. Gabby planted herself back to back with Ros and took down every insect that came too close.

"When you said pincer movement, I didn't think you meant letting them catch us in one!" Gabby yelled, taking down one of the XyrQ who'd come dangerously close to punching a hole in her armour. Her ribs throbbed in remembrance.

"So do something about it," Ros shouted back. "Cut them off."

Gabby thought quickly; they didn't have anything on them powerful enough to take down the number of XyrQ that were still storming towards them. Then she got an idea.

"Cover me," she said, dropping to one knee on the ice.

"What?" Ros said, whirling round to try to keep two advancing hordes of bugs at bay.

Gabby ignored her and just jammed her rifle into the ice, flicking it to auto-fire. It wouldn't be terrible accurate but it would at least keep the XyrQ at a decent distance for a while. Then she pulled three flash grenades from her belt and pulled some bonding tape from the utility compartment on her thigh. Working quickly, she taped the three grenades together before adding one of her spare ammo packs for good measure.

"Cover your eyes," she yelled to Ros, scrambling to her feet again. "Gonna be a hell of a bang." She pulled the pin on one of the grenades and threw it as hard as she could into the seething mass of chitinous limbs. Then she scooped her rifle up and grabbed hold of Ros's arm, dragging her to the floor.

A few heart-stopping seconds passed before the grenade went off with a boom that shook Gabby to her bones. Chunks of ice and rock rained down all around them as mantises shrieked and tried to escape, ignoring the two mercenaries in a vulnerable position on the floor. A large chuck of ice bounced off Gabby's suit, causing a warning alarm to sound in her already ringing ears.

"Move!" she shouted to Ros, and they both crawled forwards, out of range of the tunnel collapse Gabby had started.

Another few chunks of rock and ice hit them, and each time Gabby's heart skipped a few sickening beats. Eventually the rumbling stopped and things went quiet enough for them to scramble to their feet. Gabby turned around to examine her handy work.

"Hell of a boom, huh?" she said, admiring the pile of rock and ice that now sat where there used to be tunnel. Bits of XyrQ were sticking haphazardly out of the rubble, dripping gore that was rapidly freezing in place.

"Never do that again!" said Ros, sounding furious. There was a gleam in her eye that wasn't entirely anger though, and Gabby could tell she was pleased that her plan had worked.

"Sí Capitan," Gabby said, attempting to look contrite even though there was a massive grin fighting to break out on her face. "It was kind of awesome though," she dared.

A smile broke out on Ros's face. "Yeah it was. Come on, fight's not over yet. Our people still need us."

Just then the general comm crackled to life. "Captain," Ewan said, "I don't know what you did to cause that explosion, but it's just pissed the bugs off. We need back up."

"On our way," Ros said and then flicked back to the private channel. "I think there's a side tunnel up ahead. We might be able to get into one of the tunnels that runs parallel to this one and surprise the XyrQ again."

"Sí Capitan." She paused. "You sure you don't want me to do that again?"

"Maybe," Ros said and set off down the tunnel at a light jog.

There was indeed a path through the ice up ahead, but calling it a tunnel might have been too generous. It was barely wide enough for them to squeeze their suits through sideways, and Ros kept banging her head on the ceiling. Gabby had never been so glad she wasn't that tall.

"I think I know why the XyrQ haven't been using this," she grumbled.

"Yeah," Ros agreed. "I can barely get my arse through this, there's no way an eight foot bug would fit through."

Soon enough the little crevasse opened out into the tunnel proper where the eight foot bugs definitely fit through. This time they'd managed to get behind the main force in the tunnel and had the element of surprise.

"More grenades Captain?" Gabby asked.

Ros nodded. "One each, on my mark."

They tossed their grenades and were shooting almost from the moment it went off. Gabby almost went into a trance, repeating the same motions over and over again. Breathe, aim, fire. Breathe, aim, fire. Breathe, aim, fire, reload. They moved steadily down the tunnel towards base camp and their people, taking down scores of bugs as they went. Eventually the mass of insects thinned and seconds later they stepped out into the light.

When they'd left base camp less than twenty minutes previously the tide of the battle had been turning in the Irregulars' favour. That was no longer the case. Three tunnels were still open and spitting out XyrQ at a rate that seemed impossible. There were piles of their dead all over the place but they didn't seem to care; they just kept coming.

The Irregulars had been pushed back almost to the ship, and Gabby could only see seven or eight people still on their feet. Ewan had lost his helmet at some point and his head was streaming with blood. It didn't seem to affect his volume or extensive vocabulary though. Lizzie seemed to be holding her own pretty well, using her engineering skills to improvise deadly explosives while Noora gave her cover. Every few seconds the distinctive sound of Mila's sniper rifle rang out, followed shortly by another mantis head exploding into chunks.

It wasn't enough though.

Without saying a word Ros and Gabby dived in, helping out as much as they could. The Irregulars rallied, bolstered by the sight of their Captain and XO, but they were still in dire straits. Outnumbered and rapidly losing both faith and energy, there was only one way this battle would end. There were just too many of them, and there was nothing they could do against such relentless hate. Gabby had fought enough battles to know when one was lost.

Still, she wasn't about to give up without a fight. She advanced on the XyrQ, aiming for their most vulnerable bits, doing the most damage for the least expense, trying to conserve her ammo.

It worked for a while.

Then one of the mantises slipped through her defences and got too close. There was a scream down the comms she didn't have time to process before she took a XyrQ foreleg to the head.

Everything went black.

Waking up after that was honestly a surprise. Everything was fuzzy, her ears were ringing and her limbs didn't want to work properly, but even despite that she could see the battle was over. The XyrQ were gone, and the Irregulars were tending to their wounded.

Someone pulled Gabby upright and took off her helmet. A sea of ginger swam into her vision. Ewan.

"Steady on there," he said, the words barely audible to Gabby. "AJ's on his way."

She wanted to asked what happened but her mouth wouldn't obey her brain. Slowly she scanned the battlefield, putting faces to names and noting who was missing. Panic overtook her, and she struggled against Ewan's grip.

"Easy there, Gabby, easy. You'll make your head injury worse."

She fought to get her words out even though her mouth felt like it belonged to someone else. "Ewan," she said frantically. "Where's Ros?"

CHAPTER NINETEEN

ROS

When Ros drifted back to awareness, the first thing she noticed was that she was upside down.

She only narrowly avoided panicking, instead channelling all her anxiety into anger. Where the flying fuck was she, and what had happened? Her last clear memory was of seeing Gabby go down. Her stomach lurched at the thought, but she pushed the nausea aside. She could worry about Gabby when she'd gotten herself out of this mess.

A quick glance towards her feet revealed that she was suspended from the ice by some kind of sticky silk-like substance but the sensors on her suit didn't quite know what to make of it. Her feet and legs were completely covered in the stuff, keeping them immobile. Her arms were free though, and she used them to gain momentum to swing herself around, get her bearings.

Two of her mercenaries were in a similar situation—Siddiqui and Manning judging by the armour—but they didn't respond no matter how much she yelled. She hoped like hell they were still alive.

With nothing to occupy her attention and all the blood in her body rushing towards her head, Ros allowed unconsciousness to reclaim her. This time when she came to, her field of vision was full of mantis.

She screamed.

The bug reared back and chittered in a way Ros might

have recognised as being surprise if she hadn't been too busy panicking.

This bug was different to the ones she was used to. It was a lot less than eight feet tall and lacked the powerful fighting forearms that were so dangerous. Instead this insect had smaller limbs ending in an almost delicate pincer-like appendage that looked capable of some fine motion. It was a far cry from the bludgeoning fist Ros was used to.

In fact this insect was completely different to what she was used to. All the XyrQ Ros had encountered in her life had displayed a singular-focus on their mission—usually Ros's destruction—that it could only be stopped by death. This bug wasn't like that at all. It almost had a curious look on its alien features and certainly didn't want Ros dead; if that had been its goal she would never have woken up. No, this bug seemed to study her in a cool, detached manner suggestive of great intelligence.

Ros had had no idea there were different types of XyrQ, and she was floored by the idea that not all of them were mindless killing machines. She wondered what else she might not know about the XyrQ.

The bug skittered towards a corner of the cave, pausing a moment before returning with something in its pincer. A container of water. It held the container up and towards Ros, the intent unmistakable.

Suddenly very aware of the carpet-like feel of her mouth, Ros pulled her helmet off and accepted the water, drinking eagerly. Which wasn't easy when she was upside down, and she spilled quite a lot down her face and up her nose. It chilled quickly, making her shiver. When she was done, the bug took away her container and came back with a piece of silk-like substance similar to the one anchoring Ros to the ceiling. The XyrQ wiped her face ever so gently, mopping up the spilled water. This silk wasn't as sticky as the stuff around her feet.

"Thank you?" Ros said, unsure how to react. This was so far beyond her experience it was ridiculous.

The bug chittered at her—saying "you're welcome" perhaps?—before *eating* the silk and freaking Ros out. It left the cave and Ros was on her own again.

Time has little meaning when you're suspended upside down in a largely featureless cave, especially when you're alone. Ros's attention drifted and wandered. Maybe she slept, she couldn't be sure. If she did it wasn't restful sleep. Eventually the friendly XyrQ returned, this time accompanied by two of the more familiar insects.

Ros's hand went instinctively for her holster before realising it was empty.

The bugs were making clicking noises at each other, clearly having a conversation. Ros wished she had even the slightest clue what was going on. The bug that had been kind to her came over and supported her shoulders with one of its pincers, lifting her up slightly so she was less upside down. Her head was very grateful. One of the Punch Bugs, as she was starting to think of them, lumbered over and ate through the silk attaching her to the ceiling. It made short work of her bindings and then Ros's legs dropped to meet the Nice Bug's other pincer arm, the bug keeping her up in some sort of bridal hold. A really creepy bridal hold.

Ros didn't dare move.

The Punch Bug that had cut her down now started eating through the rest of the sticky silk keeping her legs together. She could see the bug's mandibles working as it devoured the silk that had presumably been produced by another one of the XyrQ and it took every ounce of self control she had not to freak the fuck out.

When her feet were free the Nice Bug set her down on the ice and gestured towards the door. Obviously she was being taken somewhere.

Her legs didn't quite want to work properly after having been suspended by them for so long, but Ros stumbled forwards anyway. The two Punch Bugs stood at either shoulder, flanking her, nudging her forwards with one of their punching arms. No matter how kind the strange new type of XyrQ had been to her, Ros was still a prisoner. Alone and weaponless accompanied by three XyrQ, the odds of escape were minute. That didn't mean Ros wasn't scanning the tunnels as she went, cataloguing every detail on the off-chance she might find the opportunity to run.

The tunnels were much like the ones Ros had seen throughout the rest of this icy rock; tall enough for XyrQ to move about easily and wide enough for them to walk at least two abreast. Every so often a new tunnel broke off, or a cavern opened up to the side. These caverns were filled with activity though, XyrQ bustling here and there doing whatever it was that they did. Ros noticed that her new friend wasn't the only one of that type of bug. If there were any other varieties, she didn't see them.

After a while the relentless trudge through the tunnels became boring, the constant click of the XyrQ's legs on the ice repetitive. All the tunnels looked the same, as did the caverns they passed, and the insects working within them. The only notable aspect of their journey was the constant decline of the tunnel; they were headed deeper into the planetesimal, that much Ros could tell, but not much more.

"So, where are you guys taking me?" Ros asked, mostly to break up the encroaching silence in her mind. Also to entertain herself. She had no illusions that one of the XyrQ would answer, and she wouldn't understand if they did. "Are you even guys?" she continued, wondering aloud. "How does gender work for you, anyway?"

One of the Punch Bugs hissed at her in a way that was definitely a warning.

"Sorry, I was just asking."

After that the rest of the journey was undertaken in silence since Ros was rather attached to her remaining limbs. Thankfully it didn't take long to reach their destination.

The tunnel opened out into the largest cavern Ros had yet seen, obviously having been built to lead here. The central cavern, at least Ros assumed it was roughly at the centre of the planetesimal given the way the tunnels had been winding downwards, was lined with walkways and bridges, with XyrQ skittering here and there doing... whatever it was they were doing. That wasn't what attracted Ros's immediate attention though.

In the centre of the cavern was the largest XyrQ Ros had ever seen.

At least thirty feet tall with a huge distended abdomen, the thing was honestly terrifying. It lacked almost all the features Ros was used to seeing on XyrQ; there were no punching arms, very little in the way of chitinous armour. The only real distinguishing feature it had was the enormous abdomen. All the XyrQ in the cavern were rushing around this one, almost as if they were dancing attendance on it. Every few seconds or so the great abdomen twitched and writhed, producing a pale, shuddering maggot-like thing. Ros could see something moving inside before each one was carried off by one of the other XyrQ. Something that looked an awful lot like one of the Punch Bugs behind her.

"Fucking hell," Ros whispered to herself, "they're *breeding*."

The enormous XyrQ must be their queen, and given the rate she was popping out baby bugs, there was no wonder they could afford to throw hundreds of soldiers at the Irregulars as cannon fodder.

She'd stopped in her tracks, staring open mouthed at the sight in front of her, but apparently the show was over: one of the Punch Bugs "nudged" her, nearly driving her to her knees.

"Alright, alright," she said. "I get it." Her shoulder blade ached where the bug's forearm had made contact.

The Nice Bug clicked and buzzed at the Punch Bug, sounding kinda pissed off. Apparently she wasn't to be damaged in any way. Which was nice. The Nice Bug took hold of her arm, much more gently than Ros would have anticipated, and guided her towards the enormous insect in the centre of the cavern. Which was the last place in the universe she wanted to be quite frankly.

"Er, hi," Ros tried, speaking mostly to calm her own mind. From a tactical standpoint she was fucked, and she knew it. Talking always kept the panic at bay and there was always a slim chance she might talk her way out of the situation. Or keep the distraction up until a rescue was mounted. "Nice brood you've got here," she said, wincing at her own words. How does one talk to a thirty foot monstrosity that probably wants to eat you, anyway?

The Queen clicked her mandibles at Ros, possibly in answer but there really was no way to tell. There was a distinct language barrier in the way.

The Nice Bug moved over to a strange looking console that Ros had assumed was just a chunk of rock at first. It poked at a few things with its pincers and a low hum started up, just loud enough to be annoying. The Queen made another round of sounds with her rather intimidating mandible. This time though, the machine provided a translation. Halting and somewhat delayed, but a translation nonetheless.

"Welcome. Human," the Queen said.

"Hi?," Ros said, utterly confused by what was going on here. "Glad we can communicate now." There was another delay after Ros finished speaking before the machine produced a series of chittering noises, presumably translating her words for the Queen.

This would be the weirdest conversation she'd ever

had, she could tell.

"You. Queen of human–" here there was just a series of clicks, the machine apparently unable to translate the word. Ros had a feeling it wasn't very nice whatever it was. "I Queen of XyrQ. We talk."

That explained why she'd been kept alive. For negotiations. Her people might not have been so lucky.

"I'm the leader of the humans, yes. What do you want to talk about?"

"You come. Kill us. Bad. You stop."

"You started killing us first. You've been attacking trade ships in this system for months," Ros said, trying to keep a handle on her anger. Yes she was pissed at the XyrQ for what they'd done but letting that show was a good way to get herself killed without achieving anything. And if she died Gabby would kill her and bring her back so Isobel could do it too. Better to be careful with her words and keep her temper in check.

"Need supplies. Build nest. Home. Too many. Start new."

Ros cocked her head to one side, trying to get her head around what the Queen had just said. They needed those supplies to build their nest here because the XyrQ homeworld was overpopulated? It made sense at least. That didn't make it right.

"You could have asked," Ros said, unable to keep the heat out of her voice. "We would have helped, sent aid to your homeworld. We could have helped you build a colony. You didn't have to kill us for resources."

She was hoping she might get through to the Queen

though Ewan's words about what the XyrQ did to the Commonwealth envoys sent to them were swirling around in her mind. Maybe they hadn't had this translation machine? She had to try to convince them that violence wasn't the answer. There had to be a diplomatic solution here. She might only be trying the tactful approach because there was no viable alternative, but it still counted.

Isobel would be proud.

"XyrQ no ask," the Queen said, and Ros thought her initial clacking sounded a bit haughty, if she was any judge of XyrQ mannerisms. Which she might well be. It was possible no one else in the Commonwealth had spent so much time in their company and remained alive. "XyrQ take. No ask."

"Why not?"

The Queen drew herself up to her full height, which was pretty intimidating. Or it would have been if not for the fact she was still popping out maggots at a hell of a rate. She might not be paying attention to it, but it was kind of distracting in the corner of Ros's field of vision. There was a nervous sweat on the back of Ros's neck.

"XyrQ no ask human," she said, the tone of the translator almost offended. "XyrQ better."

"Better than what?"

"Human," the Queen said simply. "No ask. Only take."

"It doesn't have to be like that though," Ros insisted. "There's plenty of room in this galaxy for both our species. Surely we can find a way to coexist peacefully?"

"No."

Ros sighed with frustration. "Why are we even talking if you refuse to co-operate?"

"XyrQ heard of you. Captain Lamarr. Many tales. You kill many XyrQ." The Queen tipped her head to the side, mimicking Ros's earlier gesture. It was kind of scary on a mantis that size, especially when it was staring at you with those eyes. "You. Mighty warrior. We look at you."

"Thank you," Ros said. "I think that was a compliment."

So, even the XyrQ had heard stories of the great Captain Ros Lamarr. She normally resented the level of celebrity—or notoriety—she'd achieved, but right now she was grateful for it; it might be the only thing keeping her alive.

"Kill many XyrQ," the Queen said. "Stop now. Give chance to leave. One time. Take it. Leave now."

"And my people?"

"Leave now," she repeated.

"And if we take your offer, if we leave, will you stop attacking our ships? Will you work with us to live together peacefully?"

"No."

Ros had no way of knowing whether it was a general XyrQ trait to refuse to co-operate with "lowly" humans or whether it was just this particular queen, but it was becoming apparent that there was no diplomatic solution. The Irregulars would be allowed to leave the planetesimal, by the grace of this Queen, but the attacks on their ships would continue. Novis, her home, would remain in danger, and so would the people she loved.

And who was to say the XyrQ would remain in the ball of ice on the edge of the system? What was stopping them from deciding Novis looked like a much better place to live once the Queen had popped out enough soldiers to take it?

She had to put a stop to this, but how? She was a single soldier, alone in enemy territory, with only her melee weapon available. What could she possibly do?

As she mulled over the tactical options—which were limited and carried very slim odds—she observed. The XyrQ might look like Earth mantises, but the make up of the species and the way they interacted with one another reminded Ros much of ants. The fact there were two or more varieties of XyrQ specialised for their respective jobs, the soldier for killing and the other type for other tasks. The fact they had built themselves a hive, with a Queen in charge. Ros knew ants behaved as a hive mind rather than individuals and if the similarity rang true, then the Queen was the key; without her the colony would collapse. Novis would be safe.

She had to kill the Queen. It was her only chance.

"Is there any way I can convince you to work with us?" she said, subtly casting her gaze about to finalise her plan. Her Punch Bug escorts were several feet behind her, and only the Nice Bug working the translator was between her and the Queen. She was confident she could reach her goal before any of the other XyrQ could stop her. "The Commonwealth believes in peaceful cooperation. We only attacked you in self-defence. If you agree to stop your attacks, we could provide you with the supplies you need to build your colony. Perhaps we could even help with your homeworld."

"No," the Queen said. "No peace. XyrQ no ask. XyrQ better than human. XyrQ take."

Ros surreptitiously undid the catch for her arm blade. Without her helmet she'd have to release it manually, and she wouldn't be able to ignite its super-heated edge, but the carbon-steel should still be enough to cause damage. The Queen looked much less heavily armoured than the soldier XyrQ she was used to fighting. This would all come down to timing.

"Last chance," Ros warned. "Either we come to some sort of agreement to work together, or I will have no choice but to kill you."

The Queen let out a series of clicks that went untranslated, but they sounded to Ros like laughter. "No peace. No kill XyrQ. We kill you, Captain Lamarr."

"Thank you, that's what I was waiting for."

Ros ran forward, loosening the spring-loaded blade as she went. The Queen didn't seem to know what to make of the sudden movement, and the moment's hesitation gave Ros the opening she needed.

Aided by the motors in her suit, she covered the distance quickly, and aimed for the largest target available; the Queen's distended abdomen.

Taking a flying leap, she drove the blade as deep as she could into the Queen's thoracic segment and let the planetesimal's gravity do the rest. The Queen screamed as Ros opened up a huge gash in her abdomen. A foul smelling clear liquid seeped out, and for a fleeting moment Ros wished she'd thought to bring her helmet.

After that she didn't have time to think.

The Queen thrashed wildly, whether in anger or pain, Ros didn't have time to work out. She was too busy trying not to get crushed. Ros thrust upwards with her arm and scored another hit to the abdomen though less deep this time.

Another scream tore through the cavern.

The XyrQ who had been queued up to take away the maggots advanced on Ros, their usual job now secondary to protecting their Queen. She slashed wildly with the blade, taking off a few arms. Apparently the worker bugs were nowhere near as well armoured as the soldiers.

Still, Ros was vastly outnumbered; she didn't have time to get cocky.

The wounds she'd given the Queen so far didn't appear to be fatal. She needed to find a new target, one that would cause more serious damage. The head was usually the best bet.

Stabbing in with the blade, Ros attempted to use it to climb the Queen's abdomen. It was slow going, her blade kept slipping in the gore, and she had no way to anchor her left hand.

She couldn't climb quickly enough.

One of the workers got its pincer around her ankle. Ros shook it off, but the motion cost her dearly. Her blade opened up another wound as she slid down, the meagre gravity still too much for her to overcome.

Multiple sets of pincers grabbed at her. She slashed at them to free herself. Finding her feet on the now slippery ice she ran for the control panel.

Right into one of the Punch Bug's fists.

The blow sent her flying. Her suit's chest piece was caved in, but the impact gel underneath did its job. She was winded, but unharmed.

As the XyrQ advanced on her, the Queen chittered in a way the translator finally decided it could handle. "No," she said. "Mine."

And with that she heaved her enormous bulk towards Ros, leaning down to grab her. Ros tried to wave her off with the blade arm, but all that did was provide the Queen with a new target.

Deceptively powerful jaws clamped down on Ros's arm and heaved upwards.

Ros screamed as the Queen's mandibles crushed her armour like it was nothing. And the pressure kept on mounting.

Dangling in mid-air there was nothing she could do, her only weapon useless. The only thing preventing her shoulder from dislocating was her armour, but the crushed chest piece made breathing harder.

The armour buckled about the same time Ros felt her arm shatter. Blood ran down her arm where the carbon-steel tore into her skin or her bone outwards, she couldn't tell.

Her arm felt like it was on fire.

Still those jaws *squeezed*.

Tears blurred Ros's vision as desperate sobs tore from her throat. This was it. This was the end.

The thought occurred to her that she should never

have left Erebus Station. She should never have taken this job.

Sure she would never have met Isobel, but her people would still be alive. Matty would still be alive. Surely her happiness was a small price to pay for that?

For a moment she was back there, on the Station, drinking away her boredom and getting into fights.

Her memory jogged.

The fight. Her knife!

She still had the knife she kept in her prosthetic leg. Ros had given up hope of surviving this around the time her arm broke, but there was still a chance she could take the Queen down with her. She might still be able to save her home.

Maybe this was why she'd survived as a child. Maybe this was what all the hurt and the guilt was for. So she could save Novis and break the curse.

Ros reached down with her remaining hand, fumbling with the clasps in her armour. She couldn't see, could barely think for the pain but somehow she got the leg plate off. The undersuit was more of a problem but somehow she rolled it up far enough.

She could feel consciousness bleeding away as her body succumbed to the pain and trauma. Ros grit her teeth, refusing the pull of sweet oblivion. Her hand shook as she strained to get to the compartment.

The Queen had started *chewing* on Ros's arm with her secondary mandibles. She was going to eat her alive!

"Not if I can fucking help it," Ros ground out. With a burst of energy she didn't have to spare, she reached.

Her fingers closed around the handle of the knife.

"For Novis," she said, and swung upwards.

The knife struck the Queen's eye and bit deep. She screamed, her jaws releasing Ros's mangled arm. Fighting through the pain, she swung with that arm too, driving the blade into the Queen's other eye.

Clear fluid ran down Ros's arms, burning and hissing as it made contact with her exposed flesh.

Ros screamed so hard she almost passed out.

Blindly, the Queen thrashed her head about. Unable to fight the momentum, Ros went flying, her grip on the knife slipping. She hit the ice hard and landed on one of the platforms, dazed.

The XyrQ were in a complete disarray, their Queen clearly dying, but they were ignoring her for now. That was good.

Ros cradled her maimed arm to her chest watching as the blood on her armour bubbled where the XyrQ gore had touched it. *Interesting*, she thought, on the verge of passing out. It was almost mesmerising.

A haunting wail fill the air, a sound of mourning. Ros dragged herself to the platform's edge to get a better look. The Queen was dead.

Some of the workers were biting into her flesh. Whether to try to wake her or because they had lost their minds without her, it didn't matter.

It was done. Novis was safe. Her people were safe. She could let go now.

With a smile on her face, she did.

CHAPTER TWENTY

GABBY

Convincing AJ to let her go after Ros with a serious head injury was easier said than done. In the end, her stubbornness had won out, and he'd pumped her full of painkillers. Under duress mind you. No doubt it would be noted in the medical logs.

Gabby didn't care. The only thing that mattered was finding Ros. And her head didn't even hurt that much any more.

Well, she could see straight again, which was something.

The dizziness was a bit more of a challenge, but she'd fought battles in worse shape. Probably.

"I still think you should have let me take the lead on this one," Ewan said, probably for the fifth time that hour. "You should be in the medical bay, not suited up and gunning for a fight."

"Gracias, *madre*," Gabby said. Her native language was somehow easier than English at the moment. She sighed, knowing she was being unfair to Ewan. "I know you're right," she managed to get out. "But I need to know Ros is okay, or if she's..." she couldn't finish the sentence. It was unbearable to even think about.

"I know," Ewan said, his voice kind even over the comm. "We'd all fall to pieces without the Captain."

"I need to do this," Gabby insisted. "I need to see for myself. AJ can do whatever he wants with me after, but I need to know."

Mila spat something in Russian which was no doubt a threat to kill the Captain if she died or something. One reason Gabby liked the Russian so much was her tendency to express affection via the means of death threats; the more threats you got the more she liked you. The only exception to that apparently was Lizzie, who was definitely liked but received precious few threats of violence.

In any case, Mila was probably the least of Ros's worries right now.

The team Gabby had assembled—Ewan, Mila, Lizzie out in front tracking and Noora bringing up the rear— made their way steadily through tunnels that were far too quiet. They hadn't seen a single bug since they'd left camp, which worried Gabby immensely.

"I don't like this boss," Ewan said, echoing Gabby's thoughts.

"If you say you've got a bad feeling about this I'll kill you," Noora groused.

"And I'll let her," Gabby added. "You just keep your bad feelings to yourself."

"Quiet!" Lizzie said suddenly said, throwing a hand up to signal them to halt. "Did you hear that?"

"Nyet," Mila said. "What was it?"

"A scream," Lizzie replied. "Like something was in pain. Didn't sound like anything I've ever heard before."

Gabby shared a look with Ewan, who nodded. "Whatever it was it can't be anything good," she said. "Alright team, weapons at the ready. We move fast and we move hard. I'd bet the *Star* that Ros is involved with whatever Lizzie heard, so let's find the source of that scream. Kill anything that gets in our way."

Four sets of guns and one improbably large arm-mounted cannon powered up at the same time. Lizzie pushed forwards, leading them through the tunnels at a jog. The floor had begun to slope downwards, towards the planetesimal's centre of gravity, and the Irregulars followed instinctively.

They met one or two XyrQ on the way, but they seemed distracted, as though they had other things to worry about. The team took them down with no problems.

Another inhuman scream echoed through the tunnels, this time loud enough that Gabby heard it too.

"Lizzie, can you get a lock on where that's coming from?" Gabby shouted as the team picked up their pace.

"Close enough!" the tracker called back. "There's a large cavern a few kilometres ahead, seems to be coming from there."

"The Captain?" Ewan asked.

"Almost certainly," Gabby replied. "Let's just hope we get there in time to keep her from doing something foolish."

The seconds seemed to last forever as they ran through the tunnels and caverns. Gabby's breath seemed harsh in her ears, her head pounding with every beat of her heart. She could barely see for fear that they would be too late.

A third scream sounded out, and in Gabby's mind

there was no doubt that whatever was making it was dying. An unearthly wail started up afterwards, a sound that made Gabby's skin crawl.

Where there had been too few for comfort before, XyrQ now seemed to flood the tunnels, slowing down their progress. The Irregulars acted on their orders, shooting anything that wasn't human. But there was something off about the XyrQ's behaviour, something that Gabby couldn't quite put her finger on.

It wasn't until the tunnels opened out into a small cavern that she realised what it was.

"Fucking hell," Ewan said eloquently. "They're fighting each other."

"And ignoring us," Gabby added. That was what had been bothering her. Every mantis she'd ever met had attacked her on sight, but the ones they'd met in the tunnels had seemed uninterested in the five armed mercenaries storming their territory.

"This is just too fucking weird," Ewan said.

"New orders people," Gabby barked, doing her best Ros impression. "We need to get to that central chamber as fast as possible. Shoot only if the bugs look like they're going after us or they're in our way. Our priority is to get to Ros."

Too many minutes later they burst into the central chamber, and what they saw shocked them.

"That is fucking huge!" Ewan said as swearwords in three languages came down the comm.

He wasn't wrong. The creature was like a thing out of Gabby's worst nightmare. She almost couldn't process it.

Thirty feet of XyrQ twitching on the ice, surrounded by more bugs than she was comfortable with. The monstrous mantis was bleeding out, either dead or dying, as the other insects literally ate her.

"Ugh, I feel sick," Lizzie said, sounding a little green.

"Disgusting," Mila said in agreement, an unpleasant look on her face. It had to be bad if even Mila was struggling.

"Ros did this," Gabby said. It was the only real explanation for the carnage. "We need to find her."

The team spread out, searching for their Captain. Gabby became increasingly frantic the longer there was no sign of her.

"There!" Ewan cried, pointing to one of the walkways about halfway up the room. An armoured foot was just visible over the edge of the platform as was the steady drip of very human looking blood.

The sight of the blood did nothing to calm the utter terror Gabby had felt since she'd woken up and realised her Captain was missing. There was no obvious way up there without leaving the chamber, and Gabby knew she didn't have time for that.

"Anyone got a grappling hook or a rappelling cable in their suit? I used mine."

"Here," Mila said, pulling a small gun from her belt, which admittedly was full of guns. "Never leave home without."

"Thanks," Gabby said as she took the gun. She aimed for the ice above the walkway and fired; the cable flew true and the anchor buried itself deep. She dropped the gun and pulled out her auto-ascender, clipping it to the cable and securing it. Activating the device, she zipped up the cable, armour and all, within seconds.

Gabby landed on the platform with both feet and looked around frantically. The armour and the blood did indeed belong to Ros, and it didn't look good.

She was slumped against the wall of the cavern, unconscious or worse. For some reason she wasn't wearing her helmet, and part of her leg armour had come off, revealing her prosthetic. Her chest plate was caved in, and her right arm was cradled against it, a bloody mangled mess.

"Ros!" she cried, rushing over to her fallen lover. The arm looked even worse up close, clearly shattered. The blood wasn't clotting for some reason, and something smelled foul enough to make Gabby gag despite the air filters in her suit.

What the hell happened here? Gabby thought to herself, kneeling next to her, heart in her throat.

Ros didn't react, didn't respond in the slightest.

"Oh no no no no, come on Ros." *Please be breathing, please be breathing.* She held her arm close to Ros's mouth, watching for condensation on the chilly carbon-steel. There wasn't much, but it was there. "¡Gracias a dios!"

"Gabby?" Ewan said, sounding distressed. "She okay?"

"She's alive," Gabby informed the team, and she could almost hear the collective sigh of relief. "She's in bad shape though. We need to get her to AJ ASAP."

"We'll try to find another way up," Ewan said. "Just

stay with her her boss."

"I'm not going anywhere," Gabby insisted.

The comm fell silent. Gabby yanked her helmet's visor up before pulling a first aid pouch from her suit, intending to do what she could while she was waiting for her team mates. There wasn't much she could do about the arm, but she could try to wake Ros up. They hadn't brought a stretcher with them and it would be difficult to get her back to the ship if she was dead weight. Plus Ros being conscious would make Gabby feel a lot better.

AJ packed everyone's first aid kits with a cocktail of drugs he referred to as his "special". A potent combination of stimulants, painkillers and clotting agents, it could see a mercenary through even the worst injuries, and had saved Gabby's life on countless occasions. She picked up the injector pen and pulled the cap off with her teeth, jabbing it firmly into the muscles of Ros's neck. When the injector was empty, she tossed it to the side.

Ros's breathing seemed steadier already.

"Come on Ros," Gabby said, shaking her shoulders gently. "I need you to wake up."

Nothing. Ros didn't even twitch.

Gabby tried again, slapping her cheeks gently. "Come on Ros, wake up."

Still nothing.

"Wake up soldier," Gabby barked, doing her best impression of their drill sergeant from their army days. "Dawn's a-breaking, time for waking. You've got duties to attend to."

Ros twitched and her eyes flew open. They were glassy and unfocused, her pupils like pinpricks, no doubt a result of the drugs now flooding her system.

"Gabby?" she said uncertainly. "What? I thought..." She was clearly confused and disorientated, but she was alive and conscious. The relief Gabby felt was so intense she almost wanted to cry.

"Steady on there Ros," she said softly, more softly than she ever spoke to most people. "You're hurt. The rest of the Irregulars are on their way; we're going to get you home."

Ros blinked slowly and swallowed several times, trying to get words out. "Manning and Siddiqui? Didya find them?"

"Not yet, are they still alive?"

She shrugged, and almost fell sideways, sliding down the ice. Gabby reached out to steady her, keeping her sat upright.

"Do you know where they are?"

Ros shook her head, exaggerating the motion, almost as if she was drunk. The drugs were definitely working.

"We'll find them." Gabby activated the comm. "Ewan, I've managed to rouse the Captain. She says Manning and Siddiqui are somewhere in this ice maze but she's not sure if they're still alive. Send Mila and Lizzie to locate them; I'm gonna need you to help me get the Captain back to the ship."

"Aye lieutenant," he said. "I think we're almost at your location. We'll be there in a moment. Burns out."

"We'll find them," Gabby said to Ros, whose eyes were

drifting closed again. "Hey, come on, Ros. I need you to stay awake."

"Tired," Ros said, sounding for all the world like a petulant five-year-old at bedtime. "Hurts."

Gabby glanced down at what was left of her arm. By look of it the pain level was probably closer to excruciating agony, but she didn't say that out loud. "I know it hurts, Capitan, but I need you to stay awake for me. Can you stand?"

Ros just blinked owlishly at her, like Gabby was speaking a language she'd never heard before. Cooperation was clearly not forthcoming. Time to try a different tactic.

"On your feet soldier," she said, slinging Ros's good arm around her shoulders and dragging her upwards. "That's it, come on." She managed to get Ros upright and leaning on her, despite the Captain being basically dead weight; she'd handled more cooperative drunks. If not for the assistance from her suit Gabby would never have been able to lift her. "There we go," she said. It was all she could do to keep her upright.

Ros swayed and her gaze seemed to focus on the corpse of the enormous XyrQ. A wide, slightly ridiculous smile spread across her face. "I got the bitch, Gabs," she slurred. "I got her."

"Yes you did. And you can debrief properly once we've got you patched up."

Thankfully Ewan and Noora turned up shortly afterwards, exiting one of the tunnels further down the cavern wall. There was a look of shock and horror on

Ewan's face for a brief second before he covered it up. Noora was muttering quietly inside her helmet, no doubt whispering a prayer or two; Gabby had done it often enough herself to recognise the look.

"How's she doing?" Ewan asked.

"High as a kite on AJ's special cocktail, and the arm's a mess, but she's alive, thank God. That's all that matters."

"Aye, it is," he said, moving to help support Ros's right-hand side. The injured arm was just dangling uselessly now, but Gabby could see he was being careful to avoid it.

"Alright then Ros, lets get you home," Gabby said. Noora took up point, weapon at the ready, and they set off.

It was slow going. Ros didn't seem to be able to control her legs properly, so each step was an ordeal. Gabby and Ewan basically had to swift her weight back and forth between them to get her to move. Meanwhile Ros just sort of stared off into space, barely paying any attention to her surroundings.

"Fucking hell," Ewan said after about ten minutes. "I've dealt with people pissed outta their skulls who were easier to move than this."

"Same here," Gabby said, taking the brunt of Ros's weight again. "I definitely prefer drunk Ros to this. Drunk Ros usually just wants a fuck and then to go to sleep."

"I'm not sure I needed to know that," Noora said, sounding amused.

Mila and Lizzie radioed in to say they'd found Manning and Siddiqui. Siddiqui was unconscious but still alive, but there was nothing anyone could do for Manning. Ewan cursed up a storm before contacting AJ to update him on the situation. AJ promised he'd be prepped and ready to go by the time they got there.

After what seemed like hours, they finally stumbled out into the open, where the *Mercenary Star* was sat, a sight for sore eyes. AJ, as good as his word, was waiting on the ice with a gurney for the Captain.

"Am I glad to see you Kapitan," he said.

"Arthur!" Ros cried, throwing her good arm up in the air and nearly falling flat on her face. AJ raised his eyebrows at the uncharacteristic use of his first name.

"Those drugs you put in our first aid kits are *really* good," Gabby offered by way of explanation as she tried to get Ros onto the gurney. The Captain didn't seem to want to co-operate, her non-mangled limbs flailing all over the place unhelpfully.

"Yes I see that," AJ said dryly. He and Ewan wheeled Ros into the ship and headed for the med bay. Gabby, who could really use some of those drugs herself for the pounding in her skull, followed closely behind.

"Gabriela, sit," AJ said as he prepped for dealing with Ros's injuries. "You should never have left here in the first place." Unwilling to disobey a clearly pissed off AJ, she did as she was told.

"Any other casualties?" she asked, trying to be the competent second-in-command again instead of the reckless soldier running off after her best friend.

"Potts didn't make it," AJ said, his clipped professional tone hiding the grief Gabby knew he had to feel. He'd mourn properly later; they all would. "Boy took one more head injuries than his body could take. Apart from that you and the Kapitan are my most serious concerns. Ewan, liebchen, help me get the Kapitan's armour off."

"Aye love."

"Mila and Lizzie are bringing Siddiqui back. No word on her condition yet," Gabby said.

Between them the boys managed to get most of Ros's suit off while she hummed softly to herself. She was still largely uncooperative but in the way a toddler was; sure they were never where you wanted them to be, but it was easy enough to put them back. It wasn't until AJ took a proper look at the Captain's injured arm that things took a turn for the worse.

"Scheisse!" he said, peeling part of the crushed arm-plate away. "The arm will have to come off."

That proclamation seemed to set off Ros's survival instincts or something, as she immediately panicked. Screaming that no one was going to take her arm, Ros tried to climb off the bed. Gabby immediately moved to help keep her down.

"Not my arm," Ros screamed, "I need that arm!"

Gabby grimaced as Ros thrashed and bucked on the bed, trying to wiggle out of their hold. Her good arm clipped Gabby on the side of the head, and the sudden blinding pain and wave of nausea almost sent her to her knees.

"We're going to need the restraints I think," AJ said calmly, as though he wasn't the only thing keeping his hysterical Captain from bolting. They could have been discussing the weather for all the sense of urgency in his voice.

"I'll get them," Ewan said, turning about and heading for the door.

"The *medical* restraints, liebchen," AJ said, finally sounding just a little exasperated.

"Oh, right," Ewan said, his face going red. Gabby would have laughed if she wasn't too busy trying not to vomit.

Between them AJ and Ewan got Ros strapped to the bed and pumped some more sedatives into her. It made Gabby's heart hurt to see Ros in such a state, but it needed to be done.

"Will the arm really have to come off?" she asked.

"Ja, I'm afraid so," AJ said sadly. "There is just too much trauma to the limb. I can see from here the bones are shattered, and the soft tissue damage..." He sighed. "In a state-of-the-art operating theatre on a central Commonwealth planet I might have a chance at saving it, but out here? Nein. And we wouldn't make it to the Capital in time even if I did not have other patients to see to here." He eyed Gabby in a way that made her feel like a naughty kid again. "Speaking of my other patients..."

"I know I shouldn't have gone after her," Gabby said, cutting AJ off before he could chastise her properly. "But what else could I do?"

"Nothing," AJ admitted. "When it comes to you and the Kapitan you will always do whatever necessary to find each other, regardless of the personal cost. I know this. That does not mean I have to approve."

Gabby didn't respond immediately, her gaze drifting over Ros's now peaceful form. "It's not going to be easy for her is it, coming back from an injury like this?"

"No it is not."

"I thought she was bad after she lost the leg but this, this is going to be worse."

"She had you to help her through last time. And now she has you and Isobel. It will be hard, but she will get through it. You will see." Gabby wasn't sure she believed him just yet, but he had an annoying habit of being right.

She groaned as realisation dawned. "I'm going to have to tell Isobel what's happened."

AJ grimaced. "Good luck with that," he said. "You will need it."

"She's going to be so pissed off. At both of us."

"Ja. Better you than me, I think. I would not wish to attract the ire of Governor Devereux. Speaking of the Governor, when you inform her of her partners' collective foolishness, please ask her to arrange landing permits for us. I am going to need to get the Kapitan back to Novis as soon as possible."

"I'll give Noora and Tariq orders to set off as soon as we're able."

"No, I will," Ewan said, joining back in after a lengthy silence. "You're in no condition to make command decisions Gabby." She protested but Ewan cut her off. "Don't make me get AJ to relieve you of duty," he warned.

"Fine. You're in charge."

"Good," he said and turned to AJ. "As soon as everyone's on board we'll be on our way."

"Good."

"What about the remaining XyrQ?" Gabby asked. "Could they still be a threat to Novis?" She'd hate to have gone through all this and their home still be in danger.

"We'll sort them out," Ewan said. "I've got just the thing."

AJ sighed again. "You mean that electro-magnetic pulse mine the Kapitan said you couldn't have?"

Ewan grinned, clearly unrepentant. "It'll fry every electronic device in the outer solar system. They won't be able to get off that rock ever again."

"You are a monster, liebchen."

"Love you too, babe."

"Enough flirting," AJ said. "I have a patient to see to. Do what you have to do liebchen, I shall see you later. Gabriela, you may contact Isobel but you are to come back here immediately afterwards. I want you under medical supervision for that head injury."

"Yes sir," she said, too exhausted and in far too much pain to even be sarcastic.

"Now shoo, both of you. I need the space to work."

Gabby stumbled out of the medical bay, her head swimming again.

"You gonna be alright to get back to your cabin Gabs?" Ewan asked, sounded really concerned.

"I'll be fine, gracias." Ewan nodded and headed off in the direction of the cockpit while Gabby made her way slowly to her quarters.

As soon as the door hissed shut behind her, she pulled her suit off. She wanted to be in something comfortable and pretty so she pulled out one of her favourite dresses. It took a few tries, but eventually she got it over her head.

Still woozy, she staggered to her comm unit and punched in Isobel's details. The governor answered after only a few minutes and she was a sight for sore eyes. Gabby felt such a wave of relief at seeing her face she almost cried. She could blame the head injury, right?

"Gabby?" Isobel said, frowning. "What's wrong? Do you have news?"

Gabby nodded carefully, trying not to make her headache worse. "It's Ros."

Isobel's hand flew to her mouth. "Is she...?"

"She's alive. The job's done and we're coming home but Ros... she's in a bad way Iz."

Emotions flashed over Isobel's face faster than Gabby could categorise them, before settling into something that looked like determination. Gabby had seen that look a lot over the last six months, usually just before Izzy gave some asshole diplomat a piece of her mind. "How bad?"

"She's gonna lose her arm Iz," Gabby said, and her voice broke at last, all the emotional highs and lows of the day finally catching up with her. "Ros's right arm is pretty much gone. She's in surgery with AJ right now."

"What can I do to help?" she asked. Gabby passed on AJ's message about landing permits. Isobel promised she would sort everything out and have the medical centre on Novis ready for Ros's arrival.

"I don't know what to do Iz," Gabby said when the business was out of the way. "She's gonna take this hard."

"We'll be there for her every step of the way," Isobel

said gently, the soothing quality of her voice an ill fit with the ragged edges of Gabby's emotional state. "Whatever happens we'll get through it."

Gabby wiped at her face, astonished to find it was wet. When had she started crying?

"Is there anything I can do for you Gabby?" she asked.

The sheer amount of kindness in Isobel's voice was too much for Gabby and she burst into tears properly. Isobel started murmuring soothing words immediately, encouraging her to let it all out.

Sobbing down the comm to the other person who loved Ros best, she cried for everything they had lost, and everything they had yet to face

CHAPTER TWENTY ONE

ISOBEL

Ros's recovery was slow.

The loss of her arm hit harder than anyone expected, despite Gabby having feared the worst from the beginning. Ros was a generally independent person and having to adjust to not having her dominant hand any more was a huge blow.

AJ had saved as much of the arm as he could, taking it off just below the elbow which would make fitting a cybernetic replacement much easier, but that was still weeks off. In the meantime Ros had to get by with just a bandaged stump, and the process of learning how to deal with that had been hard on everyone.

Ewan was helping as much as he could, being the only other person in the Irregulars who had dealt with the loss of an arm before, but there was only so much he could do. His injury had been years ago, and he was well used to carrying out day-to-day tasks with one hand and a stump by now.

But it wasn't just the loss of the arm Ros was dealing with; she was irritable, quick to anger, her temper permanently on a knife edge. And she was constantly tired too, which only made it worse. She wasn't sleeping well, spending hours lying in bed awake. And when she managed to drop off she suffered with horrific nightmares. Isobel and Gabby were doing what they could to soothe Ros when she woke up screaming and drenched in sweat, but they couldn't do anything about the root cause. And Gabby had her own problems to deal with, the after-effect of her head injury lasting far longer than she'd expected.

No one had mentioned PTSD to Ros yet, but they were all thinking it. AJ had advised watchful waiting for now, but he was prepared to intervene medically if necessary. It was still early days and things might get easier for Ros, especially after her new prosthetic was fitted. All they could do was wait and see.

It made Isobel's heart ache to see her so wound up and frustrated all the time. There was nothing she could do besides be patient, and be there for Ros, reassuring her of her love as often as possible.

It never felt like enough.

This was something that was completely beyond her realm of expertise and feeling helpless had never gone down well with Isobel. Things were a little tense between her and Ros and Gabby, but they were all trying. They'd get through this together, no matter what.

What they all needed was a break in routine, an opportunity to relax. Which was why Isobel suggested a day out just the three of them.

It was a nice enough day for Novis, the sun warm but not too hot and the wind as low as it ever got. There were no dust storms forecast. Isobel took Ros and Gabby to a secluded corner of her garden where they wouldn't be disturbed by anyone.

The sound of running water in the background, the gentle murmur of the wind through crops almost ready to harvest, and the sweet scent of honeysuckle on the air, the one plant Isobel allowed herself to grow for pleasure; it was almost romantic. Ros seemed in better spirits than she had the last few days, and Isobel was happy to devote herself to making the woman she loved smile.

"Would you like some strawberries love?" she asked, lifting the container. She'd packed a robust picnic, including a few off-world delicacies she'd been saving for a special occasion.

A picnic in the garden might not seem special on the surface, but it felt it to Isobel. Hence the treats.

"Sure," said Ros, reaching out for the container. Isobel batted her hand away with a coy little smile.

"Not like that," she said playfully, while Gabby chuckled in the background. She picked up one of the strawberries in her fingers and held it out for Ros to take a bite of. Some of the juice ran down her chin and Isobel had to fight the urge to lean over and lick it off. Judging by the dark look in Gabby's eyes, she was having much the same problem.

"That's good," Ros said when she'd swallowed. "I can't remember the last time I had a strawberry."

"Probably those freeze dried ones we picked up after the Sequoia job," Gabby said. "Do you remember getting drunk with Ewan and AJ, grinding them up and daring Ewan to snort the powder?" she asked with a grin on her face.

Ros nodded, the corners of her lips twitching slightly. "I do," she said. "The powder made the bastard sneeze and we ended up with red paste splattered all over the rec room. He claimed everything tasted vaguely of strawberry for weeks after that."

"The Erebus Station Irregulars," Isobel said solemnly, lifting her glass. "Professionals in every sense of the word."

Gabby's lips twitched and Isobel couldn't help it, she burst out laughing. Gabby quickly lost control herself and the two broke down into hysterics. Even Ros managed a genuine smile, something that had been far too rare since her injury.

"It's good to see you smile again," Isobel said softly, looking at Ros. The feeling of love in her heart was so overwhelming in that moment she thought her ribcage might burst.

"Yeah, well," Ros said, looking down at the ground. "Sorry I haven't been much fun recently."

"Hey, it's okay," Isobel said. "I understand. We both do." She glanced at Gabby, who nodded. "It's just nice to see you being yourself again, even only briefly. Proves that you can."

"I guess," Ros said, but she was looking at Isobel again, so she considered it a win. She cleared her throat. "Are there any more of those strawberries?"

"Sure," Isobel said, handing the container over. Ros took it with her left hand and settled it onto her lap. She reached for a strawberry and offered it to Isobel to eat. Isobel took it gratefully. As the flavours exploded on her tongue she noted that they really were good strawberries.

"Mmmm, delicious," she said in a low voice, keeping

steady eye contact with Ros. Gabby grinned as the tips of Ros's ears darkened ever so slightly with her blush.

"I don't think she's talking about the fruit, Capitan," Gabby said helpfully. "Any chance I could get some of that?"

Ros reached for the container again, this time moving instinctively with her right arm. Her stump clipped the top of the container, knocking it over and spilling strawberries everywhere.

"Fuck it!" she shouted, clearly frustrated. "Stupid fucking *useless* arm."

"Hey hey hey," Isobel said trying to forestall a proper meltdown. "It's okay. It happens."

"I wasted the strawberries," Ros said, looking about a minute away from crying.

"It doesn't matter. They don't matter," Isobel reassured her. "You're doing so well love. A little accident doesn't change that."

"I can't even pick up a plastic box without making a fucking mess," Ros said, her voice rising again. "I'm supposed be this great mercenary Captain and I can't even do that. How am I supposed to do my job?"

"You aren't," Gabby said. Isobel looked up sharply, thinking her tone was a little harsh, but she continued anyway. "Not right now at least. You were hurt and you're recovering. That takes time, you need to allow yourself that."

"But while we're waiting for me to recover the Irregulars aren't working," Ros complained.

"You know as well as I do that the Irregulars never

need to work again if they don't want to," Gabby said. "We've done enough lucrative jobs that most of us have enough put away for a rainy day that we could retire if we wanted to. And if the greener mercs on the team don't like the extended shore leave they can always move on to another outfit. Anyone who's worked for you will have no trouble finding mercenary work anywhere in the Commonwealth and you know it. So you can stop worrying about the Irregulars and just think about yourself."

"Okay," Ros said, a trace of petulance still running through her words. "I guess I can work on that. It doesn't make it any less frustrating. I swear losing my leg was easier than this."

"Yeah, that's cos you didn't have to deal with yourself. Madre de Dios you were a pain in the ass."

"Was not," Ros insisted, but there was no bite to her voice.

"Yes you were."

"Rosalind Lamarr is a poor patient," Isobel said. "Why am I not surprised?"

"Hey!" Ros protested. Gabby burst out laughing.

"Don't worry about it chica," she said through her chuckles, "you'll soon have your new arm fitted and then you can get back to normal. Before you know it, you'll be annoying us with jokes about how this job has cost you an arm and a leg."

Isobel and Ros groaned in tandem, which just made Gabby laugh harder.

"That was awful!" Isobel said, throwing one of the

slightly squished strawberries at her.

"Hey!" Gabby protested, picking up the offending item and throwing it right back. "I *like* this dress."

"You like all your dresses Gabs," Ros said. Gabby threw a strawberry at her in response. It hit the side of Ros's face with a vaguely threatening *splat*. "Right, that's it. Come on Izzy," she said, launching herself at Gabby with a playful roar.

Isobel threw herself into the fray joyfully though what she could do against two experienced combat veterans she didn't know. All that mattered to her was that Ros was laughing and smiling as she wrestled with Gabby, the frustration of her mishap completely forgotten.

Despite Isobel's complete lack of upper body strength and wrestling experience, she and Ros ended up on top, pinning Gabby to the ground and they tickled her mercilessly.

"Please no!" Gabby begged, her eyes streaming from laughing so much. "I yield, I yield."

Ros and Isobel gave her mercy and the three of them lay there in a pile, breathing heavily and grinning fit to burst. The sheer delight on Ros's face made Isobel's heart sing, and judging from the way Gabby was looking at her, she felt the same way.

It wasn't the first good day Ros had had since her injury, but they were still rare enough to be treasured. Isobel knew that after this they'd only get more frequent.

"I love you," she blurted, sitting up slightly. "Both of you. I really hope you know that. Vous etes mes chéries."

"I love you too Izzy," Ros said, pulling her close and

holding her tight.

Gabby rested her hand on Isobel's arm, the smile on her face saying 'I love you too but I'm not ready to say it out loud.'

Snuggled up in an undignified pile, the three of them drifted off to sleep to the sounds of running water. Isobel felt safe and content, surrounded by her people, her family. With Ros and Gabby next to her she always felt like she was home.

***

Isobel had been putting off planning this party as long as she could.

It didn't feel right to celebrate the victory over the XyrQ while Ros and Gabby were still struggling to recover, not to mention while the grief for Manning and Potts was still so fresh in the Irregulars' minds, but the people of Novis demanded *something* to mark the occasion. Things had been quiet since the Irregulars returned from their mission, shipments of supplies getting through with no trouble at all for the first time since ever. Isobel couldn't remember life on Novis ever being this easy, and it was all thanks to Ros and her crew. She was starting to think the curse might truly have been broken; her fellow colonists certainly believed it had been, hence the party.

She'd set up the most relaxed and casual affair she could, all too aware of what had happened the last time she'd hosted an event at the governor's mansion. Her father's death, Ros, everything.

Isobel missed her father so much it hurt sometimes, but it was getting easier. She often wondered what he'd think of her relationship with Ros, and with Gabby. Whether he'd be proud of her for what she'd accomplished in less than a year as Governor. She knew he'd be proud of the way she'd put this celebration together, that was for sure.

Benoit Devereux had always enjoyed himself at events like this.

"What you thinking about?" Ros asked, coming up to stand at Isobel's side. She was wearing an extremely well fitting suit, her right sleeve pinned neatly at the elbow. Isobel thought she'd never looked so handsome.

"My father," Isobel answered honestly. "I miss him."

Ros slipped her hand into Isobel's letting their fingers tangle together. "He seemed like a good man. I'm sorry I didn't get the chance to know him better."

"He was a good man. He gave everything to Novis, even his life in the end. I hope he'd be proud of what I've done with the place."

"I'm sure he would be," Ros said, giving Isobel's hand a gentle squeeze.

They were quiet for a moment, comfortable. Isobel let herself enjoy the feeling of Ros's hand in hers, the warmth of her arm where it touched her own.

"I miss Matty," Ros said after a while. "For all he was an annoying little shit, I really do miss him. It had always been me Gabby and Matty, right from the beginning. I couldn't imagine the Irregulars without him, and it's still strange. I'm not used to it."

"He left some tough shoes to fill."

"Yeah. We're going to try to fill them when we head to the capital for my surgery," Ros said, gesturing with her stump. "As much as it hurts to think about, we need someone else on the team. We can never really replace Matty, but we need someone to do his job."

"You'll find someone," Isobel said. "Take your time to find the *right* someone though."

"You know he was the one who brought this job to my attention?"

"I knew he was the one I had initial contact with, but I didn't know that, no."

Ros nodded, staring off into the middle distance with a pensive look on her face. "I was fresh out of a bar fight, still bleeding and the git comes up to tell me he's got a job. I could have taken his head off when he told me where it was."

Isobel winced. "We didn't have the best reputation I know."

"This job has cost me more than any other job I've done. I lost my arm, four good mercenaries, four good *people*, and I lost Matty." She sighed, before turning to Isobel with a smile on her face. "And yet I can't bring myself to regret a thing. Taking this job led me to you, and you're one of the best things to ever happen to me. And I have a home for the first time since I was a child. Is it weird I don't regret it?"

"I don't think it's weird," Isobel said, thinking of all the things she'd lost since the Irregulars first arrived on her colony, and how she wouldn't change any of it for the world. "I feel the same way."

Gabby chose that moment to wander over, breaking the slightly solemn mood by saying "you're looking very serious over here. Didn't anyone tell you this was a fiesta? Here, this should help." She handed them both drinks which looked to be of her own making and rather strong.

Isobel shook herself slightly as she accepted the glass. "It is a party, and it's *my* party, so I should probably go mingle. You two heroes might want to think about doing the same. Now, if you'll both excuse me."

She started up a circuit of the room, drifting from group to group and exchanging a few words with everyone, staying longer where she got involved with an interesting conversation. The colonists and the Irregulars were well mixed, and it occurred to Isobel that really there was no difference between the two any more; with the Irregulars being permanently based here now, they were all Novisians. The thought made Isobel smile.

Drifting through the room with her drink in hand, which really was strong she realised after her first sip, she noticed Noora had ensconced herself in a corner with several admirers of various genders. By looks on their faces, they were all utterly enraptured by what she was saying. Gabby would be so proud.

Her brother, on the other hand, barely seemed to notice there was a party going on. Tariq had spent the entire evening with one of the colonists, a woman who's name Isobel couldn't quite remember. She remembered she'd lost her husband in one of the Hellbeast attacks, and it made her smile to think of one of her people moving past that and finding happiness again. Judging by the way Tariq was looking at the woman's two-year-old daughter as she squirmed in his arms, he was just as smitten with the child as he was with her mother. It looked like Tariq had found himself a family here.

Lizzie and Mila had their own group of hangers on though for very different reasons. Isobel floated to the edge of the conversation just in time to hear one of her administration team ask "so, what is a lovely young woman like you doing with someone old enough to be her grandmother? Especially since she doesn't even want to sleep with you. What does she have that I don't?"

"Apart from manners?" Mila said gruffly.

Isobel winced and hoped she wouldn't end up having to mop his entrails off the floor after Mila was done with him. Lizzie, however, didn't look the slightest bit fazed.

"What am I doing with Mila?" she asked cheerfully, as though the question wasn't horribly offensive on just about every level. "We read, we cuddle, play board games. And she teaches me a new way to kill a man every week if she can," she finished sweetly. The man blanched and walked off, muttering excuses.

Good riddance, Isobel thought.

"By all means threaten my staff," she said to Lizzie, "but please keep the actual murders as low as possible. It's not as easy to find a decent administrator as you would think."

"Don't worry, I train her well," said Mila, pressing a kiss to Lizzie's cheek. "It is more fun to make threat and watch them run. Make no mistake though; I will kill anyone who lays a finger on my Lizzie without her permission."

"Aww, you're so sweet," Lizzie said, as though that was the nicest compliment anyone had ever given her.

"I suppose that's as good as I'm going to get," Isobel said, more to herself than to either of the other two. By this point she wasn't sure who scared her more, Mila or her protegee. She moved on before she became a witness to any more murder threats.

By the time she drifted back to Ros's side, her girlfriend was talking to Ewan and AJ. Or rather, was exchanging amused looks with AJ while Ewan gesticulated wildly about something.

"But think of the benefits Captain," Ewan said as Isobel joined them. "You've seen what mine can do."

"Ah, he's still campaigning for you to get a cannon fitted instead of a proper cybernetic arm, I take it?" Isobel said, slipping an arm around Ros's waist.

"He hasn't stopped pretty much since I woke up from the amputation," Ros said dryly. "I keep telling him; it doesn't matter how cool it would be, or how useful for my job, I have to have a proper prosthetic fitted. I need that hand."

"What could you possibly need you hand for that's better than having a *cannon*? You've still got your left hand, you can learn how to do everything with that easy enough."

"That's true, but there are some things I'll be able to do much better when I get my right hand back."

"Like what?" Ewan asked, sounding honestly confused.

AJ pinched the bridge of his nose before leaning in to whisper something in his boyfriend's ear. Ewan's face went as red as the rather fetching jumper he was wearing, which prompted both Ros and Isobel to burst out laughing.

"Well you asked," Ros said.

"I regret everything," Ewan grumbled. "Excuse me, I need to go find some whisky."

"He'll be alright after a few drinks," AJ reassured them. "He won't stay embarrassed for long, he never does, but with luck this should be the end of his little campaign."

"But the start of mine," Ros said with a wicked grin on her face. Isobel had missed that look. "You just wait, every time I wiggle my fingers his cheeks are gonna clash with his hair."

"You are wicked, Kapitan," said AJ, but he was chuckling. "But I cannot bring myself to stop you. He looks so adorable when he blushes like that."

"If you say so," Ros said cheerfully. "You should probably go make sure he doesn't drink himself into unconsciousness. Ewan Burns and an open bar are a terrible mixture."

"I shall. Guten abend Kapitan, Governor Devereux." He nodded respectfully and headed off.

"So you're not getting the cannon arm then?" Isobel asked playfully when they were alone once more.

Ros shook her head. "It's tempting, but I have higher

priorities than being able to blast three enemies apart at once in battle. I want to be able to hold you the way I'm used to again. And I miss being able to tie my own shoelaces. Doesn't matter how many times Ewan shows me the trick for doing it one handed I just can't get the hang of it."

"The prosthetic won't solve all your problems you know," Isobel warned. Ros had been putting so much stock in her new arm and she wanted to make sure she was being realistic about it.

"I know," Ros said. "But it'll solve enough."

Isobel hummed her agreement. "Where's Gabby?"

"She found a playmate for the evening, so it's just the two of us."

"Good for her," Isobel said. The arrangement the two of them had with Gabby was sometimes a little strange, certainly not what she'd imagined for herself when she was younger, but it worked. Besides, Gabby was always fired up after she'd been with someone else, and she and Ros always reaped the rewards of that.

"Shall we head off ourselves? Or do you need to stay a little longer?"

Isobel pressed a kiss to Ros's cheeks. "I think we can make our excuses. I'm all yours love."

A few days after the party saw the Irregulars packing up the *Mercenary Star* for a trip to the central Commonwealth. Besides getting Ros's new arm fitted they planned to get upgrades to the *Star* and change out some personnel, not to mention recruit a replacement for Matthew Taylor.

It was the first time they'd been off planet since the battle with the XyrQ, and while Isobel knew rationally that they'd all be fine, she was still worried.

"I'm going to miss you, both of you," she said to Ros and Gabby as Ewan carried things up and down the cargo ramp. "I'm going to miss all of you, really. I've got used having you around."

"We'll be back before you know it," Gabby reassured her. "And then we get to have enormous fun helping la jefa get used to her new robot arm." She stepped forwards to give Isobel an intense kiss. "See you soon chica," she said softly. "I'll meet you on board," she added to Ros before taking off up the ramp.

"Hey, try not to look so glum, we're coming back. This isn't an ending, it's a beginning," Ros reassured her.

"I know," Isobel said. "Doesn't mean I'm not gonna miss you."

"I'll miss you too."

"Just... be careful, okay? I need you to come back to me. Both of you."

"Always," Ros said, looking serious. "And I'll make sure Gabby is too."

"Good," she said, pulling Ros in for a kiss. "I love you."

"I love you too," Ros said with a smile. "More than I thought I could."

"Captain," Ewan called, "we're all loaded and ready to ship out. Stop kissing your lady and get your arse on board!"

"I'll be there in a minute," Ros shouted back. "I've got to go."

"Go on. Get yourself to the Capital so you can enjoy the extra fame that comes from breaking the curse of Novis colony."

Ros laughed. "I will. And I'll get my arm sorted and then I'll come right back, I promise. I will always come home to you Isobel. You are my home."

Isobel held her tightly for a moment longer and then let her go. She retreated to the control tower so she could watch the launch safely. As the *Mercenary Star* disappeared into the upper atmosphere, she smiled to herself.

Ros was right.; this *was* just the beginning, and she would be home soon enough.

Other Books by the Author

On the Rise (Penumbra Book 1)

The Whisper of the Leaves (Daughter of Duri Book 1)

Beyond the Edge of Reason

Objective Reasoning

The Emerald Mist

12 Stories in 12 Hours

In Short: A Flash Fiction Collection

About the Author

Rachel Tonks Hill always wanted to be either a doctor or writer when she grew up. Her first novel, On the Rise, was released in 2016, having been written alongside her doctoral thesis. While having a novel out fulfills the "writer" part of her dream, she hopes this doesn't mean she has to grow up. Rachel lives in Nottingham with her partner and insufficient dogs.

racheltonkshill.com
facebook.com/racheltonkshill
twitter: @captainraz

27281776R00214

Printed in Poland
by Amazon Fulfillment
Poland Sp. z o.o., Wrocław